THE GOLD IN THEM HILLS

By Trish Lacey

To Deon
Thank you for always believing in me

PROLOGUE

I was perched on a ladder, five stories high, carefully wiping centuries of accumulated grime from the cracked leather covers of all the technical books of knowledge ever printed in the world, when Seth called me. It could have been a tedious job but I found myself reading instead of cleaning; swallowing, in great gulps, all manner of information about anything and everything. There was so much to know and the funny thing was, it all made sense. The links were there, the answers to all human problems. It was incredible to think that humans couldn't see them when they were so obvious.

"Zanihaer," Seth called from the mammoth carved doors of the library. I swivelled around on my perch and saw him far below, dressed as I loved him best, completely in black – black shirt and pants, characteristic long cloak swirling about his slim shoulders, top hat. He looked dashing, his darkness to my light; floating wisps of chiffon.

"Seth. How great to see you. I'll be right down." My voice drifted down to him, thin and twittery. I slid the book I had been reading on solar systems and black holes back into its slot on the shelf and shimmied quickly down the rails of the ladder and into Seth's arms. We embraced closely and I could feel his spirit seeking mine. "To what do I owe this pleasant surprise?" I asked.

Although Seth was my guide, we did not see each other often. He had other charges under his protection still in the physical world whereas I was on rest in the upper realm and didn't need his assistance.

"It's time, Zanihaer. There is a family ready for you that fulfil your criteria."

The announcement produced a flip-flop of fright in my abdomen. I had expected to feel ecstatic but now that the time had finally arrived after so many eons of waiting, all I felt was an abrupt hollowness as if having raced with joy and eagerness towards the edge of a precipice, I had stumbled at the last and now balanced there, suspended, too afraid to leap.

After my last death in a 1947 London air raid, I had waited for the others in my group to join me, and one by one they had; my brothers Steve and Robert followed not long after by Betty and Ruth, my sisters, both killed in a car crash on a road trip to Bristol. Then one by one they had left again, reborn, refreshed and ready to carry on with their evolution. But I had grown comfortable and not wanted to follow. I'd already had five lifetimes and was tired. I was enjoying the rest.

I wondered what the terms of my rebirth would be. My preparatory interviews had not been totally successful in that I was beginning to understand how to get along and be successful in life and wanted to capitalise on what I had learned but the elders wanted me to keep growing. They saw my potential. "You could easily take a position in the court as a guide," they said, "if you keep developing. You are nearly there."

But their arguments fell deadly and stultifying on my ears and I was resolute. "I want a good family," I had announced boldly to the Council of Twelve, having learned from experience that good parents were vital for success.

My previous family had been low in their expectations of me and my intelligence had not been fostered. So absorbed were they in their own lives, I had largely been left to my own devices. If only I could take my knowledge and experience with me, I thought, and not for the first time; but that was the Achilles heel in the condition of being human. The brain couldn't cope with the baseness of life on the physical plane and so was powered down to a fraction of its capacity. Although the essence of who a person was went with them, it had to be rediscovered with each birth. It was heartbreaking to see a brilliant surgeon or musician be born into an unaware family, to see their talent remain untapped because of a lack of perception.

Then again, there were some who preferred to remain on the lower levels of enlightenment, returning again and again without even a momentary break; destroyed in one life, maybe shot under a lonely bridge over a drug deal gone wrong, only to be reborn immediately, perpetuating the cycle all over again, never advancing.

During my interviews with The Council, Meadore, the head of The Twelve had asked, "What exactly do you mean by a good family?" Such questions were difficult to answer to the selection panel as they had never been human and never would be. Everything regarding human existence had to be explained in detail otherwise all sorts of misunderstandings occurred. This time I intended to be as precise as possible. I wanted the best advantage. "I want a middle class family in America. They should have money. I want a good education. And they should be kind, encouraging and have good values – supportive. Oh, and they should be happily married. I don't want a broken home."

Meadore wrote on the parchment. "And what lesson do you wish to learn? We believe that you should be aspiring to do good in the world."

In my mind, I remembered the shape and form of service; missionaries labouring in far flung, dangerous places populated by thieves, liars and murderers. People didn't like to believe there was real evil in the world but not believing in something didn't make it less true.

I did not want to learn any more lessons that involved struggle and hardship. Life on earth had a lot to offer and some people seemed to reap all the benefits with ease. Success flew before them like a sparkling ribbon and that was what I wanted. I wanted to be successful, happy and enjoy life. I wanted to be a winner.

The still visage of Meadore locked onto me over the parchment. Hand hovering, ink nib poised mid air and fluttering like a hummingbird; he 'hemmed' before pronouncing his verdict. "We will have to consult with the High Council to ascertain whether your goal is a worthy one. You will not be allowed to exist for your own gratification. You are in possession of too much knowledge for that." He slammed 'The Great Book' shut and stood. The interview clearly over, I returned to my room and lay prostrate on my bed, mentally exhausted.

The rooms in the court were sparse but comfortable, comprising of four whitewashed stone walls and a pallet bed. The windows were merely deep arches shaped into the thick blocks. We didn't need the rooms for much. They were mainly used for retiring into for meditation or some privacy but I loved spending quiet hours sitting in the window recess and gazing out over the picturesque, rolling hills of the outer realm.

It wasn't as if we had to sleep, although we could if we wanted to. In the upper realm, physical needs were absent. In fact it was the physical needs and desires that were the draw cards for returning to earthly life. Food! In particular: coffee, bacon and eggs, chocolate, a fat steak on the barbeque. The desire to eat food never abated. For others the 'carrots' were alcohol, drugs, cigarettes (never mind if they killed them) fast cars, sex, the touch of skin on skin, human love.

Sex and love were not exactly forbidden in the upper realm. It was just rarely thought about. We touched each other constantly but in a more cerebral way. Our minds and spirits melded together with physical contact in a way that was deeply satisfying. Nature drew many back. The earth, despite its problems, was still beautiful; the natural world, rain, snow, sun and storms, the ocean, animals. I missed animals and longed to hold a cat and ride a horse again.

"Has The Council made a decision?" I asked Seth. "Have they acceded to my requests?"

Seth twiddled the gold ring on his finger. "I don't know," he said as we turned to walk the length of the corridor. "I was merely sent to fetch you."

The walk to the council rooms was not far, just in the next wing. Most of the doors into the rooms leading off from the high ceilinged corridor were closed and we did not encounter anyone else on the way. The hollow halls echoed to our footsteps alone.

Outside the door to the council rooms stood two guards dressed in red pantaloons and highly embroidered, tailored jackets. They both held a clear ball the size of an orange in each hand at right angles to their bodies. I'd heard about the spheres. It was said that within them could be discerned the motives of any action. Found guilty of malicious intent and your punishment would be to be sent back to earth with full awareness of loss and death. The woe of that knowledge filled the spirit with such despair that any chance of happiness was effectively ruined. Those children were born wailing on their first breaths, their cries echoing through the early months and years; unhappy, angry children who took forever to settle into life, always finding fault, perpetually negative, driving their parents to distraction.

We bowed in deference to each of the guards in turn and then Seth knocked. The massive doors swung inwards to reveal a long hall. A solid wood table filled most of the space and the twelve council elders sat, cloaked in richly decorated robes, along three sides of the table. Two empty seats waited on the fourth side. Seth took the chair to the right so I sat in the one to the left.

'The Great Book' lay open in the middle of the table. Meadore looked up from the scroll he was perusing and smiled at me. A thrill of excitement skipped through my heart. "Child, we have considered and granted your request. We believe there is much growth to be gained in desiring to live well and it could be that learning to live well is at least as important as any other lesson; for how can a human learn to live except through the inevitable trials of life? Therefore, we have agreed to give you a good start."

"Amen," chorused The Twelve.

Their solemn voices floated up as one to the vaulted rafters of the ceiling.

Meadore cleared his throat. "The terms are such: You will be born into an established ranching family in Wyoming. You will be born healthy and there are no hereditary illnesses in the family; although you must realise of course," Meadore peered at me over the bridge of his nose, "that many illnesses in humans are brought on by the persons themselves and that is beyond our ability to influence or control." I nodded to show that I understood. "And," he continued, "you will be who you are. All you have become will remain with you and all you will become will be your own doing. Finally, Seth will be your guide once more. Call on him and he will guide you although, as always, he is forbidden to directly intervene."

"Go well my child," said The Twelve in unison. "May God bless you in this undertaking - Amen."

The Twelve rose as one, which indicated that Seth and I do also. My heart was pounding. Was it out of fear or excitement? I couldn't tell. Over thirty years had passed since I had been on earth. What would it be like now? How would I cope? Would anyone be there with me from my group or would I be alone? What had Meadore said? A Wyoming ranching family. Were there other children or would I be the first? Questions, literally hundreds of them crowded my mind.

I packed up the meagre possessions in my room and dressed in my leaving shift; a soft, grey, draping garment that only served to cover my nakedness while I waited for my spirit to enter into the new life of the infant. Finally, I was ready and was led to the departure room by two attendants; beautiful, willowy women who took me by the hands and positioned me on a small disc of light in the centre of the room. Golden light beamed down on my head from a corresponding disc in the ceiling, bathing my shoulders and hair. The light grew. Its brilliance dazzled my eyes, disorientating me...

...Darkness. Pain. My head was being crushed. Dull noises driving me through an unbelievably narrow portal. I didn't need to breathe yet, *couldn't* breathe. Light. Bright light. Shapes against the light. Murmuring sounds. *Breathe*. I drew a gasp, burning my lungs, and then wailed as I slithered out in a rush. Space! My arms flailed about and fearing I was about to fall, I cried out; coughing and spluttering. *Was I drowning?* I felt the pressure and warmth of firm hands grasping my ankles and shoulders. I felt hunger. It gripped my stomach and my head turned instinctively, my mouth searching for nourishment, feeling softness and the warm smell of sweat on skin. Although I did not know what those smells were, they comforted me. The softness in my mouth made me suckle. Somehow I knew how to swallow. The thin trickle of life filled me and I was reassured. I opened my eyes but could only make out dim shapes. I heard murmurings and turned instinctively towards them.

"A girl, Sherman. A girl at last. Isn't she just precious? The boys will be tickled pink, - tickled pink. Do you want to hold your daughter, Sherman?" I felt myself being passed, wobbly, through the air. Then, for the first time, I smelled my father and the wood smoke earthiness of him as I was held securely against his chest.

"She's a beauty, Suzie," he said as he gazed adoringly into my still blind eyes. "Who's Pa's girl then?" He jiggled me up and down and I felt the rough skin of his finger stroke the curving moons of my cheek before he passed me back to his wife, my mother. I cried when he handed me over.

Suzie laughed "Sheriden. Let's call her Sheriden," she crooned.

CHAPTER ONE

...Birth! Nothing could ever have prepared me for the cataclysmic upheaval that wracked my body. Convulsions, not dissimilar to the wretched heaving I had experienced once with food poisoning, took over. "Pant. Breathe shallowly," instructed the midwife. But I could no more hold back the contractions that expelled my son out into the world than Moses had been able to hold back the red sea.

My darling mother, who had held my hand throughout the ordeal, was the first to hold the child. She murmured gently and laid him on my chest. A pair of dark eyes surveyed me quietly. He was perfect. An unexpected wave of pure love coursed through me as I took in his cow lick of dark hair and delicate cupid lips. At the same time, there was a lonely feeling of loss and vulnerability. "Who will look after us little boy?" I whispered into his tiny, translucent ear.

On the afternoon of the third day of my confinement, Mark appeared in the doorway of my room. My heart skipped. I hadn't seen him for months, since school finished. He was as well built as ever but looked older. His chin was shaded with stubble and he had a man's look about him. He shuffled awkwardly.

I tucked the sheet in around my waist, instinctively ensuring that none of my body parts were visible, before saying as pleasantly as I could muster, "Hi, Mark, come and have a look at your son." At this he drew closer and peered into the crib where the infant was sleeping.

"Hey little fella," he said. He placed his hand on the baby's head and the child stirred and whimpered. I swallowed the 'be careful' that sprang to my lips. "Can I hold him?" Jealousy whisked through the room and I understood that I didn't want Mark holding my son; not now, not ever.

"He's asleep," I stalled. "Maybe later - when he wakes up."

Mark straightened, frowning. "How have you been?" he ventured, uncertain of whether to negotiate the bed to where the lone chair presided or remain standing.

"Fine. And you?" The tone of my voice and the defiant gaze of my eyes challenged him to imagine differently but he could not meet my look. Instead, his own eyes ranged over some unspecified spot on the wall above my head.

"Yeah. Good. Good," he nodded.

"What are you doing? Are you working?"

"Yeah. I got a job," he said. He looked discomfited. "Do you need anything?"

My mind worked fast. We didn't exactly need anything but I sure could have done with some cash to buy a decent drink at the hospital shop. "If you have ten bucks so I can buy some diapers once we go home that would be good," I said.

Mark looked at the floor, his face clearly betraying an internal conflict. "I do but it's all I've got on me and I need that for booze. There's a party at Dekko's tonight."

Immediately, my temper flared at this new evidence of what I interpreted as his irresponsibility and self absorption. "What's more important, your son or a party?" I spoke icily, incredulous that the question even had to be asked.

"The party," he replied. "Just because I've got a kid doesn't mean I have to give up on life."

"Yeah, not for you – you selfish pig." My voice rose involuntarily as anger, too long suppressed, erupted. "I've carried *your* baby for nine months, through no fault of my own, and you've never said or done a thing."

"I didn't think you wanted anything to do with me. You knew where I was," he argued, his voice also rising as he defended himself.

Rage blinded me. "Get out you bastard," I hissed. "Don't think you are *ever* going to have anything to do with my son. I *hate* you." His face flushed a violent shade of red but he turned to leave without protest.

"Hey," I barked as he neared the door. Mark paused and turned around. "Why?" I pleaded. "Why did you do that to me? You're a popular guy. Any number of girls would have thrown themselves at your feet. Why me?"

The characteristic smirk played across his lips. "To tell the truth it was a dare," he answered. "Some of the guys thought you might be ripe for it under those jeans and boring T shirts. We flipped for it."

I held it together until he left then I cried and cried. I felt like the stupidest female that ever walked the face of the planet. The baby stirred in his crib and began wailing too so I picked him up and put him to the breast where he quickly settled into contented grunting. I wished I could have been so easily appeased. The tears fell as I wept for my own stupidity, for the future of my son and out of frustration and rage at Mark who, once I thought about it, had so cleverly side stepped any responsibility towards us.

****

A highlight of 1992 had been that as a senior student I was eligible to attend the school formal and for the first half of the year speculation had been rife as to who was potentially going with whom as their date. Becky had managed to manoeuvre her way into going on Jet's arm, a prospect I found to be faintly alarming as Jet had plans for his life and Becky had but one – to find a man to look after her. It was ironic in the light of Pa's attitudes but the idea of a facile Becky leeching off Jet dismayed me so badly that I cornered him in his room one evening to talk to him about it.

He was sitting, with long, jean clad legs extended on his bed and IPod in his ears while he expertly shuffled the controls on his Xbox 360. Jet was our family's golden boy. Smart, cheeky and rakishly good looking, I had idolised him for as long as I could remember. He pressed pause and removed his ear phones at my knock. "Come in," he invited when he saw that it was me. I sat on the edge of the bed and gathered courage before asking whether it was true that he was taking Becky to the prom as his date.

Upon hearing the question, he placed the controller on the duvet and swung himself around until he was sitting beside me. "Yeah, what of it?" he replied, cautiously.

I scuffed at the carpet with my bare foot. "I think she likes you," I confided.

He glanced at me sideways as if trying to decide how much to reveal of his own feelings. "I like her."

Surprised, I removed myself to Jet's desk and inspected the silver, sporting trophies that were proudly lined up there. I hadn't expected him to say that he liked her as well.

"What's wrong? You okay with that?" he asked.

"She's got no ambition," I replied. I didn't want to hurt his feelings and Becky was, after all, a friend. "I don't think she's right for you, that's all. She'll use you up. You'll have to look after her your whole life." I absently ran my hand over the shelf, sweeping up the fine layer of dust, allowing it to create ribbons in my palm.

Jet said nothing for a while then said, thoughtfully, "That's what a man's supposed to do isn't it? Look after his wife and kids? I'll earn the money. Besides she can work part time to keep busy if she wants to. She's already got a job at one of the dress shops in town."

I turned to face him, distressed at the thought of him throwing his life away and giving up on his aspirations. "But what about going to Uni and being a vet? Don't you want to do that anymore?"

"Yes, silly, of course," he laughed. "I'm going to start next year. It will only take four years. I'll see Becky when I come home on the semester breaks and we'll get married when I'm qualified. Don't worry, Sis," he said, coming over to me and wrapping his arms about my shoulders. "I'll still love you."

I gave him a shove, laughing despite my anxiety. "Jackass."

I saw how it was for Jet. His life and career were all planned out. Jet would make decisions based on what he wanted for himself and Becky would agree. She had done so already but then she had never wanted anything specifically for herself. She was like Ma.

In that moment, I realised that it was me who was different, me who was dissatisfied with the idea of being a housewife long before the question arose. What a bore to spend life in the kitchen and keeping the house clean when in reality you were the only one who cared about it. We kids had never cared whether the beds were made or whether the dishes were done, as long as we didn't have to do them and our bellies were full. I suddenly felt very close to my Aunty Harriet and wondered if this was why she had never married.

Ma's two older sisters were twins but they did not look anything alike. Aunty Harriet was short and dumpy with a rotund upper body shape that made her look as though she would topple over at any moment while Aunty Julie was just as short but much thinner. *Jack sprat could eat no fat. His wife could eat no lean,* I often recited disloyally to myself. They lived with Grandma and Grandpa and together ran the family hardware store.

Harriet may as well have been a man. She dressed in pants and shapeless jerseys that concealed her voluminous and shapeless figure and effortlessly flung forty pound sacks of oats about as if they were cabbages. Aunty Julie, on the other hand, was always immaculately dressed and smelled delectable. Her voice, mannerisms and hair-do were refined although I was never certain whether her hair was real because it remained perfectly immobile no matter what. There was never a single strand out of place whereas my hair couldn't even manage to stay put with a scrunchie. It slipped out in random wisps no matter how tightly it had been pulled and tugged into submission. I would have loved to have been allowed to touch Aunty Julie's hair – to check whether it was, in fact, real – but I could never bring myself to breach the unspoken barrier of good manners that prevented me from doing so.

Aunty Julie also wore make-up. Her lips were invariably painted bright red which Ma frowned upon, but I admired. It made her look glamorous. Aunty Julie managed the store accounts and handled the money. She smoked while she added up figures on the adding machine, cigarette dangling elegantly between manicured nails, her face clouded by the smoke she exhaled.

As much as I watched Aunty Harriet and Aunty Julie, neither of them appeared to demonstrate any interest in the Flagstaff males despite encountering a good selection of them every day. No one seemed to see my aunties as women. They were as much a part of the store as the bridles and sacks of animal feed that they sold.

When they visited, which they did every Sunday after church, Harriet did all the talking while Julie helped Ma in the kitchen. It was interesting listening to Harriet as she gossiped about the neighbours. She knew everything that was going on in Flagstaff and quite a bit that wasn't. She knew who was sick, whose kids were going to college and who was expecting. Good reason, as Ma said, to 'behave and keep our noses clean' otherwise 'the whole town'd be yakking about you behind your back,' such was the extent of the grapevine and how effectively news flew around the district.

With lunch over, Pa customarily drove Harriet and Julie back to the hardware store. For some reason, neither of them liked the idea of driving even though they were around cars all day long. Then again, Ma had never learned to drive either. I guess with Pa to ferry them about they didn't need to learn. Ma called driving a man's job but I think underneath she liked it that Pa went with her to do the shopping. If she had been able to drive, next thing Pa would have been getting our mother to run errands every minute of the day.

I loved it at the shop; the smells mostly – the dusty scent of hessian sacks bulging with oats and chaff, sweet bales of hay and bins of grass seeds sold by the pound while the racks of saddles and saddlery gear imparted their own oiled, leathery smell to the odours in the store. Everything in the place was evocative of wide open spaces, horses and cattle.

Harriet gave me jobs to do such as arranging the cans of oil, tools and other goods onto the shelves. She was strict about how the products were to be presented with new stock behind the old stock, labels facing outwards and the front item in line with the edge of the shelf. When I became proficient at that, I was allowed to write the prices on the new stock with a vivid. Unpacking the boxes was as exciting as opening presents at Christmas time and I learned how to mark off the goods received against the inventory and how to find the retail price against the wholesale price.

When I slept over, I stayed in Ma's old room which remained unchanged from when she was a girl. The head board of the narrow single bed was walnut veneer in elaborate Queen Ann style and already well over one hundred years old. It rose high over the top part and was edged with a scalloped trim of solid walnut. The footboard was the same shape but in addition had two cabriole posts, one on each end, that I liked to hang my clothes on. The mattress lay on wooden slats and had long ago lost its spring but after a hard day at the store, I invariably slept like a baby.

Harriet was easy to talk to and I often interrogated her about life's mysteries because she could be relied upon to give a considered answer, unlike my parents who tended to assert that 'I was too young to understand' whenever I broached a topic that they did not view as being suitable for discussion with a minor.

Ever since noticing my aunt's single status, I had resolved to ask her about it as all of the other adults I could think of were married and my curiosity burned as to the reason why she wasn't.

"Can I ask you something personal?" I asked, deceptively casual, one afternoon while we were putting away the new deliveries in the store room.

She paused from the boxes she was stacking, giving me her undivided attention. "Sure honey. What is it?"

"Why haven't you ever married?"

Unexpectedly, she gave a great belly laugh, and slapped her thighs. "Well ain't that a grand question," she bellowed. "I guess it's because I didn't ever need to. I've got my own place, a good job and money. I can do what I want, when I want and don't have to answer to anyone. I don't need a man to look after me."

I elaborated, "But what about love and kids. Don't you want those things?"

"Kids. Now why would I want kids? Lazy little buggers they are these days. I've seen them touchin' stuff they shouldn't be, answerin' back to their parents, spending their money. Nah, I definitely don't want children. Anyhow, I've got you!"

I persisted, determined to get answers.

"What about love? Don't you want a boyfriend at least?"

At this she sat down on a pallet of grass seed and removed her gloves. "Hah. Well." She tapped the side of her nose and winked. "That's my business and I aint tellin'. What about you? Who are you going to the prom with?" she asked in a deft attempt to change the subject.

My mind reeled, trying to make sense of what her answer implied. "Do you have a boyfriend?" I pressed, incredulous at the prospect.

"He-he," she chuckled, giving in, "Look girl, a woman's got certain needs, right? I ain't no nun that's for sure.

But get married and have kids, no that ain't my scene. Let me give you some advice. You've gotta be discreet. This is a very small town and everybody knows or is related to everyone else. You don't want to mess in your own back yard – got it? You've gotta go further afield and be careful. A man he can do whatever he likes and he's just sowin' his wild oats. Huh! It's a double standard for sure. A female plays the field and she's no good. Plus you've gotta take care of your health. You don't want no unplanned pregnancy to take care of."

"Take care of?" If my voice was faint it was because I was shocked. I had no idea that Harriet who seemed as sexless as a spud possessed such secret, extensive knowledge about life.

"Ya know – abortion. God! Ain't your ma told you nothin' girl?"

"Oh yeah, abortion," I said. I knew about that, sort of. Knew there were ways of getting rid of a baby like having hot baths or doing lots of exercise but of the medical aspects I knew nothing. I tried to imagine sitting in Dr Solomon's surgery and informing him I wanted a pregnancy terminated. The whole town would know about it within seconds via the great, flapping, red rimmed lips of Dr Solomon's receptionist. It gave me cold sweats to anticipate the embarrassment. Better to leave town than endure the gossip. Suddenly, the realisation dawned on me that this could be the precise reason why a couple of older girls in school *had* abruptly left during the previous year.

I felt gauche and naive but at the same time, thrilled. I was sixteen and a real life, out in the wide world, was possible. It was not unreasonable to believe that I could go to college, have a boyfriend *and* live an independent life.

Nothing out of the ordinary occurred during the following weeks and I attended classes as usual. The prom was on everyone's minds. The entire school was talking about it. I wasn't interested in going, in part because I didn't have anything to wear. I hadn't been talking to Ma and Pa much of late and didn't know how to go about getting them to buy me a new outfit for the occasion without incurring the obligation to express gratitude. It seemed easier not to go.

Not that anyone that I was interested in going with had asked me anyway. I had friends but boys never flirted with me. I was never the recipient of sultry looks cast from the corners of brooding eyes. No lanky frame ever leaned against my locker, predatory casual, like they did with the other girls, so close that you wondered how they could smell so good, hips seductively slim, sexy. That is until you saw their faces up close, white and spotty, lank hair and probably glasses too. The good looking grid iron boys, jocks, were out of my league and anyway a startling truth was that most of them were stupid and couldn't pass classes if they tried – which they didn't; believing academic success was beneath them and that they were destined for pro ball stardom.

I was saved from being too much of a recluse by my friends who hassled me without any sense of mercy if they thought my grades were getting out of hand. "You gotta 'A' again?" they'd scoff. "No one normal gets so many As. You gotta get a life girl or you gonna turn into one of those rocks you're so passionate about." So the next day after school we'd all catch the bus to the Flagstaff Mall and I'd play at being social, drink cola, look at clothes or go to a movie then catch the late bus home again.

Then, out of the blue, an unexpected incident occurred in the cafeteria. I was seated opposite Vanessa and Becky, picking at my stodgy pasta bake and discussing some scholarship forms my science teacher, Mrs Phelps, had given me, when the buff frame belonging to Mark Bronson slid into the bench next to Vanessa and I found myself at eye level with a pair of startling green eyes and fashionably shambolic mop of bedraggled hair. We all gawped. Never in the history of the world had any boy creature joined our little group.

A large hand was extended first to Vanessa then to me. "Mark Bronson," he cheerfully announced.

Not that he needed any introducing. We all knew who he was. Mark 'Handsome' as we liked to call him was well known to all the girls; notably for his skill on the football field as well as his abnormally high levels of academic achievement. It was well known that he was top in most of his classes. He managed to maintain popularity by the sheer force of his considerable, cheery charm.

"Which one of you gorgeous ladies is going to accompany me to the prom?" he asked as naturally as if he was ordering fries. He spoke generally but he was looking at me. Our mouths dropped open in unison. *Was this for real?* I looked around. Everything seemed normal but I saw that the cheer-group was looking our way which aroused my suspicions.

"Is this some kind of joke?" I said coldly. "Cos if it is, you can just crawl back to your little blondie group and tell them I said sod you."

Mark laughed a genuine laugh. "No. No joke. I've had my eye on you for quite a while Miss Sheriden Lewis."

I stared at him, uncertain. Boys just didn't talk to me, nor me to them.

"I like how you're interested in geology," he continued. "Not many girls are any good at science. But how's your math? Do you need help? If you want a hand I can assist."

His arrogance annoyed me. My math was weak but I was working on it during after school tutorials. I snapped, "I'm fine with math thanks."

"Oh. Cool. Sweet," he replied. An inexplicably irritating smirk played on his annoying, chiselled lips. "So, it's a date then." It was a statement not a question.

"Wh... what?" I stammered, confused.

"It's a date. You're coming with me to the prom. I'll pick you up at eight. Don't be late!" he quipped as he gathered up his tray. "Ladies." He bowed to each of us in turn, his gaze lingering on me a fraction of a moment longer, and then he was gone.

We exploded into chatter.

"O.M.G," crowed Vanessa. "Did you hear that? You lucky cow! Oh my god. Fancy Mark 'Handsome' asking you to the prom. You will *have* to buy a ball gown now."

I shook my head, disbelieving. "Do you think he was genuine? It seems so bizarre. He's never so much as glanced my way before."

"Who cares? Oh, he's so gorgeous. You lucky thing." She sighed wistfully and slumped into her seat. "You will *have* to look drop dead gorgeous for him," she continued. "We are going shopping."

When I arrived home I told Ma that Mark Bronson had asked me to the prom and she was ecstatic. You would have thought it was she who was going. 150 bucks materialised out of thin air for me to buy a dress and accessories and a hair appointment was also made forthwith for the afternoon of the day in question. Ma declined to come with me to find a dress but Vanessa and Becky were, of course, more than happy to oblige.

Vanessa Goodwell and Becky Baldwin were my best friends. We had met as new entrants on the very first lunch time, of our very first day of the first grade and after swapping sandwiches were inseparable from that moment on. Vanessa's father was a pharmacist and Becky's father worked in an office in Flagstaff. None of our mothers worked full time but Vanessa's mother often helped out in the pharmacy. Vanessa was my closest friend and we walked to the bus stop together most days. She had a grown up sister called Rosie who worked in a bank in downtown Dodge City and drove home on the weekends in her own car.

Becky was more reserved and sometimes I felt that I didn't know her at all but she spent a lot of time at our house because even as a young girl, she fancied Jet. Becky didn't own a horse so we spent most of our day hanging out in the stables and playing at rodeo games; our favourite pastime being to set up empty forty-four gallon drums in the main corral and practise barrel racing. Becky could ride perfectly well and gave me competition but I had the edge owing to my extensive experience, although I had to admit she looked better on my mount, Bono, than I did. She was an all American girl in the making. Her silky, blonde hair and clear, blue eyes dazzled everyone who set eyes on her. Her figure, slender and sylph-like contrasted badly, or so I felt, with my relatively plain visage.

When I was fourteen, I fell in love with Posh Spice and spent hours modelling myself on her example. Having read once that she took over an hour to get ready for school when she was a child, I felt licensed to obsess over examining my own body in the bedroom mirror; agonising over whether my abdomen was flat, my hair curling correctly and skin pimple free, whether I better suited my hair up or down, clipped at the sides or upswept in a pony tail.

I disagreed with Ma over what I should be wearing. I wanted Abercrombie & Fitch or Eagle because everyone was wearing them at school and I didn't want to be different. She wanted Macy's because it was cheaper. Much to my discontent, I sprouted in every direction and stressed over the likelihood of inheriting my build from Pa who was a solid six foot tall but I needn't have worried. As I grew older, I slimmed out so that by the time I was sixteen I was a tidy 5'6, much like all the other girls.

But I was more academic than fashion. As a child, I was always happiest when roaming about the farm, exploring and discovering the creatures that hid under rocks and bark. Trees existed to house spindly nests of twigs garnished with delicately tinted, opaque speckled eggs. And my room was filled with treasures; a fish skeleton bleached white that I had found in a stream plus various rocks carefully arranged alongside cracked and broken shells, scavenged during a rare trip to the beach. I loved nature and the workings of the earth held a fascination for me. I poured over books examining diagrams of volcanoes. The spider veins of lava reaching deep into the earth like roots and the boil-like cone of the volcano were both entrancing and terrifying at the same time.

My science teacher, recognising a passion that reflected her own, nagged me constantly about applying for Frankton University to study geology and earth sciences. Eventually, I had to tell her that my father didn't think that I was worth the cost. Curiously, she didn't seem at all surprised by this revelation. Instead, she pulled some papers out from her desk drawer and handed them to me. "They're scholarship papers. The scholarship is to Fieldwest College, not as good as Frankton but they still run a respected science programme. Fill in the forms and get them back to me and I'll do my best to get you in." She spoke as if she actually possessed the ability to do that, to 'get me in,' so I took the papers with genuine appreciation and remembered my manners and said, "Thank you."

The college question was a matter of generational difference in point of view between Pa and myself. I wanted to go to college to study geology and volcanology but Pa couldn't see the value of educating a female who would inevitably 'get married and have children.' His argument developed along the lines of: "Then you've gotta look after them. You can't go jettin' off around the world when you've got kids to look after now can you? Who's gonna look after your family if you don't?"

My retort to that was, "Maybe I don't want to get married and have kids." I didn't know whether I did or not truth be told. I hadn't even had a boyfriend yet. Fear of being fodder for the gossip machine kept me chaste. Anyone who even looked as if they might like a boy at school was ragged mercilessly. Rumours were endemic about who had done what with whom, who got drunk and slept with whoever's boyfriend or girlfriend. It was hateful, mad. Reputations were ruined overnight on the basis of hearsay. I escaped most of it because I focused on my school work, and evaded being called a nerd because I was ultra careful not to fit the stereotype. I kept my hair cut in shoulder length waves and my clothes were the trendiest I could extract from my parent's wallets. I even wore make-up, carefully applied in the girl's loos once away from Ma's watchful eyes. School was not the place to be dating boys in my opinion but I didn't see why I couldn't have a husband, children *and* a career in the future. Only Pa didn't see it that way. "You should go an' work in the hardware store once you finish school. It's as good a job as any and its family," he said.

"Pa! I've been working there since I was ten years old," I sighed, exasperation edging my voice. "Anyway, Jet's going to study veterinary science. Why can't I go to Uni too? It's not fair to favour the boys, you know."

At that he grunted. "We'll see, pet," he said as he tossed the remains of his smoke between the boards of the deck. I sighed, convinced I'd be stuck in Flagstaff forever.

As a child, Pa had been my champion but as I had grown older the stubborn will ingrained in both of us emerged and we found it all but impossible to agree on anything. The fight about going to college became a symbol of everything my father and I disagreed about. It was fight for the control of my life and I was unprepared to lose it. On one journey home from school with Pa, I was silent and pensive as the familiar scenery flicked by.

"Penny for your thoughts," he quipped looking across at me.

"Pa. I want to go to college. I want to be a geologist." I forced my voice to remain calm and reasonable. "I don't want to get married and stay at home with kids cooking and cleaning all day like Ma. I want more."

"Don't you criticise your ma," growled Pa, taking offence. "She's been well taken care of and been happy doin' so like any good woman would be. She's never had to worry about money, food or a roof over her head."

"I know, Pa," I interrupted. "I'm not criticising. I know Ma is happy with her life and you and Ma have been great parents. I could never have asked for better. But that's not the life I want for myself – not just yet anyhow. I want to learn and maybe travel and earn my own money, like Jet. It's the modern world, Pa. And why not? I like science and I'm good at it."

Pa drove, his face set on the road ahead, quiet, for a long time. "I dunno girl," he said, finally. "It just ain't natural. All girls wanna get married and have kids at some point in life. What good's all that time in college gonna do you when you're home with your little ones? It's gonna be a big waste of money."

He wasn't convinced and I didn't know what else to say to change his mind. I was left, once again, close to tears of frustration. Jet had the college idea handed to him on a plate. He would have been happy to stay home and run the ranch with my older brother, Byron but I knew Pa didn't want the boys collaborating behind his back. Getting Jet off to college was one way of getting him off the scene.

I was as smart as Jet. My grades were better. The injustice of it settled like a stodgy dumpling and as the miles sped by, the enraged frustration grew within me. All my growing up years I had been one of the kids and hadn't noticed any distinctive treatment. I'd ridden my ponies, driven the tractor and done my jobs along with my brothers, never associating my being female with our mother who was, as always, a warm presence in the kitchen, baking, while the boys and I stamped in at dusk, cold and grubby, yearning for nourishment and a cup of hot tea. And now what - because I was sixteen and had breasts I was suddenly different?

I clenched my jaw tightly and stared at the landscape rolling by. The ache in my throat, eyes and chest silenced me. My tongue felt too big for my mouth. If I spoke, out would pour black, sticky tar that would fill up the dodge and never in a million years would we ever be able to extricate ourselves from it so I shut my mouth and said nothing more.

CHAPTER TWO

Unexpectedly, shopping for the prom turned out to be fun. The riding I did every spare moment meant that my legs and waist were shapely and toned and my boobs were in proportion to the rest of my body so the gowns I tried on looked stunning, Why hadn't I noticed before that I was looking pretty hot?

I eventually settled on an ice blue cocktail dress with a straight cut neckline ruched across the bodice and held up with double shoestring straps. The skirt was a simple knee length, A line - but flipped out at the hem with a cheeky, double ruffle that peeked out from underneath. A stylish pair of strappy, white sandals finished off my ensemble and I left the store feeling like a million dollars. I couldn't wait to see Mark's reaction.

Vanessa found a gorgeous satin vermillion, floor length, formal gown with an asymmetrical shoulder that clung to her voluptuous curves like mercury. I envied the easy sexuality that oozed out of her pores. She hadn't said if she had done 'it' yet but sometimes I wondered. She seemed knowing somehow. She knew how to flaunt her body but I never actually saw her do anything more than say a friendly hello to any of the boys at school. But then we were a group. We ate together and sat together in classes and hung out together on the weekends. Maybe the fact was that we didn't let anyone else in although we didn't see ourselves as necessarily being exclusive. It was more the fact that no one ever wanted to join us so we stuck together.

As the weeks until the formal raced by, the prom committee spent hours decorating the school hall in a Jurassic Park theme (based on the must see film of the year) while I sweated my way through our mid-year exams. I needn't have worried. I sailed through them all, even math. When the results were posted, there was my name: Sheriden Lewis, at or near the top of every class. The girls gave me crap of course. "Geek. Nerd. Brainiac," they sneered, disgusted.

I wondered in what universe was it considered cool to be stupid? I *wanted* to pass. I had filled out the scholarship papers and handed them back to Ms Phelps the very next day but not heard anything since. Nevertheless, the thought of a scholarship had rekindled my ambitions. In my mind, I envisaged myself working at a gold or diamond mine, devising methods of opening up the earth and encouraging the rocks to divulge the locations of their secret, hoarded treasures to the machines. I couldn't wait.

Since the day in the cafeteria, Mark had kept in superficial contact. He liked to sneak up behind me as I walked to class and whisper 'hello' directly into my ear; which was sweet, but after the 'hello how are you,' conversation tended to stall leaving me feeling flustered. I put it down to his being a jock. Football guys were not noted for their conversation skills. Rumour had it that most of them went to parties and got wasted on the weekends or cruised around in their cars – although cruising was a grandiose term for the driving that occurred on the streets of Flagstaff on any given Friday night. We didn't even have a set of traffic lights.

When the morning of the prom arrived, I was bundled into the car and delivered to the stylist. An hour later, I emerged with an elegant French twist roll and a wispy fringe that strayed over my forehead and cheek. It took me two hours to apply my make-up but in the end I was satisfied with the results. Mark rapped on the door at precisely eight o'clock and after enduring an impromptu photo shoot directed by Ma, we made it out into the evening.

The early stars were tentatively making their appearance as dusk gathered around the lingering remnants of the balmy spring day. I felt excited and a little nervous as I climbed into the passenger seat of Mark's navy blue Chevy pickup. "Nice truck," I remarked somewhat inanely. "Is it yours?"

"Yup," confirmed Mark as he turned the key in the ignition. "Dad bought it for my seventeenth birthday when I made the team."

"So what does your dad do – you know – for a living?" I asked grateful for the opportunity to find out a bit more about him.

"He doesn't do anything now. He's retired. He used to be a cop in Dodge City but he got shot in the side of his head. The doctors had to take off the whole side of his skull to relieve the bleeding on his brain. He was lucky to live but he's lost a lot of confidence. He got a compo payout and has been retired ever since."

"Gosh! That's horrible," I exclaimed, horrified. "Is he okay?"

Mark looked across at me. "Yeah. He's okay. He can lose his temper sometimes. You have to watch out for that. But I can tell when he's getting riled up."

"And what about your mum?"

"Dead," he answered shortly, "five years ago, not long after dad's accident."

Shocked, I didn't know what to say so I shut up and looked out of the window. My brain wondered how she'd died but I didn't like to ask.

"Hey!" said Mark, reaching over and patting my knee with chummy vigour, "I'm okay. We're okay. Life goes on, right?" His grin was infectious. "And by the way, you look stunning. I was right about you."

I wasn't exactly sure what he meant by that but I was so flattered to be told that I looked stunning by Mark 'Handsome' that the unasked question lingered in my head for less than a second.

There was already quite a crowd when we arrived at the hall. The Principal and deputies were lined up like a reception committee with all the students passing along the chain, shaking hands with each as they dished out compliments like lollies.

The covert purpose of the line up was to identify the inebriates who had been boozing for most of the afternoon. Anyone suspected of being under the influence was discreetly siphoned off into a curtained enclave where they were breathalysed. The bad boys naturally counted being busted as a badge of honour and emerged making signs of victory, arms raised and punching into the air as they swaggered out of the foyer, escorted from the premises by extraordinarily large, uniformed security guys. Mark and I shook hands with the teachers, accepted their compliments and were given permission to pass into the hall that was already pumping with heaving teenage bodies straining to the sounds of the school band playing a very creditable performance of 'Mustang Sally.'

We muscled our way to the drink stand where we received some tropical punch served in a plastic disposable cup then struggled to the photo booth for the couple's photo. The music was so loud that conversation was impossible but I saw Vanessa and a girl called Amelia dancing together and waved. They waved back and manoeuvred their way through the crowd to where Mark and I were standing. "You two look divine," gushed Vanessa directly into my ear. "I hope you get voted best couple."

Amelia jiggled on the spot in time to the beat as she gazed out over the dance floor searching for who knows what – or whom. My own eyes sought Jet and Becky but couldn't locate them. As a group, we elbowed into the crush and joined in, moving our bodies in time to the beat. I let the rhythm wash over me, instructing my limbs as to the correct moves to make and we sang along to the songs at the tops of our lungs as Mark danced with each of us in turn. Other friends of his joined us. He yelled their names into my ear but I forgot them as soon as they were mentioned. We were high on the music. I kicked off my shoes against the wall. My hair slipped and then fell into its habitual shape. Sweat beaded my forehead as I danced myself into a trance. The hours flew by.

As the night progressed, Mark's hands strayed more and more to my body. It was a thrilling experience to be showered with attention by one of the more desirable boys from school. *What a gentleman,* I thought as he brought me drinks and escorted me, his hand guiding my elbow, to the supper buffet.

At eleven, the speeches were made and the prom king and queen were announced. "Fuck it," Mark muttered under his breath but I didn't know those who won and couldn't have cared less. With a final flourish, the band signalled that the party was over and a group of us drifted into the night.

The damp air felt like silk on my clammy face and arms and Mark's arm lingered around my waist as I teetered on aching feet to his truck and clambered in. Two others climbed into the back. Mark reached across and rummaged in the glove compartment, drawing out a plastic coke bottle. He took a long draught before handing it to me. I took a gulp, registering the alcohol laden taste as it slid down my throat. "What's in this?" I asked, holding the bottle up to the light.

"Bourbon. Dad's best. I've been hanging out for this." He took the bottle out of my hand and had another pull.

"Hand it over," clamoured the others. Mark passed the bottle to the back seat where it did the rounds. Once again in my hands, I took another long swig and then another. I was terribly thirsty and a pleasant feeling was rapidly enveloping my bones leaving me blissful and relaxed.

Mark turned on the engine and pulled out of the parking lot. He turned into a road that led out of town and drove for a while in the darkness. "Where are we going?" I asked, snuggling closer to him.

"To the river. It will be nice to sit out by the water for a bit don't you think?"

I agreed, feeling adult and daring. The evening was going great. Mark turned the Chevy into the car park and we piled out. The two in the back who I now knew were Sasha and Warwick were kissing in the dark so we left them to it and strolled over, hand in hand, to the water's edge. The river gurgled, friendly. The night air hit me and I stumbled slightly. Mark took my arm in his. "Steady there, soldier," he cautioned. "How much did you have to drink?"

I didn't know. It wasn't so much I didn't think. We sat on the grass, chatting quietly and then I lay back, feeling the hard, damp earth beneath my back. Mark stroked my hair softly as I lay there, then he leaned over and kissed me gently on the lips. A deep well of feeling sprang up at his touch and I opened my mouth to his and rolled towards him. He ran his hand along my leg and caressed, with feather light fingers, the inside of my thigh making me moan with pleasure. I could feel him pressing against me. *This could get out of hand,* I thought briefly. Instinctively, I placed one restraining hand on his chest. "Hang on, Mark," I whispered. "Don't go too far."

"It's okay," he breathed. "We can stop anytime you want." I relaxed a little. He responded by slipping a finger into the elastic of my briefs. At this, urgency arose in him and he passed his leg over mine so that he was on top of me, crushing me into the dirt of the riverbank. Then his mouth was on my bare skin as one hand yanked down the bodice of my dress while the other hoisted the skirt up around my waist, fumbling. I squirmed, hurting from the stones and the weight of his body.

"Stop. Mark, please stop." I spoke breathlessly; loudly, it seemed, in the clear air of the night. He placed his hand over my mouth and pressed hard and murmured, "Shhh. Stop being a baby. You want this as much as I do."

I could feel the hardness of him digging into my thigh, seeking me out. I squirmed and struggled but he intensified his efforts in response. Then he found me and rammed his way in. I felt pain but the physical pain was nothing compared to the rage that spilled out of my eyes. A moment later, he came in a harsh groan then rolled off onto his back, gasping. Returning into himself, he groped blindly for my hand, and upon finding it, squeezed. He leaned over and kissed my cheek. "Thanks babe," he said. "You were great."

I sat up and reached over and slapped him hard across the face with my open palm. "How could you do that to me?" My voice broke. Immediately, I hated the way I sounded and must have looked - a bedraggled mess of a kid. I felt the sticky ooze of him flood out of my body and instantly I desperately wanted a shower more than I had ever wanted anything in my life.

Lurching to my feet, I stumbled over to the truck and jerked open the door. Sasha and Warwick were curled up over each other, snoring on the back seat. I slammed the door shut but they didn't wake. "Take me home," I snarled to Mark once he joined me in the truck. Silently he turned the key in the ignition.

Neither of us spoke a word during the drive home but much was going through my mind. So now I was no longer a virgin. I'd 'done it' but I felt like muck and I knew I'd never be able to breathe a word of what had happened to anybody.

Because it was so late when I let myself in, the house was quiet. Ma let out a croak as I crept past their room.

"Is that you love? How was it?"

"Fine Ma," I managed to say. "I'm dead tired and going for a shower now."

I kicked my gown onto the floor and padded to the bathroom where I turned the shower faucet on full. I stepped into the steaming heat of the water and took the soap and cloth and scrubbed myself fit to take the skin off. I wanted to scrub away every trace of Mark and go back to feeling like the girl I had been yesterday; a feeling that I knew only too well was gone forever. Surprisingly, I didn't cry. And maybe, if I was completely honest, there could have been a part of me that felt proud, or something like proud. I was officially a woman.

Collapsing into the soft haven of my own bed felt like heaven and I soon fell into a deep sleep but when I woke in the morning it felt like I hadn't slept at all. My body hurt all over. Inspecting myself in the mirror I saw that my arms and legs were dotted with purple and yellow bruises. Dark shadows smudged beneath my heavy eyes and my head pounded out the rhythm of my pulse. The ball dress lay crumpled where I'd kicked it, in the corner of my room, its glory completely gone. I pulled on jeans and a long sleeved skivvy and dragged myself downstairs to the kitchen. Ma looked up as I entered. "Gawd! What's up with you?" she gasped. "You look dreadful."

"I think I'm coming down with something," I lied. Although maybe it was true; maybe I was getting the flu instead of merely nursing an unaccustomed hangover.

Ma reached into the cupboard and took down a packet of analgesics. "Here, take these," she said handing me a couple. I dutifully swallowed them and munched dryly on the toast Ma placed in front of me but my appetite was dull and the toast tasted of dust.

"I think I'll stay home and go back to bed today," I groaned. You would have thought I was 100 years old.

Ma placed her hand on my forehead. "You feel cool enough," she commented, concern creasing her brow. Suddenly, I wanted to throw myself into her arms and sob uncontrollably but she had never been the emotional kind so I restrained myself. And what could I have said? It's not like I could just say, 'by the way, I had sex, *or was it rape?* last night,' could I?

"How was the prom?" she asked. I started, then relaxed. That's right, I remembered, she didn't know what had happened.

"Yeah it was fine. I had a good time," I replied, anxious to get to the sanctuary of my room and away from any further questions. Fortunately, no one expects teenagers to be polite for long so it was easy to escape. I crawled back into bed and lay on my back, arms behind my head, agonising. What would school be like now? Would Mark say anything about what had happened? Would people talk? I wondered whether it had been my fault. Maybe I had led him on.

A chill of fear pricked my palms. Could I get pregnant? Surely not. I tried to remember health class. Could a girl get pregnant from one time? I couldn't recall. We had been too busy laughing at the fool of a nurse awkwardly demonstrating how to get a condom onto a banana.

I felt like an idiot. What had been a joke previously was now terribly serious. What an ignorant twit I was last week, yesterday. *What did I think was going to happen?* I thought about Mark and imagined how he must be feeling. Was he pleased with himself at having scored? Damn it! I was barely legal. Could he be charged?

My phone chimed to tell me I had a text. It was Becky. "U ok? Nt at skwl today?"

"Na sick. Brb Monday," I replied.

Monday felt like far enough away. Hopefully by then I would have gotten over the shock, could go back to normal and pretend that the whole thing had never happened.

CHAPTER THREE

I was changed; schooldays a blur, eyes, teeth, leaden. All I wanted to do was curl up and sleep. Mark had not been at school for weeks following the ball and even after he returned all I saw of him were glimpses of his retreating back whereas I, with no plausible excuse to hand, had no alternative other than to pull on my jeans and head for the door each morning.

Were people looking at me oddly? The cheer-girls seemed to look my way and laugh more loudly than usual while the girls in my classes left a wider berth around me as we crowded in and out of narrow classroom doorways and turned away slightly as I approached, engrossing themselves even more deeply than usual in their carefree conversations. I couldn't be sure.

Drifting through classes, I gazed out of the window, repetitively and mindlessly going over the calculations of days in my head but the numbers remained impartially brutal. There was no getting around the fact that I was late. Maybe it is just stress, I reasoned, before hope faded, before one week had gone by, then two; the implications multiplying as fast as the foetus. Microscopic cells, doubling by the hour; at first inklings, and then, fully fledged thoughts all too soon to be born into a solid and unalterable existence.

Outright fear pulled my nerves taught and snappy. Ma, full of concern, asked if I was alright more than once but I allayed her questions with stories about exams. It was easy to lie. Vanessa and Becky were not so easy to evade but as much as I wanted to, I couldn't speak the words. My throat was swollen shut. If I spoke the words out loud then it all would become real. If I stayed silent there was a chance it would go away. My grades plummeted. I couldn't produce any work. Essays and tests ceased to hold any importance for me. All that consumed my thoughts was the Armageddon gathering on the horizon.

After one particularly unproductive science class, Miss Phelps called me to her desk and handed me my paper. A big, fat C was clearly scrawled on the front in bright, red ink.

"Sit down, Sheri." She indicated the chair that was placed by her desk expressly for that purpose. I slowly lowered myself into the seat. She began. "Now would you like to tell me what is going on? Your grades have fallen dramatically. You barely passed this test. Is everything alright?"

The kindness underlying the sternness in her voice made me blush. Heated emotions, suppressed for weeks, sprang to the surface ready to spill the beans. I looked to the floor, desperately trying to come up with something serious enough to explain my poor performance.

"I... broke up with my boyfriend," I offered. The distress in my eyes was real.

The teacher sat back in her chair. "Oh," she said. "I was unaware of that. Is he a Flagstaff High boy?"

"Oh no. He's not at school. He works for Pa on the ranch," I hastily assured her.

"Well dear, these things are painful at the time but we all get over them. Meanwhile it is not worth ruining your academic record over. Please do try to focus on your work."

She meant well. "Yes Miss. I'll try," I said as I stood up to leave.

In the cafeteria, nausea competed with hunger. I scooped some fries onto my plate and joined Vanessa at a table where I silently picked at my food.

Fed up, she slammed her fork down. "For god's sake, Sheri," she exclaimed. "What is wrong with you? Ever since the prom you've been a ghost. What happened?"

I looked at her with misery and fear inscribed on my face. "Come outside and I'll tell you," I said, not daring to risk Becky finding out on account of the fact that she would tell Jet.

We pushed our way out of the canteen doors into the bright, lunchtime sunlight and out onto the back of the field where a small grove of Maple trees stood. It was quieter there as few students could be bothered walking all that way back and forth. I sat on the thin grass and began tugging up tufts of dried roots.

Vanessa sat down beside me. "Spill," she commanded.

"Mark raped me after the ball and now I'm pregnant," I whispered, stricken.

"You can't be serious," she whispered back. She leaned forward and urgently grasped my limp hands in her own vital ones. "Raped! Pregnant! Good grief, this is huge. Have you told your folks?"

I shook my head. "No. You're the first person I have told." I put my head into my hands and burst into tears.

"What happened?" she pressed.

"I don't know. We went to the river and were talking. Then he started kissing me and it just happened. I tried to stop him but he wouldn't."

"And you are certain you're pregnant? Maybe it's stress or something. That can happen."

"I'm pretty certain I'm pregnant. I've missed two cycles already. Oh my god. What am I going to do? I'm going to have to tell Ma and Pa, not to mention Mark who has avoided me ever since. And what about my future? College! How am I going to do that now? I'll have a baby to look after. My life is ruined and it hasn't even begun yet." It was a relief to give in to the heaving sobs that wracked my body. Vanessa placed her arm around my shoulders.

"I'll help," she said kindly. "I'll even come with you to tell your Ma and Pa if you like. It won't be so bad. They will know what to do and will help you. And there are options. You could get a termination or give the baby up for adoption. Don't worry. Everything will work out okay." With the optimism of youth reasserting itself, Vanessa's reassurances calmed me down and gave me hope that maybe my predicament wasn't such a calamity after all.

"Thanks," I mumbled, exhausted. Over the field drifted the sound of the siren signalling the end of lunch. Unable to face class, I contemplated phoning home and asking Pa to come and get me but my fragile emotional state couldn't handle any more stress for the moment so I lay back on the grass. If we were very quiet and stayed low, no one would notice we were here and we could always say we were studying if accosted by a nosy teacher.

The bus ride home provided an ideal opportunity for me to rehearse what I planned to say. I didn't know how my parents would take the news but felt confident that Pa would be furious and would want to storm over to Mark's right away. As fate would have it they were alone on the veranda having afternoon tea when I trudged up the steps, my heavy footsteps heralding that something was wrong before I said a word. They looked at me expectantly, my flushed cheeks and red eyes silencing questions about how my day had gone before they were spoken.

"Ma. Pa," I croaked. "I've got something to tell you." Pa paused, his cup halfway to his lips. "I'm pregnant. Mark... after the prom (I couldn't say the words) ...and now I'm pregnant." I clung to the veranda for support.

Both Ma and Pa jumped up from their chairs simultaneously. "What! What happened? How?" Their questions spilled out.

I explained as simply as I could. Even to my own ears I sounded foolish. What was I thinking of going to the river with a jock? What did I think would happen? Ma's questions echoed my own thoughts. They bundled me inside and sat me down on the couch. Pa fired questions at me and I was compelled to answer them. Shame. Pa was furious. Ma stood between us fearing Pa may belt me silly. He made me give him Mark's number and ordered Ma to bring the phone. Ma scurried away; any refusal to comply, unthinkable. She hovered nearby as he pressed the numbers.

Mr Bronson," he growled into the receiver after waiting for the call to be answered. "Mr Lewis, Sherman Lewis here. We need to meet and talk. An incident has occurred between my daughter and your son. We need to meet and discuss things." Silence ensued punctuated by, "Aha. Yup. Okay. 5:15 then." He handed the receiver back to Ma. At 5:15 we were to meet with Mr Bronson and Mark.

Cringing inwardly, I groaned "Does Mark have to be there?"

"Damn right he does," replied Pa. "He's gonna have to do the right thing by his kid."

I started at his words. Until then, I hadn't thought of Mark as actually being the father of a child, a new human life with a father and a mother. My emotions did an about flip and my absent period suddenly became a baby, an infant, with living parents. I placed a protective hand over my belly. I was going to be a mother.

Mark's father was a big man, and as flabby as his son was toned. He wore a grey singlet, once white, that barely covered the exuberant paunch that spilled over his navy blue shorts. He sat upright, his massive arms outstretched and meaty hands resting lightly on his knees. Hair erupted out of his neck, armpits, legs, nose, eyebrows and ears. He had a heavy face. The scars from the shooting were clearly visible down the left hand side.

The house was tidy but dingy and the orange - brown, geometrically patterned wallpaper, reminiscent of the seventies, had just about survived long enough to undergo a fashion revival. With a good clean, the place could have exuded a certain style. I wondered if that had been Mark's mother's touch.

Mark sat opposite, elbows resting on his thighs, head low. He did not look up when we crammed into the room and squeezed onto the one couch. No one offered us a drink.

Mr Bronson initiated the discussion. "I'm guessing what all this is about. Mark has admitted to me that he and the young lady got it on after the dance but he believes it was consensual."

He spoke slowly and deliberately in a manner that suggested his police training was coming into play.

Pa was quick to respond. "Mr Bronson. I don't see how getting an underage, innocent girl of sixteen drunk and then taking advantage of her can be called consensual."

I watched Mark but he made no response to this comment. I felt angry and couldn't understand how he could be so unfeeling.

"But that is by the bye," Pa continued. "The real issue here is that Sheri is now pregnant and Mark is the father."

That did get Mark's attention. He looked up with a horrified expression on his face which accorded me a momentary, vicious stab of glee. He was like a spider stuck in his own web. *I will keep the baby*, I thought. Mark Bronson would pay for messing with me. Shocked silence filled the room. Neither Mark nor his father had expected this.

"Sheri and Mark are going to need to discuss what they plan to do," continued Pa. At this Mark looked at me. His eyes were enormous, like those of a raccoon about to get run over by a very large truck. I would have giggled except the enormity of having to plan how to take care of a baby was too much to contemplate. The eyes of everyone in the room were on Mark who squirmed like a naughty school boy.

"What can I do?" he asked bewildered as to what might be expected of him. "What do you want to do, Sheri?"

"I'm going to keep the baby," I announced cleanly and coldly, "I'm certainly not going to *kill* it. That's murder."

Mark who I guessed had immediately leapt to the conclusion that a termination would be the best way out for him, blanched.

"I imagine you will have to get a job to support your child." I drove the arrow home and twisted it. "I can't expect my parents to look after us." My anger was shaping and directing my future like a flooded stream, carving away at established banks and charting new directions.

Devastated, Mark slumped his head into his hands. "I'm so sorry," he mumbled. "I didn't mean to hurt you. I thought..."

"Yes. You should have thought," I snapped, standing up.

Ma leapt up beside me and took hold of my trembling arm as I strode to the door and wrenched it open, seeking to escape. Bright daylight dazzled my eyes, making me blink. I had forgotten it was still day time. I stalked to Pa's truck as Ma trotted along beside me chattering out her anxiety but I heard nothing because of the pounding of thick blood in my ears.

The following week brought issues that needed dealing with. An embarrassing trip to Doctor Solomon's confirmed that I was ten weeks pregnant. The baby would be born early December. I worried about where we would live. To my huge relief, Ma insisted that I stay at home, at least initially, until we found our feet.

I think, secretly, Ma was pleased that she was going to be a grandmother but she found the gossip difficult to cope with. Her sisters, my aunties, after the initial shock, were supportive but some of the other Flagstaff ladies were not so generous. Their disapproving looks at my swelling belly as the months progressed conveyed all too clearly how disgusted they were with me, and by association, my family.

I had to decide whether I was going to carry on with school and that also was a complicated question. Vanessa and Becky clustered around me thereby providing a protective barrier between me and the other students, and I hid my growing little bump under loose tops, but nevertheless the entire school soon knew all about it. Sheriden Lewis, academic good girl had fallen from her pedestal. The polite ones asked how I was feeling. The rude ones called me 'skank' to my face. Some half admired me for being pregnant to Mark who was rarely seen without a group of defensively noisy mates surrounding him. *If only you knew,* I thought. I was a new Sheri. I couldn't be bothered with them. I felt so much older than sixteen. Melodramatic school yard gossip faded into insignificance alongside important real life topics such as how painful was it going to be to give birth, whether I was having a girl or a boy, whether it would be healthy, names, how I would cope financially and where we would live once it became apparent that we couldn't live in my room for ever more.

The summer holidays heralded yet more changes. How different we all were compared to a mere six months earlier. Jet finished school and moved to the halls of residence at Dodge City University. Pa drove him over one weekend. I wanted to go too but the pain of his departure rankled too deeply. His lucky life was so uncomplicated. It didn't seem fair. The house was unnaturally quiet without him.

During the last month of pregnancy, I lost all inclination to do anything. The late fall weather was warm and soporific enough to lend itself to quiet contemplation on the veranda and I sat there, on the step, for hours at a time, head resting on folded arms, not thinking, not doing, just being.

The rays of the sun warmed their way into my shoulders and my heavy eyes, unable to stay open, closed. Birdsong and the faraway sounds of tractors hummed in the background while my baby moved within me. At first his kicks had manifested as delicate butterfly tickles, then as fluid globs of gassy bubbles. Now the child kicked like a kangaroo joey, its watery pouch already cramped. Like Jonah in the belly of the whale - the idea made me giggle. The womb was a safe haven but soon the baby would be forced out by nature, ejected into an unsafe world, like me. I was incubating in my room but the day would come when there was no place for me at home any longer. The idea terrified me.

I thought about my mother, how she'd met my father and created a future together with him. Their life was sorted but the price was routine. For twenty years Ma had been on the ranch; Pa since he was born but I couldn't see where I fitted in and the world that once had seemed so benign now appeared to be fraught with danger. I felt as if I was squeezed into the fringes; as if everybody had their position in life secured whereas I was adrift, clinging precariously to a rickety raft on a treacherous sea of change. Belonging seemed impossible.

Once we arrived home after Jonah's birth, the peace of the countryside that was steeped into the very walls of the house calmed my frazzled nerves. Ma helped me with Jonah and loved him with all her heart. Her gentle admiration for him was evident with every movement. She picked him up and handled him as if he was made of spun glass and liable to break with any careless mishandle and giggled over his every new expression. Pa on the other hand, liked Jonah well enough but should he happen to begin crying while the news was on, I knew better than to remain in the room.

Out of gratitude to my mother, I pulled my weight more in the house, giving every appearance of settling into motherhood. And on a functional level I was but in my spirit an underlying misery squatted like a lump of mouldy bread. I had no money, couldn't drive and couldn't go anywhere. My friends, one by one, stopped calling. Isolation settled about my shoulders like a blackout blanket.

As Christmas came and went, Ma increasingly took over the role of looking after Jonah. At first that didn't bother me. Tiredness and anxiety over the overwhelming burden of responsibility for keeping a new life alive made it easy for me to feel thankful when Ma stepped in but as the months progressed I began to feel as if Ma was the mother and I was once more merely Sheri the daughter. I was in limbo, stuck in an in-between world where I wasn't a kid any longer, but neither was I an adult. Things were as they always had been, only with a new family member. I fretted about what to do for several weeks before resolving to talk to Aunty Harriet.

As usual, both aunties were thrilled to see Jonah. They trilled the usual feminine trivia about how much he had grown and blew raspberries into his Buddha-like tummy while Jonah responded with delighted gurgles and giggles. At three months old he was recognising and interacting with the people in his little world which rendered him very cute and ensured that he was the centre of attention at all times. He would be thinking the whole world revolved around him before too long.

"And how are you dear?" asked Aunty Julie once she could tear herself away from the infant.

"I'm managing fine thanks to Ma. She helps me a lot."

"And are you getting enough sleep?"

Truth was that although I was not experienced as a mother, even I had to admit that Jonah was a great baby. He slept seven hours a night, had two good sleeps a day and only cried when he needed changing or feeding. Sometimes I wondered what he needed me for. A monkey could have looked after him. I relayed this information to Aunty who nodded approvingly. Not for the first time I wondered why she had never married or had children. She seemed made for it.

Aunty Harriet appeared with steaming cups of coffee on a tray which she set onto the wooden table under the pergola. A budding grape vine, barely more than a ragged cluster of sticks, exposed us to the weak spring sunshine. The fields surrounding the store shimmered neon green and soggy from the sun showers that had been sweeping the plains all morning. Aunty Julie took Jonah inside out of the cold thereby giving us an opportunity to talk freely but I found it difficult to begin. I didn't want to sound ungrateful and I didn't know exactly what I wanted. I only knew what I didn't want. We chattered idly for a few minutes...

"I'm finding it hard being at home, Aunty," I said eventually. "I don't know what to do." Harriet waited quietly. "It's not that there's anything wrong with Ma or Pa. It's just, I don't know, I still feel like a kid myself. Nothing has changed. Ma buys everything we need, which don't get me wrong, I'm grateful for her help but..."

"You want independence," she concluded.

"Yes! Yes! I do. I have none. I'm seventeen and a mother but sometimes it's like Jonah isn't even my kid. Ma does so much for him it's like he's hers. And I can't go anywhere. I can't drive, don't have a car and we live way out in the sticks. It's terrible and I can't stand it but I don't know what to do about it."

"What about Mark?" she asked.

"Ugh. That bastard. He came to see us in hospital and you know what he said to me?" Aunty shook her head. "He said I was a dare. A *dare*! That pig. His mates put him up to it because they wanted to find out whether I was hot or not!" At that I started to laugh. It sounded so absurd, then burst into tears. "I hope he rots in hell," I snuffled into the tissue Aunty handed me.

"Okay, so he's out of the picture for now. Although I'm pretty certain he will have obligations with regard to supporting Jonah financially but that will probably mean he is entitled to have access rights."

"Over my dead body," I growled. "He's not having anything to do with Jonah if I can help it... I didn't put his name on the birth certificate! He wouldn't even give me ten bucks for diapers; said he was going to a party and needed the cash for booze."

Aunty was non committal. "Nevertheless... So what do you want to do?"

"I don't know. If I move out Ma will be upset and how can I afford to live by myself or get a job with Jonah to take care of? My life is a mess. Did you know I wanted to go to college and study geology? Miss Phelps even helped me to apply for a scholarship."

Harriet lay an arm about my shoulders and gave a squeeze. "Life hasn't worked out as you planned, that's true but it's not a failure yet. You are very young and there are lots of options. You could go flatting, put Jonah in day care and get a job."

Flatting and a job sounded good but I felt uncertain about putting Jonah into care. An unfamiliar concern about the quality of other families and children he would be in contact with, and an anxiety about hygiene and whether he would be have his diapers changed and be fed on time, tripped through my heart.

Harriet was still talking, "I will find out some information. You never know. There could be some government assistance you can get. And as I said, I'm certain Mark has responsibilities in that department. Meanwhile you could start making enquiries about flats and jobs."

"But if I get a job, how will I get to it?" I fretted.

"Don't worry about that right now. You can deal with that when it happens. One step at a time eh?"

Her words gave me hope that maybe there was a solution and that my life could go forward even if it was in a different form to that which I had hoped for. I hugged Aunty tightly. "Thanks for everything," I whispered. She always was wise.

Once home, I fed and changed Jonah then asked Ma if she could watch him while I went over to the stables. It was good be outside in the sun. I calculated it had been almost a year since I had ridden Bono and I wondered how I could have left him for so long. Bono was turned out to pasture but he stood obediently as I approached with his lead rope and halter hidden behind my back. I held out a piece of bread which his soft nose snuffled up out of my hand. Then having tricked him into being caught, I tied him to the fence and commenced grooming his rain matted coat.

The weak sun held warmth and Bono rested with one fetlock bent, soaking up the rare attention. With his coat smooth and hooves picked clean, I slipped on the bridle and saddle. The girth barely fitted into the last hole. "Time for you and me to get back into shape," I scolded.

For a ride, I decided to go and see Pa in the far home paddock where Ma had told me he was digging a new dam with Byron. We set off at a walk, our unaccustomed limbs, mine still feeling somewhat wobbly, easing into the rhythm. A feeling of blissful wellbeing settled over me. It felt good to be alive and I could literally feel the tension and anxiety dissipating. My mind, which rambled constantly over my situation in frustrating and unproductive cycles, cleared; taken up with the task of negotiating the terrain. For a while I forgot about everything except the horse beneath me and the joy of a perfect afternoon.

My first pony had been given to me in a much simpler age. I was four years old and it was my birthday. Pa carried me outside with one calloused hand covering my eyes. "Don't peek now," he instructed. I shook my head solemnly. Excitement and suspense chased the chocolate cake around my belly. Then there was my pony – a pretty, grey welsh mountain pony with a fringe so long it hung almost down to his nose.

Squealing and kicking, I squiggled to get free but Pa set me on the ground and held my hand firmly. "Now you gotta approach him quiet like or you'll spook him."

I jumped up and down on the spot, unable to contain my joy. "What's his name, Pa, what's his name?" I demanded with impatience.

"Jackie," he replied. He lifted me onto the pony's back and set my feet into the little clogs of the pony pad.

My brother led me around the yard. "Faster, faster, Byron," I commanded. I flapped my short legs feeling supremely confident, as though I could have galloped off there and then but Byron, after casting a glance at Pa, replied that I needed to have lessons first, to learn how to ride properly.

He took it upon himself to teach me and there began a golden summer of playing around with horses where I learned how to look after Jackie; how to brush him and feed him hay and cornmeal. I loved taking a gift of an apple or slice of bread which I hid in my pocket. His snuffling nose following the scent would nudge against me and pull at the fabric of my clothes, whereupon I would pull out the treat and hold it out to him with my palm held flat, as taught, in case his teeth mistook my fingers for the tiny morsel of deliciousness.

Usually, taking care of Jackie was fun but sometimes I didn't feel like doing my chores especially if I was lazing on the carpet, watching the television or drawing pictures. Pa would ask whether I had settled Jackie for the night. Then I would whinge and try to coax one of my brothers into doing my jobs but they never would. "Jackie is your responsibility," they'd reply. "We have our own horses to look after." So grumbling and complaining I would kick out into the dusk, fling Jackie's hay into the net and leave without so much as a pat on his scruffy neck.

Byron proved to be a good, if demanding, teacher as he yelled directives: "Heels down! Elbows in! Watcha doin' - pushin' a buggy? Turn those wrists out." And years later, I would still be able to hear his voice crowing in my ear from the centre of the corral while I trotted in circles trying to do everything at once.

Under his guidance, my skills progressed so that before long I was allowed out from the corral, although for safety he kept me on a lead rope twisted around the pommel of his stock saddle as we rode all over the ranch. By the time I turned five I was a competent rider and after that, all three of us would ride out of a morning on the weekend and be gone for most of the day. With three thousand acres to ride over there was always plenty to do.

In the distance, I saw Pa and Byron with the tractors and nudged Bono into a gentle trot. When Pa saw me approach he climbed down out of the cab. "Good to see you out on Bono, Sheri." His kindly smile, full of love for me, tugged at my heart.

"Yes. It's a beautiful day. I forgot how much I missed riding. But we are both so unfit and fat."

He laughed at that then explained the dam to me and how it would mean we could keep more cattle on the flat during the intense, desert heat of summer. It seemed like a good plan.

That evening with Ma happy in the kitchen and Jonah lying on the mat with his diapers off and squinting at a picture book propped up by his side, there was nothing for it but to lie on the sofa and watch television. My body felt deliciously tired and I felt happier than I had for months. I waited till the ads were on then I said to Pa, knowing that he would relay this information to Ma, that I'd had a good chat with Aunty Harriet and was planning move to town once I found a flat and a job.

"There's plenty of time for that, Sheri. You know you can stay here as long as you want and need," he responded.

"I know, Pa, and I am grateful for everything but I'm going to be eighteen soon and I can't just live here and do nothing with my life."

Pa looked at me and I understood there were things he would like to have said but didn't know how.

"I'll be ok, Pa. Promise."

After dinner, before Jonah and I went to bed I sought out Ma and found her in front of her dresser brushing her long, dark hair. I released the brush from her bird-like fingers and took over, gently sweeping the brush in long curving strokes. We observed each other through the mirror.

"I just wanted to thank you for everything, Ma. I couldn't have done it without your help. You've been amazing. I never imagined that having a baby could be so hard."

She reached behind and squeezed my hand. "Darling, that's what family is for; to love and support one another through life. A baby at seventeen and no husband; that's not what we hoped for you, Sheri, but that's how it turned out. One thing we can always count on is for life to throw us problems."

"You have a good life though, Ma?"

"Yes dear, I can't complain. Your Pa has been a wonderful husband and father. I have been very blessed."

As much as I loved Ma, I'd always had difficulty understanding how she lived her life. When I was very young, my mother was just someone who existed for me, the background song who made sure my clothes were washed and ensured that I was fed. I never thought of her as a human being in her own right. Looking back, I can now see that she was the quintessential American mother and home maker. She kept our house in a state of pristine perfection. Fresh prairie flowers cut straight from her garden could be relied upon to grace the large pottery urn that resided in the marble tiled entrance hall of our home and her vegetable gardens, defying the bitter winters and arid summers, were the best in the district.

The homestead had been built by Pa's grandpa when the area was settled by the whites (after first muscling out the indigenous Indian tribes who were living there) in1908. It had been one of the first in the area to be constructed out of milled cypress, and from the outside upheld the barn like appearance, typical to Wyoming homesteads, of a large, central part and smaller wings on either side. The high roof, steeply pitched to facilitate the dislocation of snow during winter, had been extended at some time to cover a deep veranda that ran the length of the building.

The interior had been modernised by Pa but retained a deeply rural ambience that was only emphasised by the dark leather and timber furnishings and trophy stag heads mounted on the walls. An exception to all this masculinity was Ma's formal sitting room that exited off the entry hall. As children, we were forbidden to enter this room being, as it was, decorated in tones of white and pastel green and furnished with the family antiques.

Ma was born the third and youngest daughter, after my twin aunts. Pa first saw her when he went with Grandpa Lewis to buy supplies and was instantly smitten by her shy smile. As Mr Granger loaded sacks of oats and barley onto the dray of the truck, Pa cast surreptitious glances at our mother who was only fifteen at the time. Four long years went by with the two young lovebirds making puppy dog eyes over the counter but once Ma was nineteen she was deemed old enough to make up her own mind so Pa went cap in hand to Mr Granger to ask for Suzie's hand in marriage. The year was 1967 but things were done the traditional way in Flagstaff.

As a girl, she attended the local Flagstaff school and was a fair enough scholar. She read a lot of books which Mr Granger didn't think much about and dallied with the idea of being a journalist, dashing off a couple of articles to the Flagstaff Press which was printed on Tuesdays and Thursdays but once married, she'd settled into her expected role as a rancher's wife and that was the end of any ambitions she might have harboured.

They were married in the Flagstaff multidenominational church; the same church that we had attended as a family every Sunday morning throughout my childhood. I'd never liked church and found it boring, although

I couldn't help but admire the way the sun streamed through the stained glass windows giving the risen Jesus the mirage of a halo.

The pews were hewn out of solid trunks of imported Oregon Pine and were as hard as rock. The building itself still looked exactly the same as it had when Ma and Pa were married in it and all of us kids had been christened at the very same alter that Rev Monty, the kindly old pastor who'd presided over the Flagstaff parish for thirty years, leaned on every Sunday.

CHAPTER FOUR

That night, I lay in bed wondering how I could make moving happen but no matter how I went over it in my head, the problems posed cancelled each other out like the proverbial chicken and egg dilemma. To get a job I needed care for Jonah. For that I needed a job. I also needed a place to live, and furniture, and transport. Who would have known that adult life was so difficult to organise and needed so much cash?

Suddenly I felt guilty for all the designer clothes and shoes I'd demanded over the years; clothes I couldn't even fit into now. I figured that in the morning I could at least begin to find out about child care costs and start looking for a flat. Hopefully, as Harriet had assured me, something would turn up.

Just as I was dozing off, my phone beeped to say I had received a text. It was Vanessa. "U awake?" I read.

"No, lol," I text back.

"Hey I'm moving to Dodge. Sis got me a job. Wanna cme?" My heart kicked up the pace a notch.

"Maybe. Where we live?"

"Gotta flat. Share costs?"

"OMG totally interested."

"OK. Ph tmrw 2 confirm details."

Dodge City. I could hardly believe it. What a stroke of luck. What a coincidence. I lay back on my pillows resisting the urge to run into Ma's room and tell her the news. "We'll soon be outa here," I whispered instead, into the dark, to my comatose boy.

Once set in motion, events moved quickly. My share of the rent was $75 per week plus expenses. I found a day care centre for Jonah and made an appointment to apply for a position at the local supermarket. Both places were within walking distance of the flat but in opposite directions. I would have a bit of walking to do until I could afford a car but I was so excited I didn't care.

Barely two weeks later, Vanessa's father drove us over with a trailer piled high with our belongings following along behind. Ma bought me a load of groceries and baby things and handed me $500 to tide me over. Now that Jonah was on formula he cost more but at least my body was my own.

I hugged my parents and Byron goodbye, not really noticing the way Ma nuzzled into Jonah's neck, or the way she clutched his squirming body close to her heart as if trying to absorb everything about him to feed what would now be her memories. I feel sad now, looking back, at how blithely I plucked him from her, from she who had in truth been more of a mother to him than I had; how glibly I took her beloved grandchild from her and plonked him in the car seat, leaving him there for another half hour while we yakked our goodbyes, not noticing how Ma's eyes strayed to the car where Jonah waited, growing fractious. There was a lot I didn't notice back then.

Our flat was fabulous. The end unit in a ground level set of six, it sported two bedrooms. I drew the smaller of the two but it was adequate space wise and held the advantage of opening out through stiff, unused French doors into an overgrown back yard that sprouted winter toughened grasses from the cracks in the crazed concrete.

The wallpaper was a dusty pink, floral number and a heavily patterned carpet in florid red and green swirls covered the floor. Despite looking as if a garden gnome had picked out the colour scheme, it was brilliant to be playing house. Our own place! The sensation was heady.

I sat Jonah onto the carpet in the hallway whereby he promptly fell over and banged his head on the skirting, so I found a blanket and a couple of pillows and set him up properly with some toys before helping Vanessa unpack our little kitchen. Sure the stainless steel tub was scratched, the taps grubby and the lino cracked but we barely noticed as we arranged our few tea cups, glasses and plates and packed the cupboard with the groceries.

In my room, I positioned Jonah's cot at the end of the bed. Our clothes I arranged in the wardrobe. I didn't have a set of drawers but in the end the room looked alright – and it was mine. The lounge only took a minute. Vanessa's dad had bequeathed us a couch that had been stored in their garage and a television so even though we didn't have a computer or a table, we had the basics. By the time we vacuumed the floor, it was time for dinner.

Because I'd recently spent so much time in the kitchen with Ma, I was the logical choice to act as chief cook and bottle washer for our first night in so I filled our one pot with water and peeled some potatoes.

Jonah sat in his high chair and sucked on a rusk, smearing it all over his face and leading me to marvel at how grubby babies were. That thought led me to realise that I would have to do some washing the following day and that we had no soap powder. Although there was a washing machine that came with the flat, I had no idea whether it worked.

The enormity of what moving out meant hit me like a slap; no mother to do the washing, or cook when, no questions asked, I made myself scarce from the kitchen. No one except us to earn the money, budget, go shopping or pay the bills. Cripes, I didn't even know how to pay a utilities bill.

Feeling a rush of panic, I hurried to phone Ma, needing her to reassure me like a little lamb dashing back to its mother when startled. But when I flipped my cell phone open and dialled the number, the automated voice informed me that my balance was insufficient to make the call.

Deflated, I slumped down onto a chair. We were literally on our own. Jonah chose that moment to commence grizzling so I found a wet wipe with which to wipe his face. He grinned up at me and then rubbed his eyes, smearing his skin with even more dissolved rusk.

"Come here you little grub," I said as I lifted him out of his high chair. *Phew he needed changing.* I took him to my room and lay him on the bed where he gurgled and kicked, trying to roll over. I located his diapers and with the pack of wipes, began the unpleasant task.

"What the hell is that smell?" called Vanessa, emerging from her room.

"It's only Jonah. I'm changing him now."

"No its not - it's burning." Instantly remembering the potatoes, I hurriedly finished changing Jonah and dashed into the kitchen where Vanessa was already inspecting the dried and charred remains, welded to the bottom of the pot, that were creating the acrid stink.

"Oh heck. What a disaster," we laughed.

Vanessa tossed the pot into the sink and turned on the tap. The water splashed onto the scorched metal with a demented sizzle.

It was late and we were tired so after rugging Jonah up and popping him into his stroller, we let ourselves out of the flat and walked to the corner shops where we bought two dollars of chips at the diner and a packet of soap powder on the way home from the all night Hypermart.

The next few months flew by in a hectic muddle. Vanessa left in a flurry every morning at seven thirty to catch the bus into the city centre and returned home at around six each evening while I struggled to get Jonah and myself sorted. I didn't know how to organise everything that needed to be done and usually managed to forget something important.

Somehow I located the childcare centre in the next block. It looked rather stark and uninviting as a concrete parking area took up the entire front of the building. Inside, I was met by a hearty, middle aged woman with dyed, reddish hair. "Mrs Betty Skate," she announced, hand outstretched. "And this is?"

"Jonah," I filled in. "And I'm Sheri."

The large room seemed to be filled with hyperactive little bodies darting this way and that so I clutched Jonah to my chest, afraid to let him loose in the melee. Betty explained the programme but it went in one ear and out of the other. What I wanted to know was whether each child had their own sleeping cot and whether there were any other teachers but Betty was busy explaining that the babies had a sleep between 12 – 3 pm and I felt too shy to interrupt.

The other children looked happy enough and seemed to know the routine. As mothers arrived, their children hung their bags on what appeared to be designated spaces; judging by the individual drawings obviously created by childish hands that hung above each hook.

I took the enrolment forms from the woman. The fees were twenty dollars a day and a quick calculation of my finances told me that while there would be enough to cover everything, there would not be a lot left over. I wouldn't be buying a car any time soon that was for sure.

For a fleeting moment I thought about the dreams I'd had of money, travel and an exciting career. What a letdown. Not that having Jonah was all bad. He was very cute and I loved him but when I imagined being stuck in our little flat forever it couldn't help but feel like I'd been given a life sentence.

Nevertheless, the following Monday I started my job at the Dominion Road Hypermart and walked Jonah the mile to Betty's in the morning and left him there, screaming and red faced, tears streaming from his clenched eyes and snotty nose while I hurried away, praying that I wouldn't cry myself, already missing him. Why was being a mother so damn hard? Sometimes I loved him so much my heart physically hurt but on other occasions, he irritated me so much I had to deliberately leave the room for fear of smacking and hurting him.

We fell into a routine and I found I liked going to work. It was the first real job I'd ever had and I was surprised to discover that I didn't miss Jonah as much as I thought I would. In fact, I enjoyed getting away from him and having myself to myself. It had been so long since I'd led any kind of individual existence I'd forgotten what it was like.

My job was a checkout chick. On my first day, the supervisor, a chubby guy called Greg issued me with my uniform, an acceptably smart smock pinstriped in beige and red. All the work I'd done in the hardware store with Aunty rendered learning how to work the scanner and the till easy and I enjoyed scanning the items, packing them into bags and the chit chat that went along with the job.

Most of the customers were regulars and were very friendly. They recognised me as being new to the store and were full of questions as to where I was from. The older women were especially interested to hear about Jonah and one even offered to look after him which gave me something to think about as he seemed to be constantly suffering from a cold or some other kind of ailment despite the season moving into summer.

Vanessa effortlessly established a circle of friends and they were often at the flat during the evenings. The boys brought drinks which the girls cadged off them and it was fun sitting around in the back yard drinking and swapping bullshit stories. The girls loved Jonah and he loved clambering over them. I suspected they liked having the opportunity to impress the boys with how good they were with babies.

Once the conversation died, and the majority of the booze consumed, the boys pulled out their little packets of weed and rolled skinny joints, passing them around unmindful of the communal sharing of spit and other germs. At these moments, I usually left them to it citing work in the morning. Truth was, I had no heart for drugs of any kind. I just didn't feel the urge to smoke anything – not even a cigarette. If the others thought me to be uptight, no one ever commented; and I was never hit on either. There seemed to be an unspoken agreement amongst the boys that exempted me on account of motherhood from the usual messy entanglements generated by unthinking youth.

Most Friday and Saturday nights, Vanessa and the others went out clubbing but I had not accompanied her so far. After having Jonah in day care all week I felt too guilty about leaving him with a babysitter at night as well. Plus, I didn't want to date. I kept boys at arm's length. I supposed it had something to do with Mark but also the boys we hung out with, in their late teens and early twenties, were simply too immature for me. Having Jonah and working and flatting had made me grow up. I was only eighteen but I looked, acted and felt much older.

We went home for Christmas of 1994. Vanessa's father collected us and we made the two hour trip back to Flagstaff under a leaden sky although the snow held off. The sight of Flagstaff's familiar roads and the bright, cheery lights of the hardware store and pharmacy glowing in the gloom filled me with nostalgia.

Finally Pa's truck came into view; his bulky shape within. I realised I'd been peering out of the window of the car, straining for that first sighting. "Thanks a million, Mr Goodwell. Happy Christmas, Nessa," I prattled off.

The minute we pulled to a halt, I had Jonah's car seat unclipped from the seatbelt. He stirred at the brush of the cold air against his warm cheeks. I grabbed my bag from the seat and hoisted it over my shoulder. Pa, noticing our arrival, opened the door of his Dakota and strode over to help. I flung myself at him awkwardly, my bundles held at impossible angles while I hugged him tightly, reluctant to let him go. "Pa. Oh Pa," I sobbed. "I've missed you so much. I'm so glad to be home. How's Ma?"

He held me close. His heavy jacket smelled divine, of smoke and hay and horses. "She's fine, darlin'. C'mon, it's cold out here. Hop in the truck." I settled Jonah into the king seat and buckled him in.

I had only been away since April but it felt like years. Ma, wiping floury hands on her apron, hurried out to greet us the moment we pulled up in the driveway; overjoyed to see Jonah again, hugging us to her before ushering us into the glowing warmth of the living room. Byron, looking like a fully grown man introduced me to Louisa, his girlfriend, a petit woman with straggly blonde hair who said, 'Hi,' in a quiet voice.

Ma had dinner ready and waiting and the golden roasted pork belly topped with crackling that burst in the mouth and sweet deep fried apple fritters tasted delicious after the months of more basic fare that Vanessa and I managed to rustle up between us.

The dining table chatter naturally revolved around Jonah and how much he had grown. He was past one year old and was pulling himself up on chairs, balancing on the balls of his feet like a ballerina. Ma said that was a sign he would be walking soon. He was not talking yet but could identify various things and knew what tractors and motorbikes were. He accepted Ma quickly and was soon pulling her nose and trying to dislodge her glasses but with Pa he was more cautious. "Don't worry, Pa," I reassured him. "Jonah will be following you around the ranch in no time."

"We've missed you, Sheri," said Ma. And I had missed them too. It was good to be home.

The next morning I rugged Jonah up against the cold and walked with him to the stables. He had seen pictures of horses in books but I wanted to show him the real thing. The horses were stabled in the barn and would remain so during the worst of the winter. With or without snow, the winds gusting across the open plains were vicious.

Bono nickered when he saw me and searched for the apple that his snuffling nose informed him was in my jacket pocket. I handed it to him and he took it, crunching messily while the froth slobbered from the corners of his mouth in streaming strands. I rubbed his hairy forehead but Jonah leaned away and clung to my hair, eyes wide as he took in the sight of the animal. I inclined Jonah towards Bono. "Horsey, Jonah. Pat the horsey." After a moment he reached out and touched him, his stubby little fingers clutching unsuccessfully at the short hair on Bono's forehead. "Horse, Jonah. Where's the horse?"

"Os," said Jonah distinctly. I laughed out loud with excitement and joy. Jonah had said his first word and I had taught him.

"Good boy, horse."

"Os," he repeated, delighted at this novel way to gain approval from his mother.

I let myself into the box and lifted Jonah onto Bono's back. Bono stood stock still but inclined his head sideways as if straining to see what the little creature wobbling about on his back was. "Good boy, Bono," I soothed as I stroked his neck.

"Looks like he's a natural."

A masculine voice spoke behind me and I turned to see a cowboy. My eyes took him in and automatically slid down to the pair of very fine handcrafted leather boots that clad his narrow shins.

"Who are you?" I wanted to know. I hadn't heard him come in.

"Name's Luke." He extended a leather gloved hand over the stable door. "I help on the ranch."

That was news to me. Pa hadn't said anything about it. Luke explained that he was taking care of the horses and cattle while Pa and Byron were busy with the dam which made sense. Jet's and my departure had no doubt left a labour void. Resettling Jonah onto one hip, I unlatched the half gate and stepped out into the barn.

"I'm about to feed the horses and muck out," Luke explained. I gathered that must be true because in his hand he held the feed bucket. Not having Jonah's stroller with me I sat on a straw bale and perched him on my lap. I was finding Luke interesting and wanted to know more about him.

"Why are you still here at Christmas?" I called out. "Don't you have a home to go to?"

"Nope," said Luke's voice from inside the feed room. "My folks are in Los Angeles. I always wanted to work on a ranch and I love horses so I came out here 'bout six months ago and straight away landed a job with Mr Lewis."

"That's my Pa," I informed him. "I'm Sheri, his daughter."

He popped his head around the door. "Pleased to meet you, Sheri. I figured it was you though. Your Pa talks about you a lot."

More interesting news." So where do you live?"

"I got lodgings at the Bentley's next door. I drive over each mornin'. And I'm coming to your place for Christmas dinner. Your Ma's a great cook."

He winked at me when he said this but I felt a flash of irritation and disappointment. I didn't want an outsider at our Christmas gathering. Before I could comment, Jonah arched his back and let out a discontented grizzle. Seeing he had a stick of straw poking out of his mouth, I scooped my finger in and removed the wad of mangled hay. Reluctantly, I said it was best that I be getting back. Jonah was more than ready for breakfast.

As I returned to the house, I mused about how old Luke was and how I could find out. I then realised that he hadn't asked anything about where Jonah's father might be. Pa had probably told him all about it already. I groaned. Back in good old Flagstaff where everybody knew everything and if they didn't, saw no harm in asking someone who might know, or else made it up. I was distracted from further conjecture by the sight of a blue, four wheel drive bouncing towards the homestead. Incredibly, when it pulled to a halt it was Aunty Harriet who climbed out of the driver's seat.

"Aunty Harriet," I exclaimed. "You're driving! How? When?" We hugged enthusiastically causing Jonah, who was squashed into Harriet's ample chest, to let out a cry of protest.

"Well I thought here was me tellin' you to learn to drive and to make a change and here I was too damn scared to get behind the wheel myself." She laughed in the exuberant manner particular to her.

"And she drives like a maniac," commented Aunty Julie as she came up behind Harriet bearing a suitcase in both hands.

I couldn't believe it. The car was a very tidy Suzuki Jimny; not new but not that far off. "I'm so jealous. Please teach me to drive Aunty," I begged. "I can mostly. I've driven Pa's truck up the farm but that's not driving, driving. Please can we go to Flagstaff and drive in the car park or something?"

Harriet stalled in the manner of adults saying she wasn't fully licensed yet so she didn't know whether she could, legally, but she said she would think about it and I had to be content with that.

She whisked Jonah from my arms and ferried him inside so I gathered the bags of groceries from the back of the jeep and with our arms full we marched up the steps and into the house. Naturally, Aunty was very interested in how we were getting on in Dodge and it was satisfying to be able to tell her that we were managing fine.

A few hours later, Jet and Becky arrived. I hadn't seen Becky in over a year and was secretly gratified to notice that she had picked up weight. Her neck was disappearing into her chin. I wasn't sure why I felt a sense of maliciousness towards her. I felt that she had somehow ingratiated herself into my family and that she wasn't good enough for Jet but in my head I knew that was unreasonable. She was superficial but why should that bother me so much? It didn't explain my antagonism. Nevertheless, we exchanged polite greetings. I complimented her on her dress and she complimented me on Jonah but there was an underlying current between us. We circled each other like gladiators eyeing each other, testing the strength of the opposition.

With the house full, and Jonah being passed from one effusive female relative to the next, I was free to catch up with Jet. He looked as handsome as ever in his striped shirt and low rider jeans and wore a stunning silver longhorn buckle on the hips. I almost wished we weren't related. In response to my questions, he told me that he was passing his papers and planning to specialise in farm animal science so that he could come back to the ranching lifestyle in the future. He lived in a dormitory with three other guys. They had a lot of fun. When Jet rose to fetch a new beer from the fridge, I moved closer to Becky.

"What have you been up to?" I asked. "Are you still at school?"

Becky laughed. "No. You know I always hated school. I was glad to finish. I've been working at 'Jenniez' in town. We've got some great gear in for the winter. You should come and have a look. I'll get you looking fab' in no time."

The barb seemed ill concealed. "I haven't had money to spend on clothes for ages," I explained. "Jonah takes up all my spare cash."

'I'd love to have a baby," she cooed. "They're so cute. You know I was totally jealous when you told us you were pregnant."

"It's not all great. Jonah's a lot of work and I can't just leave him. He needs watching all the time."

"Doesn't Mark have him?" The question appeared innocent enough but a pricking feeling in my hands warned me to tread carefully.

"No," I replied. "Mark doesn't have anything to do with us."

Becky seemed surprised. "Really? That's not what he's saying."

"What do you mean," I demanded.

But Becky backed off and refused to elaborate any further. "Nothing, except... I must have got it wrong. Forget it."

At that moment Jet returned. "What are you ladies looking so serious about?" he asked as he inserted himself between us.

"Nothing," we chorused. She hadn't really said anything wrong but my happy mood was dented.

The next day being Christmas day, I rose early and sought out Ma in the kitchen. I hadn't had a chance to talk to her since I'd arrived home. She was stuffing an enormous turkey and its pale skin quivered obscenely as she packed fragrant seasoned breadcrumbs into its cavity. I switched on the jug and set out the cups in the old routine.

"I'm so glad to be home, Ma," I said. "It's been good flatting but it's been difficult too. Life is so hectic."

Ma chuckled. "I remember when I was first married. I made a loaf of bread and it turned out like a brick. Your Pa varnished it and we used it as a door stop for an entire year." The image was comical. I couldn't remember a time when Ma couldn't cook.

"I burnt my first batch of potatoes," I confessed. "We had to throw away the pot."

Ma laughed. "Are you happy, Sheri?"

She wanted to know but I couldn't exactly reply. I wasn't unhappy but was I happy? There were too many things in life that were taxing like having to walk with Jonah every morning and evening through all kinds of weather to take him to day care. I could cope more easily with the difficulties when they affected only me. They hurt more when they affected Jonah too.

"You are a mother, Sheri. That's what mothers do. They worry about their children."

"Did you worry about us?" It didn't seem possible. We'd had the run of the farm and pretty much done as we pleased.

"Of course, I still worry about you but you have to be allowed to live your own life."

I like my job," I said to lighten the mood. "My colleagues and the customers. The work is easy, though it doesn't pay much. I should look for something else but it suits me because I can walk there and if Jonah's sick I can stay home with him and they can get someone to cover for me."

"When Jonah starts school it will be easier."

Goodness knew where the school was so I changed the subject. "What do you think of Becky?"

"She seems a good match for Jet. He's happy with her." Ma's voice suggested that she wasn't about to say anything negative about her future daughter in law. Understanding that Ma would always support all of her children, even if one turned out to be an axe murderer, I abandoned my aim of finding out what Ma really thought but I couldn't help stating my view.

"She bothers me."

"Why? You were such good friends for so long. Can you get out that bag of potatoes please?"

Comprehending, I did as requested and began peeling. Ma, meanwhile, set out two more cups and made a fresh pot of coffee for Pa and Byron who appeared five minutes later. They sat at the breakfast bar and discussed the Reader's Digest version of the day. Because it was Christmas, they would only shift the cattle and feed the horses and be back in time for breakfast. I contemplated asking to go with them but a peek out of the window at the threatening sky put me off. I wouldn't want to get out of the truck so there was no point. Instead, while they were gone, Ma, Harriet and I cooked bacon, eggs and baked beans for the nine of us.

At 10 o'clock the doorbell rang and in came Grandpa Granger dressed as Santa and carrying a pillowcase flung over his shoulder for a Santa sack. Grandma followed, clutching a baking dish. I felt a flash of inadequacy. I had bought Ma a lovely mauve pashmina, and Pa, a bottle of aged Bourbon Whisky but I hadn't had the money to buy for anyone else. Not that I needed to worry. After five minutes of frantic gift giving and paper tearing my angst was forgotten.

Jonah was, without a doubt, the biggest recipient of toys in the west, including a blue plastic ride on trike with black wheels. He couldn't wait to try it but once seated could only rock back and forth unsure of how to propel it forward. Ma gave him a push and he squealed in unrestrained delight.

Becky and Jet gave me a $200 clothes voucher to be redeemed at Becky's work place and my aunties gave me a gorgeous duvet cover set printed with a chocolate and ice blue paisley design. Pa handed me a small box which I tore open expecting to find a pair of earrings or the like but which revealed a small pewter horse figurine to which was attached a key chain and key. The room fell silent and I looked at the key, puzzled as to its significance.

"What's this for, Pa, the safe?" I joked.

Everybody laughed but their eyes willed me to guess. I stood up. "You're not telling me it's a car are you?" But how could it be a car? I hadn't seen a car anywhere.

Harriet spoke. "You'd better go and look." I walked to the window and peered out. All I could see was Auntie's Jimny, and Grandpa's SUV. I was confused. "What do you see?" she prompted.

"Your car...." Understanding went 'plunk' in my brain. I gasped. "No. You can't be serious. That's *my* car?" Harriet nodded. I heard myself screaming. Then everyone crowded around, hugging me and patting my back.

"We're proud of you, Sheri," said Pa. "We thought you could do with a hand."

I jumped around the lounge like a banshee then dashed outside to sit in my car. Although I wasn't licensed to drive yet, I was still able to admire the interior and adjust the seat and rear view mirror. There was even a CD player that had the mp3 symbol stamped onto the black plastic trim. I sat out there for half an hour, until the cold chased me back inside.

For lunch we joined the formal dining table with the family one so that all twelve of us would fit around it. Luke arrived at midday bearing a crate of cold beer. I set the table, taking particular care with the arrangement of the napkins and glasses. It looked like a work of art. The crystal picked up the reflected light of the candles so that they shimmered like diamantes against the highly polished silverware. Ma's centrepiece, a highlight of the Christmas table for as long as I could remember, took centre stage. A luscious red and green creation, silver and gold dusted pinecones framed a velvet covered, plastic model of Santa and his reindeer. Complete with gift laden sleigh and snow encrusted fir trees it seemed to invoke all that was sentimental and delicious about a winter Christmas.

We stood together around the table and held hands while Pa intoned the grace. Then once everyone was settled, Ma and I ceremonially carried in the platter of glistening roasted turkey surrounded by aromatic mounds of glazed apricots and pears. Grandma's large casserole dish filled with creamy, cheesy, potato bake along with piles of hot, roasted vegetables and greens complemented the bird.

I found myself positioned at the end of the table next to Aunty Julie and opposite Luke. Jonah sat beside me in his high chair where I fed him spoons full of mashed sweet potato and gravy. I chatted to Aunty Julie who informed me that the hardware store was going well and that Grandma and Grandpa had bowed out of the business over the last year and were considering going on a cruise. I guessed that was what people did when they got old; they retired and went on holidays. As

Aunty chattered on, I endeavoured to keep an ear on the conversation between Byron and Luke, waiting for an opportunity to join in. After a while I managed to ask Luke whether he had any brothers or sisters. Luke smiled and his eyes twinkled cheekily.

"I have one sister," was his reply. He didn't elaborate but his silence invited me to ask further questions - if I was interested, that is.

I couldn't help myself. "And what does she do?"

"She's married and has a three year old daughter. They all live in L.A. Congratulations on your car by the way."

"Thanks. Now I just need to get my license to drive it. I was hoping Byron could take me into Flagstaff on Tuesday." I smiled at my brother hopefully.

Byron replied, "I would, Sis, but we are lining the dam on Tuesday. I can take you on Friday."

I was disappointed. If I wanted to drive my car home to Dodge I needed to get some practice in and get the paperwork done, pronto. My face must have fallen because Luke, seeing I was bummed out, offered to take me instead and agreed to pick me up on Tuesday morning.

Pa was planning on driving Harriet and Julie back to Flagstaff on the Monday so I took the opportunity to go with them so as to have a look in Becky's shop and spend the clothes voucher. Pa dropped me on Main Street. The day, though cold, was clear and the weak sun, making a valiant effort to infuse a little warmth, created puffs of steam that wavered thinly upwards from the rivulets of water that trickled down the gutters of the roadside.

I pushed Jonah along the footpath. He was as immobile as a snowman with his head tucked into a beanie that had fur flaps to cover his ears and his hands swathed in woolly mittens. Becky was behind the counter tagging some new garments when we arrived. She seemed genuinely pleased to see us.

Over the next half hour I tried on various outfits. Everything looked so gorgeous to my fashion starved eyes it was difficult to choose. I eventually settled on functionality rather than pure desire and chose a light, chocolate coloured, bomber style padded jacket, matched with a grey wool, pencil skirt and teal blue, polo neck sweater. Deciding to wear the jacket, I peeled off my old coat and placed it in the bag all the while wishing I had money for shoes.

Voicing my goodbyes and thanks to Becky, I pushed Jonah to a nearby cafe where I ordered a cappuccino and gave him an opportunity to escape his pushchair and climb over the seat. It was delightful in the cafe. The smell of baking pies and cakes infused the warmth, creating a homely sense of wellbeing. *Coffee is such a cheap pleasure* I thought. There was something indulgent about spending half an hour sipping a hot drink and reading a magazine.

The people inside the cafe were doing various things. Some were reading the newspaper. One woman was tapping away on a laptop which made me curious as to what she was writing. A group of four, two men and two women were clustered into one corner of the room, animatedly discussing something. One of the women had a diary open in front of her into which she periodically made notes. *Probably a business meeting*, I decided.

The door opened and a scruffy young man walked in. He glanced my way, then looked again more closely. After placing an order he walked towards me.

"Sheri," he stated. I nodded. "It's Mark."

Thin and unshaven, he was unrecognisable as the buff jock he had been in school. His faded jeans looked as if they needed a wash.

"I didn't recognise you," I exclaimed. "What have you been doing?"

"Not much; just odd jobs here and there. I quit my last job; too boring."

Quit or was fired?

The waitress brought his coffee. He emptied three sachets of sugar into the cup and stirred vigorously, causing the coffee to slop into the saucer. He asked what I was doing and I explained that I was working and flatting. I didn't say where but led him to believe it was in another part of Flagstaff. He nodded absently, the whole while watching Jonah.

"How's he been – the little fella?"

"His name's Jonah and he's good, almost walking. He said 'horse' the other day."

"Good. Good. I would like him to stay with me one weekend. I'd like to know my own son."

I didn't reply. I had thought about this topic over and over but couldn't come to any firm conclusion. On the one hand, Jonah did deserve to know his father but on the other, I distrusted Mark and did not want him influencing Jonah, nor did I want him phoning me or arriving unannounced at my flat. I didn't want anything to do with him at all.

"You don't pay child support," I said slowly, remembering what Harriet had told me. "I don't see why you should have Jonah if you don't contribute anything towards his life.

"I could pay child support," he countered. "How much is it?"

I didn't know but said I thought it could be about $300 a month. Mark shrugged and said he didn't earn much. I explained that the arrangement would have to be legal so we all knew where we stood but I was secretly banking on Mark not being motivated enough to organise anything.

"Hello boy," he finally said to Jonah who slunk down beside me and stared at his father with two fingers in his mouth. The silence stretched between us but then conversation had always been awkward.

"Did you have a hard night last night?" I asked, coldly.

Mark chuckled and it was a dry hollow sound. "Yeah. Yeah, you could say that," he said without volunteering any further information.

Getting anything out of him was like getting blood from a stone. He spoke cryptically so that what he said could have meant anything. It exasperated me to be forced into asking yet another question and his reticence made me suspicious. That's the problem when people are cagey, I thought. You put two and two together and get five.

I considered whether the conversation was worth the effort but decided that if Mark did want to organise to spend time with Jonah, then it behove me to know as much as possible about his lifestyle so I persisted. "Why? What did you do?"

"Oh. Just me and some mates. You know...." he left the sentence hanging but I was unwilling to let him get away with it.

"No. I don't know, Mark. What? Did you get high, hire some hookers? Explain it to me." To my own ears I sounded like a mother scolding her wayward son.

"We just had a bit of fun. Nothing serious. Chill."

I saw I'd get nothing further out of him. "That reminds me. I saw Becky at Christmas time." He flinched ever so slightly but then waited, unresponsive. "She came with Jet for Christmas lunch. You know she's dating Jet, eh?"

"Yeah. What about it?" he said. His whole attitude exuded studied nonchalance.

"Nothing really but she said that you'd said you were paying child support and visiting Jonah, which obviously you aren't."

"Nah, nah," he countered. "What I said was that I wanted to."

That made sense and Becky had said she could have got it wrong but somehow it all seemed off.

"Do you see Becky much?" I asked.

"No. She's one of the girls in the group I socialise with, that's all." He leaned back and tapped at his pocket, looking for smokes, then remembering he was in a no smoking area, he stood up. "I'd better be going," he said.

When he had gone, I realised that he hadn't even asked for my number. I looked at my watch. It was two in the afternoon. There was just enough time to go and sit my theoretical learner driver test.

CHAPTER FIVE

Seated at the wheel of my very own car on the following Tuesday morning, I felt very adult. Luke watched while I went through the preliminary routines of adjusting mirrors and seat belt. I'd left Jonah with Ma. The last thing I wanted was to have him grizzling and causing distractions. I turned on the ignition, flicked on the indicator, and slid the car out into the road. Driving was not hard. I'd driven the truck many times on the farm but usually only in low gear. Driving on the road was faster that was all. Under Luke's tutelage, I practiced hill starts, reverse parking and changing gears. The hour passed quickly.

"Can I buy you a coffee?" Luke offered as we parked for the final time.

It was my second trip to a cafe in as many days but one can never have too much coffee. While we were waiting for our drinks to arrive, Luke asked me about Jonah. I explained as succinctly as I could.

"He's a sweet kid," was all he said. I was relieved; having been afraid he would judge me for being so stupid. I went on to describe my meeting with Mark the previous day and voiced my suspicion that something didn't ring true about him. Luke had nothing to add but advised that I should trust my feelings. "Instincts," he explained, "are rational. Our subconscious notices tiny clues and responds to them before we can consciously explain them. It's like with horses. Have you ever been riding and thought 'go left,' and the horse turns before you even do anything?"

I nodded.

"It's as if the horse read your mind but in fact, the horse didn't read your mind. It just felt the subtle shift in your body position before you made the conscious move. It's a safeguard for humans to protect us from harmful people and situations. Always listen to your instincts, Sheri."

"Listen to you, you guru," I teased.

Luke grinned. "My mother is into metaphysical things and she got me interested."

Although it was reassuring to hear his explanation, this type of thought was new to me. Ma and Pa were as natural and physical as the land they lived and worked on and accepted everyone at face value. But I had been terribly hurt by Mark and the experience had revealed to me the person underneath who was vastly different to the handsome and charming young man he portrayed to the world. I had seen beneath the mask. It seemed to me that Becky was not who she said she was either but so far I didn't know in which way. When I thought about it, I realised I had never trusted her in the same way that I trusted Vanessa.

"The trouble is it is hard to know who the real person is. Is Mark charming and successful or is he an irresponsible player?"

"What does he do, Sheri? There will be your answer. Don't believe what guys say, believe what they do. Actions speak louder than words as they say."

The advice snapped Mark into focus. Who Mark was, the drinker and ball playing womaniser had been there to see all along only I hadn't been able to see past his charm. I'd been so flattered to be chosen for the prom by one of the most popular boys in school that I had ignored my suspicions.

I groaned out loud. "I have been an even bigger fool than I thought," I confessed.

"No, Sheri. Don't blame yourself. You were very young and didn't know better. But he did. The guy plays mind games. He knew what he was doing. And he's not the only one. You have to be careful."

"Have you ever been duped by a woman?"

"No," Luke said wryly. "But my mum went through the same thing and the result was me. So I know what she went through with my dad."

"Did you see your dad when you were a kid?"

"Yes. When I was ten I wanted to meet him. I think every boy wants to know his father. Mum organised for me to spend the weekend with him but it wasn't very successful. Dad lived alone and the house was dingy. He watched TV the whole time. It was pretty bad."

"But are you glad you know him?"

"I think so because I don't have any unanswered questions. I remember being very angry at Mum for a while."

What Luke said gave me a lot to think about with regard to Jonah. It was good to have a man's perspective.

"You are very smart," I said. "How old are you by the way?"

Luke fiddled with his napkin, folding it into squares. "I'm twenty six," he said. "My birthday is in February."

"An Aquarian." *And nine years older than me.* "I'm a Leo. Do you believe in star signs?"

Luke laughed and stood up, ready to leave. "My mum does. Are we ready to go?"

We didn't talk much on the way home. I was driving and needed to concentrate. But I had learned a lot from Luke and imagined that we would be friends for a long time to come. It already felt like I had known him all my life.

I wondered why he hadn't married. He was reasonable looking. He had a clear, if somewhat swarthy, complexion, short black hair, average height, slim build. He dressed well and had a sense of style. Most of all, he was very understanding. It seemed weird that no one had snapped him up. *Maybe he was gay?*

The rest of the week sped by. I practiced driving as much as possible in readiness for the trip back. As much as I loved being on the ranch, I was feeling rejuvenated and ready to return to the flat.

Once home, life quickly settled back into the old routine but I couldn't stop thinking about Luke. He was unlike any other man I had met. In fact, I hadn't known there were men like him. Not that it made any difference. Hoping to find a man didn't bring one to my door. I complained to Vanessa about it.

"Yeah well, you do have a 'do not disturb' sign on your forehead,' she advised somewhat caustically.

"What do you mean?' I demanded.

"I dunno. You have a kind of reserve about you. If you want a man you have to encourage them, be friendly."

I thought it was probably true. I didn't encourage men and I wasn't friendly to them because I hadn't met anyone I wanted to let into my life yet. After all, it wasn't just me, there was Jonah to consider too. The man would have to not only accept Jonah but also love him and be a good dad to him which effectively eliminated most of the boys I met. Vanessa enjoyed playing the field and I bumped into a different male looking for juice in the fridge almost every weekend but I couldn't bring myself to do the same and having Jonah sleep in my room didn't help.

The months of my life dropped off the calendar and with each week I grew increasingly bored and broke. Any challenge my job had ever provided had long since been mastered so that my day mostly consisted of counting the hours until I could go home again. I was also lonely. Vanessa was rarely home. Having fallen in love with a Brazilian guy called Santos, she spent most nights at his place.

Part of the problem was Jonah who had turned into a handful, a small bundle of inexhaustible energy that possessed an innate knack for being naughty. Having outgrown his cot, I had squeezed a single bed into my room for him but he would not stay in it. No sooner had I tucked him in than he was up for a drink of water or to go to the bathroom. He drove us crazy. Usually, I ended up letting him fall asleep on the couch. It was easier than fighting the battle. It was the same in the supermarket. Saying 'no' to Jonah usually resulted in his flinging himself to the floor in frenzy and if I had little patience, Vanessa had none. "For goodness sake, give the kid a lolly and shut him up," she'd snap when Jonah threw the inevitable tantrum. Jonah seemed to know exactly what to do to get his own way and I felt powerless against him.

Without Vanessa, the others came to the flat less often so my social life, as poor as it had been before, was rendered virtually non-existent. Empty, quiet nights followed each other in dreary succession. I needed a boyfriend and yearned for a hug. An intense desire for human touch plagued my spirit. I felt restless and agitated and found it impossible to sleep.

Luke had awoken something within me and I found myself looking forward to seeing him again but when I returned home to visit, he wasn't there. Pa had finished the dam and was once again able to handle the farm with Byron, so Luke had left and Pa could not say where he had gone. The disappointment I felt confused me. I was not attracted to Luke and was not in love with him so the sting of his not leaving his contact details was as difficult to explain as it was to ignore.

I bought the papers and scoured the employment sections looking for a new job. The selections were limited; office jobs, waitressing, bar work, even exotic dancing. Nothing seemed desirable and once again I cursed the stupidity that had cut short my education and relegated me to the unskilled labour market.

A position as a real estate assistant caught my eye. That could be interesting, I thought. I pictured myself smartly dressed in corporate attire, heels, hair in a chic roll showing the houses, emphasising their good points and down-playing the bad. There would be forms to fill out, deals to make, people to call. *I could do that.* The agency was in St Kilda's, an up-market suburb in the hills overlooking the lake.

Still not owning a computer, I found a pen and paper and wrote out a Curriculum Vitae by hand, planning to take it to the internet cafe on the weekend and type it out. Jonah, intrigued at what was keeping me occupied at the table for so long, climbed up beside me and grabbed at the papers, forcing me to get up and find him some scrap paper and his crayons to keep him amused for five minutes. So, in between keeping Jonah occupied, I wrote my resume in a silent flat, on a red Formica table, under a naked light bulb and made it as glowing as I could without actually lying.

Once my CV was printed, I decided to catch the bus into the city and deliver it by hand. I wanted to see exactly where the agency was and hopefully meet someone with influence. On the day, I dressed carefully and took special care in applying make-up while Jonah, naturally, tried to fiddle with everything on my dresser. After repeatedly ignoring my commands to leave things alone, I snapped and smacked his bare leg. A welt, in the shape of my hand, appeared on his chubby thigh. Guilt slapped me back and Jonah screamed loud enough for the neighbours to hear so, with my blood pressure rising rapidly, I hauled him by his arm outside of my bedroom and into the hall. I slammed the door shut and thereafter was compelled to finish my couture accompanied by the sound of Jonah screaming insanely and drumming at the door with his feet.

Ignoring his cries, I proceeded to the kitchen to organise some snacks and a drink for him and packed them in his travel kit. Jonah toddled after me into the kitchen, flung himself on the floor and screamed louder than ever but I ignored him. I knew if I dealt with him then and there I would smack his little backside so hard I would regret it. I put the jug on to make coffee. There was half an hour until the bus came. I stood over the out of control child, and then thought to crouch down to where he lay on the floor where I heard, with surprise, my mother's voice say firmly, "Stop crying right now or I will give you something to cry about."

To my amazement, Jonah stopped screaming and stared at me, eyes wet, the cries captured in his throat emerging as hiccups and gulps. "We are going for a ride on the bus, Jonah, into the city. Mummy is going to look for a new job and she wants to see the place she wants to work. So you have to be a good boy for mummy, eh. Are you going to be a good boy?'

Jonah nodded mutely.

"Okay. That's good. Good boy," I said. I picked him up and he clung to me. I wiped his face and tugged on a pull-up, just in case. Abandoning the coffee idea, I strapped Jonah into his stroller and set off for the bus. During the ride, he struggled to keep his eyes open. The tantrum had worn him out. I kept him awake hoping he would fall asleep in his stroller instead – which he did. I realised with a flash of pride how much I had learned about being a mother. I was getting pretty good at it.

The agency was easy to find and was only a short walk from the bus stop meaning I could commute if I was unable to find a new flat immediately. The street was pretty and had a village feel to it. There appeared to be a number of boutique shops interspersed with cafes and even a small park. I imagined how nice it would be to live in a place like this and the flat seemed even drabber beside that thought. I pushed open the door and went inside. An attractive blonde woman who looked to be in her early forties said hello in a breathless, girly voice.

"Hi. My name is Sheri," I said. "I saw the ad' in the paper for the real estate assistant position and I thought I would deliver my CV myself."

"Oh. Yes. I'll hand that in for you." She held out her hand for the envelope.

"Actually, I was hoping to meet the person who is doing the hiring, if that is possible, please."

"That is Steve Carnegie. But...we don't usually do this. I'll see if he is in."

She tottered away on a pair of extraordinarily high heels and disappeared behind a closed door. I took a seat and waited. When she emerged again, a tall man dressed in a suit, followed.

"Steve," he said without offering me his hand.

I took a deep breath. "Hi. Thanks for meeting me. My name's Sheri and I wanted to meet you because as you can see, I am young and have a two and a half year old son. But I did really well at school and would have gone on to University except for what happened. I have been working in Sunhill for the last two years and now I'm bored with my job and need a change. If I get the job, and I hope I do, I will move here and put Jonah in day care over here too. Oh, and I am more than willing to work for free for a couple of weeks so that you can see if you like me, which I am sure you will." I handed him my resume which he took. He looked abashed and not a little disconcerted. I supposed they didn't usually get earnest young women pleading their case in person.

"Thank you, Ah..."

"Sheri."

"Yes. Thank you, Sheri. Most interesting. We will be in touch." He turned away so with that I left. I had done as much as I could. Thankfully, Jonah had slept like a cherub through the whole process.

Out in the midday sun, I went for a wander down the tree lined street. Well dressed women with obedient children in tow browsed the shelves. *How did they do it?* I wondered. Jonah would have been running up and down the aisles touching everything he could see. I would have to lift my game if I hoped to make it here. My country background and life in the poor districts had not exactly prepared me for the trendy lifestyle.

Jonah stirred and grizzled in his stroller so I popped into the nearest cafe and ordered a cappuccino for me, a milkshake for Jonah and a sweet bagel. I spotted the bathroom and took him, thereby pre-empting the need to change him later. He sat contentedly on my lap and we ate our food while I related to him all that had transpired. I don't know how much he understood but he seemed to be listening.

Jonah was asleep by seven thirty, exhausted by the day's events so I poured Vanessa and I a glass of white wine. "How's it going with Santos?" I asked as we carried our drinks into the lounge. To my consternation, Vanessa flushed then began to weep silent tears that rolled over the curve of her cheek. I moved closer and put my arm around her shoulders. "Hey, what's the matter?" It had been so long since anything had gone wrong in Vanessa's life, I thought at first that maybe she had put on weight or was growing a pimple but she shook her head. Devastation was evident in every sad bend of her neck and with every flop of her dejected hands.

"I think Santos is seeing another woman. I think he's cheating on me."

"No!" I exclaimed, not wanting to believe that anyone would want to hurt darling, loyal Vanessa. "How do you know? What makes you think that?"

When Vanessa replied, her voice sounded weary. "He's been really secretive about his cell phone. And he's been working late – a lot."

"Have you talked to him about it?"

"Yes, but of course he denied it. Then he got angry with me and accused me of not trusting him. How I became the bad guy, I don't know."

I handed Nessa her glass. "Here, have a drink."

We sipped in silence for a moment. "Is there any way we could find out for sure? You know, we could follow him or something. What's he doing tonight anyhow?

"I don't know. Nothing. He said he wanted a night in. Some mates were coming round. He didn't exactly say."

"Man, if we could get someone to come over and babysit Jonah, we could drive over and have a look, see what Mr Santos is really up to."

Despite herself, Vanessa laughed. "We could ask Deena." She rummaged for her cell phone. Deena said she would be right over.

Fifteen minutes later, Nessa and I were in the Jimny and heading over to Santos' house. It was just on dark when we pulled up in the street opposite. There were no cars in the driveway and no lights on. It looked like no one was home.

"Go and knock on the door and ask if you left your cell phone there," I instructed. "That won't seem unreasonable."

Vanessa did as I suggested. I watched as she pressed the doorbell but the house remained in darkness.

"What now?" she asked as she climbed back into the car.

I turned on the ignition. "Let's go for a little cruise." I drove slowly down the road towards the suburban shopping centre that I knew was a quarter of a mile ahead. We circled the block; past the hotel and the gas station, but of Santos there was no sign. The street stretched ahead, dark and empty. He could have been anywhere.

"Stop! Stop! There's his car," cried Vanessa, pulling on my arm and indicating a new Hummer parked outside an all night convenience store, twenty yards up the road. I pulled abruptly into a space. We slunk down in our seats and watched.

"There he is," she said.

Sure enough, I could see his figure outlined against the light of the mart, surrounded by a group of guys. "Get down. Get down." He had pushed the door open.

At that moment, a Camaro appeared; bright orange paint and racing stripe prowling noisily along the street. A loud series of 'bangs' rang out. "What the hell!" I exclaimed, imagining the Camaro had backfired.

"OH MY GOD! Sheri – Santos has been SHOT!"

The Camaro roared past and I glimpsed a pair of dark eyes as they oh so fleetingly brushed past mine. *Had the occupants seen us*? I watched the disappearing glow of the Camaro's tail lights in my rear view but it did not return; did not perform a quick u turn and return to see whether those really were eyes that the driver had seen peering out of the parked car waiting silently in the darkness.

A life and death drama was playing out on the sidewalk. Within the glowing circle of the shop lights we could see Santos leaning awkwardly, half sitting, slumped against the door where a wide smear of blood described his descent. He was clutching his shoulder while gesticulating men crowded around him.

"We've gotta get out of here right now," I said, horrified at the thought of being caught up in the fallout from a drive by shooting. I turned on the ignition and carefully pulled out, hoping that if I drove normally no one would ever remember seeing us parked on the side of the road, witness to all that had occurred. Once we were past the shop I planted my foot on the gas pedal and raced for home. My hands were shaking so badly it was a miracle we made it. There were so many questions, none of which Vanessa could answer. The irony of it was that it didn't look as if Santos was cheating after all, only the reality was looking much worse. I parked the Jimny around the back out of sight and we fell into the house.

"That was quick," said Deena.

We garbled out the story. "We have to think this through," I said. "We have to make a plan. I say we act as if nothing has happened until we see what comes up on the news. Once we know what the police know about Santos, then we can decide what to do next."

Neither of us got any sleep that night and despite having the television on all the next day nothing appeared on the news until the late edition at 10.30 on Sunday night. Vanessa and I huddled on the couch, eyes glued to the screen.

"Wannabe drug lord, Santos Haviera, was shot and injured in a drive by shooting in Sunhill last night. Police are asking that anyone with information that might help the investigation to come forward. Haviera, who is wanted in several states on possession charges, has been taken into custody."

"Thank God he's only injured," sobbed Vanessa.

"He's a drug lord," I gasped. "Holy crap, Vanessa, you've been screwing a drug lord. And I saw the vehicle driven by his attackers. It was an orange Camaro."

"How do you know that?"

"Byron has a Camaro," I said. "When you grow up with two brothers you learn a few things.

"What now?" asked Vanessa once she had calmed down.

"I think you should phone Santos and say you have seen the news and that you're shocked and scared," a fact that was true. "And then I think we should go home to my place for a few days. I'm too freaked to stay here anyway. What if those guys know who you are or saw my car? They could come looking for us." The vision of those empty, dark eyes replayed in my mind.

Vanessa wanted to know whether I was going to phone the cops about the Camaro but all I could say was that I didn't know although I had already wondered whether I could phone anonymously. I really needed to talk to Pa about it. I was out of my depth.

When Vanessa phoned Santos, the phone went to voice mail so she spoke into the machine the message as planned. We then worked frantically into the early hours of the morning packing up the Jimny with everything important but all the while taking care to ensure that the house didn't look as if we had abandoned it. Finally, I gathered up Jonah and strapped his sleepy body into the car seat. Having done all we could, we drove off into the night.

It was five in the morning when we arrived in Flagstaff and pulled up at Big Berta's Roadhouse for breakfast. Jonah was very quiet, no doubt disconcerted by being in a diner so early in the morning. The mid October day was dawning clear and crisp and the horizon grew brighter with each passing moment. The smell of fresh coffee and frying bacon made my mouth water. I realised that despite the circumstances that had precipitated our wild flight, I was having more fun than I'd had in a very long time. Even Jonah was behaving better with so much going on. Maybe he'd been as bored as I was.

We were home by six. Pa and Byron were just emerging from the porch when I pulled up and were clearly surprised to see us. "Hi Pa. Hi Byron," I said, giving them a hug. "Something has happened. We need your advice." We all trooped back into the house and settled ourselves around the table. Ma whisked Jonah off while we described everything that had occurred. To my relief, Pa didn't think we had anything to worry about and said that he would go and have a chat to Sherriff Longridge later that morning and pass on the information about the Camaro. It felt good to relinquish the responsibility.

After a day or two of lying about recuperating from the recent sleepless nights, Vanessa and I had a conversation. I described the real estate job I had applied for and expressed my dissatisfaction with our cramped living quarters and the general monotony of my life. "I need to have some fun," I complained. Only I didn't know how to achieve that. I still had no money and still had to look after Jonah. Essentially, nothing had changed. The only real difference was that now I was twenty years old and my teenage years were gone. I wished I could turn back the clock and do it differently. I would be smarter, less trusting, would look out for myself more.

"Look after yourself now," said Vanessa. "Get Mark to have Jonah for a while." But giving up my son was something I was literally unable to do. Whatever turn my life took next, Jonah would have to come with me.

On Wednesday, deeming that the drama would have settled, we drove back to Dodge. When we let ourselves into the flat, we saw that everything was as we had left it. I collected the mail. There was a letter from the agency. I ripped the envelope open. It read; *we regret to inform you that you were unsuccessful in your application.* I crumpled the letter up and threw it into the bin. "Didn't get the job," I informed Nessa. She didn't comment. What was there to say?

Had I been brave enough, I would have handed in my resignation when I went back to work on the Monday and placed my belief in something turning up. But my fear of having to crawl home yet again if unable to find a new job, held me back. The move would smell too much of failure. I would have to stick it out until something changed.

What changed was that Santos was released on bail. Violent banging awakened us from sleep in the middle of the night. I crept to the door with Vanessa huddled right behind me, clinging to my dressing gown like a toddler. "Who is it?" I called.

"Santos! Open up."

The moment the key turned, he barged in. His shoulder was heavily bandaged. "Have to stay with you, darlin'," he said addressing Vanessa. "My place is a bit hot right now." So saying, he carted his bag into Nessa's bedroom and dumped it on the floor.

"Fix us a coffee, sweets," he instructed. I ignored him but Vanessa put the jug on. He flung his body into a lounge chair and sat there jigging his leg up and down.

"Isn't it dangerous for us with you being here?" I asked. My mind popped with an image of armed thugs bursting in without the polite preliminaries and terrorising us all. But as usual, Santos was only able to see the situation in the light of how it affected him.

"Those guys who jumped me, were busted through a tip off. The whole Mandez clan are after me now," he said, missing my point entirely. "Have to lay low for a bit."

I pulled Vanessa aside. "He can't stay here. What about us?"

Vanessa shrugged. She said she loved Santos and didn't have it in her to turn him out. So much for looking out for herself, I thought. However, my own anxiety over Jonah being placed in danger served as the impetus I needed to hand in my resignation after all. To Greg's enquiry as to what I would do next, all I could reply was that I didn't know.

The following two weeks living with Santos proved to be impossible. He ate our food without reservation and expected Vanessa to run around after him as if she was his personal assistant. Understandably nervous about leaving the house, he had Vanessa running off to the lawyers, filing his parole reports and dashing to the bank during her lunch breaks while he reigned from the couch like the king pin he believed himself to be. Meanwhile, his underlings all but moved in as well. They filled the place up with their loud voices, drinking and swearing, relegating Vanessa and I to the kitchen.

"Come with me," I begged. "You're going to get destroyed here." But Vanessa was reluctant. She believed Santos needed her.

'He's using you. He's using us. He doesn't care about us. We are just a convenience to him. He's costing us a fortune."

My appeals fell on deaf ears.

As the days moved closer to my departure, my anxiety became overwhelming. I still had no idea of what I was going to do but I packed our things anyway. The boxes stood about like off duty soldiers. My final pay included two years of holiday pay and came to over $3000, enough to give me a new start, but because I had nowhere else to go, there was nothing for it but to go home to Ma and Pa's yet again. As I travelled the highway east, I vowed that the next time I left home it would be for good. I would find my place in life, would make it work, and that it would be great.

CHAPTER SIX

Ma and Pa, bless them, accepted my rocking up unannounced with equanimity and I once again fell into the easy sense of belonging and peace that life on the ranch accorded me.

True to my prediction, Jonah, now he was nearly three years old, idolised his Grandpa and endeavoured to follow him everywhere. Long hours passed when I didn't see him at all and Jonah benefitted immensely from the country life. Helping Grandpa drive tractors and bang in nails was hard work for a small boy.

Bono, too old for service, was permanently turned out to pasture so I had to content myself with riding the farm hacks but I roamed over the ranch much as I had in my childhood and took great pleasure in remembering. I felt as if I was far away from the girl passionate about rocks and science I had been four short years ago.

The freedom from daily responsibility and activity gave me the time I desperately needed to think about my situation and what I wanted and it soon became apparent to me that I wanted to find my own way in life. I wanted to move on. As much as I loved the farm, I did not want to live in Flagstaff. I wanted to be somewhere bigger, somewhere where people were not so involved in their neighbour's lives, where I could live freely with a certain amount of anonymity.

****

I was hanging out the washing, tussling with the sheets, one windy afternoon, when Mark appeared with a tall, dark haired woman by his side whom he introduced as Sophie. He had come, he said, because he'd heard I was back and he wanted to organise time with Jonah. He told me he was working in construction and was able to pay $100 a week in child support. In return, he wanted to be able to arrange to have Jonah for weekends and special days.

As I stood there, clutching my hoodie around my shoulders, I understood that the time had finally arrived when the right thing to do was to relinquish some of the control of Jonah and allow him to have a relationship with his father. As much as it aggravated me to see Mark pulling himself together with another woman in a way he had been unwilling or unable, to do with me, that wasn't Jonah's fault. Nevertheless, when I pictured Mark and Sophie intent on creating a happy family unit with Jonah in the way that I had not been able to, the envy was bitter in my throat.

Mark pulled one hundred dollars from his wallet and handed them to me, 'to prove his good faith.' I took the money. My son needed new winter clothes. Jonah was out with Pa so they promised to return in the morning. He would need to be introduced to Mark but I had no doubt he would cope. He'd spent so much of his short life in care it was a wonder he even recognised me as being his mother.

With my mind and heart in turmoil, I went for a walk along the stream that meandered through the farm. I marvelled at the twists and turns that had been thrown my way. So much was out of my control. Mark was Jonah's father, and no matter how much I might wish that the ground would open up and swallow him, there was no changing that fact, just as there was no changing the fact that I was alone. But my heart ached. It ached for the family life and consistent male influence that I was unable to give Jonah, ached for my youth spent raising him and ached for my inability to get a decent job. It all seemed too hard and too unfair. I sat by the stream and watched the water, mesmerised by its perpetual bubbling, and tried to think of a way to once and for all escape from Flagstaff and to create a good life for myself and my son.

Mark and Sophie returned the following morning to take Jonah for the day. I set my son down on the deck and crouched down beside him. "This is your daddy, Jonah" I explained. "He wants to take you out." He leaned into me, uncertain. "Say hi to Daddy. You're going to go in the car." I fetched Jonah's car seat and settled him in.

Having expected to feel sad as the car pulled away, I was taken by surprise by the lightening and freeing sensation that washed over me. The entire day stretched ahead, empty of demands on my person. I considered what I might do and failed dismally to come up with anything. "Why don't you go and see Harriet," suggested Ma who was baking muffins in the kitchen. "I know she would love to see you."

I made myself a cup of coffee and settled on my favourite step on the veranda to contemplate my options. Rambo, one of the farm dogs wandered over and lay down beside me, inviting me to fondle his ears while I gazed out over the stark fields. If Mark was to be a permanent fixture in Jonah's life, then I needed to live within a sensible proximity to him. Dodge City was too far away.

In my mind's eye, I assessed the other local towns as to their viability and my mood quickened as the thought occurred to me that as much as I wanted to live in a bigger city, I was probably not suited to the city lifestyle. It wasn't where my heart lay. After all, as I reasoned it through, I had never been one to focus on my appearance. It took conscious effort for me to apply make-up and style my hair. The relaxed attitudes of the country suited me better and there was no denying that the countryside and horses filled me with the greatest joy whereas the colourless suburban lifestyle depressed me.

I considered the town of Melvin which was forty five minutes from Flagstaff. I didn't remember it as being much bigger than Flagstaff, but then I had only been there once with Pa to a pastoral show. It was, from memory, pleasantly situated. I decided to spend the day driving over and having a look at the town to ascertain its suitability as a place to live and work.

On the way, I called in at the hardware store to photocopy my resume. Harriet was offloading a new order of corn seed in readiness for the spring planting, stacking the hessian sacks in neat piles in the dusty store room. She was pleased to see me but was too busy to stop and chat. Grandma, Grandpa and Julie, she informed me in between sacks, had gone on a cruise around the Pacific. She was running the store by herself. I offered to help for a few weeks until they returned; an offer she accepted.

Melvin turned out to be much nicer than I remembered. The streets were lined with towering oaks that were at least a hundred years old. And unlike Flagstaff which was dead flat and looked as if it had been randomly dropped out of the sky, Melvin had natural boundaries. A range of violet hills flanked the north and a lazy green river cut through the business district. The centre of town was vibrant and busy. There were even small skyscrapers housing offices and banks. I was surprised to learn that Melvin was the commercial centre for the region and the economic hub of the oil and mineral developments within the state of Wyoming.

After buying a newspaper, I went into a crowded cafe and ordered a hot chocolate with marshmallows. The warmth seeped into my bones and chased away the cold. I shook open the awkwardly large sheets of paper to the rental section. Although it wasn't worth organising a place to live at that moment, with it being only a few weeks until Thanksgiving and Christmas, there seemed to be a variety of places to rent around the six hundred a month figure.

Out on the street, I saw that there were several real estate agent offices and no doubt there were others in locations farther afield. Having brought five copies of my resume with me, as I came to an office I went in and offered them a copy. No one had any vacancies at the present time but several agents agreed that the property market had been buzzing of late and that it was not inconceivable that they would take on new staff in the New Year. Greatly encouraged, I returned to the Jimny and climbed in, all the while thinking it was incredible how energising having a direction in life was.

When Mark didn't return Jonah by the agreed time of five o'clock, I was furious. It was bitterly cold out and driving after dark was treacherous. I phoned Mark's cell phone but it went straight to voicemail. *I'll wait an hour*, I thought. After all, Jonah could have been asleep. But when 6pm rolled around and there was still no sign of them, I was frantic as well. Grizzly scenarios of the car crashed into a lonely ditch and Jonah slowly freezing to death where no one could find him played out their dramas in my head as I paced the house, anxiously peering out into the night searching for the welcome sight of headlights. I would have gone to Mark's to look for them but was afraid of unwittingly passing them in the dark. At 8.30 the sweep of lights past the window signalled the approach of a car. I pulled on my coat and boots and wrenched the door open. Mark was lifting Jonah out of his car seat. He was fast asleep. I handed the sleeping child to Ma who hurried him inside. Once they were gone, I turned to Mark.

"Where the hell were you?" I snarled. "I was worried sick. Five o'clock we agreed. You're three and a half hours late."

Mark snarled back. "Chill, Sheri. We had a great day and he was asleep. I didn't want to wake him."

"You could have phoned me. I phoned you. Why was your phone off?"

"My battery was flat."

The useless man. "Has he been fed and had his bath?"

"He went down at four. He'll probably be hungry when he wakes up."

I could have hit Mark at that moment out of anger at his irresponsibility and his blatant disregard for, and disruption of, the routines I had established with Jonah. I turned on my heels and stalked inside with the car seat, slamming the door behind me. In the kitchen, Ma had an egg boiling in a pot on the stove while Jonah sat, red cheeked in his booster chair, sucking hot milk out of a kiddie cup. I left them there and went upstairs to run his bath.

It was almost ten by the time Jonah was tucked up in bed. As I kissed him goodnight, I asked him whether he'd had a good time with his dad. Despite myself, I was full of curiosity as to what they had done all day. "Dada," said Jonah. I reminded myself he was only just three. I couldn't expect too much.

****

Thanksgiving in 1996 ended up being bigger than Christmas. By the time Christmas came, we'd had ten inches of snow and travel was virtually impossible. Jet and Becky came home for Thanksgiving. Jet had finished his college courses and was a qualified vet, specialising in farm animals. He was looking for a position and an opportunity fell into his lap.

Unbelievably, Aunty Julie had met a man on the cruise and they were planning to marry. Frank, an oil prospector who had made several financially lucrative strikes in his long career, was sixty four years old. The family met him a week before Thanksgiving. We all went out to dinner in Flagstaff and found him to be distinguished looking as well as charming. His first wife had died from cancer six years previously and he had two grown up children from the marriage. The couple were planning a quiet registry wedding before embarking on an around the world cruise for their honeymoon.

Julie looked stunning, and happy. I had never seen her so animated as she was that evening. She touched Frank's arm and smiled into his eyes as they communicated their plans. The luminous brilliance of the ruby necklace and earrings that adorned her neck glittered in the lamp light and played with the faux fur collar of her red, woollen cardigan, emphasising the elegant slenderness of her shoulders. I wondered whether they were gifts from Frank.

Grandma and Grandpa, also confirming their decision to leave the store and retire into town, presented Jet and Becky with the opportunity of taking over. Jet intended to establish his own practice and work from the store as a vet while Becky took over Julie's role and the management of the accounts. According to everybody concerned, it was the perfect solution.

Much to my own disgust, I couldn't help the feeling of jealously that rose within me. Forgetting that I myself had chosen to walk my own path and sought to find my own place in life, I could only summons disappointed envy towards Jet and Becky, and even Aunty Julie and Frank, over the ease in which their lives appeared to be paved with opportunities whereas I'd had to fight for everything. It was only with great effort that I managed to swallow the clench in my throat and smile my approval.

So like a turn on a kaleidoscope that reveals a new pattern, we were all changed once more. In the New Year, Julie married Frank and left for her new life in California. Jet and Becky moved into the hardware store and I packed up my trusty Jimny and drove to Melvin where I had found on the internet, a small two bedroom wooden bungalow on the outskirts of town for six hundred a month.

A house is an intensely personal thing. The artist Hundertwasser regarded a person's house as an extension of their identity, as much an expression of individuality as skin, hair or clothes. I loved my house from the start. It was small by American standards, and old; maybe even one of the first houses built in Melvin. Constructed squarely out of sky blue painted weatherboards it had high ceilings and a wide veranda that was perfect for relaxing on after a long day. No doubt the veranda reminded me of home but there was pleasure to be had in the fact of it being my own chair that took centre stage beside the front door. More of a couch than a chair really; it was a bulky, overstuffed, horsehair creation I'd found at the junk shop for a few dollars. The arms were wide, and had curved, ring stained, wooden tables on the ends of them where you could place a coffee cup or a bottle of bourbon. A couple of cushions and a blanket made it comfortable and also served to cover the floral fabric that had long ago faded into sepia like an old photograph.

The kitchen in the house was functional, the oven grimy. I opened the door to the cooker and peered in, then shut it and never opened it again in all the time I lived there. I didn't fancy cleaning it so I just abandoned it and used the stove top and microwave instead. The windows were the old fashioned, wooden, slide up type and were low enough to the ground to climb out of. Draping swaths of gauzy floral and lace curtains fell to the floor and brushed sweeping arcs in the dust.

There was always dust in the house. Being on the town boundary, it looked out over the rocky, scrubby landscape towards a range of purple, brooding hills. The hills affected the house and cast heavy light into the living room, especially on stormy days when the tumultuous clouds took on the same violet hue.

The owners had rewired the place after a minor fire had almost got out of hand and burned the bedroom down. Since then, the main bedroom had been redecorated in the same vanilla and floral theme as the rest of the house. Although the feminine, romantic look had never exactly been my style, in a stroke of inspiration and design coordination, I bought an antique iron bedstead and installed it in the room. The paisley print duvet Aunty had given me for Christmas clashed with the other patterns in the decor so I also bought a plain cream textured cover. A thick rug on the polished floor boards completed the fabrics and the results were very pleasing.

Being late winter, it was still very cold. The roses and other unidentifiable bushes in the tiny front garden pointed their bare brown sticks into the white air. Even rugged up, steaming Milo in hand, my breath puffed dragon-like into the weak sunlight but I was as content as I had ever been in my life. In a strange way I felt at home and at peace. The feeling lasted the entire week I had allowed myself for moving in – until the realities of daily life reared their viperous heads. *If only I never had to work, life would be great*, I thought. I could just spend my days doing the things I enjoyed. But like everyone, I had rent to pay and food to buy so I needed a job and Jonah needed to be cared for while I did that.

I found a child care centre for him. More of a pre-school, they actually had a curriculum. The centre manager explained that each child could write their own name, cut with scissors, recite the alphabet and count to ten by the time they started school. This was Jonah's last year before starting first grade but I had never considered that he could learn such things before then. "Oh yes," asserted Ms Gilmore with dynamic, positive energy. "With proper teaching, children as young as two can learn to read." I instantly felt like an inadequate mother. I had scarcely thought about teaching Jonah anything about reading and now worried as to whether he was already disadvantaged before he even started. "Better late than never," she chirped. "We will soon have young Jonah up to speed. I'm sure he'll catch up."

I slunk away convinced that Jonah was in better hands than mine; my mind already darting ahead to what I would wear to the interview I had at ten. A real estate office in the centre of town had rung to say they had an office assistant position available and I had leapt at the opportunity because ultimately I needed a job - any job, although I did have some reservations at the thought of being stuck inside collecting mail and making morning teas. But beggars can't be choosers as they say and I consoled myself that once employed opportunities to improve my situation would probably arise.

After pulling on the trusty outfit I'd chosen at Becky's, I tugged my hair into its customary pony tail, secured it with a black velvet scrunchie, then surveyed my appearance in the full length mirror; slim, tidy, conventional; brown hair, bushy eyebrows, candid blue eyes, a flush of tiny freckles across my nose. Nothing remarkable but not exactly plain either.

A scrimmage in my drawer located an aged lipstick. I styled the fudgy tip onto my lips which then seemed to glow pinkly like huge, pink, clown lips so I wiped it off and smeared them with a slick of Vaseline. A make-over was desperately needed but there was no time at the present. I had to get going. With my bag on my shoulder and the keys to the Jimny clutched in my hand, I dashed out of the door.

"Click. Click. Click." Instead of starting the car, the turn of the key in the ignition produced a sound that emphatically declared that the engine was not going to turn over. My heart sank. *No, no, no. - Not now you son of a seafaring bush pig.* I pumped the gas pedal and tried again but the same thing; a disastrous clicking sound where there ought to have been the roar of cylinders kicking into life. *How could this happen?* I'd only just pulled up in the driveway barely half an hour earlier. I tried again but the engine was not going to turn over without intervention.

I pulled the hood and peered in, trying to think what could be wrong. *It could be the power,* I reasoned as I jiggled the battery leads. They looked pretty corroded. There were globs of white granulated fluff accumulated around the terminals. I flicked it off with a stick and twisted the leads from side to side. They seemed tight enough. I tried turning the key once more but there was no change. I dithered. Time was ticking on. I would either have to call a cab or phone and change my appointment. I knew I didn't have the number, or cash for a cab, but I looked anyway, just in case. Nor did I know the name of the place, although I knew where they were. I could picture the office in the street. I had reached a dead end and there was nothing further I could do about it. I'd have to get the Jimny going and then go into town and make my apologies. *They may even phone me when I don't turn up,* I thought; though it wasn't going to be a good look that I was so disorganised. Re-entering the house, I removed my skirt and pulled on a pair of jeans. I'd previously seen a garage about half a mile down the road so I set off to walk to it.

The workshop, when I arrived was quiet. The building faced the road and the morning sun reached halfway across the cleanly swept floor. Tools hung neatly on the boards above the workbenches alongside which a burnished gold Pontiac Trans Am stood with the hood up. A radio playing classic hits hummed in the background. I called out, "Hello, anybody there?"

At my call, an attractive middle aged woman appeared dressed in navy blue overalls. The sleeves were tied around her waist and in her hands she held a spanner and a rag. A red chequered scarf was tied around her head. From underneath, wisps of fine blond hair escaped. Blue enamelled earrings dangled from her ears and voluptuous breasts pushed out her tight T shirt which had a picture of two puppies emblazoned across the front. She grinned at me and said, "Beryl's the name. How can I help you?"

I am ashamed to admit it now, but I looked about the workshop for a man. "I need to talk to a mechanic about my car," I said. "It won't start."

"I can help. What's happening?" she responded.

"Are you a mechanic?" *Was my voice incredulous?*

She sighed. "I own the garage. And yes I am a fully qualified mechanic. So if you would like to tell me what the problem is, maybe I can help you."

At that I warmed to her completely. "Sorry. I was a bit surprised. I've never met a female mechanic before. But sure - when I turn over the engine it makes a clicking noise." I explained how I'd suspected it may be the battery but that twisting the leads hadn't made any difference.

Beryl nodded. "You are probably right," she said. "The battery could be dead."

"I don't see how. I only just pulled up in the drive a minute before."

"They can go at any time," she responded. She found a new battery and charged me seventy bucks.

Compelled to unburden myself, I explained how I'd missed a job interview. "No doubt I've blown that chance," I complained.

She asked where I was from so I told her a little about Jonah and Pa's ranch; said that I'd moved here to start a new life and that I lived just up the road.

"And you know a bit about cars?" she probed.

I knew a bit, probably more than I thought I knew. She stared out over my head as if thinking. "I could offer you a job here," she said after a moment. "I need someone to help out with the basic stuff, you know, cleaning, answering the phones and taking payments, that sort of thing." She left the offer hanging.

I thought quickly but was unable to prevent a wide grin spreading across my face. "I'd love to," I said. There was something about this woman that appealed to me with her feminine sexiness that contrasted most shockingly with the masculine role she played. "Yes," I continued almost laughing aloud. "I'd love to work here. Thank you so much for the offer."

We shook hands. "Okay," she said. "It's a deal. See you tomorrow."

The workings of TooGood's Garage were simple. Beryl was a widow. The late Thomas Toogood had died of congestive heart failure only a couple of years previously and Beryl had chosen to carry on the business rather than close down, a decision that made sense as even a widow has to pay bills. She had two sons, neither of whom was interested in the workshop, although the elder son, Owen, owned and operated a towing company which played a complimentary role with TooGood's, especially with regard to crashes and breakdowns which were conveniently towed directly to the garage. Owen had a full bodied wife of foreign origin and a pale, willow slender, daughter who looked like a fairy. Owen himself was a big man who reminded me of Mark's father. Sitting driving all day didn't do much for a man's waistline.

Beryl employed two male mechanics, both youngish guys called Karl and Lloyd. Karl, I couldn't get on with. His chauvinistic attitudes made themselves apparent on the first day when he ordered me to 'move my tight arse and make him a coffee.' I was cleaning the tuning machine at the time and his comment paused me mid wipe. I was fairly confident that making him coffee was not a part of my job description but not wanting to create a disturbance on my first day, I pretended that I hadn't heard him. A few minutes passed. Then, clearly annoyed, he called out again, louder this time. "Hey, new girl. Get me a coffee."

I looked up. "My name's Sheri. And I don't think making you coffee is my responsibility."

Karl reacted by raising his voice. "Look sister. You make the coffee if I say you do. You're not doing anything important so get to it."

As much as I didn't want to have a show down so soon, I saw that if I didn't stand my ground I'd be running around after the guys and making coffee as if I was their own mothers so I put down my rag, looked Karl straight in the eye and said, "No. What did your last slave die of? Get your own damn coffee."

He swore under his breath. "Bitch."

I heard him but I let it go. He wasn't worth the effort but thereafter our relationship went from bad to worse. He undermined my every move. If Karl was to be believed, I was responsible for every thing that ever went wrong; every tool left lying on the bench or hanging in the wrong place and every nut that fell through the engine onto the floor.

I let his ranting go straight over my head. To my mind he was an arsehole and I refused to play the game. And if after a particularly hard day I went home and had a cry in the bath, I never let on. I knew he realised he was out of line because he never did it in front of Beryl. Ironically, Beryl was big on respect and didn't have any patience with what she called 'male bullshit.' "Cut the crap," was her favourite saying and it effectively stopped Karl in his tracks but then she was the boss and he knew perfectly well which side of his bread was buttered.

As the weeks passed and Karl saw that there was no point in badgering me because I wouldn't cave, the attacks eased off into a kind of grudging acceptance of me as an actual human being, although he would never call me by name, preferring some kind of diminutive such as kid or girl, even though he couldn't have been more than five years older than me.

Lloyd was okay on his own but he wasn't much of a talker. We'd sit in the weak sun while he smoked a skinny roll-your-own and the feeling would be semi companionable. From our sporadic conversations, I discovered that he'd been born and bred in Melvin and had not actually left the town, even once. His first job had been at the Crispy Chicken Diner where he'd worked as a cook and kitchen hand for a few years before Beryl had offered him an apprenticeship through the local trade school.

I was interested in this fact because as time passed I became increasingly interested in the idea of learning to be a mechanic myself. I had been somewhat surprised and pleased to discover I knew most of the basic workings of the internal combustion engine. I knew what spark plugs were, and how to set the gaps, where the sump was and how to drain oil. It seemed I'd learned a lot by simply tinkering with cars alongside my brothers. The more I thought about it the more I liked the idea of knowing about such a masculine topic. It never ceased to tickle me when Beryl gave that sigh of hers and explained to the clients that yes she was a mechanic. I wanted that for myself.

Also it was obvious to me that there were opportunities for business development within the garage. Beryl's cliental were predominantly automotive with a certain emphasis on classic American muscle cars but the location of the workshop, being on the town boundary and within close proximity to the countryside, leant itself to diesel and agricultural machinery repairs.

Broaching the idea with Beryl one lunch time, she heard me out then said, "So are you deciding on a diesel mechanical apprenticeship?"

I hadn't exactly thought that far but an innate sense of opportunism kicked in and I said 'yes' anyway.

Beryl pondered. "I'll have to think about that," she said. "It would pose certain difficulties because we don't have the right equipment or tools. We don't even have a heavy duty welder but I agree that there is a need for the service. And you can charge ranchers. They're all loaded when it comes to farm expenses."

After several months of proving myself, the boys began to entrust me with incidental tasks that assisted them such as flushing radiators, installing new leads or finding parts. It was interesting work and there was a huge amount to learn. My nails broke down to stumps and my hands took on a grey tinge that defied all efforts with the scrubber at night but I didn't mind. I enjoyed the work.

Women tended to frequent the garage because they felt less likely to be ripped off by some guy telling them stories about the repairs their car needed. They trusted Beryl to tell them the truth, which she did – usually. Business is business.

The rule seemed to be that if you could book a bigger job for more, then why wouldn't you? I didn't fully agree with the philosophy because that had been me on the receiving end in the past but whether or not they could get away with their version of the truth appeared to be the determining criteria.

I met Maisie at the garage. Maisie was a fitness freak with short, dark hair cut into a sleek bob and a gymnast's body. She thought her car was running rough so I got her to pull the hood and fire it up and saw right away that the spark plug leads were cracked and split. It was only $20 for a new set and I had them fitted in a heartbeat. She was terribly impressed and we got talking. As is so often the way when you connect with someone, we could have stood chatting for an hour but I had to get back to work. She put my number on her cell and promised to give me a call as on Saturday afternoon she and a group of her friends were going to a pub in Melvin. She invited me to join them.

I said yes but this posed a problem of what to do with Jonah as I hadn't organised a babysitter for him yet. To this, Maisie confided that she had two kids of her own and that I was welcome to leave Jonah at her place. I was thrilled to finally meet another woman in the same situation as myself.

At six, I picked Jonah up from pre-school and was handed a little booklet by the duty teacher. I had a flick through the booklet after dinner. It was report which said that Jonah was making progress but that he had a tendency to push other children over and monopolise the toys.

Samples of work were contained therein and Jonah's out of shape renditions of the letters of his name made me smile. A letter was also enclosed asking parents to contribute towards an up-coming gala day. I dismissed the letter immediately because there was no way I could attend. It wasn't as if I didn't want to, I couldn't, what with work and all; and I couldn't imagine myself doing anything with the other women anyway.

I didn't exactly advertise the fact I was a solo mum but my absences must have made the fact plain because they never included me in their coffee mornings or play dates or whatever it was that they amused themselves with during the days while their husbands worked.

On the Saturday, Maisie answered the door at my knock dressed in a short leotard and a sweat top. She looked as if she had been exercising. Inside, her house was large and spacious and I estimated it probably had five bedrooms and three bathrooms. I'd never understood the American preoccupation with having a bathroom for every bedroom. Didn't people get sick of cleaning them? *Maybe they paid a cleaner.*

The family room where the kids hung out was also huge and devoid of furnishings, except for a couple of beanbags randomly dotted about the floor; little molehills in a desert expanse of grey designer tile. A massive, flat screen television dominated the entire wall at one end of the room into which was plugged a Playstation surrounded by a scattering of games. The whole room imparted a feeling of emptiness. Even my shoes clip clopped so loudly on the tiles that I felt compelled to walk on tip toe.

A young girl of about fourteen years old slouched on one of the beanbags. She was very thin and her matchstick legs were engulfed by an oversized pair of ugg-boots. A striped woolly beanie with ear flaps and dangling, beaded tassels obscured what appeared to be a petulant face but then she was busy texting on her cell phone and so maybe had a problem with her boyfriend. She didn't look up when Maisie introduced her as Stella the babysitter.

I placed Jonah on the floor next to Maisie's kids. Scottie, the elder of the two was expertly manipulating the controls of the Playstation while Laura looked on with glazed eyes. Jonah shuffled closer to Scottie and made a grab for the controls but Scottie expertly fended him off with his elbow. I hoped that Jonah wouldn't cause any trouble.

While the kids settled, Maisie led me into the kitchen and poured a coffee. It was warm in the kitchen, a muffins and cookies kind of place, although none were apparent. Maisie told me that she was twenty eight years old and currently single. She had been married, young, to a body builder and together they had managed a gym until she had discovered her husband having it off in the office with a female client. She now made a living working as a personal trainer and selling health products on the internet.

We drove into Melvin in her car and when we arrived at the pub, there was already a crowd of around ten people gathered. By the time I figured out it was actually Maisie's birthday it was too late to do anything about it other than concentrate on being sociable. I found myself sitting next to a solid looking guy. "Eric," he said, offering his smooth, white hand for me to shake. I picked him to be too softly built for a gym junkie so was not surprised when he revealed himself to be a stock broker who worked for one of the investment companies in town. Even in this informal setting he wore a pin striped, business shirt and grey pants, although no tie. As we chatted I found myself noting his open, clean shaven face, short hair, full nose and curved lips, then cursed myself for once again being haphazard with my dress. Sure, I looked tidy and presentable in my tight blue Levis and white shirt but not, I was certain, attractive.

When I caught up with Maisie in the ladies bathroom, she winked suggestively into the mirror, teasing. "You and Eric seem to be getting along famously."

I giggled like a school girl. "He's nice. I really do need some help with make-up, hair and clothes though. I look a fright. Do you know anyone?"

Maisie smiled into the mirror. "As a matter of fact I do. I have a friend who's a beautician. She does all my make-up and she matches the colours to your complexion. I'll give her a call. She might be able to fit you in tomorrow."

I tussled momentarily with my old enemy guilt. Damn it if he didn't yawp on in my ear whenever anything to do with leaving Jonah came up. As if reading my mind, Maisie continued. "Bring Jonah to my place and we'll leave the kids with Stella again. Don't worry they'll be fine."

Jonah would be okay, wouldn't he? Sure, I hadn't really seen him all week but he was safe and in good hands with Stella. It wasn't as if he was going to come to harm. Plus, I really did want this for myself. "Thanks," I said resisting the urge to throw my arms around her and burst into tears of gratitude. "Shopping tomorrow it is. I can't wait."

On my return, I was a little surprised to see Eric still sitting where I had left him. I'd expected that he would have moved on. He leaned into me when I resumed my seat and Maisie perched on a bar stool opposite.

"Where did you get to?" he wanted to know.

"I was chatting to Maisie. We arranged to go shopping tomorrow."

"How about a late lunch afterwards? My treat at Trilby's on The Avenue." With a sweep of his green eyes, he included the both of us with his offer.

"Great idea," agreed Maisie.

I could only but concur. "Cheers," I said raising my glass. And so it was arranged, just like that.

As the evening wore on, I found myself really enjoying the party. At around eight o'clock a band arrived and set up in another, larger area off from the main bar. Ignoring my protests, Eric hauled me up to dance and it soon became apparent why. He knew all the moves whereas I, never having been very coordinated, could only do my best to copy. In the end I gave up trying to get it right and clapped, kicked and hip wiggled with abandon. It wasn't exactly elegant or in time to the music, but Eric found my efforts to be insanely funny and we both spent much of our time on the dance floor giggling hysterically.

We staggered out together into the night air just before midnight. Eric gave me a chaste kiss on the cheek. "See you tomorrow," he said.

Maisie and I fell into the car. We didn't say much on the way home and when the car pulled up into the driveway I remembered my son and wondered how he had got on. I needn't have worried. He was conked out on a bean bag.

The next morning, more than little hung over, I was back at Maisie's with Jonah who was more than a little grumpy. He grizzled about everything, pushing away his breakfast and refusing to lift his feet so I could pull his pants on. His mood didn't improve when he realised that I was going to leave him with the babysitter again. I left him throwing a violent tantrum on the bare tiles. Stella, of course, was texting while Scottie merely turned up the volume on the television to drown out the racket.

Once headed into town, I quickly forgot about him, or rather, put him out of my mind. This was my time and I wasn't going to let Jonah spoil it. Maisie's kids were fine with a baby sitter so he could be too.

The appointment was at Maisie's friend's home where she had a room set aside for a parlour. The woman's name was Donna and she was perfectly presented. I mused that it probably wouldn't be a very good advertisement for her services were she to be otherwise. "Thank you. It's very kind of you to give me an appointment," I said as I deposited an air kiss on her soft, downy cheek.

"No worries," she twittered as she directed me to a chair. "First I'm going to do your colours," she said. I didn't know what that meant so I waited expectantly as Donna pulled out a swath of fabrics. "What colour jewellery do you normally wear, gold or silver?" she asked.

I didn't really wear much jewellery at all but I guessed I mostly wore silver. In response, Donna laid a slip of silver paper against my skin, and then swapped it for a piece of gold. "Hmm," she murmured. "I think silver does suit your skin tone best. You definitely are fair rather than dark, but not completely white. There is some olive in your skin and you do have a bit of redness in your cheeks so I would say that you are a winter type which means that black, white and blue colours should suit you best.

She turned her attention to the make-up kit while Maisie perched on the desk and commented, "You know you are really very pretty. Well, not pretty – striking. You have beautiful eyes and bone structure."

Donna agreed. "You should cut your hair to more shoulder length or shorter so you can see your cheekbones better."

I didn't know about cutting my hair short. It was customarily long and had never been anything other than trimmed my entire life.

The beautician was applying eye shadow. "I think the browns will look very nice on you, with cream highlights over the brow. They should bring out your blue eyes beautifully."

I was gratified to observe that she was right. It did look nice and natural, not at all overdone. She applied an antique pink lipstick and the dusky rose hue made a huge difference to the overall look. It made all the other make-up gain relevance. "The trick," Donna explained, "is to highlight either the lips or the eyes but not both at once. It's a bit like clothes. You should mix and match. Either wear a patterned top and plain skirt, or the other way round, but not all plain and definitely not all pattern."

I turned my head this way and that. It was a new me that looked out from the mirror; an older, more confident and sophisticated me. "I love it," I pronounced.

Donna recommended a hair dresser and I made a note of the name and number, figuring to make an appointment for the following week.

After that, Maisie and I drove into town. All the boutiques were open so there were plenty of options. My job demanded that I wore jeans or shorts and a T shirt under my overalls so I needed outfits suitable for trips to town and for socialising. With plenty of guidance from Maisie, I finally selected a gorgeous charcoal grey, merino jersey that crossed over at the front and a mid calf, panelled burgundy skirt. To go with the outfit, I found a pair of cute, leather, ankle boots that fastened up the front with a row of toggled buttons.

Eric gave a whistle when he saw us but his eyes were on me. He touched my shoulder briefly and lightly kissed my cheek. "You look amazing," he murmured. I blushed slightly with pleasure. We seated ourselves at the table indicated by the smart waitress and surveyed the menu which revolved mostly around deli style and pasta dishes. I agonised over the open steak sandwich or the pasta carbonara before deciding on the steak, suddenly nostalgic for farm reared beef perfectly cooked to Ma's mouth watering standards. We ate our meals in the filtered sunlight and chatted.

I addressed Eric. "How long have you lived in Melvin?"

"Three years now," he responded. "I moved here after I finished my Master of Business in Dodge City. What about you?

"Only a couple of months."

"She works at TooGood's," chimed in Maisie.

"What do you do there? Work in the office?"

I shifted in my seat, inexplicably shy. He was so suave I didn't know how he would perceive me once he knew I had a manual job. "No, I help out in the workshop. I had an interview for a position in real estate but my car broke down. Beryl offered me work so I took it."

"She fixed my car in ten minutes and it only cost twenty bucks. That's how we met," said Maisie.

"Well I'll know who to call should my car break down then." He raised his glass in a silent salute.

He didn't ask me about where I had lived before and I was glad. For some reason I didn't want to tell him. Dodge City was so long ago it felt like it had happened to some other girl in some other life.

"How do you and Maisie know each other?" I asked.

Eric smiled. "I'll let Maisie answer that one."

Maisie said, "Pig," then laughed. She turned to me. "Don't take this the wrong way but Eric and I had a little fling, a very brief one, when I first separated from my husband..."

Eric interjected. "Don't listen to her. No we didn't. I've known Maisie most of my life. We went to school together and I was friends with her brother when we were kids. We lost contact for a couple of years then I went to the gym one day and there she was taking the class."

I accepted his explanation and when he asked for my number as we made ready to leave an hour or so later, I gave it to him. Why wouldn't I have? He seemed a nice guy. There was a lot to be said for nice.

Another week; Jonah at childcare, non compliant. Mrs Gilmore tried bailing me up with a list of gripes on Monday afternoon. "Pulling hair... Grabbing toys...Won't do as he is told." Her complaints pecked at my ears like chickens pecking at wheat.

"Sorry. We had a very busy weekend," I explained hurriedly, desperate to get home and put the dinner on.

"Important... Sleep... Regular bedtimes." Her words chased me out to the Jimny where I buckled Jonah in. She was right of course but I didn't want to hear it. I wanted some of my life for me too and Jonah just had to fit in.

After work on Thursday, I took Jonah with me to my late night appointment with the hairdresser; a trendy young woman with dyed, purple/black hair from which sprang bleached white highlights. Initially, she cut my hair into a shoulder length bob but when I looked at myself in the mirror, I realised that long hair of any sort simply wasn't practical.

I'd spent most of the week doing oil changes; undoing sump nuts, draining the thickened black oil and replacing with new. It was messy work. The oil splashed as it hit the tray so that smudgy droplets ended up dotted through my hair and splattered over my face and overalls.

"Cut it off short," I instructed, my mind made up.

I was left with a shaggy cut, slightly longer at the front than the back. It made me look different, like an urchin, and my head felt free. Jonah looked at me sideways, uncertain, but since he had witnessed the whole deal, he knew it was me.

With the weekend rushing up, I made plans. Maisie had already suggested that we go out Saturday night and I felt pretty certain that Eric would call sometime soon but I was thinking of Vanessa. I hadn't heard a thing from her since I'd left the previous October. Now it was almost May. I'd sent a couple of texts and tried to phone but there had been no response. The calls had gone straight to voicemail. I'd heard nothing further about Santos either. With curiosity and lurking anxiety growing exponentially the longer I didn't hear, I decided to pack the Jimny and drive over to see for myself. Who knew whether she would even be there in the old place? Maybe she had gone home or moved elsewhere.

We set off early Saturday afternoon and Jonah fell asleep almost immediately, lulled into unconsciousness by the warmth. I had forgotten how far away Sunhill was and how long it took to get there; then as the streets of Sunhill emerged before me, I marvelled at how little it had changed. There were the same broken street signs, the same dull brown fences and the same loose lidded rubbish bins standing forlornly on the same dusty street corners. I turned into the street where the flat was and pulled up in the driveway.

The grass was calf high and the trash can lay on its side, spilling plastic bags and snail nibbled milk cartons onto the path. Like a cliché, a thin cat darted away at my approach. The curtains were closed and silence wrapped around the flat like a shroud. I rapped on the door and the sound reverberated through the afternoon air. I knocked again, harder this time. *Was that a slight stirring inside?* After trying the door handle, which yielded under my touch, I pushed lightly and the door swung open. "Hello?" I called into the acrid gloom. "Anybody home?"

From the doorway, it was impossible to recognise any of the furnishings. About to turn and leave, I heard a low sigh. "Hello. Vanessa?" I called again. A figure shambled into view from the direction of her bedroom and I stared at the apparition in shock. The figure was the same size and shape as Vanessa but her dark hair was bedraggled and fell in lank strands about her shoulders as she clutched a blanket around thin shoulders with one hand and fingered a cigarette with the other. Incredulity lent an edge to my voice. "Vanessa, is that you?"

The woman grumbled as her bare feet scuffed the floor, barely audible, "Yeah. Who wants to know?"

"It's me, Sheri. Good lord! What happened to you?"

Vanessa peered at me. "Oh. So it is. Your hair is different. Come in, I guess." She led the way into the kitchen and flicked the jug on. I collected Jonah from the Jimny and followed her into the once familiar room. Dishes clogged the sink and food scraps littered the trash and bench tops. Vanessa, seemingly oblivious to the mess, sat at the red Formica table and puffed on her cigarette. I could not believe the change in her. I settled Jonah on my lap where he groggily sucked his thumb.

"How's Santos?"

She shrugged. "In jail."

That information made me feel a bit better. At least he wasn't about to suddenly turn up. "What happened? I'm sorry but you look like shit. Are you okay? Why are you living like this? Are you working?" In response, Vanessa silently extended her left leg out from under the table and hoisted the blanket to reveal a home detention bracelet. I had never seen one up close. The chunky contraption was locked securely around her ankle and its single neon green eye winked maliciously.

"How?"

"Santos robbed the drug store. I was driving his car but turns out he was under surveillance. The cops got us before he even left the store." She giggled and stubbed out her butt in an overflowing saucer. "I didn't know he was going to do that," she continued quietly, "but the cops didn't believe me of course."

Presuming she meant the very same drug store where Santos had been shot, I was stunned by the sheer stupidity of the man, and while on bail too. "But why?"

"He wanted cold tablets."

"And he couldn't just buy them?"

"I dunno. They use the ingredients to make something else, I think. He must've needed a lot because they caught him with boxes of the stuff."

It was too much to take in. From a bright, beautiful, vivacious woman to this wreck in eight months seemed impossible.

"But golly, Nessa - the dishes, the mess. This isn't you."

She shrugged again and within the gesture was futility and helplessness. "What's the point?" she said.

I was at a loss for words. The situation was beyond me. All I could do was clean the kitchen with Vanessa helping me in a fashion then leave my number with her. Instructing her to call me if she needed me, I drove home, shattered by what I had seen.

Thoughts ran around in my mind. My first instinct was that she could come and stay with me but I didn't know whether she was allowed to change her address or even the extent of her relationship with Santos. I certainly did not want him turning up at my house now any more than I had in the past. And then there was the question of room to consider. Jonah had the only other bedroom and I couldn't say that I wanted to disrupt that arrangement.

The problems associated with helping Vanessa by allowing her to move in with me were cumbersome but if I was completely honest, I would have had to admit that although large, they were not insurmountable and that the real root of my reluctance lay in a desire to protect my own situation. I had walked a long, hard road to date and was only now getting on my feet. My job was enjoyable. I had some money spare each week and I had made some friends. I didn't want to jeopardise those things. And hadn't she had the opportunity to come with me in the beginning? Yet she had turned that down out of a sense of misplaced loyalty to Santos. Would she act any differently now? *I doubt it,* I told myself.

An unpleasant feeling of being selfish niggled at me but I pushed the feeling down. Why hadn't her father taken her home? Maybe he didn't know. The thought occurred to me that perhaps Vanessa was also a user. After all, it must be difficult to keep away from the stuff when her boyfriend was a dealer. The more I thought about her grey pallor and smudged eyes the more convinced I became that she was and that the trembling hands, stilled by cigarettes, were not merely the result of being stuck at home bored all day.

The next morning, I looked up Mr Goodwell's number in the directory and dialled.

"Yup," said his voice after what seemed like an age.

"Hi. It's Sheri Lewis here – Vanessa's friend." I took the 'hrmph' on the other end of the line to indicate that he knew who I was. "I saw Vanessa yesterday and wondered if you had seen her lately? I was shocked to tell you the truth."

"Yeah, I've seen her."

"Don't you think she's in a state and needs help? I don't know what to do about it though. What do you think?"

When he responded, Mr Goodwell's frustration towards his wayward daughter was evident. "Look, she's got herself into that mess. She can get herself out of it. Anyhow, I tried but she's too caught up in that loser boyfriend of hers. You won't get anywhere." Clearly, any ideas I had of rescuing Vanessa were a waste of time as far as Mr Goodwell was concerned.

That should have been the end of it but I couldn't put her out of my mind. I worried at her situation like a terrier trying to dig a rat out of its hole. What was it about Santos that had such a hold on Vanessa? I had never believed that he loved her. She was useful to him that was all and he could use her because she allowed him too. I couldn't understand why she didn't say no. Maybe she was afraid of him. I was afraid of him. You never knew how far the fingers of his criminal life might extend; far better to have nothing to do with him. *Even if it meant cutting one of my oldest friends loose?* Maybe if she had a safe place to go where she could feel certain that he'd never find her she would feel confident enough to leave. Was there anywhere that safe? Somehow, I doubted it. Men like Santos knew everything. That was how they survived.

CHAPTER SEVEN

Crisp mornings preceded warm, balmy days during that all too brief interlude of spring perfection before giving way to the stultifying heat of summer and the attendant threat of tornados. Not that we were hit by many in Melvin. According to the meteorological reports, we were too far to the east and although tornados did sometimes touch down, they were much smaller than those experienced through the centre of the country in the aptly named Tornado Alley. The trees in the city were in full bloom and I had never seen such a profusion of blossoms ranging from deepest crimson through to the palest, translucent shades of white. Beryl said they were fruit trees. Apparently the hot, Melvin summers favoured the growing of stone fruit.

That week, Beryl presented me with the good news that she had approved my training as a mechanic at Melvin Tech'. I would study two days a week and work at the garage the other three and a half. She smiled maternally as I threw my arms around her neck. I knew I was lucky. "You won't regret it," I promised.

Looking forward to studying something again, I went straight down to the campus to pick up a book list and course outline. The course didn't commence until after the summer break but I wanted to get an early start on the reading. While chatting to the student advisor, I discovered that over the summer, the school also ran a night class welding course so I booked myself in for that too; figuring that if I could weld, I could also do light engineering jobs on farm equipment and machinery.

In my visions, the garage grew. I saw newly commissioned signs directing customers to the different departments for the different services offered: a tyre bay, engineering, diesel... but Beryl was cautious. "One step at a time," she said when I shared my ideas with her.

Lloyd and I were sitting in the midday sun eating our sandwiches when Eric called. It had been two weeks since our lunch in Melvin and I was beginning to think that he had changed his mind about me. "Long time, no hear," I said once he'd announced his name.

"Yeah... Sorry about that. I've been out of town. What are you up to on Friday night? Do you want to go to the speedway?"

I hesitated, thinking immediately of Jonah and how he would love to go to the speedway too but that would mean telling Eric that I had a son, something I'd not done yet. Besides which, taking Jonah with us would be so much easier than organising yet another babysitter and much less guilt inducing for me.

"Are you there?"

"Yes. Sorry." I stood up and moved away from Lloyd whose eyes followed me with curiosity as he winked and mouthed, "OOO, who's that?" I gave him the fingers.

"I'm just moving away from the guys I work with," I said into the receiver. "Hey, there's something I haven't told you about me yet." My heart fluttered nervously which was silly because what was the worst that could happen? "I have a son called Jonah. He's four years old." I could feel Eric's surprise bounce off the satellite and into my cell phone. "Um, I could try and get a babysitter but really, he'd love the speedway too." I could imagine the thoughts filling Eric's head: okay, not much chance for romantic overtures and definitely not much chance of sex.

"Sure, why not?" he conceded, after what seemed like a long pause.

He arranged to pick us up at six o'clock on Friday and we were ready and waiting for him when he rolled up in his beautiful, silver Audi. My eyes were drawn to the mag wheels which were of burnished stainless steel and unusually shaped, like a knights templar cross. The interior of the vehicle was pristine and I made a mental note to clean the Jimny before allowing Eric to even see it. I couldn't imagine his immaculately groomed self ever being in proximity to such lowly things as food stained, child seats. I affixed Jonah's booster cushion to the seatbelt and buckled him in.

"Wow. Look at you," whistled Eric as I slid into the front. I had forgotten that I'd had my hair cut since I'd seen him last but conscious that this was my first real date with a man in my life, I'd dressed with care in a new pair of skinny black jeans that showed off my slim legs to best advantage and a cream, cowl necked skivvy teamed with a tailored jacket. I had also taken the time to apply make-up, as taught, and all was complemented by the lovely accompanying feminine fragrances of perfume and hair products.

"You like?" I queried, shamelessly fishing for more praise.

"I like."

He expertly reversed the car out onto the road, looking immaculate himself in grey pants and an open necked, white shirt. A grey jersey was slung on the back seat.

"I thought we could get a burger there," he suggested, which sounded good to me. I felt ridiculously happy like youth firing on all four cylinders.

Never having been to a speedway, I was impressed by the size of the stadium. Even though racing wasn't due to start until 7pm the seats were already filling up, especially in the top tiers where I assumed the view to be better.

Eric stood in line for the food while I held firmly onto Jonah's hand, terrified that if I let him go he'd be swallowed up by the throng and I'd never see him again. But Jonah, probably terrified of getting lost himself, attached his arms to my legs, taking in the sight and sound of so many people, and the stockcars spinning practice laps in the arena, with wide eyes. When Eric returned, we walked around the edge of the stadium until we came to the corner stands.

"Up here," he directed. "Most of the action occurs on the corners." I climbed a couple of steps and then moved to take a position on the fourth row which was almost empty. "No, further up. We'll get hit by mud here," he said, thereby explaining why the top tiers were so full compared to the lower ones. We settled into seats in the tenth row. Below us, others, who obviously didn't know about the mud, were making themselves comfortable in the seats we had shunned and were engrossed in wrapping themselves in blankets and distributing cushions. "Watch and laugh," said Eric.

I wished I had thought of bringing some padding as the moulded seats were hard. As if reading my mind, he unpacked a couple of self inflating cushions from his backpack and handed one to me. I threw him a grateful smile. He distributed the burgers and drinks, a cola for Jonah and coffee for us, and I organised Jonah with his food before tucking into my own burger. It was hot, greasy, saucy, oniony and altogether delicious.

The sun, sinking behind the far reaches of the stadium, imbued the light with a golden hue and cast enormous, elongated shadows onto the turf area in the middle of the track. The scene appeared surreal; one of those moments of sheer wellbeing that imprints itself into the psyche and becomes a benchmark against which all other similar moments are measured. *This is happiness,* I thought. And the realisation was all the more precious because it had snuck up on me. Without my knowing, I'd been getting happy. My little house, a good job for a wonderful woman who believed in me, a new look, friends, a date; it was all perfect. A lone tear taking an advantage of the breach in my defences, sprang to my eye. I took a deep breath and hauled in my emotions. Eric would think I was a twit if he knew but as if sensing my mood, he turned to me and asked, "Are you okay?"

I nodded and smiled brightly. "Yes. Happy and having fun."

He patted my knee. "That's good."

Once the action began, conversation proved impossible as the noise of the stockcars revving their way around the track was outrageous. The saloon cars, V8's roaring, were especially thrilling and race followed race in quick succession.

With the stinging smell of fuel and cordite exhilarating my senses as well as my mind, I wondered what it took to own a car and race it. It would be good for business as I saw that each car had the logos of their sponsors painted on to the doors. The boys would love the idea I was sure.

I placed a one dollar bet with Eric. "Select a car," I instructed as the entrants ran their warm up laps. "If your car wins, you get the dollar, and if mine does, I get it." Somehow that seemed to jinx the cars as one after another our selections ended up broken down in the middle of the field.

Eric's mud predictions proved correct. As the cars drifted through the bends, showers of mud and dust were flung out from twenty sets of wide tyres, pinging the heads and shoulders of the spectators in the front rows who tried valiantly to protect themselves behind their coats and rugs. A chunk of solid mud even slammed into the space between our seats. It sounded like a gunshot and I was relieved that it hadn't hit Jonah on the head.

As the evening grew chilly, we huddled together under a blanket for warmth. I snuggled into Eric and plied Jonah with food and drinks to keep him occupied until tiredness overcame his will and he fell asleep with his head on my lap.

By the time all the events had concluded, it was late and the creeping line of headlights that snaked out of the gates and into the night was slow to disperse from the stadium. It was past eleven when Eric pulled into my driveway and turned off the key.

"Thank you so much," I said. "I had a great time and Jonah too. Thanks for letting him come with us."

His face glowed dimly in the reflected light from the headlights. "No worries. I had fun as well."

We leaned into each other and brushed lips against cheeks. "I'll call you," he said.

I lugged my sleeping son out of the car and as I fumbled for my keys, Eric reversed out of the drive and left.

The next morning, I couldn't wait to get to the garage so as to broach my ideas about racing a super saloon car with Beryl. I found her in the office and quickly pitched my idea. She loved it and called the boys. Karl was highly enthusiastic.

"I could drive it," he informed the rest of us. Typically, he had a cousin who raced a V8 drag car and knew how the systems worked. Before thirty minutes had passed, Karl had allotted himself the tasks of finding the car, driving the car and being head mechanic, along with Lloyd of course, and I was effectively cut clean out of my own idea. But as much as it stung, I had to acknowledge that in reality, I had little to offer the project. I couldn't drive well enough to compete. I wasn't even qualified and would a woman in the racing world ever be taken seriously anyway? The best I could do for now was to watch and learn and see how the project developed.

Because Beryl was the one who would be footing the expense, all work and purchases had to be approved by her. And as much as Karl would have liked to make the decision about which car to buy it wasn't up to him so I had some chance of finding the right vehicle. Not that I knew that much about high performance cars, which makes and models, how they were modified, it was all new to me. Byron would know though. He'd always been nuts about cars and I hadn't seen him for ages, nor Ma and Pa for that matter. It was time to pay them a visit.

I toyed with the idea of phoning Mark, to let him know that Jonah and I would soon be in Flagstaff for a day or two, but decided against it. He had not been in contact with me at all since I'd left and as expected, the promised child support had not eventuated. Even if he didn't have my number he could easily have found out what it was by asking Ma. So much for wanting to be a father to Jonah, I thought with derision.

The following Friday evening, after work, I packed the Jimny and drove the forty five minutes back to Flagstaff. This time when I drove into town, it did not affect me at all. I saw the square fronted shops and the wide, quiet streets and felt removed. It could have been any town in any county. I arrived home in the dark. Ma was there, framed by the light that glowed from the lounge, small and neat as usual. "You've cut your hair," she exclaimed when she saw me; and Pa also, as large and comforting as ever. Another homecoming, different again. I was no longer confused or anxious. I had a direction and that knowledge gave me confidence.

Jonah, older, full of words, chattered away to Ma who crouched down to ask him, "What have you been doing young man?"

And Jonah, syntax perfect, replying, "I go to preschool now and I can write my name."

"Wow! What a clever boy. And what is your name?"

Jonah giggled, uncertain, "It's Jonah."

"Jonah! What a fabulous name. And what's my name?"

"Grandma," he reassured her.

Ma gave him a big hug. "Of course it's Grandma. Do you want a drink?"

"Cola. Jonah wants cola." He jumped up and down on the spot unable to contain his glee at the unexpected relaxation of rules that allowed him to have cola on a Friday evening. At home, I'd discovered that the best way to deal with Jonah's many wants was to have strict routines; one bottle of soda which Jonah was allowed to have over the weekend and takeaways only on Tuesdays. So far, he had accepted the rules.

Ma had food ready; Cajun chicken served with new baked potatoes and jam sweetened vegetables. I vowed to ask for some of her recipes as the necessity of getting something into the stomach in short order tended to make me a boring and repetitive cook. Like ghosts, Byron and Louisa materialised once the food appeared on the table. They were living in Jet's old room but work had begun on a new home for them nearby. I looked forward to seeing it.

"How are Jet and Becky?" I asked once we were all gathered around the table.

Ma answered as she passed the potatoes. "They're good. Jet has a lot of work on. He's rarely home. Farmers call him up all hours of the day and night. I don't think Becky likes it."

"I told him to take the phone off the hook," Pa growled. "He shouldn't be at folk's beck and call all the time."

"Yes, but you know, if an animal needs a vet it needs a vet. It doesn't matter what time it is," countered Byron.

"How is Becky?" I asked Ma.

"She's good. Hoping to fall pregnant, I believe, although it would be nice if they were married first. Not that anyone seems to worry about such things these days."

"And the store... and Harriet?"

"The same. Yes, all that goes on as usual. You know that Becky is running the office I think?"

Not much had changed then. I told the family about my job at the garage and my plan to train as a mechanic.

In a curious role reversal, Pa, encouraging now in a way that he had never been when I was younger, said, "Good on you girl. You'll succeed at anything."

While Ma, expressing disapproval at the idea of her daughter in such a male dominated and unladylike career, could only comment, "Playing around with machinery, that's a dirty job. What do you want to do such a dirty job for?"

Not really having an answer for that, I didn't reply. It wasn't as if I had exactly chosen the career. I'd fallen into it more than anything so I addressed Byron instead. "We're looking to buy a V8 super saloon or at least a car suitable for modification."

"They're usually purpose built," he clarified. "Why do you want one?"

I explained how I'd been to the speedway and thought owning a racing car would be good for advertising Beryl's business. "We have two guys, mechanics, plus Beryl who is a mechanic herself and then me - although I'm a trainee, so we've got loads of people to work on the car in down time, and Karl, one of the guys can drive it... or anyhow, he has a cousin who is involved in V8 drags and knows all about it... It's true!" I exclaimed, noticing the looks of disbelief being unsuccessfully concealed by my family. "You just wait and see. I start my course in July at Tech' and meanwhile I'm going to learn welding at night class over the summer." Even to my ears my protestations sounded as if I was trying to convince myself as much as them. But hadn't that always been the case?

The next morning I sought out Louisa and asked her to show me their building site. She was such a quiet woman that taking to her was hard work but her pride in their prospective new home was evident.

The site was about a quarter mile from the main house and hidden from view by a grove of pine trees on the other side of the sheds. The concrete pad was down, as was the timber framing that defined the rooms. "The roof goes on next week," said Louisa as we stepped over the front door stoop. She named each room as well as the names of the fittings that were due to be installed within. It all went over my head. I had never heard of 'Miele' appliances or 'Jado' taps but one thing was clear, the house would be designer everything. This was one woman who knew her Dacor from her General Electric.

I wondered who was paying; probably Pa seeing as the house was on his ranch but building a house for Byron intimated that Byron would inherit the farm when Pa passed on. I supposed that was hardly surprising considering that Byron was the eldest son and he had been working with Pa for years already. But where did Jet and I fit into that plan? The ranch must be worth millions. It would hardly be fair if Byron inherited outright. *No wonder Louisa was with Byron*, I thought uncharitably. She was onto a good thing.

As much as I yearned to be involved, Karl and Lloyd effectively contrived to shut me out of the racing car project. The newly purchased car, a stock standard '82 Chevy Monte Carlo, stood in the yard with the hood open while Karl and Lloyd leaned over the engine. I joined them, along the side of the car where the angle of the hood forced my body into a 45 degree slant. Karl was asking: "Where are we going to get a rolling chassis fitted?"

I knew the answer to that having passed such a business on a daily basis during my sojourn in Dodge, and so suggested coolly, "Cavandash's Motorsport in Dodge City." Without changing the direction of his eyes, Karl continued speaking directly to Lloyd. "Do you wanna come down on the weekend? We could also go and get some prices on tubing for a roll cage. Forty meters I reckon should do it."

Feeling completely ignored, I hovered, hoping that they would invite, and therefore include, me but the fact that they refused to even glance my way told otherwise. Let down, I wandered into the ante room and pulled on my overalls. Changing tyres it was then.

My first day of course that afternoon proved to be no better and did nothing to dispel my depressed mood. I felt like a tyre with a slow leak. uninspiring cream walls adorned with a few disconsolate posters tacked carelessly askew advertised the virtues of life as an apprentice mechanic but the fresh skinned teen whose pale face beamed out from the posters revealed him to be the model he was and bore no resemblance to the scraggy and spotty visages of most young men I knew.

The chairs, arranged in rows along the tables, rapidly filled up with male students who chatted amongst themselves and rocked back untidily on chair legs which didn't look up to the task of remaining upright, while I, the only female in the room, sat and waited patiently.

Twenty minutes late, the lecturer, wearing blue jeans and a green T shirt, finally turned up and took his place at the front. He had a generic look to him and could have been anybody's uncle. I estimated him to be at least forty five due to his broad face and expanding middle. His ruddy cheeks, no doubt the result of too many steaks and beers, were framed by a closely trimmed moustache in such a way that the greying line formed a box around his mouth giving him an incongruous Latino appearance.

His broad American voice twanged out. "Right we will begin. My name is Ross Verrant and today we will be talking about the internal combustion engine first developed by Karl Benz in 1886 and massed produced by Henry Ford in 1908..."

He continued on without pausing. Half of the class bent to their books but a significant number of lads continued their talk and laughter for the remainder of the lesson. It was worse than at school and it took all my self control to prevent myself from hissing my disapproval out loud; although I did cast some angry glares in their direction. To my amazement, the lecturer exhibited no desire to control the class and didn't seem to care whether his students passed or failed. He merely delivered the theory and let the students make of it what they could.

After three weeks of lessons, I'd had enough. It seemed that a certain level of understanding about engines and how they worked was required that I didn't possess. After putting up my hand to ask what the boys clearly thought was a stupid question, and trust a girl to ask it, (judging by the sniggers that twittered around the room) I felt reluctant to ask again so the pace of the lessons continued to move too fast for me.

I needed the teacher to slow down and explain the definitions of unfamiliar aspects and terminology as without such knowledge I was all at sea. As a consequence, I found the class boring and one day, after yawning my way through yet another three hours of my life, I realised that not only did I not understand, I did not care to understand.

Later that night, at the kitchen table, I went over my options. I needed another job. That much was clear. But finding work isn't easy and finding a job secretly is even harder still. I did not want Beryl to know I was job hunting but the stumbling point was that I couldn't exactly cite Beryl as a referee if she didn't know I was planning on leaving.

Call it woman's intuition. She somehow worked it out because she called me into the office one Friday afternoon and demanded to know what was going on. I felt my face flush with heat. *Had someone said something to her, a potential employer contacted her?*

"Well something's up," she said when I stood there, mute. "You spend all day just doing the basics. You haven't taken on a new task for the last three weeks. I thought it might be a family issue. Give her a break Beryl, I said to myself, she's probably got a family problem to take care of, but now I'm beginning to wonder. So what's going on, Sheri?"

While she talked, my mind rifled through all the appropriate responses I could come up with before settling on the truth. "I find it hard with the boys," I complained. "They cut me out all the time. It's the same at course. They think I'm stupid because I'm female and I've had enough of it frankly."

Beryl gave a sharp laugh then leaned towards me, forearms resting on the desk in front of her. "Now girl, why are you caring about what those mutton heads think? You know you're more than up to the job."

It was the perfect opening. I had given her a reason; now all I had to do was deliver my decision but until that moment, I hadn't even known I wanted to leave. "I don't know – maybe," my voice said. "But I've decided to look for another job anyway. I'm sorry. I don't think this is the career for me though I am really happy that you gave me the opportunity to work here."

Beryl's face creased into a wry frown. "If you have to go, you have to go but I won't say I'm not disappointed," she said as she stood and moved around the table to give me a friendly hug. "If you need a reference, just get them to call me," she added.

It seems to be a law of the universe that once a path is chosen and the first concrete steps towards a goal are taken, that things fall into place. True as can be, that very week I received a call from Melvin Western, a real estate agent's office on Highgrove Street, to invite me for an interview. The meeting could not have gone better and by Wednesday I got the blessed call to advise me that I had a new job.

At the initial briefing, I was told that once a three month trial period was successfully completed, I would be sent to the Academy for training. But to begin with, I was buddied with a senior sales agent so that I could begin to learn the basics of how to take listings and evaluate the selling price of properties.

After being constantly hot and grimy, it was a distinct pleasure to have a reason to dress with style and do my hair and make-up each morning and the fact that we were out and about each day, inspecting and listing properties, was also a pleasure. I was partnered with Vivienne, a stunning, curvaceous blonde woman whom I gathered to be in her early thirties. She had been selling real estate for over ten years and was the top income earner in the team. To me it was obvious why as she had a friendly, easy manner which disarmed and charmed every potential vendor.

On our travels around the city, Vivienne told me her story. She had been born in Las Vegas, the daughter of a professional dancer mother and a musician father but despite the glamour, life was hard and a constant hustle for gigs that paid for longer than a couple of weeks. The family shifted regularly and it was not until she was eight years old that social services finally caught up with her rampant truancy and placed her in foster care where she thrived on the stability. After attending college, she landed her job at Melvin Western and there she had stayed. Strangely, she remained unmarried and still lived at home; a fact I found vaguely disturbing.

The sales offices weren't large but they were modern and airy. Each member of the team had their own room but I, being junior, was merely allocated a desk with a computer near to the front reception area where the receptionist, a prickly young woman called Savannah, spent her days. Every morning, a briefing was held where the agents shared information regarding new listings and clients. The properties Vivienne mostly dealt with were upmarket and some were worth millions of dollars. The competition to be the one to successfully sell them was cut throat.

On my first day in the field, we drove in her Ford up into the winding hills that surrounded Melvin to photograph a glorious, hacienda style mansion that had been listed the week previously. Emerging from the car, I saw the city spread before me and could well imagine how beautiful the scene would look at night with the lights from the city punctuating the darkness.

The owner was out but Vivienne had a key. "Sometimes professional photographers are hired to take the photos for these high end homes," she informed me as we stepped into the cool, marbled entry. "But in this case the owner felt disinclined to pay the extra."

I set up the tripod and camera in the living area while Vivienne moved professionally about, adjusting cushions, straightening curtains and moving objects so as to present the room in a stylish and uncluttered state. While I did not consider myself any kind of expert, I had always held an interest in photography and had taken it as a subject at school. I particularly enjoyed the thrill of being in the dark room and seeing the images emerge from their chemical bath for the first time.

Because I was adventurous with my shots, artistic even, the results were sometimes hit and miss but the pure excitement of a shot that worked perfectly made the defeats worthwhile. And that was the core premise of photography wasn't it? The seeking of the perfect shot; not always obtained the first time, sometimes requiring hours of waiting for the right light conditions to reveal the contrasts and inherent qualities of the scene before the lens, and fraught with disappointments - but the joy when a shot turned out perfectly!

With all that I had learned about photography rapidly returning to memory, I adjusted the focus and checked the view for composition while analysing the scene for the aesthetic components (which necessitated shifting a vase of gloriously scented lilies along the bench a little), then took the shot.

Outside, the photographs required the best angle to be selected as the house was so expansive it was difficult to fit everything into the frame in a meaningful way. I wanted to highlight the magnificent views and managed to get a great photo from the curving decks that led off the living area. A set of glass doors opened up the entire wall so by pulling over the barbecue and positioning it closer to the outdoor table setting, I managed to emphasise the area's desirability as an outdoor entertainment area.

Back at the office, I inserted the camera's SD card into the computer and uploaded the images to Photoshop where I cropped and enhanced until I was pleased with the results. Within a week, I was given the task of taking all the advertising photographs for all of the agency's listings.

Having finally organised my working situation satisfactorily, you would have thought that life would be sorted but I found that keeping all areas of life in harmony to be an impossible task. Like a juggler trying to keep the balls of home, work, money, relationship, Jonah, family, friends and myself in the air; at any one time, one or more of the balls could be counted on to be lying on the ground in desperate need of remedial attention.

****

After six months of friendly dating, Eric, it seemed, had moved in. We hadn't discussed it. He merely stayed over more and more frequently until one morning, as I swished his shavings out of the bathroom sink, it dawned on me that we were living together. *Did I mind?* He paid his way in that it was usually him that paid for the food and often he who cooked it; and if he was home before me, he picked up Jonah. He didn't shout. We never argued. Sex was satisfactory, if infrequent. We were from the start like an old married couple, flatmates, brother and sister even. I didn't think I loved him though. *Was being friends a good enough reason to live together?* He was a good man. It didn't seem right to kick him out because I wasn't in love with him, because of a lack of passion. I didn't want to hurt him.

Meanwhile, Jonah had started school at Melvin Elementary and had initially settled in well. But of late, the accusatory phone calls from school that had once occurred intermittently, easily explained away as a bad day, were becoming a weekly event. Jonah had stolen another kid's lunch money. Jonah had not completed his homework. Jonah had scribbled all over the desks with a vivid...

"And where did he get the vivid from?"

He stole it from the teacher's desk.

If there was something naughty to be done, Jonah had a sixth sense for it. He wasn't always bad. He could be sweetly helpful, funny and clever. It was easy to blame the school and the teacher for not keeping the vivids locked away, for not dealing with the issue adequately at the time, for not ensuring Jonah did his homework. He always told me he had none and I accepted his story because after a day at work, I didn't feel like doing homework with him. Not all students are as academic as I was, I told myself. And anyway, didn't boys prefer physical activities to reading and writing?

He went home with Maisie and her children after school and from there, either I or Eric collected him sometime after 4 o'clock. This was a pleasant interlude in the working day for me as Maisie usually put the kettle on and we would then lean comfortably at her beautiful, solid oak, kitchen table and chat about our respective days over cups of steaming coffee.

When I told her that Eric had all but moved in she looked pleased. "He's a great guy," she commented. She held a nail up for close inspection and finding a flaw, nibbled at it with her neat teeth. I wondered, and not for the first time, why Eric was not with Maisie. They seemed much more suited to each other than Eric and I. Both were...image conscious. Both of them cared about how they looked, worked and lived to a degree that was not a natural part of my makeup.

Jonah was rarely sick, so when he came down with tonsillitis I didn't feel too guilty about staying at home with him. After a visit to the doctors, I tucked him up on the couch with his Playstation. Outside, the day was cool and overcast. I made some toast and brought it to my son who took one bite before flinging it across the room where it landed butter side down on the rug.

"Jonah! – don't do that," I exclaimed, as any mother would.

"My throat hurts," he wailed.

I retrieved the toast and rubbed at the oily mark with a kitchen sponge.

"I want noodles. Get me noodles...."

Excusing his behaviour on account of his being unwell, I returned to the kitchen to boil the jug. Then, taking the antibiotic syrup the doctor had prescribed, poured a dose into the measuring cup supplied.

"Here's your medicine. It will make you feel better," I said as I held the cup out to the boy who promptly knocked it out of my hand and onto the carpet where the syrup joined the toast mark and made a sticky burgundy splatter.

My son's red and contorted face screamed at me. "NOODLES. I want NOODLES."

Irritated, I slapped his arm then fetched a paper towel to place over the mess.

"Naughty boy," I scolded. "You need your medicine." I poured a fresh dose then sat him on my knee, noticing he was a lot bigger and stronger than he had once been. Holding his arms firmly, I held the cup to his lips but he struggled so hard, arching his back and turning his compressed and reddened face aside, that dose went flying too.

His displeasure erupted into a full blown tantrum and his violence found targets. A well aimed kick sent the footstool skidding across the room where it collided against the television and with a flailing arm, he swept a vase laden with flowers off the side table to join the other detritus on the floor.

Horrified, I grabbed the screaming banshee that was my son, dragged him to his room and flung him onto the bed. "You can stay in there until you calm down," I yelled over his wailing. But barely had the door closed than he yanked it open.

"Get back in there you horrible rat bag," I shouted.

We tussled for possession of the door handle until I was finally able to prise his fingers from their grip, push him in, slam the door shut and hold onto the knob firmly.

"I *hate* you! I *hate* you!" Jonah yelled as he vainly tried to tug open the door until, realising he was defeated, he began drumming at the door instead with his feet.

Concerned that he might kick a hole in the veneer, I shouted back, "STOP THAT you naughty boy," and stood for some time holding onto the knob until eventually the noise subsided and the house fell silent. I waited for a while then opened the door and peeked in. He was asleep, rosy cheeked and damp haired, on his bed.

It would have been okay if this had been a one-off incident. I could have overlooked it; explained it as an outburst generated by overtiredness and illness but I had to acknowledge that his aggression was a part of a developing pattern of rebellious and defiant behaviour that had been slowly growing in magnitude since he was a toddler.

Not long after he got over his bout of tonsillitis, I was called in to the school by the Principal for a meeting, a restorative justice conference they called it, because Jonah had hit another kid in his class with a baseball bat and broken his arm.

There are some situations in life that are truly humiliating and have the power to make you cringe for years afterwards, and this was one of them. The skinniest and palest boy I had ever seen sat between his parents. His Biafran arm was weighed down by a thick white plaster cast from which frail fingers emerged like twigs. Black rimmed glasses dwarfed his elfin face.

In stark contrast was his mother, a sturdy woman with short, russet blonde, coiffured hair. Disc shaped earrings with white enamelled centres grabbed at her ear lobes. On the other side sat Mr Adams, a thin man with a hound like appearance.

Mrs Adams did all the talking and began by outlining Jonah's misdemeanour and describing how 'hurt and angry' they had felt about their boy being so badly injured by a child who was obviously 'somewhat of a problem already.'

The Principal explained that the event had happened during sports. Jonah was batting during a game of baseball and Caleb was backstop when Jonah had hit Caleb on the arm for 'no apparent reason.' At this point, Jonah who had so far sat silently through the proceedings suddenly leaned forward and announced defiantly, "He wouldn't throw the ball back."

I glared at him. "You don't hit somebody just because you don't like what they do."

"Why not? You do," he retorted, clearly referring to the incident of the previous week.

I felt like I had been physically punched. Was I the worst mother in the world? The Principal looked at me and I could tell he was about to speak.

"Not with a bat," I hissed. "I don't injure you."

He interjected. "Do you make a habit of physically punishing your son, Ms Lewis?"

"Only a slap now and then when he deserves it. I don't beat him."

"Children learn how to behave from their parents. While slapping children to punish them is not illegal, it is not recommended in current literature." His voice dripped with accusation.

A deep frown creased his brow and Mr and Mrs Adams looked at me as if confronted for the first time with a real, live gargoyle. I could feel my face blushing bright red in mortification.

"I'm busy. I have to work," I explained, lamely.

Jonah was ordered to write a letter of apology to the Adams' and was stood down from school but all I could think was: what am I going to do with him for three days? Justice deemed to have been served; the Adams' were shown to the door while Jonah and I were indicated to remain. My fingers picked nervously at the seam of my trousers.

"I would like to recommend a child psychologist for you to see," said the Principal as he returned to the vast expanse of his desk. "I think you and Jonah would benefit from working through some of these issues." He wrote a name and phone number on a piece of paper and handed it to me. I tucked the paper into my bag without looking at it. "Jonah is still young and I think it is possible to effect a change in this negative cycle of interactions that you have fallen into. If we don't act now to change these destructive patterns, the consequences could turn out to be dire in regard to antisocial behaviour in the future."

I was intimidated and shocked into silence. Was he saying that Jonah's poor behaviour was my fault?

"He doesn't have much contact with his father..."

"While that is unfortunate - a boy needs positive male role models in his life, there are many one parent families in today's world and aggressive behaviour is not always a natural consequence; a fact which should give us hope, Ms Lewis."

I left the school, cheeks flushed with shame. "I have to work. Why can't you just behave yourself?" I snarled at Jonah as I hurried him to the car.

It wasn't my fault, I told myself as I drove home. I was doing my best. Pa had whacked me from time to time as a kid and I had turned out alright hadn't I? I thought about a time when I was ten and had gone across the road after school to the store with my friends instead of going straight home as was the rule.

"Catch the later bus," they had cried. So I had stayed with them and we had gone as a group to loiter outside the shop. The target was some homemade toffees that the shop keeper sold. They were wrapped in waxed cup cake papers and every so often one of the toffees held a nickel captive within the sweet.

Two of the boys, Jude and Rory, entered first and engaged the shop keeper in a lengthy discussion about which sweets they wanted from the selection available while we girls slipped in quietly and hovered nearby. Then, Tiffany feigned interest in what was going on with the boys as I surreptitiously stole handfuls of the toffees and slid them into the pockets of my over apron. The deed done, we coolly retreated to the park where we divided out the contraband loot between us.

With cheeks stuffed full of toffee, I caught the late bus home, carefree in the belief that we had gotten away with it. But one look at my father's face and demeanour told me that he knew. I had no idea how. We had believed ourselves to be cleverly covert. It was only in hindsight that I realised that we lived in a very small town. Within an hour of us leaving the shop, Mr Bennett had phoned all of our parents and reported us. Pa gave me a minute to confess before he slapped the backs of my legs so hard the welts stayed there for the rest of the afternoon. But what Ma did was far worse. She marched me into the shop after school the very next day and made me apologise in person to Mr Bennett. With my face burning, I had stammered through my punishment. To make matters worse, I was made to work in the shop for a whole Saturday to pay for the stolen goods. Thinking about that now, I wondered if whether it wasn't so much the smack that had punished me but rather facing Mr Bennett.

The smack was expected, but knowing that Mr Bennett knew my father well enough to phone him, and that he thereafter knew my father's daughter to be a thief, had hurt. ·

That evening, I recounted to Eric what had happened but he didn't seem concerned. "It's just a phase that Jonah's going through," he said. "Don't worry about it." I wanted to believe he was right so I willingly put the whole issue in the 'too hard' basket and forgot about it.

CHAPTER EIGHT

We stumbled along to the end of the year with things continuing as they were. Fall transmogrified into winter but the rain came rather than the snow. The roads, houses, trees and the end of my nose all dripped water. I kept the fire burning.

One morning, Eric, sick of being constantly cooped up indoors, moved in close, stretched his arms around me and murmured into my ear. "How about you and I go on a holiday, somewhere sunny, like Hawaii?" It was a great idea, especially considering that I had not stopped working since Jonah was born. "Why don't you see if Jonah's father can have him for two weeks, or your parents? That way it will be a holiday for him too and we can have some time to ourselves."

He kissed me languidly and we stood arms entwined for a few moments until I broke away to phone Mark who answered after a couple of rings. He sounded well and friendly as he said, "Hi. How are you? How is Jonah?"

"That's what I'm phoning about. He's good, but we've had a few ups and downs over the last year. He can throw some massive tantrums if he doesn't get his own way and he hit a kid at school and broke his arm."

"Why didn't you tell me?" he demanded.

There were many reasons. Mark was barely involved in Jonah's life and there was nothing he could practically do anyway. And if I was totally honest, I might have said that I didn't want to give him any reason to accuse me of being a bad parent. But I didn't say any of those things. I only said, "Sorry. I think it's just a stage he's going through. You know how it is. Life goes on. We got over it. Hey - I was hoping that Jonah could come and stay with you for a couple of weeks. It's the holidays soon." I could feel Mark's resistance over the line so I pressed the point before he had a chance to protest. "Please man. The kid should spend some time with his father and I still have to work. It's hard enough when he's at school."

I lied. We were going on a holiday but it wasn't as if I was given to lying. The fact is that some people can't be told the truth.

Mark agreed that Jonah could stay with them so when the day arrived, I drove to Flagstaff and took the opportunity to call in at the store. I hadn't seen Harriet, Jet or Becky for months. The big surprise was that Becky was heavily pregnant. I vaguely recalled Ma telling me Becky was expecting some time ago. How I could have forgotten such a momentous thing? "A Christmas baby like Jonah," I squealed as we embraced.

She looked radiant; Jet too. The outdoor work suited him. He had broadened out and buffed up. Harriet, the same as ever, was planning a trip to visit Aunty Julie in the New Year. With Becky there to help in the store it made time away easier. Naturally, I was quizzed over what was going on in my life so I filled them in on the good parts and glossed over the rest.

Leaving Jonah who hovered behind me, suddenly shy, with Harriet, Becky showed me the nursery, my old room, once Ma's, now ready to make way for a new generation. She had decorated it beautifully in white with lemon accents.

A stunning wooden hand crafted cot stood near the window. It had little padded cushions around the sides that were tied with cream ribbons into delicate bows. My eyes took in the comfy chair with tri pillow at the ready, thermostat heater and throw rugs, stacks of diapers - unopened yet - on the change table and my heart constricted. From the care she had taken, it was evident that Becky was excited about the prospect of being a mother; that she yearned to meet her unborn child and delighted in the preparations for her infant's arrival; an experience vastly different from my own.

In a flash of clarity, I understood the devastating impact the circumstances of Jonah's birth had had on me and how I felt about my son. Becky was in love with her baby already which was in stark contrast to the dread that had culminated in Jonah's birth. I tried to say, "It's beautiful Becky," but instead, burst into violent tears. Becky was immediately all concern. "What's the matter, Sheri?" she prompted as she placed a kindly arm about my shoulders and pushed me into the chair.

"I'm so jealous, and sad," I wailed. "It's all beautiful and you want your baby so badly, and you and Jet love each other. It wasn't like that for me and everything is still hard. And watching you – I've only just realised how badly the circumstances of his birth has affected how I relate to Jonah. I love him but I don't love him the way you love your baby already." *And I don't really love Eric either,* my heart added. Even though we were living together, I didn't love Eric the way Becky loved Jet.

Becky made consoling noises. "Shhh. Of course you love Jonah. You probably just need a rest. A holiday would do you good. You work very hard. You need to take a break, relax and enjoy life."

"We *are* going on a holiday. Jonah's staying with Mark. But I haven't told either of them we're going so you mustn't tell Jonah. He'd never forgive me. He's angry with me enough. I don't want to make it worse."

"There you see? Believe me; a holiday will make all the difference. But I wish we had known you were struggling. We could have helped more. You always seem to have everything covered."

Becky was right. Not wanting to be a burden to the family, I tried to be independent. That was part of it. I also wanted to prove I could manage my own life, prove I wasn't a failure. And on the surface, it looked like I had everything sorted. I had a good job which I loved, I had a good man in Eric and Jonah was, to all appearances, growing up satisfactorily but at the core of me I knew that my relationships with Eric and Jonah were all wrong. I had never experienced adult love and therefore had never experienced feeling loved either. Recalling the feeling of pure love that had washed over me when Jonah was born, I wondered where that had gone. *Trampled under the unrelenting realities of bringing a child up alone, that's where.* Becky handed me a tissue and I blew my nose.

"Thanks. Sorry. I'm okay now. I will be okay; just feeling sorry for myself I think. You are right. I need a holiday. It will make all the difference." I felt exhausted and drained as if every drop of fluid had been sucked out of my cells.

Harriet, sensing a crisis, insisted I leave Jonah with her, happily unpacking boxes much as I had done at his age. Echoes of those fondly remembered times reverberated around images of long, hot, dusty days, stacking the new stock carefully on the shelves, and later, learning how to check the goods against the invoice and writing the retail prices on the labels. I'd felt so grown up and important.

Life had become so complicated and these wide open plains that seemed attached to my heart, dredged up well controlled emotions. I thought about Luke and wished he was here. He would have known exactly the right things to say to restore my unbalanced equilibrium.

The weather closed in as I drove to Ma's, and the rain battered landscape visible through my windshield, reflected my mood precisely. My throat and chest hurt with what felt like pent up grief. Was it grief? Was I grieving after all these years? Grieving for the carefree girl I once was with my future uncluttered and straight before me, grieving for the poor start my son and I had endured that could never be rewritten, and grieving for the love within which a child is meant to be brought into the world?

By the time I arrived at the ranch, my emotions were largely under control. It was amazing how much of an expert I had become at putting on a brave face. "I've got a terrible headache," I offered by way of explanation for my reddened eyes, remembering that other time long ago that I had used that very same excuse. If Ma made the connection she gave no sign. And here I was still bawling about it almost a decade later. It was so good to see Ma and Pa; to sit on the veranda with a comforting hot drink and to talk about the farm and about Jonah.

"He's a real handful for me and I don't know how to deal with him," I said. "I don't think I ever have. He gets angry with me and then I get even angrier with him. Sure, I provide for him but we don't do anything fun together. I wouldn't know where to begin. All he likes to do is play on the computer or Playstation and I'm so busy..."

They listened while I got it all off my chest then Pa said, "Maybe it's time to consider lettin' Jonah go and live with his father for a while to give yourself a break. You've carried the burden for a long time, Sheri. You're only human and can only do so much. I think you need some time to be carefree and to have some fun without the responsibility of a child to worry about."

I know at first I had been so angry with Mark that I would rather have walked to New York than let him have Jonah but now that he had grown so much, almost eight years old... It would be such a relief to lay down the tools for a while, to be able to look after myself and sort out how I wanted to handle my relationship with Eric. I wanted to live but what I was doing wasn't living. It was pure grind. Jonah with his father was definitely something to think about.

When I picked my son up from the store in the morning, it was snowing soft white flakes that drifted gently through the air to settle on cheeks and shoulders. I drove to Mark's in a flurry of anxiety. I hadn't seen him since moving to Melvin and I wasn't sure how Jonah would respond to being left with his father after being so long apart so when Mark opened the door to my knock looking relaxed and happy, I was pleasantly surprised. Sophie invited me in for coffee but I made my excuses, citing work in the morning, while Jonah hefted his bag down to his room.

"We're going to have a great time, eh buddy?"

"Yeah man. Too right," came the boy's disembodied voice from down the hall.

I handed Mark a box containing Jonah's Playstation and a twenty dollar note for him to spend. After saying goodbye, I climbed back in the Jimny and drove home.

****

'Paradise.' That was the only word to describe the Hawaiian Island of Oahu - 'Paradise.' The palm trees lining the boulevard, the turquoise blue arc of sky stretching into an azure infinity and the roaring ocean; it was all postcard perfect. Dimly remembered snapshot memories of shell collecting and sand in the crotch of my bathing suit, surfaced.

The towering waves had to be seen to be believed as the thunderous, pounding walls of water collapsed almost lazily into churning mounds of foam that shook the beach and could be heard from our room in the hotel.

"Oh my god, it's amazing," I exclaimed on first sight; my eyes taking in the expansive, super king bed, *room to move – bliss,* flat screen T.V *with cable* and views of the coast that could be seen in their entirety from the floor to ceiling windows. "This must be costing a fortune," I said to Eric.

He took me in his arms. "Don't worry about that," he replied. "It's on me. You're worth it."

One thing led to another as they say, and after an hour or so, having tested the bed, we made our way down to the lobby where Eric insisted I select a new swim suit from the resort store.

The shop, obviously geared towards ill equipped tourists, stocked bikinis in every size and style imaginable. After trying on several pairs, I finally settled on a padded suit in a hot pink Hawaiian themed fabric.

Initially, I felt shy exposing so much flesh in public but once on the beach I felt overdressed, being as it was, full of the most stunning women; long legged, tanned creatures in the skimpiest costumes, some topless - and wearing nothing more than a tiny thong – who paraded up and down or reclined in the sun on vibrantly patterned beach towels.

We found a spot and sat there with the other observers of the action on the waves; watching the young, and not so young perform death defying feats on their boards. As they paddled out, they valiantly climbed the swells that towered above them and I found myself holding my breath, convinced that they would lose the contest between man and nature and be hurled back onto the beach, only to see them pop over the forming crests of the waves at the very last minute.

Once out there, bobbing lazily over the sweeping swells that rolled in from the Pacific, they waited patiently for the perfect wave to form; instinct directing them as to the right time to paddle furiously in order to catch the wave that surged away from them. And having committed themselves, there was no turning back. They had to ride the wave or be crushed beneath it. So they rode, down the twenty to thirty foot wall of sheer power, board slicing oh so cleanly into the teal, their agile bodies bending this way and that as they directed the board through the tube of water, as smoothly shaped as a plastic pipe, which formed behind them as the crest of the wave curled over.

And the shock when a rider fell off; the anxiety that churned in the belly until the board popped back out of the foaming froth like a cork, the surfer nearby, still attached to his board by the strap.

We ate the most delicious food out on the hotel balcony in the warm evenings where the romantic glow of gardenia scented candles complemented the deep shades of magenta and pure orange created by the setting sun. The evening buffet was a smorgasbord of delicacies featuring barbequed lobster tails nestled in perfumed dressings and juicy, fat steaks sautéed in hand prepared sauces that competed for selection with colourful, tropical salads and creamy desserts.

I could feel the tension of the years slipping away as we slept, swam and ate our way through the long, warm days. We drove to the other side of the island and visited Pearl Harbour, now a memorial museum. There was a guided tour so we climbed into an inflatable dinghy that took us out to a platform built over the where the Arizona sank. We could see her dimly beneath us; a sleeping ghost ship.

The guide told us that over 1000 men were still entombed therein. "Horrible to think of all those sons, brothers, husbands and lovers, cold, dead and waterlogged forever," I commented to Eric; imagining my own son down there. I wept a tear for the heart-breaking loss experienced by all those mothers that I would never meet or know. They would have mostly passed over themselves by now. It happened sixty years ago, after all. I thought of the mothers and fathers reunited with their long dead sons and daughters. *That is if there is a heaven.* But if no heaven, no life after this one, what did life mean? What was the purpose of it? The futility of it all seemed sad and depressing.

The next day we cruised to Hawaii Island, the largest island of the group. Having organised a hire car, we drove to the Volcanic National Park. Because of recent eruptions, the viewing platform was out of action so we paid the fee and boarded a launch that took groups out into the ocean side to see where the volcano and the Pacific met.

Bright orange and red lava ran in sticky streaks like overheated treacle down the blackened volcanic rock and into the sea which steamed and hissed violently as the superheated molten rock cooled and solidified. Some streams had cooled into smooth, ebony sausages that had the appearance of giant toe bones while others were crusted over into rough mounds like broken loaves of bread. The winking glow of the still molten rock broke through the darkening skin of the formations making me wish I had a stick to poke and stir at them with.

Back at the information centre we perused the displayed photographs of previous eruptions. One image showed a fissure on the mainland spewing a quarter mile long, curving arc of crimson lava straight into the sea. In another, the main crater could be seen filled up with molten rock like a bowl of tomato soup.

Nearby, we held hands and wandered through a petrified forest where eruptions had flown through many eons ago leaving the tree stumps, the parts that had been too thick to reduce to carbon, encased in grotesque blackened casts. Primordial and eerie, the surrounding ferny areas were entirely cloaked in moss. We came across a small, semi submerged house. The flow had occurred in 1990, stated an information plaque and the lava was now cold. You could walk on it, so we did and peered down into the windows that were positioned lower than our waists.

That night it rained and I tossed and turned restlessly, my dreams haunted by soldiers drowning in viscous tar as they were carried along by a creeping tide of black into the washing machine jaws of the ocean. There, they cried out for help but their feeble voices were silenced by the relentless beating of drums being pounded by swarthy and fierce looking Hawaiian men clad in loin cloths.

Tired and sticky, the following morning we drove inland, to Aloha Ranch, so as to go horse riding. Eric was not a fan of riding but fortunately he was a good sport about it. "As long as we don't go too fast, I'll do it for you," he said as he kissed me lightly.

The day was hot and humid so I kept my window down to allow the cooling breeze to waft around the car's interior as we drove through a Jurassic landscape of palm trees and rampant undergrowth punctuated by sinister, rocky outcrops.

"Are you sure we are going the right way?" I wondered aloud, thinking that it didn't look as if the road went anywhere civilised. But eventually, the thick bush parted and gave way to scattered pockets of cleared land. "There it is, Eric," I declared as I noticed the sign.

We drove up a recently graded dirt track. On both sides were paddocks where groups of grazing horses ignored our approach. We pulled into the car park next to a cluster of sheds and two corrals, one of which was set up with a few jumps and barrels and the other holding two horses.

A sun browned man wearing an American Stetson and a stunning pair of tan, leather cowboy boots emerged into the daylight from of one of the huts as we climbed out of the car. He looked familiar and with a jolt that hit me right in the heart and left me ice cold and panicked with fright, I saw that it was Luke. I couldn't speak for shock but my limbs acted of their own accord and propelled me forward where upon, at the precise moment that recognition dawned in his eyes, his own arms fell open and into them, I fell. "Sheri." His arms squeezed my body, clinging tightly.

I buried my head in his shoulder. "Luke! I didn't know where you were."

"What are you doing here?"

I pulled away and we stepped apart as the proprieties of social convention reasserted themselves. "I'm here on a holiday with my partner, Eric." I turned to indicate Eric and beckon him closer. He was standing somewhat aside and the look on his face expressed his confusion as to what the display he had just witnessed must mean. They shook hands as men do on such occasions and feigned a polite friendliness.

"What are *you* doing here? – Luke was working for my Pa when Jonah was born," I told Eric by way of explanation. "He taught me how to drive and took me for my driving license."

"My father owns this ranch but he's been ill. When the manager left, he asked me to come instead. That was a year ago."

"This is my first trip to Hawaii and I absolutely love it. It's incredibly beautiful." I waved my hand about, indicating the trees and sky.

"How is Jonah?"

"He's with Mark while we are here but he's doing okay. We have our ups and downs. I'm always busy with work and everything so we have a few issues but we're coping. I am thinking of letting him live with Mark next year, if Mark will have him. He's nearly eight now and we could both do with a break from each other."

Luke nodded thoughtfully. "And you are going for a ride?"

"Yep. But Eric isn't a rider so we need something safe for him."

"I brought some horses in earlier." He uplifted a couple of halters from a rail and handed one to me.

I followed Luke into the corral where the two horses stood and waited patiently. I broke the silence, "So is there a Mrs Luke? And any little Lukes?"

He chuckled. "No, Sheri. Though if I met the right woman...." He left the comment suspended in the air like an invitation. My heart leapt. *What did he mean by that?* "What about you and Errol?"

"Eric." I corrected. *Was that deliberate?* "We were dating but we recently seem to have drifted into living together. He's a good guy. This holiday was his idea. He's paid for most of it."

"I'm glad you are well and happy."

Luke slipped the halter over the head of a pretty palomino mare and I slipped mine onto the head of a chunky piebald gelding. Horses in tow, we led them back to the hitching rail where Eric was waiting.

Luke pointed to one of the nearby sheds. "Saddlery is in the tack room, there. Your horse is called Figaro, Sheri and this one is called Pica."

Neatly organised, the saddles sat on proper, designated saddle trees with each horse's individual bridle hanging above. Upon locating the correct gear, I carried it out into the saddle area. Luke, prepared Pica while I brushed Figaro's glossy back, saddled him up and looped a lead rope around his neck in case Pica proved to be too much for Eric to handle.

Once we were mounted, Luke gave us directions. We were free to ride all over the ranch which was riddled with tracks, but our destination was a waterfall towards the north eastern corner of the property where we planned to enjoy the picnic lunch I carried in my backpack. "Don't worry about the time limit," said Luke. "And the ride is on me. Enjoy yourself and I'll see you when you get back."

I waved goodbye and he watched as we rode off into the still and silent bush. The horse's hooves clip clopped peacefully as we walked single file along the trail. My limbs immediately fell into the familiar rhythm but I could see the tension in Eric's body as he clung with one hand onto the horn of his stock saddle. I was glad that we could not immediately ride together and talk as my mind was full of the meeting with Luke.

As the absolute peace and tranquillity of the setting seeped over me, it proved difficult to picture my Melvin life. *The extreme weather, either freezing or sweltering, why do I live there?* My mind toyed with the image of living in Hawaii and I pictured myself working in real estate; *some of these places must be worth millions,* and being able to be friends with Luke, *maybe even more than friends.* But what about Ma and Pa, and Eric and Jonah? *It's not as if Hawaii is only in the next county or state.* It would be almost impossible to get home for visits and too expensive anyway. It would mean cutting ties with everybody. Logic said the whole idea was a pipe dream and not something that could be realistically turned into reality. *But the lifestyle, the warmth, the semi rural living that anyone outside of the city limits enjoyed with horses, swimming, and the stunning vistas wherever one looked.*

Eric's voice jolted me out of my reverie. "How's your horse?"

I hadn't thought about it. Horses and I were one but I twisted in my saddle and looked back at Eric and Pica who were ambling along about ten yards behind. "Yes, good. What about yours?"

"She keeps stopping and trying to eat."

I laughed, suddenly realising the meaning of her name. "Just pull her head up and kick her along if she tries. If you shorten your reins she won't be able to get her head down." He pulled up beside me and I showed him how to hold the reins so that contact was kept with her head while still allowing free movement.

We walked along, quietly. I thought that Eric would ask about Luke but he didn't mention it. Not that there was anything to learn. After all, we had only met a couple of times and Luke had made no moves. He hadn't asked me out or anything.

We'd been riding for an hour or so when the faint thunder of cascading water first reached our ears. A few more paces and we were out in a wide clearing. The sun was high overhead and the secluded basin of land was bathed in bright sunlight that twinkled and sparkled off the water that plummeted from a terrific height into a dark green pool. The scene looked so much out of a long ago age that I half expected a couple of raven haired, Hawaiian maidens clad in leis and grass skirts to appear from amongst the rocks that were fringed with luxuriant, tropical plants.

Once dismounted, I unsaddled the horses then led each to the pool to drink before hitching them to some nearby trees. Eric, meanwhile, spread out the blanket under the shade and unpacked the picnic.

"I don't know about you but I'm starving," he said as he laid out the feast provided by the hotel kitchen; comprising of a crispy fresh baguette, cream cheese and ham, deep red tomatoes and a lettuce. A knife was included as was fresh butter. We lay back on the blanket and sipped cold diet coke.

"My thighs are killing me already," Eric commented. He pulled his pants off and inspected the insides of his legs where the seams of his jeans had rubbed angry welts into his skin.

I laughed, remembering all the times in the past that I had suffered the same pain and taunted him in reply. "Don't worry. You won't really feel the worst of the effects until tomorrow or the day after."

"Why haven't your jeans rubbed your legs?"

"I don't know; maybe because I sit stiller when I ride. I don't really move my legs unless to tell the horse what to do. My legs grip the horse and only my body moves."

"I never knew there was so much to riding. I just thought you just got on and the horse did everything."

He rolled towards me, looking so ridiculous lying there in his stripped briefs that every time I looked at him, the vulnerable state of his appearance made me smile.

"Having fun?"

Feeling a rush of tender affection, I assured him I was having the best time in my entire life. He placed his arm on my waist and leaned into my body for a gentle kiss then reached into his jeans pocket. "I have something to give you." A small, velvet jewellery box was placed in my hand. Heart pounding, I carefully opened the lid to reveal the most beautiful white gold, channel set, diamond ring.

Eric was looking at me with eyes full of adoration and hope. "I love you. Marry me?"

"Yes," I said. "Yes." He slipped the ring onto my finger. *He is a good man. I could do much worse,* I thought.

Sleep was impossible. From the moment of our engagement, Eric assumed a propitious manner; and if his arm strayed to my back more often, if he held my hand in public and called me his fiancée, surely he had the right. I should have been feeling ecstatic. I was living every woman's dream.

Riding back to the stables, he had even led the way, a small detail that did not go unnoticed by Luke whose glance intuitively slipped to my left finger; although he made no mention of the ring that now rested there, casting about rays of dazzling brilliance with every flick of my wrist. It had taken every ounce of will to prevent myself from slipping my hand into my pocket.

Luke and I had unsaddled the horses together but our conversation was wedged against an invisible wall as if all the questions we wanted to ask each other were concertinaed into a tight, unutterable bunch. *Give me your business card,* I wanted to say as he turned aside. *Will you be returning to the mainland or staying here?* And as I waved goodbye and climbed into the passenger seat of the car: *Will I ever see you again?* Eric turned the key in the ignition and reversed out of the parking lot a satisfied man but Luke was disappearing as he led the horses away. If only he had said something - made some kind of sign; but he hadn't and therefore I had nothing to go on. I didn't know how Luke felt about me, if anything, and was not even certain how I felt about him. There was a real connection between us, that, I knew, but what exactly was the nature of that connection? I was not particularly attracted to him. *He is quite short and not that good looking, not my type physically. But he wears great boots and knows horses. He is in tune with the land. He is wise. He is always the one I feel the need to talk to when I can't make sense of life.* Constricted tears gathered in the back of my throat. *Why was I crying?* My heart ached.

Later that night, sleepless once again, I slipped out of bed and padded softly into the lounge, leaving Eric snoring lightly. The curtains were still open. It was very dark outside. I put the kettle on and made a cup of tea. *What did I want?* I had everything a woman could desire, a great job, a wonderful man who obviously loved me and wanted to marry me, a supportive family, money, travel. What more could I possibly want? *You are just being a stupid, stupid woman,* I told myself. *You need to snap out of it.*

CHAPTER NINE

Once home, I drove out to pick up Jonah. The weather was freezing. It was the worst part of winter and dirty, slushy, snow lay piled up in haphazard heaps on the sides of the road where the plough had pushed it. My engagement ring sat snugly in my pocket where I had slipped it off. I wasn't ready for congratulatory hugs just yet.

At Mark's, the potbelly fire was going and the house felt cosy and warm. Jonah and his father were playing on the Playstation and neither looked up as I entered. "How's he been?" I asked Sophie as we stood in the hallway.

"Really great," she replied. "Mark has enjoyed having him around. You know we can't have kids. We've been trying IVF but no luck yet."

She looked downcast and I felt a rush of warmth towards her. She was trying hard to make a decent life with Mark. Then suddenly, my voice was articulating the words I hadn't intended to voice as yet. "It's been very hard for me and Jonah. We have both really struggled and I think he is sick of me. I was thinking that it might be a good thing for Jonah if he was to live with you and Mark for a while - maybe for a year when the new school year starts. My folks on the ranch would be available for babysitting; and if it didn't work out then he could come home again. Perhaps you could talk to Mark about it?"

Sophie considered this proposition. "Okay, I will. It would be an adjustment but he is no trouble to have around."

"He will be eight years old soon. He's growing up fast. The hardest part is over. Give me a call, or if I don't hear from you, I'll call Mark in a couple of months. I think it would be best for Jonah. He's getting to the age where he needs his father around to stop him getting out of hand."

I went into the lounge and saw that Jonah was packing his game into his backpack. His face was scrunched into a scowl.

Mark was saying, "Yeah buddy. I'll see you soon, okay?"

"But I don't want to go home. I want to stay here." He looked up and saw me. "Can't I stay here mum?"

I ruffled his head. "Not today, darling. Later, in the summer break probably."

Mark agreed. "Not today. You have to go back to school and learn stuff, and play football. But I'll see you next holidays, right?"

Jonah accepted this reasoning and although clearly unhappy about it, gave his father and Sophie a hug. "Thanks for having him," I said as I ushered him out of the door and into the bitter blast of the outdoors.

"How was your stay?" I asked once we were on the road with the heater running on full.

"Good."

"Did you do anything interesting? Go anywhere?"

"We went to the movies."

"Oh good. Nice. Anything else?"

"No."

I sighed. Back to normal we were.

****

On Monday morning there was a knock at the door. It was Beryl so I held the door open in invitation. "It's good to see you. Come on in."

She stamped the slush off her boots before removing them. "I wasn't sure if you would be home."

"We've just returned from Hawaii. Jonah's at school and Eric's at work but I don't go back till next week.' I led the way into the kitchen. "What brings you here?"

"And what's this?" She grasped my hand and held the ring finger up into the light. "Are you engaged?"

"I guess so." I flicked the kettle on. "Tea or coffee?"

"Coffee please. How exciting. Are you happy?"

I shrugged. "I'm not unhappy. It's just – I don't know – I don't feel the excitement. It feels like we're an old married couple already. I don't know what that means."

I busied myself with the little coffee making ritual, placing out the cups and spooning in the coffee powder, then pouring the water and milk before carrying the cups to the kitchen table.

"I am detecting a certain lack of enthusiasm," she said. "Don't you love Eric?"

"I don't know - sort of. I'm not madly in love with him." I told her about Luke and our unexpected meeting in Hawaii.

"Are you in love with him instead?"

I laughed. "No. I don't find him attractive. But I do think about him a lot, especially when I really need someone to talk to because he always knows exactly the right thing to say. Life makes sense when I am around him. It's like being home."

"How does he feel about you?"

"I don't know that either. I can't work him out. When we are together it feels completely right to me but I don't know whether he feels it too. He's never said anything or made any moves."

"Well honey, in my understanding, if a man loves a woman he won't let anything stand in his way. But then, what do I know? Sometimes, it can feel as though you know a person even though you ain't ever met them before. Some people say that it's because we've known them from a past life. That's why they feel so familiar."

I had nothing to add but her theory did describe the defining quality of the relationship between Luke and myself, a kind of knowing or understanding of each other that, inexplicably, was irrefutable as a fact. We sipped our coffees and Beryl changed the subject.

"How's your new job going?"

That question I could answer. "I finished my training about six months ago and got three new listings before I went on holiday. Real estate is booming just now. I've never made so much money."

"You will be able to buy your own place soon."

"I have thought about it but I want to buy land. I wouldn't like to buy just a house in the city. But Eric's not a farmer so we have kind of stalled on that topic too. I want horses again. I really miss them."

"What about a motorcycle. An 'iron horse' as they call them."

I hadn't considered that option but it was a good idea. Besides, I was going to have to do something about transport very soon. The Jimny, as faithful a servant as she had been, was beginning to fall apart. I was currently driving Eric's Audi as much as possible.

"Anyway, I came to let you know that the boys have finished the car and they're racing it for the first time next weekend at the track if you'd like to come. I've got a corporate box. If you and Eric would like to join us for drinks and nibbles, you would be more than welcome."

"Is Karl driving?"

"Yes. He's pretty good too. We've done some test runs and he's made good times but of course that's been without other drivers on the track so it's anybody's guess how he'll go on the night. Him and Lloyd have done a great job on the car. It looks fantastic." She handed me three passes on lanyards. "Wear these and you'll be allowed into the pit area. We will be there about two hours before racing starts."

The following weekend, the three of us duly made our way to the track; the very same arena where Eric and I'd had our first date going on two years ago now. Eric draped his arm around my neck and drew me close. "Bring back memories?"

We flashed our VIP cards at gate security and were waved through. "I could get used to this," I laughed.

A sign on the other side of the arena said 'Pit Area' so we headed towards it. 'The Pits' turned out to be merely a section of bare ground behind the stadium, crowded with a chaotic jumble of cars as well as guys dressed, or partially dressed, in brightly coloured, racing suits.

I scanned the crowd searching for familiar faces, eventually spotting Beryl talking to a reporter. We thrust our way through the mass of bodies and machinery over to where she stood watching as the press photographer packed away his equipment. "We're getting a write up in the local paper," she said. "That will be good for business."

"Front page, hopefully," I said.

Jonah was eyeing off a nearby bright yellow Chevy with an appreciation inherent in his boy genes. "Is this the car?"

"Indeed it is, my dear. Would you like to ride in it?"

"Would I ever!"

Karl was rubbing over the paintwork with a chamois. It looked amazing; in perfect condition without a scratch or a dent. No doubt that situation would not last long. The body of the car was decorated with logos and advertising with 'TooGood's' emblazoned across the bonnet in pride of place.

I introduced Eric and Jonah to Beryl and the boys. "Congratulations on your engagement," said Beryl to Eric as they shook hands.

Jonah looked up. "What's engagement?"

"Eric and mummy are getting married," I explained briefly.

"Why?"

Kids! "Because Eric asked me and I said yes. Look honey; let's talk about this when we get home. Things are a bit busy here right now. And you want to go for a ride in the car – right?"

Jonah accepted the diversion but his expression was thoughtful and suggested he wasn't going to forget about this conversation in a hurry.

Beryl extracted a helmet from the back of the car where the rear seat used to be and positioned it on Jonah's head. She then lifted him into the passenger seat and adjusted the safety harness about his small shoulders as best she could. Jonah's body was jerking this way and that in a manner that communicated his excitement.

"Don't touch anything, Jonah," I cautioned, half afraid that the array of buttons and switches on the dash would prove too tempting for his twitchy, eight year old fingers."

Eric handed Karl his helmet and leather gloves. "See you soon, mate," he said as Karl inserted himself through the window space and settled into his seat. He pressed the ignition button and the car 'vroomed' into life. It sounded guttural; a sound no doubt attributable to the straight through performance exhausts, and grumbled out of the pits for the warm up laps. All around, muscle cars were awakening and manoeuvring into position at the exit gate.

"I have to go to the box," said Beryl. She had invited her sponsors to join her and they would be gathering there already.

Eric, observing my indecision, urged me to go, promising to wait there for Jonah.

The corporate box was about the size of a lounge room and looked like one too. A bar, well stocked with wine and spirits, lined the back wall while two sets of chocolate, leather couches were positioned facing each other over glass topped coffee tables in the main space. Floor to ceiling window panes dominated the room and delivered panoramic views of the track where the super saloons, about twenty of them, circulated tamely, although every now and again, one of the drivers would plant his foot sending sprays of mud out over the crowds that were slowly filling up the grandstand seats. I could see that the TooGood car was already well dotted with dirt.

On our entry, a waiter proffered us a tray from which I selected a fluted glass of chilled champagne and a delicate vol-au-vent filled with a creamy tuna mousse. A group of four men and two women said their hellos to Beryl and then smiled politely as she introduced me to Reg Norris from 'Pro-Performance Exhausts and Engineering,' Rex Burton, a financier from the city and Jarrod Kitchener and Sam Monk , co-owners of 'KONK Spray Painters and Panel Beaters.' The two women, who introduced themselves as Jasmine and Yolanda, clasped my fingertips with professionally manicured claws and shook gingerly. Introductions over, the men resumed their conversations so the other women and I drifted over to the impeccably clean windows and watched the cars as they continued their conditioning of the track.

As TooGood's car came around, I waved instinctively before catching myself. Realising that Jonah would have been unable to see me, I half chuckled. "My son is riding in the car with Karl," I offered by way of explanation.

The women eyed me up and down. "You have a son. How nice," one purred. *Yolanda?* They looked remarkably similar. Both were slim and wore their long, blonde hair loose around fully made up faces that were enhanced by expertly shaped eyebrows. On close inspection, I realised that one was quite older than the other. Her neck area, always a giveaway, was beginning to crepe with age. "Is he your only child?"

I nodded. "Yes, one is enough."

"I've got two myself," said the younger woman. "Two girls - Brittany, who is seven and Sarah, five."

To which Yolanda responded, "I have a twenty year old son who's in New York studying performance and a girl, Gillian. She's still at school." Her voice was tinged with pride.

The two women fell into a discussion about the merits of the various schools in the city.

"Which school does your son attend?" asked Jasmine.

I said the name of the local school, "Melvin Elementary."

"Ah. State." The women exchanged a meaningful look that I took to communicate their tacit understanding that I was not in their league. I felt myself taking offence. *Condescending bitches.* Where were Eric and Jonah anyway? I'd seen the cars leaving the track over ten minutes ago. At that moment, the door swung open and the two breezed in accompanied by a blast of winter air.

"Mum. Did you see me?" exclaimed Jonah whose cheeks were flushed with cold and excitement.

"Sure did. I waved but you couldn't see me, I don't think." I removed his coat and gave him a sandwich from the tray on the table.

Yolanda was speaking. "How do you know Beryl?"

"I used to work for her. The car was my idea although you'd never hear that from the boys."

"As a receptionist?"

"No. As a mechanic. But I never qualified. It was too much of a lad's club for me so I left. Now I work at Melvin Western Real Estate in the city. I have a few listings of my own but my main job at the moment is staging the homes and taking the photographs."

Feeling more confident with the topic of conversation I asked the women where they worked to which Yolanda sniggered in response, "Work darling. Haha. Oh no. I don't work. Rex does all that.

"Yes our job is to look nice for when we attend these functions with our husbands," chipped in Jasmine.

A life without working was hard to imagine. What did they fill their day with? I wondered. *The gym and shopping no doubt.* But how did they get their husbands to agree to it? I could just imagine what Eric's response would be to a suggestion that I stop work in order to spend my days making sure I looked nice. Yet these women managed it. What was the saying? *Trophy wives.* I created a mental story of their lives. *Rich. Daddy works in banking. Mum stays home and looks glamorous. Private schools.* Not so different from my own story really, but for a small, defining difference in upbringing and attitude that allowed them to be kept women and drove me to be independent. *It depends how you want to live life,* I mused, realising I would hate to live like these women, dependent on their husbands for their facials and gym memberships. One thing my life had forced upon me was financial self reliance. I knew I could survive without a man. I had been forced into becoming independent because I'd had to look after Jonah. There had been no one else. A feeling of pride at having made it washed over me. I had succeeded without anybody's help and owed nobody anything. The feeling was empowering.

Back at my desk the following week, I sifted through the stack of memos and files and saw that Vivienne had sold the Hacienda Mansion. No doubt about it, that woman was a pro at her job. I also took three calls as a result of a leaflet drop I had undertaken the week prior to Hawaii, so once morning briefing was over, I gathered my keys and paperwork in preparation for the listing interviews. Vivienne noticed my ring and immediately wanted to hear all the details. "I'll tell you over lunch," I protested as I pulled my hand free. "I really have to go now."Outside, a frigid wind screeched across the plains and carried my breath away. The good old Jimny, loaded up with antifreeze, started first go and I rubbed my mittened hands together briskly while I waited for the engine to warm up.

My phone rang. It was Ma. "Becky's gone into labour," she said. "Jet's taken her into Melvin maternity. They thought she'd be better there, just in case."

The news I was going to be an aunt filled me with joy. "Ok. Thanks Ma," I replied. "I'll go in and visit after work. I've got a couple of new listings to take care of just now."

"We will come over later too but we'll stay in a motel."

"No, stay with us and come for dinner," I offered.

With the gears in four wheel drive, I reversed out. It was already difficult to remember the warm climes of Hawaii. Funny how you anticipate a trip for so long and then the moment is here, and quickly gone, so that all that remains are memories that diminish in colour and clarity as the days pass and the old routines reassert themselves.

My first appointment was at a semi rural address on the edge of the city boundary. After quarter of an hour crawling up and down the road, straining to read the faded, or nonexistent identifying details, I found the faint remnants of a name on the mail box and pulled into the driveway. The house stood in the manner typical of American properties, plonked squarely on the land with little fencing to indicate any boundaries. At my knock, a shapeless woman, I guessed to be in her late fifties, answered the door. I noticed she had beautiful, long, grey hair but it was limp and carelessly twisted into a loose bun on the back of her neck giving her an unkempt appearance.

"Hi. Mrs Cartwright? I'm Sheridan Lewis."

The woman held the door open and I stepped into the living area. First impressions: gloomy and quite grubby, fly spots dotting the walls, yellowing ceilings. A pile of clothes jumbled haphazardly on the floor, worn carpets.

"Would you like a coffee?" the woman offered.

"No thanks. I just had one." I couldn't imagine anything from that kitchen touching my lips. "I will have a quick look through the house if you don't mind?" Confirming my expectations, it needed a lot of work and a good clean. "How much did you want for it?" I asked once we were seated at the cluttered kitchen table.

"I don't know. My husband died and this place is too big for me now. It's got a hundred acres with it. What do you think its worth?"

The revelation that the place came with land surprised me and cast the whole deal in a more positive light; not that one hundred acres was worth much around here compared to the huge ranches that surrounded Melvin. There was little that could be done with a land holding so small other than cut it for hay or run a couple of horses.

I made some notes on the property listing sheet. "Are there any out buildings Mrs Cartwright?"

"Call me Mary. There's a hay barn and a stable, though they're both in a bit of a state. We had horses here when the kiddies were small but that was over twenty years ago now."

I asked to see the buildings, so she led me into a dingy laundry where she pulled on a heavy coat and gumboots. She handed me a pair. *Her old husband's?* They came up to my knees and flapped around on my feet but it was better than heels in this weather. To the rear of the house stood a winter naked grove of trees.

"Peaches, plums and cherries," Mary said.

A fractured path cut through beneath the ancient boughs and I imagined how pretty it would look in spring with the trees smothered in pink and white blossom. The orchard path emerged into an open paddock where the buildings, sad and neglected, waited dismally.

The woman pointed into the distance where the dull, purple foothills climbed up from the plains. "There's gold in them hills," she declared. "My brother found a nugget in the stream once - only a small one, 'bout the size of a nickel; but nonetheless – a nugget."

The barn, understandably, was empty. She pulled on the doors which dragged on the ground, barely supported as they were, by fragile rusty hinges. Inside, disturbed dust motes hovered in the dim streaks of light and as my eyes adjusted, I took in the stable boxes, tack room, concreted middle section and sundry gear and tools that had mummified into museum pieces where they were last put down. The place smelled musty, but underneath, friendly and familiar; a smell of chaff, hay and other horsey things. *With a good clean out...*

Later that afternoon, I drove over to Maisie's to collect Jonah. "Mum's at the supermarket," Laura informed me. She was lounging on the couch while watching Nickelodeon cartoons on television and didn't look up.

I phoned Eric before leaving. "Meet us at Melvin Maternity. Becky's having her baby. She's probably had it by now. And bring a bunch of flowers."

The traffic was slow. It had been snowing on and off and cars were slewing about the road whenever an incline or a set of lights caused a loss in momentum. We manoeuvred carefully past a car spinning its wheels in the mush, its rear end swinging from side to side. I didn't want it to hit us.

"Look at that, Mum," Jonah cried observing a three car pileup on the side of the road where a Toyota and a Ford had slid nose first into the side of a parked BMW. At only four in the afternoon, the day was already darkening and the streetlights cast wet reflections into the yellow puddles of light that encircled each lamp post like a fallen halo.

In contrast, it was warm and cheerful in the lobby of the hospital and I jigged about on the spot to speed up the circulation while waiting for Eric to arrive, which he soon did, swirling little snow flurries off his coat as he moved. Together, we negotiated our way through the maze of hospital corridors until we found Becky's suite. I pushed open the door and saw she was in bed, propped up with pillows.

"It's a girl!" she said when she saw us. And she held up the tightly swaddled bundle of baby that lay in her arms for inspection.

Jet, who was seated in the chair beside the bed, rose when we entered. A shy smile of satisfaction hovered on his face.

"Congratulations!" I held my brother tightly then hugged Becky carefully. "Well done. Was it awful?"

She rolled her eyes and I knew exactly how she felt. I took the tiny parcel from her arms. It was difficult to remember Jonah being so small. The little sweetheart opened her cupid lips and gave a delicate yawn. "Oh, she is so cute." I sat in Jet's vacated chair. "Look, Jonah. This is your new cousin." Jonah looked on from a distance, dubious as to the value of this female infant. "Have you chosen a name yet?"

"We thought Lorelei Suzanna. Suzanna after your ma."

"She's gorgeous," said Eric his face alight with delight. "Congratulations."

I didn't know Eric was so keen on babies, I thought as he vigorously shook Jet's hand and pecked Becky on her cheek.

"One day this will be us," he murmured in my ear as he leaned over my shoulder and gazed at the little creature in my arms. My heart skipped a beat. *Surely, he wasn't serious.* But looking into his face I could see his happy family vision of the future plainly visible. Well, that was definitely not the vision I'd had in my head only a few short hours earlier.

The guy has a right to children, said my inner voice, a voice I promptly banished. That was a guilt I did not need. He must have seen the look of dismay in my eyes because he dropped the subject just as the blessed sound of approaching footsteps announced the approach of Ma, Pa, Byron and Louisa who bustled into the room bearing hugs all round.

Ma, spotting my ring immediately, exclaimed loudly over its cut and brilliance which prompted Becky and Louisa to do the same. I accepted their congratulations with an inner reluctance, manifested as an outer briskness which I struggled to keep under control. When Lorelei began to grizzle, I decided it was time to leave. "I'll get some food sorted and see you soon," I mouthed to Ma as I carefully placed her new granddaughter into her outstretched and welcoming arms.

The family trooped in after eight, chilled and windblown while outside, in the darkness, the rising wind whistled an eerie moan around the eaves. Eric turned on the television where a weather map showed a storm was brewing. It was going to be a rough night.

At dinner, I told Pa about the small holding I'd seen that day. "I think it could be bought for under $200,000 but it needs one hell of a lot of work."

Byron, with his mouth full of pizza, wanted to know what I would do with it. "The land is pretty poor out there and not much use for anything."

Pa agreed. "I doubt you'd even get a good cut of hay off it. It's quite stony, though you could plant it in lucerne."

"I thought I'd run horses," I responded, not realising that I was speaking as if I was seriously considering buying it. "It's got a good set of stables and a huge barn, probably from when it was part of a bigger landholding. I could agist other people's horses too, just to make a bit of income... set up a jumps arena maybe."

Eric, to whom all this was news chipped in, "When do you plan to do all this work? You're busy enough as it is." He looked and sounded irritated.

He had a valid point. I was busy. But the more I thought about it and talked about it, the more the idea appealed to me. "I could always borrow enough to get started with the renovations and pay a builder. If it was tidied up, it would be worth a lot more. I might even make a good profit if I sold it again. Plus it's got gold in the hills. Mrs Cartwright told me. She said her brother found a nugget in the stream."

Ma laughed. "Oh Sheri! You and your gold! Remember how Sheri was always looking for gold on the farm, Sherman?"

Pa addressed Eric, "She spent a whole summer once panning for gold in the stream on the ranch!"

Eric looked at me. A teasing smile played about his mouth. "Did you find anything?"

"Of course not," I snapped. It wasn't a big deal. Every family has these embarrassing stories that they drag out at inopportune times but I felt belittled; although it was true that gold and gemstones had held an intense fascination for me as a child. I'd found it incredible that secretive pockets of precious metals and diamonds lurked within the ground innocuously cloaked in trees, grasses and bushes and read avidly whatever I could find on the geographical clues that indicated the whereabouts of these treasures. In truth, I couldn't wait to ride up into those hills and fossick about.

Much later that night, the house was silent. Every available flat surface held a prone, sleeping body and Pa's snores reverberated about the darkened rooms. Eric lay beside me with his hand resting in its favourite position on my belly. It was warm and comfy under the duvet and my eyes were stuck shut, ready for sleep when Eric spoke. "Do you not want another baby now, or not want another baby ever?"

Although, he had the right to ask the question, I did not want to answer it. For one thing I was sleepy and for another I did not want to upset him so I said, "I don't know. Just now? Honey, I feel like I am only now getting over Jonah's birth and working out what I want in life and how I want to live it."

He rolled over onto his back, effectively separating us. "I'm not getting any younger, Sheri, nor are you. If we leave it too late we will be too old to put the effort in, and we can't just have one. We'd have to have at least two so they have each other to play with."

"Mmm. But I keep thinking about that farmlet. I'm so excited about it and I know we can afford it. I'd be able to have a horse again and we could get Jonah a trail bike. I know he would love that. He'd have such fun."

"When the last child goes to school you could go back to work then. You'd be back at work by the time you're thirty five."

I sat up in bed with aggrieved emotions rousing within me. "My job, my career, would be down the gurgler by then," I protested. "I'd have to start again."

Eric, sensing my change in mood, forced his voice to sound reasonable. "It's not like it's a real career though is it?" An agitated noise erupted from my throat. "I mean," he hastened to add, "anybody could do it. You could study something more important while at home with our babies." He sounded pleased with himself as if he had solved a complex equation all by himself.

Now I was really cross. "All very well for you to say," I snapped. "It's not like you'd be the one to stay home 24 / 7 and look after them, and what about money?"

"I will pay the rent and bills. I'd support you. I'd expect that..."

"No! What about MY money, for the things I want, like a new car, or a horse or even clothes or shoes?"

"It's not like you need much. You've got savings to keep you going. We'd manage."

He wasn't listening to me. He didn't hear me. Neither of us was prepared to hear the other. The discussion veered at crossed purposes as if we each had our own dialogue that we felt compelled to vocalise. Like two people on opposite ends of a bridge, we refused to meet in the middle.

"The thing is, Eric, you are not seeing me as a person in my own right. I'm not an extension of you and I don't see why I should have to put my life on hold just so that you can be a father."

Now we were really arguing. "For god's sake, Sheri," he cried. "You're so selfish. All you can think about is yourself."

"*I'm* selfish!" the idea was preposterous. "*You're* the selfish one you son of a bitch." I was hissing now, my voice low, conscious of the other sleeping inhabitants of the house. "You don't ask my opinion about anything. You just moved right on in, popped out a ring when my guard was down and now you're going to assume that I will breed for you! Get knotted you jerk."

"So what are you saying – that you don't want to marry me now?" The argument was moving fast and spiralling out of control.

I leapt out of bed. "I don't know. I don't know," I gasped. "I'm confused."

At that, Eric, suddenly deflated, resumed his habitual solicitous manner as precipitously as if he had put on a sweater of a different colour and pattern. He patted the bed, begging me to sit. "What is it, Sheri? What is the problem?"

I perched on the edge. "It's just as I said. I'm only now sorting myself out since having Jonah. You know I wanted to be a geologist? I begged and pleaded with Pa to let me go to Uni' to study science but he said what was the point? I'd be a wife and mother anyway. Well his prediction proved right on that score." I laughed a bitter laugh. "But I never wanted to just be a wife and mother. I never did."

"All women marry and have children," said Eric. "It's natural."

"Not all. Cripes. You sound just like Pa." *He was a lot like Pa come to think of it.* "Some women, like Becky, are born mothers. All they want to do is look after their kids and their man. And that's fine, for them, but I've always wanted more: money, travel and stuff."

"So why did you have Jonah then?"

I'd never discussed the manner of Jonah's conception with anyone other than my family, Luke and Vanessa and I couldn't bring myself to confide in Eric now. The old shame at my naivety and stupidity silenced me as much as it ever did. "Jonah was an accident, as you know. Who the hell would get pregnant at sixteen on purpose! Once he was born, Mark was too immature and uninterested in him but I felt responsible.

Now that he's older and I have some freedom back, why would I want to tie myself down again?"

When Eric finally spoke, his voice was low and conciliatory. "Well, Sheri, I'm thirty already and I want to settle down and have a family of my own before I get much older but I guess we could get married and wait a few more years to have kids."

He thought he was compromising and the plan was reasonable. *So why did my heart sink?*

"Okay," I agreed, thereby deferring the issue yet again. In my defence, it seemed easier to carry on than to force an ultimatum.

The household woke in the morning to find eight inches of snow had been dumped on the city in what was soon hailed as being 'the biggest snow fall of the decade.'

"Did you know that every snowflake is formed around a dust particle?" announced Jonah who was developing a fascination for facts.

"And every snowflake looks different to any other snowflake," added Louisa.

"Every one!" repeated Jonah, the idea of the uniqueness of every snowflake beyond his comprehension.

"Why don't you get out your microscope and have a look," I suggested.

They went off to locate the necessary equipment for the experiment while Ma and I cooked bacon and scrambled eggs for the seven of us.

"Were you two having words last night?" Ma asked nonchalantly as she turned the bacon over in the frying pan.

"Oh no, did you hear that? I'm sorry," I said. "We never argue. I don't know why Eric chose last night to pick a fight."

"Is everything okay?"

I outlined the gist of the argument to Ma who listened without commenting. When I finished she spoke. "One thing I can tell you Sheri is that people are who they are. I am fifty years old and I like the same things today that I did when I was young. People don't change much."

"A leopard doesn't change its spots in other words?"

"Something like that. We might modify our behaviour or learn how to manage situations differently, but essentially we stay who we are no matter how old we get."

"So who am I?"

"Only you can answer that my dear."

I told Ma about Hawaii, how beautiful it was. "And you'll never guess who we bumped into – Luke!" Ma looked mystified. "Luke! You know, who worked for Pa when Jonah was born." I had a sudden urge to talk about him, to speak his name within this context where it was safe and socially acceptable. "What a coincidence eh?"

"There's no such thing as coincidence, love. Things happen for a reason."

"Don't tell me you believe in fate now, Ma?" I scoffed. I didn't believe that there was any reason for anything. It was all chance and choices.

Everyone departed en masse the morning after the thaw and the house felt peacefully empty as I gathered my bag and keys. However, any feelings of serenity were quickly abandoned as once in the car, Jonah chose the moment to bring up the subject of our engagement again.

"Mum, why are you and Eric getting married?"

I reiterated what I had said previously. "Because he asked me, honey."

"But Mum, why aren't you and Dad married?"

My scalp prickled in fright. I had always assumed that we would have this conversation, had rehearsed it even, but now it was in front of me I didn't know how to handle it. How truthful should I be?

"Your dad and I didn't get on," I explained. I controlled the words so that they came out naturally, but the way in which my fingers gripped the steering wheel and my eyes peered out of the windscreen, revealed that driving was taking every ounce of effort.

"Didn't you love Dad?" he asked. *The poor kid.* I could hear the wistful tone in his voice. He had never before given any indication that the fact that we weren't together upset him but it was only natural for the child to want his parents to be together.

I tried to soften the words but there really was no way to explain that could possibly make the truth any easier for him to accept. "No, and he didn't love me either. But we both love you," I hastened to add. Jonah stared out of the window and watched the cars and houses as they flicked silently by.

"I don't want you to marry Eric," he said quietly.

I asked the fateful words, "why not?" already knowing what the answer would be.

"Because he's not my dad," Jonah replied.

I glanced across to where he was glaring at me with defiant eyes and was forced to curb the impulse to laugh, he looked so fierce. "But you and Eric get on well, don't you?"

"I hate him," he shouted. Now Jonah made a grimace, pulling his lips back to show his teeth, all in a sweet, bright line.

"No you don't." I countered. "Don't be silly. You and Eric are fine together." I pulled the Jimny up at the curb and turned to face my son, leaving the engine running. We were at the school, a cubic arrangement of buildings that clustered around a central administration block and parking area. The scene looked chaotic with a multitude of cars pulling in and out in a routine that was enacted twice a day for the duration of the term.

Jonah reached for his back pack and shouted over his shoulder as he shoved the door open. "He's not my dad and he can't tell me what to do."

"Jonah!" I cried after his retreating back. But he only slammed the door behind him and then he was gone, blending into the hundreds of other uniformed children streaming into the building.

Back at the office, the job list indicated that I had two new listings to stage and photograph; one, a slate and stone four bedroom family home and the other an inner city two bedroom apartment. The family had already moved out of the home so I made a call to the agency's house dressing supplier and booked an appointment.

Selecting a house lot of furniture with which to dress the house was expensive but experience had already taught me that a furnished home sold faster than an empty one because prospective purchasers liked being able to visualise where their furniture could be positioned. By late morning with the furnishings chosen and due to be delivered the following day I phoned the tenants of the apartment. The call went to voicemail so I left a message.

With nothing else pressing to do that morning, I popped into the hospital to visit Becky who was engrossed in bathing the baby.

"She is so beautiful," I sighed, taking in her exquisite fingers and toes, all clenched up in opposition to the feel of the water. She had obviously been screaming because her little face was livid with indignation. How cute her fury seemed.

The nurse arranged a towel on the bed and then watched Becky as she gripped the back of the baby's neck and little ankles firmly and lifted her out of the water. Lorelei shuddered her tiny arms as she was swaddled in the towel. I strained to remember. It didn't seem possible that I had held my own son's tiny body in the same way or dressed him in stretch 'n' grows the size of dolls clothes.

Once Lorelei was snugly trussed up like a papoose, Becky settled back against the pillows and put the baby to her breast where she snorted and grunted like a contented piglet. I tickled the baby's toes and they clenched involuntarily.

"I wish I lived closer so I could see her more often," I said wistfully.

"Mum's coming to stay for a couple of weeks," Becky replied. "So that will be good, to have some help."

I reminisced, remembering bringing Jonah home for the first time. I'd laid him in his crib and he had promptly gone to sleep. The relief I'd felt was indescribable. I don't know what I would have done if he had cried.

Becky looked up from Lorelei's dozing face, "Hey, you'll never guess who sent me a message on Facebook the other day – Vanessa!"

I was shocked. "How is she?" I recounted to Becky the last time I had seen her; what a mess she had been.

"Well, she seemed great." Becky responded. "She suggested that we get together in the beginning of February because she's going to visit her parents for a week or two."

I estimated it had been five years or more since we had all been together and I wondered how she was now. Our last meeting had been such a debacle. I couldn't wait to see her.

CHAPTER TEN

After much nagging, Eric reluctantly agreed to drive out and inspect the property. I handed responsibility for the listing over to Vivienne, citing a conflict of interest, and we converged on West Range Road one Saturday morning for the viewing. The dinginess was, if possible, even worse than I remembered. After being shut up against the winter weather for so long, the house reeked of mouldy mustiness and grime and Mrs Cartwright herself looked like she needed to be in care as surely those were the exact same clothes she had been wearing the last time we'd met.

Jonah wrinkled his nose, "Eeew..." My fingers dug into his biceps and cut short his complaint. Eric wandered through the house while Jonah and I tagged along behind but the expression on his face as he surveyed the cobwebbed and fly spotted ceilings, and opened and closed the dark intimidating recesses of the cupboards, said it all.

"I know it's nothing to look at now but it has potential don't you think?" I prompted.

"It's disgusting," Eric growled back. "You can't seriously believe you will be able to fix this place up." He opened the door to the oven which promptly fell off in his hand. "It's past it."

I agreed about the stove. "We'll buy new appliances, and even a new kitchen and bathroom if we get it for a good enough price."

We moved into the wash house and huddled there on the vile, cracked and peeling lino while we argued in whispers.

"Everything needs redoing. It'll cost at least fifty grand and it's not worth it. You can get a spec house for that. You may as well push it over and rebuild."

"We could live in a trailer while it's being done," I suggested, then immediately cancelled that thought. *Winter cramped up in a trailer with Jonah – I don't think so.*

"A trailer! Cool," exclaimed Jonah, his ears pricking up.

"Eric all but stamped his foot in frustration. "I am NOT living in a trailer. Look, if you want to buy a place, why don't we buy a place in town? We could get a modern house for the same money, three or four bedroom with en suites, properly insulated and heated. I bet this place doesn't have either." He kicked at the stained lino to emphasise his point.

At the intellectual level, I knew Eric's arguments made sense. Who would put themselves through it? Stripping walls, painting, plastering; the ancient lino tiles that would chip off into tiny pieces as their reluctant grip was prised from the floors, the leaks that would inevitably reveal themselves in the roof, guttering and plumbing; not to mention the rewiring. Eric was right but still....

I thought about the house all of the following week. By my reckoning, it must have been at least a hundred years old so one afternoon I ventured into the city library to see what could be learned about its history.

'Shaun,' read the name tag of the research assistant who fiddled with the keys of his computer at my request.

"Is this it?" he asked. He turned the monitor to face me and there on the screen was a grainy black and white photograph of the house. The source of the photograph was a back in history article from the Melvin Community Chronical dated the 20th October 1989. He skimmed through the blurb, "...built by Fred Sinclair in 1899...Lodge-pole Pine...Oh listen to this - It was half destroyed by a freak tornado in 1985..."

That was almost twenty years ago. The tornado must have occurred while old Mrs Cartwright was living there. The boxy shape of the house, the four sets of windows staring like eyes, looked much the same only the land surrounding the homestead was densely planted with a grove of towering Maple trees. *Had they blown down in the storm?* I peered closer, noticing a veranda attached to the house that was no longer there. Ornate twin columns rose up on either side of the front door, providing the supports for the covered portico. It was bizarre to think that the woman had never bothered to have it rebuilt.

A family stood awkwardly to the side of the entrance. The man, *Fred Sinclai*r? tall and broad and wearing a top hat and tails, looked like he was attired for a wedding. The woman, exaggeratedly petite beside him was dressed more plainly in a high necked gown that could not conceal the fact that she was beautiful. Thick, jet black hair was piled up high on her head and she stood erect, eyes forward, with her hands resting elegantly on the shoulders of two little girls, *twins?* They looked about the same size, and decidedly Indian, as was their mother. My spine and fingers tingled. *Who was this family and what had happened to them?* I checked my watch. There was no time to pursue the story further. It was four in the afternoon and I had to get going.

The weeks slipped by into early March. The fields, trees and gardens shone verdant neon green and the boughs of the cherry blossom trees that punctuated the landscape, normally unnoticed, popped into showy view, heavily laden with voluptuous, white and pink tinged, blousy clusters of blooms; the invasive, heady scent of which permeated the air.

Becky had organised for us to meet up with Vanessa for lunch at Denny's Cafe in Flagstaff and I waited with excitement and a certain amount of trepidation for the allotted day to arrive. The old familiar sense of belonging engulfed me as I drove into the town that never changed. We three had lived a whole life here as children but so long ago now that it felt like something I'd once read in a book.

I pushed open the heavy, glass doors to the eatery and there was Vanessa with Becky. "Oh my god. You look amazing," the two of us screeched in unison; and *she* did. The Vanessa before me was a complete transformation from the wreck of a woman I had encountered previously. Her appearance was polished from the luxurious mane of gently curling, dark hair that cascaded down her back and floated elegantly over her slender shoulders to the plum red, sheath dress that clung to her curves; *and were those Jimmy Choos?* Two solid gold bangles jangled on her wrist and a very large diamond encrusted cross dangled between the creamy arcs of her cleavage.

Both of us cooed over Lorelei who was sleeping soundly in her baby buggy before alighting about the table, chattering like seagulls. "All together again, like old times," toasted Becky once the drinks were brought. A brief silence ensued while menus were scrutinised and selections made.

"So you're not with Santos any more then?" I asked once the waitress had gone.

Vanessa flicked her luxurious hair and gave a delicate laugh, "Oh, yes I am."

I was surprised and wondered what had happened to change her situation. "But last time I saw you..." I let the question trail off, conscious of the fact that there were aspects of the story that Becky was not privy to.

"That was pretty bad," she concurred. "But when Santos was in jail I decided that I was sick of being treated like a drudge so when he got out I told him it was over. I kicked him out. But within a week he was at my door; oooh I love you babe... oooh let me come back...give me another chance...you know the thing. Heavens, he was such a baby. Anyway, I set down some rules: none of his mates in my house, he keeps his business dealings to himself, and aah," she giggled. "I said I expected a few gifts." She jangled her bangles and winked.

I took a sip of my drink to gather my thoughts while Becky asked, "Are you engaged or planning any kids?"

Vanessa looked at her as if she were mad. "Hell no, I'm never having any - but I'm sure yours are great." She turned to face me. "How's Jonah by the way?"

"He is fine," I assured her before proceeding to fill her in about Eric and concluding with my doubts about whether or not I should marry him.

Becky gasped. "Why not? He's such a nice guy and I thought you were happy with him."

I explained. "I am, kind of, but we are more like flatmates than an engaged, in love couple and we want different things. He wants more children but I don't and I have seen a property I want to buy; only it is semi rural whereas Eric is a city guy, so we don't seem to be able to agree on anything at the moment."

"Give him the flick," instructed Vanessa firmly. "Life's too short to spend it with people who can't contribute positively. What happened to that other guy you were seeing?"

I wasn't sure who she was referring to.

"That cowboy guy," she insisted.

"Luke! I wasn't dating him."

Vanessa looked puzzled. "Oh," she said. "I thought you were."

"No. But you'll never guess. I bumped into him in Hawaii." I began to recount what had happened.

I heard a weird story about him," interrupted Becky. I paused in my narration, curious to hear what she had to say. "Apparently, he was married....or about to be married... anyway, she went nuts and left him." I was shocked. *Why? And how did Becky know that?* "I think she was from one of those old settler families and they didn't like their daughter dating a native."

"Why would that matter these days," I interjected feeling irked by her comment. "He's practically white himself. Anyway, you should see Jonah's class. Only about half of the kids are white American, all the rest are Mexican, Indian or Hispanic."

Becky, clearly not finding the turn the subject was taking to her liking, abruptly changed tack and addressed Vanessa. "Where are you living? And are you working?"

Vanessa explained that she and Santos were living in Dodge City and running a club together there but that they were looking to expand and establish a second club in Melvin. She described their set up. Patrons bought tickets to a cabaret show and a set menu dinner. After the dinner and show, the stage was lowered and turned into a dance floor while the showgirls socialised with the patrons and encouraged them to buy drinks. "The venture is highly profitable," she said.

Becky's sour expression communicated the fact that she did not approve of Vanessa's line of work either. "Sheri is in real estate," she announced, as if by so saying she could convince Vanessa that a career change was in order.

"Really!" exclaimed Vanessa, missing the point entirely. "While I'm over here, I'm supposed to look for a building. I'll come in next week and see what you've got."

I met her at the office. She was with Santos, who proved to be as arrogant as ever, and looking much as he had previously except for a new heaviness about his frame. He didn't offer his hand and I wondered whether he remembered me but if he did, he gave no sign of it. Vanessa looked immaculate and exuded confidence despite the way her shapely legs teetered precariously in their patent leather platforms.

The first premises I wanted to show them was right in the centre of the city with a high profile frontage on two main streets. "It's only up for lease," I explained as I unlocked the door to the office Chrysler, a chunky black and chrome beast that drove like a sports car. "But you never know with these things. You could always make an offer if you wanted to buy." Santos slid his python-like body into the front passenger seat, leaving Vanessa to sit in the rear.

It was only a few minutes' drive to the location and I thanked the gods of car parks under my breath as I pulled into a vacant space in front of the building. "There is parking underneath and also a parking building around the corner on Channing Street," I advised as I fitted the keys into the locks and opened the door into a small foyer. A flight of concrete steps, once painted forest green but now scuffed and worn in places, rose up in front of us. "The space is on the second floor." I indicated for Vanessa and Santos to go ahead.

The stairs led into a bare room where polished wooden floors, despite showing many chips and scratches, reflected the light that streamed in from the floor to ceiling windows and made the space appear vast. There were no fittings except for a bar counter, denuded of taps, that ran along the rear wall.

Santos strolled about the room, inspected the bar and looked out of the windows which offered a panoramic view of the street below. "It will look amazing at night with the lights," commented Vanessa. He grunted and went to inspect the bathrooms.

I imagined what it would be like to live in such a place and realised it would make a great studio for an artist or a musician who needed space and no neighbours. *The bar could be converted into a kitchen and a shower installed in one of the bathrooms.* I made a mental note to talk to Vivienne about it should Santos decline.

Santos re-emerged into the main room. "What else have you got?"

I had two other listings, and I showed them, but to all present it was evident that it was the first property that held the most potential. At the end of the tour, Santos growled, "I'll be in touch," as he walked over to his Porsche. "You commin' or what?" he snapped at Vanessa.

She looked at me. "Do you want to go for coffee?" It was almost lunchtime.

"Sure," I agreed. She relayed this information to Santos who looked mystified as to why she would want to socialise with the agent but he made to climb into his car anyway.

"Don't take all day," he ordered across the car's roof.

Vanessa ignored his comment and joined me in the Chrysler. "I can run you wherever you want after," I offered.

"Of course," she replied. "Effing man thinks he owns me."

I voiced my concern that he would be angry if she was late back but Vanessa merely laughed. "Well he'd better not upset me because I might have to buy something to make myself feel better."

Her comment made me laugh. She was so naughty. But inside I wished that I could maintain more of an attitude like hers. Men, in my experience, were always commenting about how women dressed and the amount of time or money they spent on getting their hair or nails done. But really, why should a woman care what a man thinks about those things? I reasoned.

A conversation of a week ago popped into my head. I had painted my toe nails a bright azure blue, thinking the colour looked pretty and summery. "You look trashy," was Eric's only comment. Crushed, I'd rubbed the polish off and thrown the bottle out. What would he have said if I'd told him to stick it where it fits? I wondered; probably nothing. What could he have said?

"Do you think Santos suspects it was us who dobbed him in all those years ago?" I asked once we were on the road.

"He's never mentioned it but I don't have anything to do with his stuff, his deals and his associates and all that. As far as I'm concerned, as long as he doesn't bring any of it into our home and leaves me out of it, I don't care. He can do what he wants."

I wondered at her attitude. Santos was wealthy, that was evident. What were the chances of his gaining his wealth through legitimate means? The more I thought about it, the more alarm bells rang.

"Don't you worry about getting caught up in something bad?"

Vanessa's eyes narrowed and I could see she was tiring of this line of conversation. "No," she answered. "Why should I? Santos is not a bad person you know. He gives me a great life and usually treats me well, and when he doesn't, I tell him where to get off so you can stop worrying. I'm fine."

I wasn't convinced. I remembered the drive-by and those dark eyes brushing over me, not registering.

"Be careful," I cautioned. And I would be careful about how involved I got with them as a couple. I wouldn't be going to their house for dinner that was for sure.

The year rolled on towards May when Jonah was meant to be going to stay with his father but I had heard nothing and that was Mark in a nutshell; big on charm and talk and small on action, always going to do something yet failing to follow through. It felt as if we were in a deadlock, as if each of us had our own agenda and that whatever either one said or did acted in opposition to the other and prevented either of us from moving forward.

I vacillated by the phone, trying to decide whether to call him or not. To call meant opening the door to the reality of Jonah going to live with his father. And as much as a part of me eagerly relished the thought of freedom from responsibility, another part of me was becoming increasingly aware that my relationship with Jonah was in need of remedial attention before it ended up permanently broken. Although I had no real clue as to how that should or could be accomplished, instinctively I was aware that Jonah and I needed to spend some real time together and that we had to start talking beyond the 'what did you do today' level.

I pictured myself and Jonah in various scenarios like the day we would get a puppy, or a horse to ride, or some chickens and imagined the feel of his hand sliding under the stoic broody feathers of the hen's body as he collected the eggs. As a child I had enjoyed animals and the freedom of life on the ranch but Jonah had not been given any of the same opportunities. I remembered sitting Jonah on the back of Bono, now long gone, and realised that was the last time I had truly delighted in my son and the thought gave me a pang of regret.

Outside, the brilliant day bathed the landscape in sunshine. Fully awake from its winter hibernation, the ground sprung vital signs of life renewed with even the tiniest, most unimportant weeds in full bloom. In the distance shimmered those plumy hills that I had come to love; and nestled beneath them like a secret, the farm that was mine in spirit if not yet in actuality. I made a decision. If Mark called me, then I would talk about it, but if not, I would let things unfold as they may.

I ordered an independent valuation of the property which came in much lower than I'd expected at $140,000. Vivienne suggested that I put in a slightly lower offer so my trembling fingers signed the contract. Later that day, she bustled back into the office with some news. "Old Mrs Cartwright passed away on the weekend and the family have decided to auction the property in about a month's time when they have cleared out her stuff."

Life is full of surprises and disappointed shock rattled through me at the arrival of this unexpected curve ball. It was disconcerting that one so recently alive should now be gone and even though I knew nothing of her other than the few details she had shared with me, it pained me to think of the insignificance of her life.

Vivienne was making encouraging noises saying, "It could work in your favour." I checked the date on the calendar, noting that the auction coincided with the end of the school term. "Why don't you make the offer anyway," I suggested knowing that properties often sold prior to auction, and if the property failed to meet the reserve, then my interest as a potential purchaser would at least be known.

To gauge the competition, I went along to one of the open homes where three parked vehicles indicated at least two prospective purchasers. The house, if anything, had been rendered in even a worse state with the removal of the furniture with decades of stain and fading evident where armchairs had squatted and pictures had hung.

In the kitchen, a woman wearing track pants and a T shirt was gingerly prising open a cupboard with one finger while her husband looked on. "Careful! A mouse could jump out," I quipped.

The woman stepped back, concern that this was a distinct possibility evident in the crease of her brow. Up in the corner of the ceiling, above the stove, spread a rust coloured stain. I studied it intently.

"Is that from a leak?" I mused aloud as if speaking to myself.

"I think it is just from the stove," countered the man, but he inspected the mark a little more closely just to make sure.

The other couple were in the yard. They were young and the woman, frail looking and pale, was discussing the gardens with her man as a stiff gust of wind blew little spinney's of dust about the fruit trees and sent showers of petals swirling into the air. The woman watched as I scuffed a shallow depression into the ground with my shoe. "Cripes. This ground is as hard as rock," I laughed, hoping that any gardening fantasies she may have been harbouring would be dispelled.

My watch said it was three thirty. Earlier than usual, but I was too hyped up to return to work so I called in at Maisie's to collect Jonah. Eric's Audi was parked in the driveway. "What are you doing here so early?" I asked when I saw him in the kitchen nursing a freshly brewed coffee. He kissed the cheek I offered to him. "I had enough for one day so I thought I'd pick up Jonah instead," he explained.

"Snap." I laughed, still high on adrenaline.

With the auction looming, I had to organise finance in order to be in a position to bid so Vivienne pulled strings and booked me an appointment at Fannie Mae, one of the largest mortgage brokers in America.

A few days later, I nervously faced the banker across a broad mahogany desk, the expanse of which was only blemished by a telephone. "Normally," intoned Mr Borrows seriously, *Mr Borrows – seriously!* "we would require a guarantor for the loan, but considering your savings record, *forty thousand dollars,* and your employment record, *nearly ten years fully employed,* plus the valuation of the property, we will be able to pre approve you for finance up to $150,000."

It was a better outcome than I had expected and my grin must have communicated my glee because he rose to his feet and shook my hand. "Congratulations," he said. "If we can be of any more assistance, please don't hesitate to call."

I waltzed out of the office amazed at how simple the process had been. I had expected to have to argue my case but instead had been offered the money on a plate with barely a question asked.

The auction itself was held outdoors, in the front yard of the house and when the Friday of the auction arrived, it was easy to go along without telling Eric who remained oblivious to my recent activities. I arrived early but by 10 o'clock the grassy area was already filling with people although it was impossible to ascertain how many were potential bidders and how many were merely observers.

The day was perfect; clear and still and the bright, blue arc of the sky randomly dotted about with pure white, fluffy clouds hovered above, forming a shining backdrop to the proceedings. The garden lady and her young man were present. I could see them standing close together whispering but of the kitchen couple there was no sign.

After signing in and receiving my number – 125 – painted in black on a white plastic card, a strong sense of being in exactly the right place settled itself in my being. Everything felt as it should be. A gentle breeze lifted wisps of my hair and flicked at the hem of my skirt while far off, the hum of a tractor buzzing faintly and the twittering of nesting birds could be heard as they squabbled in the one remaining Maple tree.

The auctioneer, whom I knew as Mr Clarkson, took his place at the front of the group and after some tapping and squeaking of the microphone, he called the group to order. People, in ones and twos shuffled closer. This was it... He began with a spiel about the property and then opened the bidding at $150,000. With no takers, he dropped the figure by $10,000 then dropped it again. I held off. Vivienne had instructed me to allow the price to find its minimum level. "If the property is passed in, negotiations will ensue," she had said.

The auctioneer was working hard to entice someone to start the bidding. "I'll start at $120,000 and take $5,000 increments," he announced.

The young gardening man raised his ticket. "BID," yelled the nearby bid spotters in unison. I raised my ticket in response and our bids swung back and forth until they reached $135,000 against me. The garden man consulted the garden woman while the auctioneer waited expectantly to see what the young couple would do.

I wondered if they had reached their limit. At that moment, a strong gust of wind swept briskly through the gathering and rattled the windows of the house. The front gutter bounced once, violently, then precipitously fell off and clattered noisily to the ground.

Involuntary titters flew around the group. "It's your bid, sir," urged the auctioneer, sensing that he was losing momentum. The young man shook his head, declining to bid any further. "I will confer with the vendors," the auctioneer said before heading indoors where I presumed they were witnessing the proceedings. After a few minutes, he emerged out of the gloom. "Ladies and gentlemen," he began.

I held my breath.

"I am pleased to announce."

My heart pounded.

"That the reserve has been met."

Oh my god I have bought a house.

"And the property is sold to number 125." He slammed down his gravel and the people clapped then began moving about again like enchanted statues released from a spell.

How did I feel? Light – I felt light. I could have walked on water, jumped over the moon or kissed the ground. I could have danced naked in the moonlight, wept, hugged a tree or performed cartwheels. Instead, I walked demurely over to where Mr Clarkson was organising the sale and purchase agreement for me to sign and told him I would pick the keys up from the office once the deal had settled. He shook my hand and wished me luck.

The place was mine! My house, my stables, my broken gutter! What timing for it to break off like that! *It probably saved me ten grand.* I drifted back to the Jimny in a daze. Now all that remained was to tell Eric what I had done and that was a conversation I was not looking forward to one little bit.

Sometimes, the only option is to come right out with it; to grasp that awful truth by the horns and wrestle it into the open. There would never be a right way to tell Eric that there was not going to be 'us,' that because our visions of the future didn't match we therefore had no future together. He would never understand it. Better to just say it and be done with it.

I felt faint with anxiety the entire evening as I prepared dinner so that by the time we were seated at the table eating, I was all but having a panic attack. The clock showed the time - 7.05 when I literally took a deep breath and said, "I bought the farm."

Eric's fork, bearing a load of chicken pasta to his open mouth paused, mid air, before being slowly lowered to the plate. "What!" he croaked. "You did what?" A flush of blood radiated the skin of his cheeks.

"I bought the property yesterday for $135,000."

"And you didn't think it was important to tell me?"

Although his voice remained calm, I could tell he was angry. But that was Eric's way, calmness at all costs. Odd, I had never realised until that moment how much that irked me. My throat constricted. It was rough to get the words out, to force them through the swelling in my neck. They came out small and feeble. "I knew you didn't want to do it so I bought it myself."

He asked the fateful words. "What about me?"

"I don't know about us, Eric. I'm sorry but I don't want what you want. I don't want any more children. I want the farm and to give Jonah..."

He slammed his open palm onto the table causing the plates to jump and a fork to clatter on to the floor. "What are you saying, Sheri?" he demanded. "Are you breaking up with me?"

Good grief, I didn't want to say it. I didn't. I wanted him to get the picture, to get mad and break up with me, or storm out and slam the door, or shout at me to get stuffed. I felt like the most unappreciative and heartless of women as I squeezed the words out through agonised teeth, "I'm so sorry but it is over." Saying something made it real and I was making our split real.

I slipped the beautiful ring off my finger and placed it on the table between us where its brilliant lustre glowered at me accusingly. "I will move into the house with Jonah next week. You can keep this house if you want, or not, whatever you prefer."

Without saying a word, Eric stood up and stalked, stiff backed, into the lounge, leaving the ring where I'd placed it. I cleared the dishes and resisted the impulse to run after him, to throw my arms around him and make it right and tell him that it was all a mistake, and that I was sorry, sorry, sorry.

We were a torn page. One minute, the script of our life together was readable and the next we were ripped down the middle and the words made no sense. In a heartbeat, we had lost the right to communicate. We were instant strangers.

I washed and dried the dishes then went into Jonah's room where he was watching television. I sat on the bed.

"I bought the farm," I said.

Jonah shrugged without removing his eyes from the screen.

Too tired to explain the ramifications, I left him there and went to bed myself where I tried hard to ignore the empty space beside me as I reassured myself that I had done the right thing and attempted to relax enough to go to sleep...

CHAPTER ELEVEN

...Ellis had been here. I placed the bag of groceries I'd been carrying on the table and inspected his handiwork. The new custom built kitchen was looking superb. Gently, I smoothed the palm of my hand over the polished granite bench-top and marvelled at the coolness of it, admiring the slipperiness, like silk sliding over bare skin. *Ellis' hands have touched these surfaces.*

The wall oven, startling in its newness, gleamed speckled enamel and buffed chrome when I opened the door. I breathed in the unused smell of it. *Like a virgin, touched for the very first time.* Like me. That's what it felt like with Ellis. The cupboards, military accurate swung open their doors on ergonomic hinges to reveal pristine, white, laminated shelving. I was tempted to unpack my things there and then but it would have to wait.

I drifted down the hall to Jonah's room, expecting to see him lounging on his bed but his room was pretty much as it had been that morning. Only his school uniform was different, lying carelessly discarded on the rumpled duvet. *He must be outside then.* Heels clacking on slate tiles, I went into the washroom where I exchanged my shoes for riding boots.

The walk to the stables hadn't changed much as yet. The broken path still meandered through the orchard, only now there was a fenced home paddock where I could keep the horses confined. The late afternoon sun beat down with a stifling stillness. It had been a scorcher of a day.

Through the wide open barn doors, I could see Jonah laying in broken sunlight on a bale of hay with Ruff, our new Labrador puppy, stretched out on his back beside him. I had taken Jonah to the animal re-housing centre the day we had moved in. He'd been so angry and disappointed at the state of his room, which despite a thoroughly professional clean still looked tatty and run down, that I'd hoped the diversion would cheer him up.

When Jonah had knelt beside the cage where Ruff and his three siblings were housed, it had been honey coloured Ruff who'd tottered over and licked at Jonah's fingers through the wire. We were both smitten but he and Jonah were instantly inseparable with Ruff quickly abandoning his own bed in favour of his new owner's. Now the little pup was growling and nipping indignantly at a stalk of straw that Jonah was tickling his nose and mouth with. I leaned against an upright beam.

"Have you packed your bag yet?" As usual, all I received in response was a shrug and a grunt. Jonah was going to his father's for two weeks but this time, instead of eagerly looking forward to the stay, I suspected he had only agreed to go because Ruff was allowed go with him. I hurried my son along, impatient to get him out of my hair. It had been a long four months.

I shouldn't have been surprised to discover that Eric had moved straight in with Maisie after our split, after all they had known each other far longer than Eric and I, but the event stabbed of betrayal. Not only did it feel as if Eric had stolen Maisie's friendship from me, it also disrupted my ability to leave Jonah at Maisie's after school. I managed by leaving work earlier or sometimes taking him with me. And it meant completing the majority of my paperwork at home but at least the solution worked, mostly.

Jonah had seemed more upset about moving out of town and leaving his friends behind than anything else as he had struck up friendships with a lanky, cheerful boy called Bradley and a lad called Tommy, the son of a hospital radiology nurse. Neither of their parents demonstrated any inclination to do their share of running the boys around so more often than not, it fell to me to do so. Some days it felt as if I lived in my car.

I had not expected to cry over breaking up with Eric, it having been my decision, but the separation had hurt and I missed his steady presence. Now and then, in weak moments of yearning, I found myself reaching for my phone, fingers poised above the keys and debating whether I should or shouldn't text him. I had even gone so far as to type in words and phrases and it had taken great presence of will to snap the phone shut and toss it into my bag. From him, I heard nothing and his absence left a hole that confused me. I couldn't understand why I thought about him so much.

Ma had been disappointed when I phoned her. She badly wanted me to find a nice man to settle down and be happy with and on one level I wanted that for myself but on another I was sceptical as to its feasibility. My experiences had taught me that the reality of the happy family was not love all the time; it was love some of the time. Other times, it was frustration, irksomeness and annoyance. It was restriction and a loss of freedom. It was being unable to make your own decisions and dashing home to cook dinner after a hard day while he sat on the couch and watched television. It was having to account for, and answer for, everything I did while he swanned in and out at any time without ever feeling the need to explain himself. It was a double standard that annoyed me and I wondered whether it was even possible for me to live harmoniously with a man.

Clearing up the stables had kept me busy and my mind off men, until I met Ellis that is. Ellis with his lithe, tanned builder's body, brilliant white teeth and swath of dark hair that he tied back with a scrap of elastic. I'd come home at lunch time to meet him and explain the kitchen job when, as if in a movie, our eyes met and our breaths took in appreciative gasps. A clammy sweat broke out on my forehead as I walked under the clearest blue sky towards him, my hand outstretched. Our fingers touched and electricity coursed through them. "Sheri," I stammered, once I'd remembered my own name.

"Ellis," he had replied as his blue eyes twinkled in the knowledge of his effect on me; the same effect that I had on him, apparently, as I had found out barely an hour later. My belly tightened and my knees weakened at the thought of the physical intensity he had brought me to. I felt alive. Every nerve tingled with aliveness while a tight knot lingered in my abdomen where I literally ached for him and calculated the hours when I would see him again. Not on the weekend, I knew that much. He went home on the weekends, wherever 'home' was; but it was easy for me to slip back to the farm during the week days, to 'check on progress,' and to fall into the jumbled bed that hadn't been made for weeks.

Now the summer loomed ahead with Jonah away and Ellis working on the house while I was technically on holiday. Not that I wouldn't work at all. The market was far too busy for that. Everyone agreed that they hadn't seen a property boom like it. Values were rising rapidly and buyers were snapping up properties unseen.

****

Mark wasn't home when I dropped Jonah off and Sophie didn't invite me in so I called "see you later," to my son's retreating back and drove out to Ma and Pa's. The front door was open and Ma emerged onto the porch wiping her hands on her apron. She's looking tired, I thought. We hugged and went indoors where it was cooler. "Pa and Byron will be in soon," she said as she glanced at the clock. The teacups were out and the timing of the teapot down to the minute after decades of practice.

Right on cue, I heard the clumping of the men's boots on the veranda and water splashing in the basin. Then there was Pa's bulky shape to hug and the feel of his bristly cheek against mine. I let the peace and pleasure of the farm and being home settle around me as the chatter of farm life wove itself between us; a feeling that I only dimly realised I was trying to recreate in my own life. An honest feeling. The honest comfort of the rural life.

Once home, my own house felt empty. Amazing how the absence of one boy could echo through the quiet rooms. I kicked around in the kitchen, tidying up and arranging the groceries in the cupboards but outside the sun was blazing and presently, deciding the day was far too good to waste, I pulled on my riding boots and headed over to the yard where Jasper, my recently acquired ten year old bay gelding, stood slumped under the lone Maple tree. I'd bought him cheap from a teenager who had lost interest and although he was not the best mount, he sufficed. His ears perked up at the slice of bread I offered him and he allowed me to slip a halter over his head.

My objective was to scout out the back of the property. I hadn't been up there yet and I was curious to see it. From the stables it didn't look as if anything was there as the land was flat right up to the boundary but Mrs Cartwright had claimed that at least ten acres climbed into the foothills where her brother had once found the nugget of gold.

Jasper's gait was lethargic with the heat as we followed the right boundary fence; a solid, five wire, post and batten affair on the other side of which the Bowman's land, all 2500 acres of it, stretched westward with nary a living creature in sight. A meadowlark warbled high overhead but there were no other sounds. We could have been alone in the world. The sun beat down and I was glad of the broad brimmed Stetson that shaded my face. Before long, the fence veered left at a right angle to the base of what appeared to be a wash.

I dismounted and untied a lead rope from around Jasper's neck then secured him to the fence where he could graze on the dried tufts of grass while I explored. There was no gate that I could see so I clambered over the wires, taking care not to snag my jeans on the top barbs as they strained and creaked under my weight. On the other side, the ground sloped gently upwards, stony and uneven while the wash, a narrow channelling, maybe ten meters wide, was defined by a chaotic jumble of bleached, white stones that spilled out in a fan over the paddock. Larger stones and even small boulders could be seen further up. I deduced that severe weather and floods had caused the stony beach to be flushed down the watercourse although when this had last occurred, I had no idea. It looked as if the stones had been there for a very long time.

Concentration was required as I picked my way over the rocks that rolled and shifted under my feet. The surrounding scrub was dry and thorny. A spiky leaf tip pierced my thumb, drawing blood. The stones I disturbed with my boots didn't look anything special, just the granite bedrock that was common to the area. I stumbled and clambered up the dry watercourse, debating whether to continue. If I slipped and hurt myself, I would be stuck up here and no one would ever know. But my curiosity was burning. I could see a broken plank of wood jutting out from the dirt which indicated something man made had once been up there.

Figuring that the safest route appeared to be up the left side of the stream bed which was also the inside curve where there appeared to be fewer loose stones and more bedrock, I clambered up. It was hard work with the sun beating down and not so much as a sip of water but it wasn't far. After fifteen minutes, I pulled myself up over the edge of a dry cascade only to see the stream bed curving to the east in a sweeping arc while the western flank swept out in a broad flat curve.

I knew that the inside curves of alluvial streams were prime spots for gold to collect but there was nothing to indicate that it was actually so. Towards the edge of the stony flat, tucked under some bushes, lay a small bundle of decaying planks much like the broken piece I had found earlier but without pushing into the scrub there was no way of ascertaining where the planks came from. A little breeze rustled the leaves. It was totally silent and a little eerie. I felt perishingly overheated and in dire need of a drink. Whatever else there was to find here, it would have to wait for another day when I was better equipped.

After scrabbling and sliding down the mini waterfall, mostly on my backside, it was a relief to climb up on Jasper and ride home. He trotted most of the way and would have cantered but I held him back not wanting him to expire with heat exhaustion. Once in the yard, I led him to the trough where he splashed his muzzle about in the clear water and hoovered in great gulps of the liquid so that it moved in a visible blob down his gullet. Finally, his thirst quenched, he rubbed his sweaty forehead against my shirt before blowing his snotty nose over my shoulder. It was late in the afternoon when, tired and filthy, I retired to my house where I showered and made an egg on toast before falling into bed with a cup of tea to watch TV But I was too tired to keep my eyes open so it wasn't long before I switched the television off and fell into a dreamless sleep.

Hours later, through the dimness of my subconscious, my brain registered that my phone had gone off. I switched on the light and had a look.

It was Ellis. "Wats up," the message said.

I looked at the clock – 11.30 pm. What kind of a time was that to text? I texted my reply, "sleeping, where r u?"

"Out with sum m8s want a visitor?"

He was out but didn't ask me out? A brief pang shot through me that I ignored at the thought of Ellis in my warm bed.

"Sure," I replied.

An hour later when I was drifting into unconsciousness for the second time, I heard a vehicle slow on the road and pull into the driveway. Hobbling out of bed and pulling my robe about me, I shuffled off to open the door. In the silence of the dark, he stood, swaying, slightly drunk but looking hotter than ever. He stepped into me, then sliding his cold hands beneath my robe, he caressed my waist. His alcohol scented mouth sought mine as he walked me backwards into the house. I took his hand and led him to the bedroom.

"You are lucky Jonah isn't here."

"I know. You told me. He's at his dad's."

He chucked his clothes off onto the floor and slid naked under the covers. I slipped in beside him where he was already turning urgently towards me.

In the morning he was gone and I only vaguely recalled him speaking of work. I stretched my limbs luxuriously and revelled in the feeling of relaxed well-being coursing through my veins. *How little I know of him. I don't even know his last name.* Yet we had been tumbling intimately in the sheets for two months now. The shiny Sunday stretched into the distance. I sent him a message. "You left early?" He didn't reply.

On Monday morning, as much as I wanted to stay and talk to Ellis once he arrived (although I had no idea when that would be) I had some calls to make at the office. Santos had contacted me to say that he wanted to lease the building but that there were conditions.

Once at my desk, I dialled the number provided and arranged to meet with his solicitor at an address on the northern side of the city. I drove out into the suburbs. It had rained during the night and the foliage of the plants and trees glistened with plump drops that would soon evaporate.

Upon finding the entrance to the property, I guided the car up the winding concrete driveway. Leafy calla lilies, aflame in shades of orange and yellow bloom, fluttered like a flock of exotic birds in the wake of the car as it wound its way upwards. I could almost feel Santos' eyes bearing down on me from his fortified castle. From up there he would be able to survey everyone who came and went. The drive spilled out onto a wide car park area in front of the four car garaging. The mansion – it could be called nothing else - loomed above; two stories high, square, imposing and blindingly white. I wondered whose place it was. *Didn't Vanessa say they still lived in Dodge City?*

It felt unnaturally quiet on the hill. Not even birdsong punctuated the gentle rustle of the palm fronds that towered over the garden greenery. Locating the path to the front door I made my way up, noting discreet security cameras positioned on the corners of the building. I banged the wrought iron knocker and the sound echoed within. After a few moments, I heard movement and a house keeper opened the door. She was short and neat and wore her dark hair in a tidy bun on the nape of her neck. "Ms Lewis?" she asked in lightly accented American, "Come in. Mr Haviera's solicitor is expecting you."

I stepped into a functional foyer. Several coats hung on a coat rack and a bouquet of umbrellas resided in a carved wooden vase. There was also a low table with a seat attached upon which sat a telephone. The maid opened a door that led off the area and motioned with a wave of her hand for me to enter. Inside was a sizeable room, sparsely furnished with a table and a couple of easy chairs but the room held little personality and gave no clue as to the inhabitants of the house.

The maid indicated that I should take a seat and then left, closing the door behind her on the way out. The silence was unnerving. I wanted to get up and move about and look out of the windows but a fear of being somehow caught out made me stay put and wait. After a few minutes, the door opened and a small, thin man entered the room. "Ah, Ms Lewis," he said as he held out a tiny hand for me to shake. "I'm Gerald Brown and I am representing Mr Haviera's interests today." He laid his briefcase on the table and drew out a sheaf of documents. "Mr Haviera likes the property and feels it will suit his needs but he wishes the owner to effect some repairs and maintenance on the property." He laid the papers in front of me and using his pen as a pointing device, indicated the conditions. "Namely, that the taps on the bar be replaced and the bar area modernised, the flooring replaced and the bathrooms redecorated."

I pointed out that landlords were not usually given to repairs and maintenance on their buildings preferring to see outfitting as being the lessee's problem.

"I understand," said Mr Brown, "but my client is prepared to sign a nine year lease being a three year term with two rights of renewal which would of course be subject to rent reviews at the conclusion of each term."

The lawyer signed the offer and handed it to me. The whole meeting had taken less than ten minutes. We shook hands and I said that I would get onto it straight away. After spending the remainder of the day in pursuit of organising the details, I was exhausted but I managed to arrive home in time to find Ellis packing tools into his battered truck. He had been repairing the weatherboards on the outside of the building and anchoring the gutter once more to its rightful position. I offered him a cold beer and we sat on the deck and drank. I badly wanted to ask him about his life but there was a tension between us, an invisible barrier that did not invite questions.

"Did you know the house had a veranda once?" I said, seeking safe ground. "It was blown down in a tornado years ago."

Ellis peered up at the eaves. "Oh yeah. You can see the stubs of the beams where they were attached. The house must be old I think."

"At least a hundred years." I praised his work in the kitchen. He looked pleased. "How long have you been building?" I asked.

"About five years." He took a swig on his bottle. "I completed an apprenticeship under George Woollett, an old guy. He's dead now. Last year. He had a heart attack."

"So you work for yourself?" It was a question but one that I knew the answer to. "Do you employ anybody else?"

He smiled. "Nope. I do it myself. It's easier that way."

We pulled on our beers. The sun peeked out from gold edged clouds bathing our faces with instant heat.

"Where do you live then?"

"In town." His voice was smooth and pleasant but he did not volunteer any further information.

"And I suppose you bonk all your female clients?" I teased.

He leaned towards me and aimed a peck at my cheek.

"Not all of them," he retorted cheekily. "Only the pretty ones."

I wasn't sure whether to be pleased at being called pretty or hurt at the intimation that I was only one of many conquests. Instinctively, I wanted to challenge him on it but I had only known him a couple of months and didn't feel I had the right to ask. It wasn't as if we were officially together after all.

The next few days were taken up with setting the house in order and the daily chores with the animals. Ellis was working on the bathroom with the plumber so there were no opportunities for illicit afternoon romps in the bedroom. It was his last job. The house was in sound repair and all the major work completed. Only redecorating was left to do and I figured I could paint and wallpaper as well as anybody.

In between installing the new shower unit and basins, I commissioned Ellis to construct a chicken coop; a walk in affair with a roosting house and three laying boxes. Then I drove to the house of a local breeder and bought half a dozen virginal pullets in various shades of white and red. Their black, beady eyes peered at me from smooth heads, the promise of their little combs merely a rubbery nub of pale flesh. I let them go in the fenced yard and they tentatively stalked about the enclosure uttering slow, raspy croaks. For several evenings I had to go out and place the slower learners on their perch, then they all got the idea and I didn't have to do it anymore.

By the following Friday afternoon, the plumber was connecting the pipes to the mains water supply. He poked his head out around the door to where I was pouring cold drinks in the kitchen. The cooler weather from earlier in the week had passed and the temperatures were testing. The doors and windows stood wide open in order to catch the faintest breeze. "Should be all done in an hour," he called. I took the drinks into the bathroom where Ellis was sealing the screw holes in the new laminate panelling. They took the chilled glasses from the tray and drank thirstily. Sideways, I watched Ellis and wondered whether we would still see each other. It seemed unimaginable that we wouldn't as the physical connection between us was a tangible thing, like an invisible cord that joined us together. But when the men emerged from the bathroom, it was in unison and they had their tools in hand. The plumber spoke. "All done. If there are any probs' give me a call." He handed me a business card. 'Bob's Plumbing,' It read.

I smiled at Ellis and looked at him in a way that he might interpret as being meaningful. "And what about you?"

He smiled back. "Yep. All finished too. The painting needs doing but everything is watertight. Maybe leave off using the shower till tomorrow to let the sealer set properly but after that she's good to go."

The two men walked out to their respective trucks and I followed Ellis to his. Anxiety was making my heart pound uncomfortably. "Will I see you again?" I asked; suddenly shy, as he arranged his tools and equipment in the back of the tray.

"What?" His air was distracted. He had pulled out his phone and flipped it open.

I repeated myself and steeled my voice into a harder, colder shape. "Will I see you again?"

'Of course," he said casually. He climbed into his truck and slammed the door shut. "I'll call you." He turned the key and revved the engine, then reversed out of the driveway and sped off down the road. Bob, who had been parked in front of Ellis, swung his truck about and followed suit; giving a brief salute as he left.

Be cool. Be cool. My heart and throat felt constricted, tight. I didn't want to cry. And maybe his leaving so functionally, as if I was just any old client, didn't mean anything anyway. He couldn't very well kiss me in front of the plumber - and he did say he would call. Maybe he would call. I didn't know where I stood. That was the problem. Too upset to go back into the house, I headed over to the stables and spent an hour on Jasper riding barrels at a trot and slow canter. He was stiff and awkward but the energy expended slowly subsided the hurt rage so that my breath came more freely.

Over the next few days, while I waited for Ellis to call, I redecorated Jonah's room and the physical activity kept my mind occupied as I scraped, peeled cleaned and painted. The carpet, a disgusting, musty heap of fibre, I gladly consigned to the pile of demolition debris in the paddock ready to be burned once summer was over, and replaced it with a tightly woven, hard wearing carpet in a chocolate chequered pattern that complemented the stone coloured paint on the walls. But my phone, always nearby, remained silent. Eventually, unable to stand the tension of not knowing any longer, I sat on the end of Jonah's bed and texted him. "How are u?"

Ten minutes later, a reply. "Busy."

"Do you want to come over?"

'Can't soz. I'm in Chadwick."

Chadwick was a small town about forty five minutes away. I breathed with relief. So that was why I hadn't heard from him. He was working away. "Shall I come to you?" I typed.

"If you want. Highway Motel, main road."

In an ecstasy of excitement, I dashed about the house throwing underwear, spare clothes and toiletries into a travel bag. I rummaged in my wardrobe and flicked through my clothes before settling on a low scoop neck tank top and jeans.

The evening gathered behind me as I drove through deserted country roads with the top thirty hits of 10KO Live blaring on the radio. In no time at all, the dim streetlights of Chadwick came into view and the GPS announced that I had arrived. I found the motel easily and pulled into the car park. "I'm here," I texted.

A door opened and I saw his silhouette framed by the dim glow of the lamplight from the room. The motel room was seedy; a plain, bare space dominated by a sagging bed carelessly covered with an over washed pink quilt, ugly shower and toilet, separate kitchenette with a microwave, hot plate and jug, greasy pizza box on the bench top, cardboard remains of a beer box on top of the rubbish tin. My eyes swept the room as I entered and took it all in. He aimed a kiss at my cheek as I squeezed past him and missed. I stood, arms folded, uncertain, as he flopped back on the bed. The television was going and he patted the bed beside him to indicate that I should join him. I sat tentatively on the edge feeling inexplicably restless. "How have you been?" I asked as I jumped up again and looked in the fridge – a small carton of milk, that was all.

"Yeah good," he replied. "Busy."

"So where are you working?"

He yawned and ran his hand through his hair. "Oh, just reroofing some lady's house in town."

"Do you have any food?" I demanded. Feeling agitated, I wanted to goad him. He lay there so unknowing of how I was feeling that he irritated me.

"Na. Sorry," he said without looking up. He picked up an open can of bourbon from the bedside table and swallowed a mouthful. I was hungry, not having eaten since lunchtime and this was not going how I had envisaged. "Have you had dinner?" I asked.

"I had the rest of that pizza," he replied. "There's a diner down the road if you wanna go and get something."

I sat in the lone chair and contemplated him. Was this all there was of him? When he was building he had seemed vitally alive, but here relaxing, it was as if all of his personality had drained away leaving him faded and empty. *What was I doing here?* I stood abruptly.

Ellis looked over, startled. "What's up?" he asked.

"I think I'll go home," I said.

His expression was genuinely mystified, and maybe he was. "Why? You just got here."

I was bored already but didn't want to say it.

I picked up my bag. "Look, you're tired," I deflected.

He rubbed his eyes. "Yeah, I am. Sorry. But you don't have to go."

He didn't seem to realise that I had any expectation other than to lie down beside him on the ancient quilt and watch television. He truly had no idea that I might have liked to go out to dinner or at least be offered a drink.

'No its okay," I continued, trying to make my voice sound gentle and understanding rather than accusing. "Call me next week." Though I doubted he would. I made no move to kiss him and he made no move to get up.

"See ya," he said. Then, "Thanks for coming," he added quickly as if in afterthought. I closed the door behind me and climbed gratefully back into my Chevy.

On the outskirts of town, I spotted a McDonald's and pulled over. The bright lights of the interior spilled cheerfully out over the tarmac. I ordered a Big Mac Combo and found a booth. It felt strange to be eating at McDonald's without Jonah. My thoughts picked at the tangled subject of Ellis. I figured it was over and just a fling after all although it seemed unbelievable those two months of intense sexual intimacy could be nothing deeper than just that.

Outside the window, the headlights of vehicles flashed by in both directions and I wondered where the people were going. The dark night surrounded the little McDonald's oasis of light. Nothing could be seen beyond the shadowy reaches of the car park, where within my Chevy sat squarely. I felt a flash of pleasure. I'd bought the truck so as to transport my supplies and felt like a real adult while driving it.

A sudden yearning for home welled over me and I saw myself boiling the jug and making a cup of hot tea in my gleaming new kitchen, and the glowing cosy nest of my bedroom. I had achieved a lot in the ten years since Jonah was born. *Ellis and I would never have made a good couple.* Already, he seemed very young to me. *I want a man who is my equal.* Eric had been my equal financially but not in vision. He was too traditional. He would suit a woman like Becky, a real wife and home maker.

What I needed was a man to go forward in life with. *To what end?* I envisioned myself in the future; ten years hence, nearly forty, and saw a beautiful home, lilies in a vase in the hallway and the acres of my ranch stretching out in all directions, horses grazing in the paddocks. *But not Ma and Pa's life!* Not thousands of acres filled with thick headed Herefords; a smaller property. A horse breeding property or one devoted to horse sports? Barrel racing, horse racing and a like minded man to share it with. *Not a city man, a banker or even a mechanic.* He would have to have the skills and passion to manage and train the horses and we would have to keep our jobs until the horses were making enough money to support themselves, but the idea filled me with excitement. I would start a horse sport enterprise. I didn't know how it would turn out but I knew how to start. I would buy at least one good horse, maybe two if I could afford it, and begin training them in readiness for the barrel racing event at the Melvin Rodeo as a part of the Melvin Agricultural Show.

Finding a good horse at a price a normal person could afford proved to be more challenging than I had imagined. After much reading of horse trading magazines, I found a promising Quarter Horse / Morgan gelding, ten years old, in Mercy and headed off to make the four hour round trip a few days later.

It was surprising how quickly the landscape changed as I drove south. While still flat, the prairies were much greener and nowhere near as stony. Groves of mammoth trees dotted the plains, planted no doubt over a hundred years ago by the early settlers. Everything looked immaculate. Even the fences delineating the grand, wrought iron gates to the region's properties were constructed from stained timber and sported well maintained garden beds planted along their perimeters.

The GPS guided me to the entrance of 'Stanford Ranch' which looked much like the others I had passed, only the paddocks by the road were dotted with brood mares grazing while their pretty foals lay dozing in the sun at their feet. It was all very picturesque and I thought with a pang of embarrassment of my own place which would only ever appear dilapidated next to this established luxury that photosynthesised money through every blade of grass.

The Chev's tyres crunched up the sweeping driveway until they came upon a sprawling homestead that reminded me of Scarlett O'Hara's Tara, so white and 'southern' was the style of the building. As I pulled up, a short and sturdy woman with closely styled dark hair emerged on to the wide veranda. She waited for me to approach before extending a smooth hand. "Sooky," she said. She turned, and led me down a meandering landscaped path to a small paddock where a grey horse, tied to a railing, stood waiting patiently. He pricked his ears at our approach and his manner was alert and interested as we breathed each other's breath by way of introduction.

I couldn't help but exclaim, "What a lovely horse!" Standing around 15hh, his head and neck were almost completely white but tiny flecks of chocolate dotted the remainder of his body, deepening slightly as they spread across the curve of his flanks.

I stroked his silky neck and asked, "Is he part Appaloosa?"

"His mother was. His sire was a Morgan cross. What were you wanting him for?

I explained that I wanted the horse for barrel racing. "I did it as a kid, for fun but I'd like to give it a proper go."

She nodded in agreement. "Tiddlywinks would be perfect for that. He's done it before, a little. He's got the breeding."

"So why are you selling him?" I asked.

"He's a gelding; sorry boy," she laughed. "And no one rides him anymore. He's a good horse going to waste, aren't you darling?" She rubbed his forehead. I could see that she felt affection for him and that it would be difficult for her to part with him. "My son used to ride him but he's gone now," she added, wistfully. "Actually, I'm sorry that we gelded him but when he was young, he looked to have a short back. His conformation was not one hundred percent, don't you know, but he grew out of that. Now you would never tell. Well, we can't keep all of them, can we?"

I felt certain that I would take him but I went through the appropriate checks of teeth, legs and hooves. He was in perfect condition.

"I've brought my gear. Can I try him?" I asked.

Of course that was fine and it struck me as I settled the saddle onto Tiddly's back that if I was as thorough in checking out the suitability of the men I dated, I would have a lot less trouble with them.

The horse's gait proved to be comfortable and he responded to my commands promptly. I took him through a series of figure eights and his leg changes were smooth and practiced. Whoever had trained this horse had done a very good job. Feeling confident that we would quickly come to understand each other, I walked Tiddlywinks back to the fence.

"You can certainly ride," commented Sooky.

I slid off. "I have been riding all my life, mostly on the ranch, nothing competitive. It will be new to me." I ran up the stirrups and pulled the saddle off his back while Sooky produced a rag from her pocket and rubbed him down where he had sweated under the blanket.

"Where's your ranch?"

"Pa's ranch. My name is Sheriden Lewis. My Pa is Sherman Lewis from Flagstaff."

Sooky looked at me strangely and gave a short laugh. "Sherman Lewis – well I'll be. I went to school with Sherman. He was a few years ahead of me. All the girls loved him."

No way! I looked at this woman afresh. *Why was it always so difficult to imagine one's parents as anyone other than your own mother and father?* "I'll tell Pa I met you," I said. "What was your surname name again?"

"Stanford."

Oh Yeah.

"I married Hank. Tell him I married Hank. That will tickle him. I married Hank and came here."

Small world.

I said that Tiddlywinks was perfect for me and that I would take him.

"Come on in and have a drink and we can talk about the details," she said.

The house was as elegant inside as it was on the outside and my newly appreciative eyes admired how the expansive, naturally cool tones of the marble bench tops complemented the blonde oak of the kitchen cupboard doors turning them into features in themselves.

"Right, let's talk business," said Sooky as she poured chilled tea into two highball glasses and added ice direct from an ice maker built into the refrigerator door.

"If you give me your bank account, I can do a direct online transfer," I offered. "But I don't know how to get him home. I don't have a float. Can you deliver him?"

Sooky's elfin face creased into a frown. "Oh dear... yes... that could be a problem... Hank is very unwell at the moment. He has diabetes, don't you know, and he's having a terrible time with his kidneys.... I don't know." She sighed, a troubled sigh.

"Do you have a float I could borrow? I have a tow ball on my truck."

She thought about it. "Yes, we do. I guess you could borrow it." Her voice trailed off.

"I'll come and get him on Sunday then and bring the float back the next day," I said. It would mean two more trips but I couldn't think of any other option.

During the drive home, my mind organised solutions for the difficulties involved, namely, that I would need to take the day off work on Monday as well as phone Ma to see if she would have Jonah for a few days. As planned, two days later, with work and Jonah taken care of and the money in Sooky's account, I headed back to Stanford's.

The float was in the barn and together, Sooky and I manoeuvred the hitch onto the tow ball and secured the safety chain, lights and towing mirrors. I lay on the ground and peered at the under chassis which was predictably rust free. Likewise, all the mats and boards were in good condition. Slowly, I towed the float forward until it was in the yard and well clear of the barn. Sooky lowered the ramp and I filled the hay net with hay. Tiddly, who was tied up and waiting nearby, nickered softly, sensing change was in the air. Sooky had already bandaged his tail and put on his rubber boots ready for the long trip so all I had to do was settle a brand new anti sweat rug over his shoulders before she loaded him in. He walked up willingly and together we hooked up the back chain and closed the ramp. We were ready to go.

Sooky had a little tear in her eye and looked undeniably downcast. "Don't worry," I consoled her. "He will be good with me. I'll look after him and you can come and visit whenever you want. I'm on West Range Road in Melvin. I'll send you an email."

"Oh my, I'm such a baby," she half giggled. "Don't mind me."

"Are you going to the Melvin show?" I mentioned that Pa was entering a bull in the cattle section and that I was hoping to have Tiddly ready in time for the barrel racing in the rodeo.

Sooky said she would keep it in mind. "But Hank, you know, he is so terribly unwell."

Given that I hadn't seen another soul, I wondered how she managed this sprawling ranch with her husband being out of action. In a rush of earnest empathy, I grasped her small hands in mine, feeling an inexplicable connection with this gentle woman. "If I can help with anything, please let me know," I urged.

I waved goodbye and cautiously pulled out. Initially, waves of fright pricked at my scalp and hands at every unfamiliar creak and groan. I could feel the weight of Tiddly as he shifted and moved but as we both settled into the ride, I felt myself relax. The float towed smoothly and the V8 engine of the Chev' purred like a contented cat. Half way home, I pulled over to check on the horse who was munching on his hay. His ears pricked up as I opened the little side access door and poked my head in, showing him to be fine, so we continued on. Nevertheless, it was with relief that I pulled safely into the driveway of home just as the sun was sliding down on to the horizon.

The alarm woke me from deep sleep the following morning as scheduled. The night before, I had merely unloaded

Tiddly into a stall and left him there with a mixed hard feed. Before making the return journey to Stanford's, I wanted to introduce him to Jasper so I could set him free in the paddock and clean up the float. When Jasper saw Tiddly, his head shot up and he trotted importantly over to the fence. The two horses breathed into each other's nostrils and Jasper gave a territorial squeal. I pushed open the gate and it necessitated a certain amount of dexterity to push Jasper out of the way and manoeuvre Tiddly in without getting squashed. On Tiddly's release, the two horses careened off across the paddock, tails high. I wished I could stay and watch them but the day was ticking on already so I loaded the rack with a fresh wedge of fragrant, lucerne hay and left. The horses ignored me. They were too busy rubbing each other's shoulders with their teeth as they stood neck to neck under the tree.

CHAPTER TWELVE

Work was crazy during the summer of 2001 and with three lucrative deals going unconditional in one week, I was fast running out of properties to sell. I had two thousand flyers printed and then went door knocking which resulted in several new listings and numerous enquiries but with so much money to be made, competition for the few available properties on the market was fierce. Even within the office, the more unscrupulous agents thought nothing of poaching the potential clients of others and I had been dismayed to once find my own clients tucked up cosily in Nathan's office instead of waiting for me, as expected, in the waiting room, when I was five minutes late for the appointment. I had glared at him through the window but he hadn't even the grace to look ashamed. It was everyone for themselves.

Vivienne and I met for lunch, ostensibly to talk about the situation, but girl talk was getting in the way...

"Have you heard from him?"

"No but it's only been a week."

If he were really interested, surely he would have called by now?" Vivienne was speaking and her voice was tentative. I could see that she was trying to let me know, gently, that she believed the affair had merely been a sexual fling for Ellis and as much as I didn't want it to be true, common sense told me she was probably right. The trouble was I couldn't even rightfully complain about feeling used because hadn't we both jumped into bed without any kind of (unromantic) discussion or clarification of what we expected from each other, or even of basic ground rules? I had just assumed that the attraction was mutual and that it meant something more but he, clearly, had not felt the same way.

"So what's with you?" I probed coyly. "Who's new in your life? You know you're a very dark horse, Vivienne. I hardly know anything about you."

At this she shrugged her slight shoulders and shifted uneasily. "Oh, you know me, nothing much, just work, work, work. And so saying, we really should get on and discuss what we are going to do about those nasty boys stealing our clients." She glanced at the delicate bracelet watch that dangled loosely about her wrist. "Time is ticking on."

She flicked a brief smile and the effect was like sun coming out after rain. She really is beautiful, I thought, but at the same time, I felt somewhat crushed at her reluctance to share anything about her life. I'd thought we were becoming friends. Apart from Becky and Vanessa, I had to confess that I found friendships a struggle. It wasn't just the time factor, although some would have considered my life to be hectic, the fact was that most women with children Jonah's age had at least ten years on me while most women my age were either still childless or just having their first babies. *The things you have no idea that you need to think about when you fall pregnant at a young age.*

Vivienne's immaculately manicured fingers toyed with the bread knife as she continued. "We need to work together and look out for each other and I think we could do that by coordinating our clients better. For example, say if you were out of the office and expecting a client and I was in, then I could greet the client for you and 'hold them' so to speak until you return and vice versa. That way the boys can't just go up to them and poach them from under our noses.

I nodded. It would mean we would have to keep each other informed as to our movements and schedules but the extra trouble would be worth it. I shared what I had accomplished with the flyers to which she added the comment, "Another thing I have done before is drive about and put a flyer advertising my listings in the mailboxes of homes for sale through other companies. I read once that over seventy percent of people who sell a property buy their new one within ten miles of the old one."

It felt good to be collaborating with Vivienne because even though I had gained my real estate sales licence some time ago, and was considered a fully qualified member of the team, it had taken considerably longer to actually feel accepted.

As I drove past the Lumberton Road property that afternoon, I noticed that the door was open, so upon seeing a parking space handy, I quickly pulled in and headed over to check on progress. "Hi. I'm Sheri, the property manager," I said in response to the curious looks cast my way.

The builders were hard at it and the bathrooms in particular were already vastly improved in appearance with the black and white tiled floors and freshly painted, pale lime green walls creating a pleasing contrast to the dewy, pearlescent white of the Japanese styled, porcelain basins. The only criticism I felt applied to the high curving tap spouts. While elegant and attractive, I knew that they would splash water everywhere once turned on. Chromed spot lighting bounced bright light off the full length mirrors and I could imagine the women, gaudy and giggly, reapplying their lipstick and tizzying with their hair before heading back out onto the dance floor.

Emerging from the bathroom, I bumped into Santos. Unaccountably, I felt guilty even though I had every right to be there. "Santos!" I exclaimed, heartily. "I saw the place open and came up for a nosey. It's all looking fabulous. What do you think? Are you happy with it?"

Santos' eyes roved absently about the room implying that he would rather be anywhere else except talking to me and his uncalled for demonstration of distain provoked within me a shudder of irritation and annoyance at his arrogance. "It's a perfectly valid question, Santos," I snapped, "but if it's too much trouble to have a conversation with me, I will go and leave you to it."

He started and I was gratified to see a tinge of pink flush over his neck. "No. What?" he grumbled. "It's all fine. Thanks."

I wanted to ask after Vanessa as I hadn't seen her for months but he wasn't a man you could hold such a basic conversation with, besides which, he had irritated me so thoroughly I had no further inclination to stand there and make small talk myself. Honestly, the man was a Neanderthal and I didn't understand what Vanessa saw in him. He so naturally believed all women were beneath him; yet Vanessa wielded power over him and kept him in his place. Her power, it was her beauty and sexuality surely, that kept Santos interested. Well, whatever she was doing, I wasn't. I couldn't even keep an air head like Ellis interested.

At home that night I studied myself in the bedroom mirror. If I wasn't glamorous like Vanessa or Vivienne, I also wasn't homely like Becky. I looked like I was, a busy working mum. And what is wrong with looking like that? I asked myself, unable to think of anything.

After conducting two showings on Saturday morning, I drove home eager to saddle up Tiddly and have a ride. It had been a week already since he had come to live with us and this was the first time I'd had a spare moment to spend with him. It was also my last free day before bringing Jonah home and I could not say I was looking forward to having him back because there is nothing quite so awkward to accommodate as children at home during school holidays when you have to work.

Tiddlywinks was filthy and it took me a fair while to brush all the dirt out of his speckled coat. Once having done so, I paced out the paddock and arranged the three barrels I had collected previously so that they were roughly the correct distance apart. There are rules governing such things, and while I wasn't completely sure of the finer details, I remembered the formulae Pa had told me when I was little, of 90, 105 and 60, being the number of feet between the barrels and the score line respectively; although these dimensions were readily made longer or shorter in a competition course. I also knew that for the professionals, a fast time was around sixteen seconds but it would take a considerable amount of work before Tiddly and I were able to ride a course that speedily.

After an hour of riding clover leaf pattern, first at a trot, then at a slow canter, Tiddly and I were both sweating profusely and it was with relief that I unsaddled him and hosed him down unmindful of the splashes that soaked my jeans and shirt. So involved were we in playing with the hose that it was only a fortuitous glance that drew my attention to a figure loitering by the back door of the house.

"HOY!" I shouted as loudly as I could. The figure paused and then, identifying the direction from which my shout had originated, waved. A few moments later, Ellis' battered truck bumped into view. This was a turnaround! I turned off the hose and scraped the excess water from Tiddly's flanks with the edge of my palm before tying him up in the shade of the barn to dry. The truck shuddered to a noisy halt and Ellis, sexy as ever, sauntered over to where I stood, taking care to avoid the puddle of water that was slowly dissolving a manure pile on the track.

'Well," I said. "What brings you here?" I was a little dumbfounded. Having come to the conclusion that I was just a fling, and having essentially cut him loose, it was disconcerting to find him within my close proximity again.

"I was passing by and thought I'd drop in," he replied. *Passing by? Going where?* Unfortunately, I hadn't noticed which direction he had been travelling in. The conversation faltered and we both stood there, eyes fixed on the ground, feeling awkward. Ellis scratched his head and commented, "Nice horse," while indicating Tiddly with a nod.

"Yes. I bought him last week. I'm planning to try him in the Melvin Show. Do you ride?"

"Me? Nah. I've had nothing to do with horses." He patted his pocket in a move that indicated a habit of looking for smokes, but then, as if remembering that I didn't smoke and may not approve, he ceased the action and folded his arms in a manner that was faintly protective. "What are you doing now?" he continued.

"I was just going to clean up and then go and make some tea," I replied. "Why? Did you have a plan?"

"No. Not exactly. I was passing by and thought I would see what you were up to," he explained for the second time. Plainly, he was communicating in some form of 'man-speak' and I had to interpret the code. Was he testing the waters; seeing how reciprocal I was for sex? I almost burst out laughing. How completely the wheel had turned. Now I held the cards and was in the driving seat.

"I don't know, Ellis. I've been having second thoughts. I don't think you're right for me. That is, I know we're not together or even dating but I don't want a relationship that is only about sex."

I could see that he was taken off guard. He had assumed that because I was hot for him I would fall into bed again without a second thought. How the dynamics of our relationship had changed in a few short weeks.

'Yeah, yeah, right, I get it. But I broke up with my girlfriend...." His voice trailed off as he realised the confession had not come out as intended.

"What girlfriend is this?" I asked. "Were you with her while you were with me?"

His eyes flicked this way and that in panic. "Yeah but it wasn't working out. We were having problems."

"So she gave you the flick!"

He looked guilty; much like Jonah did when he was caught with his fingers in the biscuit tin.

I sighed. "Look Ellis, I had a good time with you and if you had said back then, a few weeks ago, that you would have liked us to keep dating I would have said yes - but you didn't. You just left and I didn't even get a text. You didn't even ask me if I wanted a drink for crying out loud."

"I couldn't," he protested.

"Yeah. Because you already had a girlfriend," I snapped. "Thanks for telling me." At that moment, something within me rose up; a cold, calculating shard of power so sharp that it made me want to chop him off at his feet. I wanted to hurt him even worse than he had hurt me. I wanted to win.

"Anyway," I continued, "once a cheat, always a cheat. You are obviously not trustable, and I'm over you so you should probably go. You're not man enough for me."

'If that's the way you feel," he responded. Without saying goodbye, he strode over to his truck and flung himself in. And if I had to gauge the extent of his upset by the quantity of gravel his tyres sprayed outwards as he spun his wheels and left in a thick haze of dust, I could count my grievance fully satisfied.

I let Tiddly go with a sense of lightheaded relief and headed back over to the house. As I was cutting across the paddock, my phone rang. It was Felicity Nugent, a realtor from Jepson's Real Estate, a competing firm in town. She was calling to say that one of her clients, who had attended one of my viewings that morning, was ready to make an offer. I smiled as I calculated my portion of the commission to be in the vicinity of ten thousand dollars. I would install a new wood burner and replace the insulation on that. Life was good.

...And back to reality. I got the lowdown on how Jonah had been from Ma in the quiet time before the men came in for lunch.

"He's been good," she said. "But he doesn't say much."

I agreed. "No. He's not a talker."

"It's difficult to know what's going on in that young head of his." She came over to the table and sat down opposite to where I was sitting and took both of my hands in her own. "Honey, does Jonah ever seem angry to you?"

My heart sank. "Why, what's he done?"

"Nothing exactly... it's just... I don't know... He doesn't just not speak much, when he does speak, he sounds angry. Like yesterday, I asked him if he wanted some more ham, and he said 'no,' only he said it, 'NO!'" Ma growled out the word as if it was the tenth time she'd been forced to answer the same question and was sick of it.

I knew what she was trying to say and I knew that was how Jonah often spoke but not ever having discovered a reason for it, or a way to resolve it, I had resigned myself to accepting his short temper as a personality trait.

"Does he talk like that to Pa?" I asked.

Ma replied that she didn't know but knowing Pa was not much of a talker either, I imagined that they communicated even less than we did so it probably was not an issue between them.

I rubbed my eyes with the heels of my hands. "Look Ma, I've been aware of Jonah's propensity for... um... churlishness... for a long time. I guess I've never felt like we're together on the same page or that I understand him. That's partly why I bought the farm; so that I can share with Jonah some of the fun with animals that I had growing up. And even though we've only been there a few months, I think it's a good idea that will work. I'm hoping that because we have more to talk about, because of looking after the animals, that we will talk more in general. But you know, maybe I should ask him outright if he is angry. Maybe he is. I don't know why he should be, but kids! Who knows? But yeah, you're right, Ma, and I am aware of it. Actually, I've been worrying about him turning into a rebellious teenager if I don't make headway in getting it sorted now."

My face must have communicated my despair over the emotional wellbeing of my son because Ma came around the table and gave me a hug. "Oh Sheri, you have done so well, such a good job. And kids - you never know how they are going to turn out."

I sighed as I couldn't help but feel I was to blame. After all, I was the one he had lived with and he'd been in care so much. Only I didn't know how I could have done anything differently. If I'd stayed at home with him, I wouldn't have been able to buy the farm. And I was so proud of it; the house, the kitchen and bathroom, they looked great. "I'll try and talk to him more over the next few weeks before he goes back to school," I said to Ma. We were going to be spending plenty of time together anyway.

At that moment the stomp of the men's boots could be heard on the veranda. Jonah led the way and he came over to where I sat and leaned into me.

"Hi darling," I said as I touched an arm about his boyish shoulders. "Have you had a nice time?"

"Can we have chicken takeouts for dinner?" was his reply.

It was only on the way home that I realised that I'd forgotten to tell Pa about Mrs Stanford.

A few days later and Ruff was hanging his sheepish head in disgrace while I berated him in my gruffest voice. "Bad dog, Ruff. BAD DOG!" The mangled corpse of one of the ladylike little pullets lay at our feet. It was Jonah's fault for leaving the door to the coop unlatched but the responsibility for such a tragic death was not something I wanted to place on the shoulders of a nine year old boy.

Jonah had been surprisingly amenable to the idea of having chores to do and had leaned over the table with interest while I had written the list, namely: to feed the hens and collect any eggs once they started laying, and feed Ruff; and now a new task, to spend time training him.

"We can't blame Ruff," I explained to Jonah who was staring with distressed fascination at the gory sight of the chicken's bloodied entrails. "He doesn't know that what he did was wrong but he is going to have to learn some manners so we may as well start now."

I clipped the leash onto Ruff's collar and handed the end to Jonah. "Dogs are pack animals which means they live in groups and they need a leader or a boss dog to tell them what to do. We are Ruff's pack and you and me are his leaders. We are the boss of him," I explained, recounting what I had learned on television from Cesar Millan's dog whisperer show. "If we don't teach Ruff how to behave and tell him what to do, he will do whatever he likes and might even begin to try and tell *us* what to do."

Jonah laughed. "Tell us what to do. How can he do that? He can't talk."

I thought quickly. "He might growl at us when we try and get him to do something he doesn't want to do, like get off the couch."

Some moments are light bulb moments – epiphanies – when something 'clicks' and that which was previously clouded and uncertain suddenly snaps into focus and becomes crystal clear. At that moment, I *heard* the words I was speaking and the dynamics of dog training meshed with my lack of understanding about child rearing and I realised:

Raising a child was much like training a dog! As I continued on, the words continued to resonate with me. "You have to get Ruff's attention. See how he is watching the chickens?" And indeed, Ruff was staring intently at the remaining hens who were blissfully scratching in the dust, ignorant of the fate of their lost mate. I pulled at Ruff's ear and spoke his name. He turned his head briefly and turned away again so I continued to pull on the loose skin on his neck, speaking his name, until eventually he fixed his gaze on my face, tongue lolling, as if to ask 'what do you want?'

"That is what you want from Ruff," I told Jonah, all the while remembering with horror the countless times I had thrown comments, requests and orders across the room, over the television and Playstation and even down the hall, to Jonah. Barely once could I recall ever going to him and getting his attention before talking to him. It was with a deep sense of alarm that I explained to Jonah, "Once you have got his attention, you can tell him to do anything because he will be listening to you."

Ruff, being young, proved to be a quick and willing learner. I taught Jonah how to make Ruff wait patiently for Jonah's permission to eat his dinner, to sit, and to stay as well as various other tricks and commands.

As for myself, having identified a massive hole in my parenting style, I found myself caught out repeating my bad habits every five minutes. It was terribly time consuming to physically walk over to where Jonah was and actually hold a conversation with him but I was gratified to discover that the more I did so, the more the atmosphere between us improved.

A rough routine evolved that juggled domestic chores, the animals and work, interspersed with Jonah staying overnight at his mates houses and them staying overnight with us. Also, from time to time, we saddled up Jasper and I began teaching my son how to ride. Much of this had to be performed on the lunge rein as we did not yet have an enclosed corral. However, maybe because he was older, Jonah did not possess the natural affinity for horses that I had expected and we both found the process of learning to ride a fraught one.

He was excessively rough on Jasper and was forever yanking at the animal's mouth and kicking him harshly. His constant man handling made me snap at him and I grew impatient at his bullying attempts to control the animal. After a couple of tense sessions, both he and I were ready to call it quits.

"Why are you always so angry?" I demanded after one particularly gruelling lesson whereby Jasper, flustered and anxious at Jonah's aggression, had become skittish and backed up when he was meant to be walking on. In response, Jonah, flapping the reins and kicking wildly, had resorted to shouting abuse at the frightened creature. Forced to intervene, I had marched over to the horse's head and ordered him off.

"He wouldn't go!" cried Jonah in a highly passionate state.

"Yeah, well if you'd stop kicking the poor animal. You can't treat a horse like that. You've got be gentle; firm but gentle. How would you like it if you were constantly kicked and shouted at?"

We faced off in the paddock. Jonah's features were contorted in rage.

"You yell at me all the time," he accused.

"Cos' you don't listen. Everything I say goes in one ear and out the other."

"That's because you're always telling me what to do. You're so bossy." The kid was close to tears and valiantly trying to hold his emotions in check.

My heart melted. "Oh, Jonah, you're a kid! Parents have to tell their kids what to do or they'd never do anything."

'But you don't have to yell."

At that moment, I didn't really believe that I yelled that much but in a flash of insight, I recognised that this was a defining argument and not the time to dismiss my son's impassioned assertions so I bit back the instinctive words of defensive protest and chose my next words carefully. "Okay...I'm sorry if I yell at you too much but that still doesn't explain why you are so angry."

'Because I'm not stupid, Mum. I know what to do. You don't have to tell me." At that, the tears overwhelmed his defences and flinging his hard hat to the ground, he bolted back to the house.

So as to give him time to calm down, I brushed Jasper and released him into the paddock with Tiddlywinks, stocked up the hay racks, and closed up the barn for the evening before returning home. Inside, all was quiet so I went down the hall to Jonah's room where he was lying on his bed. The habit in me wanted to say, 'go and have a shower' but in the uneasy silence I was afraid of saying the wrong thing and sparking a fresh emotional outburst so I sat gingerly on the end of the bed and asked him if he was okay.

A small, "Yeah."

"Well, I have been thinking about what you said and I guess you are nearly ten and are growing up. I don't need to be telling you things like when to go and have a shower or when to feed Ruff. I should trust you to be responsible. I'm sorry if I get it wrong, Jonah, but you are my only kid and I am still learning how to be a mum, okay?" It was the most honest I had ever been with him.

Jonah nodded.

"You know I love you," I said.

Jonah nodded again, then, for the first time in his young life said, "Love you too, Mum."

Feeling wrung out, I left him lying there and went into the kitchen to fix a drink. I had thought that the baby stage was hard, and it was in a physical sense but this new stage was something altogether different. Jonah was indeed growing up and evidently needed more mature interactions. He needed to be talked to and given genuine responsibilities. Who he was as a person with his own individual set of likes and dislikes demanded to be respected. It wasn't good enough anymore to shuttle him along around my life without any negotiation.

With my idyllic daydreams of my son and I riding and competing together in the trash and replaced with the sad realisation that Jonah no more belonged to me than I belonged to my own mother, I felt an overwhelming desire to forget about the whole issue but that was one cat that was never going back into the bag.

All too often during the following weeks, I caught myself yelling directives down the hall, or discovered Ruff loitering anxiously in the kitchen waiting for his dinner long after Jonah was in bed fast asleep. But over time, the apologising (on my side) and the getting out of bed to complete his chores (on Jonah's) abated as the new ways of relating became established.

And then it was September the eleventh and we watched the news in horror as two planes were deliberately crashed into the twin towers of the World Trade Centre in downtown Manhattan and the new words: terrorism, al Qaeda and Osama bin Laden were released onto the American national psyche. Overnight, the electronic games my son played took on new meanings as I observed him hunting bin Laden and shouting "die terrorist" at the television screen. Then one day he announced, "I'm going to be a Marine when I grow up."

In my new role as respecter of individual freedom and identity, I was at a loss as to how to respond to this. Like most Americans, I viewed the men and women serving in the armed forces as heroes but did I want my son to be a hero? Most certainly I did not!

"But you will have to kill people and you might get injured or even killed yourself."

"I don't care," was his passionate response. "I want to catch terrorists and kill bin Laden."

How to explain the raw brutality of violent death in a foreign land to a child to whom death was merely a satisfying splotch of red on a computer game?

For a month after the attack, sales were dead. It was as if the entire nation had given a collective gasp of unimaginable shock. We were bewildered as to how anyone could have committed such an inhumane act and astonished at having been caught napping. How had it happened? How had no one become alerted to the plot? Our generation, unused to war, our instincts for suspicion dulled, were naive and innocent and it was with a sense of astounded injury that we learned of the virulent hatred for all things American that had precipitated this outrage. In the aftermath, troops were dispatched to Afghanistan, airport security was tightened considerably and an insidious sense of Muslims as being shit stirrers in the world sprang up like Knapweed and was just as deeply rooted and difficult to eradicate.

With very little going on in the office, I was free to spend the time required on Tiddlywinks in order to prepare him for the barrel race; and as the days passed, we began to gel as a team so that he responded to my thoughts, sensing the subtle shifts in my body and limbs before I consciously articulated them.

I also spent a pleasant afternoon in 'Western Gals,' a rodeo store in town, selecting a gorgeous teal blue tailored shirt, a cream Stetson encrusted in glittering rhinestones and a pair of dark brown hand carved boots that immediately brought Luke to mind. The entire ensemble cost me $745 but I felt it was worth it.

On the day of the Melvin show, Jonah and I were up before the first light. I cooked bacon and eggs for breakfast as a special treat, followed by hot chocolate for Jonah and coffee for me. The year was closing and the stifling heat of summer had reluctantly yielded to the damp cool of autumn. Spicy scents of mouldering leaves and dewy grasses assaulted the nose as I shone the narrow beam of the flashlight through the chilly gloom of dawn. Accompanying us, the tentative twitters of the early birds punctuated the darkness, accentuating the crunch of fallen leaves underfoot and as we edged past the debris pile, a rustle told me that rats were finding the rubbish heap to be an attractive home for the winter.

"We'll burn that pile next week, Jonah," I commented.

"Cool!" was his enthusiastic reply.

Tiddly nickered softly when he heard the barn door open and he bobbed his head over the stable partition with ears pricked to show his interest in the early morning shenanigans. Jonah transferred our pile of gear to the entrance while I bandaged Tiddly's tail and affixed boots to his fetlocks in preparation for the trip.

At 7 o'clock, as arranged, Pa rumbled up the driveway with the transporter. Once he had dismounted from the cab, we hugged briefly and I breathed in the old familiar smoky, earthy smell of him that I loved so much. He ruffled Jonah's hair. "How are you, boy? You gonna put that stuff in that there box," he said indicating the compartment in the truck that was purpose built for such equipment. Jonah hurried to fulfil his task and Pa took a look around the barn. "You got the place lookin' pretty good kiddo," he commented.

I led Tiddly out and Pa and I loaded him into the transporter. It was a different set up to a float as we walked directly into the body of the truck. Pa's two prized Herefords, housed in their own stalls, placidly chewed hay while they watched, unperturbed by our installation of Tiddly on the other side. The remaining space was taken up with a kitchen unit and a built in table as well as several open plywood boxes within which supplies of hay, grooming gear, tack and various rugs were stored.

It had been years since I'd been in the transporter and the twin fragrances of hay and manure brought to mind the occasions when our entire family had slept in the truck with the animals. You wouldn't think that it would be possible to sleep with horses and cattle munching, snorting and belching all night long but it was those events that comprised the very fabric of my memories. I never felt so close to my family or my ponies as I did when we all slept under the one roof, way out in the middle of nowhere, in some small, unidentified country town.

With the show being held in Melvin, we did not have very far to go so within half an hour we were reversing the procedure. It was a perfect fall morning. The Liquid Ambers and Maples had turned into flaming heads of red and yellow and were already creating sprawling drifts of spent leaves around the bases of their trunks.

Pa parked the transporter in the area designated for entrants in the livestock competitions, next to the Jefferson's truck which had their name emblazoned right across the full length of the side. They were an old and wealthy family and as a child, I'd always wondered whether they were related to President Jefferson. Even now, I was none the wiser. Pa greeted Mr Jefferson with a "Howdy" and a touch to his Stetson and received the same in return.

I entered the truck and attached a halter onto Tyson's grizzled head. He'd been handled since he was a knock kneed calf and stood patiently while I attached the lead rope to the running ring under his chin, then followed obediently as I led him down the ramp and over to a three sided pen where I tied him up before returning for Bronson. Jonah was despatched with a bucket to fill at the tap while Pa scattered a thick layer of hay about the pen so that should the bulls lie down, their groomed hides would remain clean.

Jonah, having observed the outline of the fairground erupting from the tops of the trees, was keen to explore and I felt sorry for him when I told him he would have to wait until I could go with him. I'd had my brothers to roam about with and could well remember the delicious sense of freedom we had experienced as we'd wandered around the show grounds, perusing the exhibits, riding on the rides and stuffing our faces with sauce smothered hot dogs, fries, soft serve ice creams and billowing pillows of pink cotton candy.

The layout of the grounds had remained essentially the same over the years. In the southern corner, where we now were, was the cattle section where long rows of calves and bulls of various ages and breeds sat or stood in pens like the ones our bulls were occupying. To the front of the pens were three judging rings where the events took place. In various sheds, dotted about, other competitions were held where entries of flowers, vegetables, baking and preserves as well as poultry and fleeces battled it out for coveted blue ribbons. It is difficult to explain why these exhibits that reflected the ordinariness of rural life were so interesting but they were very popular.

Towards the entry gate stood the machinery exhibits where big companies displayed their newest models of tractors, harvesters and other implements in the hope of sales. To children, the machines appeared gigantic as their little heads only came up to the hubs of the back wheels. Once, I had loved sitting in the driver's seat, pretending to drive. Jonah would love it too, I thought. These days, diggers and earth moving equipment were also on display as were the latest models of farm utilities and other vehicles.

Food stalls randomly dotted the show grounds but there was also a beer tent and a large pavilion where tea, coffee and a sit down lunch could be bought. It was also the site where the Harvest Festival Dance would be held later on in the evening being, as it was, close to the sound stage where a variety of country and western bands played throughout the day.

A rough grove of scraggly Sequoias separated the main area from the events side where the crowd pleasing competitions of tractor pulling, ploughing, shearing and wood chopping took place. The rodeo arena, where Tiddly and I would be competing that afternoon, was also there.

Contented crowds of people milled about and Jonah and I soaked up the relaxed and social community atmosphere as we inspected the tractors, scoffed hot dogs and marvelled at the speed of the shearers blades as they slid over the prostrate bodies of long suffering sheep leaving them tender and surprised. The fairground beckoned so we headed over and spent an hour or two shooting at targets with inaccurate air rifles, popping plastic balls into the gaping mouths of gaudily painted plaster clowns and colliding with each other on the dodgem cars. But the morning was passing all too quickly and a glance at my watch told me that I would have to go soon and start getting Tiddly ready.

"Sheri. Is that you?" said a voice beside me.

I turned and saw...

"Luke! Fancy seeing you here." In sync, we moved in and hugged. As we separated, I pulled Jonah in closer. "You remember Jonah?" Then to Jonah, "You were just a baby when Luke saw you last. What are you doing here? I thought you were still in Hawaii."

"My father passed away. I came home for the funeral and to help my mother." He glanced at my left hand which was resting on Jonah's shoulder.

I noticed the glance and addressed his unspoken question. "Yeah, no, that didn't work out. I bought a small farm though. It's not much, only 100 acres but I've been doing up the house and bought a couple of horses. In fact I am going back to Pa now. I'm entered into the women's barrel race this afternoon. Are you here by yourself? Why don't you come and see my horse? And Pa would love to see you."

Luke smiled. "Okay," he replied.

We turned together to walk back to the transporter and I snuck a sideways peek at him as we walked. He looked good; lean, toned and relaxed - and older. It suited him. "Nice boots,"

I said noticing the gorgeous pair of light tan calf high's gracing his lower legs.

"I was just going to say the same to you," he laughed.

I felt light hearted. "Wait until you see me in my gear, that is, if you're going to stay. Come and watch if you're not busy or got other plans."

"No, I'm not doing anything," he said. "I'd love to."

We approached the transporter. Tyson's pen was empty so I looked over to the ring and saw Pa there in the line up with three other glossy beasts and their owners. Tiddly's ears pricked up when he saw me. "He's probably sick of standing here," I said.

Luke reached out and rubbed Tiddly's forehead. As he did so, his arm brushed mine and my heart skipped a beat in response. *What's this?* I scolded myself. *Are you so sex starved you're going to hit on your friends now?* I breathed deeply hoping to quell the sudden light headed breathlessness I was experiencing but Luke was looking at me with a strange expression on his face and when he spoke, his voice was incredulous. "I know this horse." My mind hit a blank. *What – How?* What did he mean 'know' the horse? Had he seen Tiddly at another show or something?

Now, Luke was laughing and patting Tiddly like a long lost buddy. "Hello Tiddlywinks old boy."

"Tell me," I demanded. "How do you know Tiddly?"

"I should know him. He was mine! Where did you get him from?"

"From Stanford's Ranch, from a woman called Sooky who's married to Hank. The farm's in..."

"Mercy," he finished for me. "Sooky – Sarah, is my mother and Hank is – was, my step father."

Click, click, click. It all fell into place. Hank who was so ill he passed away. I remembered Luke mentioning in Hawaii that his father was ill. But Luke – a Stanford, heir to a vast and very impressive ranching operation, plus another property in Hawaii. How could he be in line to inherit so much wealth and Pa not have known about it?

"I trained Tiddly. He was my horse," Luke continued.

I snapped my mouth shut. It was almost too much to take in. Somehow, his being so much more than I had thought changed everything. For all the years I had known him, I'd assumed he was 'just a cowboy' working his way up in life much as I was. But now, to discover he was old money...and Stanford, that beautiful homestead that would one day be his... and didn't he say that he only had one sister and that she was married? I felt as if I had been doused in cold water. *He will want a partner who is so much more than I.*

Pa saved the situation by appearing at that opportune moment leading Tyson who was wearing a blue ribbon around his neck. "You won! Congratulations!" I exclaimed. "You remember Luke? We bumped into him at the fairground."

"Howdy," said Pa. He extended his hand and the two men shook.

"You'll never guess, Pa. The woman I bought Tiddly off is called Sooky Stanford and she's Luke's Ma. She knew you back in school. I meant to tell you but I forgot. She married Hank and he's Luke's stepfather but he passed away recently. Tiddly, can you believe it, was Luke's horse. He trained him." The words tumbled out in a rush.

Pa nodded sagely. "Ah, Sarah Addison eh? I remember her. I heard about Hank's passing. So you're her son. I'm sorry for your loss."

"Thank you, sir," replied Luke.

"So who's looking after that ranch?"

"Larson, the manager, is there but I've been helping out, of course."

Pa grunted, then headed over to secure Tyson back in his pen while I said I'd better get Tiddly ready. If I didn't get on I would be late.

Luke asked, "Do you want me to go with Jonah to the stands?"

"That would be awesome," I replied, grateful that I wouldn't have to leave Jonah with Pa after all.

I rode Tiddly over to the arena and was gratified by the admiring glances that were cast my way. My teal shirt and rhinestone encrusted, cream Stetson complemented the speckled grey of Tiddly's coat, perfectly. Once at the arena, things got busy and I had little time to think about Luke. I registered and received my number then guided Tiddly into the warm up area where I proceeded to ride him in figure eights, changing pace and direction frequently, until he was paying close attention and responding to my commands fluently.

I heard our event called over the PA system and guided Tiddly out through the exit gate and into the waiting corral where about fifteen women were already waiting. One group of stoutly middle aged riders, who obviously knew each other, were chatting loudly amongst themselves. Assessing the competition, I was surprised to see that I was one of the youngest competitors; nevertheless, I was confident that we would acquit ourselves adequately. I patted Tiddly's neck, as much to reassure myself as him. The nerves were kicking in and I was keen to get into the ring and my first round underway. Riders were called into the arena and one by one they completed the course. Some were undeniably good, others not so. Eventually, our turn was called and I walked Tiddly to the starting point and touched my hat to the judges.

The timer counted down to the starting bell which rang shrilly. I kicked Tiddly into gear and he leapt forward. We galloped to the first barrel and in no time at all it was before us. I tugged on the right hand rein and threw my weight into the barrel. One stride too many took him slightly wide but we recovered and headed to the second barrel. *Ooops, too close!* I felt my stirrup brush the barrel which teetered alarmingly but mercifully stayed upright. A dash to the third. A slight slip. *Thank heavens for new shoes.* Then the bolt for home. By that point, adrenaline was flooding my body and excitement was high. 24 seconds! I laughed in exhilaration and slapped Tiddly's neck enthusiastically. "Good boy," I cried as he skidded to a halt. "Good boy."

"Nice ride," said one of the women as I re-entered the corral. With the grin on my face stretching my cheeks so widely they hurt, I looked over at the bank where Jonah and Luke sat side by side. They were looking my way so I waved whereupon Jonah, seeing me, jumped up and waved back.

We rode two more rounds but were unable to beat our first time and so being off the pace for a placing, I returned Tiddly to the trailer where I brushed him down and refilled his hay net and water bucket.

Pa was relaxing in his camp chair chatting to Mr Jefferson. He held a coffee mug in his hand and I would have loved to join them but Jonah and Luke were still on the hill so after filling him in, I headed back to the boys to watch the rest of the event.

Luke looked up and smiled at my approach. "I was beginning to wonder if you were coming back," he said.

I sat on the grass beside him. "Of course, silly, I was just sorting Tiddly out. Hey - you must come and visit me. We could go for a ride. You can ride Tiddly because I've also got another horse. I bought him for Jonah but that didn't turn out so well."

Luke turned to Jonah. "Don't you like riding?"

Jonah replied sourly, "No."

I laughed. "Yeah, we had some 'fun' trying to learn, didn't we?"

"Horses are stupid. They don't do what you want them to do." He sat up and shielded his eyes from the sun which was embarking on its descent for another day. "Mum, can I get a drink?" he asked.

To think of it, I could have done with a drink myself so I dug in my pocket and pulled out a $10 note and handed it to my son. "Get two flat whites and you can get what you want with the rest."

He jumped up and headed for the food truck that was parked at the top of the hill. Once he was out of earshot, Luke said, "He's a good kid."

I sighed. "We've had our moments. At times it has been really hard."

The second round of the barrel race had begun and the riders were providing a challenge for each other.

"You and Tiddly did well out there," said Luke.

I felt inordinately pleased at his compliment. "He went well for a first go," I replied. "He's a great horse. You did a bloody good job. Do you like my shirt, and how about my hat?" I took my Stetson off and handed it to him for a closer inspection of the rhinestones.

He peered at them closely for a second and then handed it back. "Very nice," he said politely.

"I still can't believe that Sooky is your mum. Oh, and I am so sorry about your father."

Luke shrugged. "Thank you. He was sick for a very long time. It was expected."

"That doesn't make it any easier. Were you close to your father?"

"My step father actually," he corrected. "I respected him. I'm closer to my mother."

I could understand that. I'd felt very warm towards her myself when I met her and liked her instantly. "She's going to have a laugh when you tell her that we know each other. I can't believe it myself, bumping into you like this – again! You pop up in the most unexpected places Mr..." I realised I didn't know Luke's last name. Addison was his mother's name. Stanford was his stepfather's name. "I don't know your last name," I confessed.

"It's confusing isn't it? It's Hawken and I could say the same to you, Ms Lewis."

I threw a piece of grass at him. "Its fate," I laughed, recalling another conversation of many years ago.

Luke chuckled also then added, quietly, "Maybe it is."

Jonah appeared with the coffees for us and a cola and donut for himself. The hot drink slid down my throat like nectar. "Mother's milk," I grinned. "So are you staying here now, on the Mainland?"

Luke thought for a moment. "I'm not sure. It depends." I waited for him to elaborate. "It depends on what Mum wants to do with the Hawaii place for one thing."

I wanted to press him further but he had turned his attention back to the event which was now on to the final round. There were three competitors left and all made fast times until the first rider on a thickly built, bay gelding knocked over a barrel and was eliminated. The crowd gave a collective groan of sympathy and the rider threw her hands up in frustration but that was all it took, one small error of judgement and you were out. The remaining two women battled it out between them until one won with an impressive time of eighteen seconds by which time I was beginning to shiver. The sun was low and a chilly breeze ranged over the contours of the land.

"We should be getting back to Pa," I said reluctantly. The three of us lurched to our feet, ankles and knees stiff from sitting for so long on the hard ground. "Are you coming to the Harvest Festival Dance tonight? We are going. There will be food and everything. I think we're going to drop the animals at home first and then come back. It's in the pavilion and starts at 7 o'clock."

Luke was shaking the pins and needles out of his legs. "I'll find out what Mum's planning and make sure she is alright. But it was great to see you again, Sheri. Bye Jonah." Then, with a wave of his hand to me and a ruffle of Jonah's head, he turned and left us standing there, watching after him.

CHAPTER THIRTEEN

The Harvest Festival dance was in full swing by the time we returned in the Chevy. Pa had purchased meal coupons for us earlier in the day so the first thing we did was leave Jonah to secure a table while we redeemed the vouchers for plates of food. It was a meat lover's feast offering a choice of braised beef cheeks or spit roasted pork with crackling so golden and crispy that I could all but taste it through sight alone. The meals were served with deep fried potatoes, sweet potato mash, pumpkin, peas and gravy. As an extra side, the pork was also served with a dollop of sweet, caramelised apple sauce.

Meanwhile Jonah, much to his glee, had connected with a group of friends from school so he gulped his food down before tearing off with them to play hide and seek by torchlight in the shadows; my instructions that he return regularly falling on deaf ears. The pavilion was crowded with people seated on every available surface, including the boulders lining the path outside. Many ate standing up while juggling their paper plates, plastic cutlery and paper napkins.

A stream of unmelodic squeaks and groans emanated from the microphones of the band who were busy setting up their instruments on the sound stage as Pa and I ate and drank and watched the crowd, many of whom I recognised through my business dealings at work. A quickening of my pulse announced that I had observed Luke threading his way through the melee so I stood and waved to catch his attention. He made his way over. "You came!" A wide smile spread over my lips.

"Yes. Mum's here too. She's over there chatting to Mrs Dawson." He waved his arm in their general direction and then sat down beside me whereupon Pa, having seen some of his buddies at the bar, excused himself now that I had someone else to talk to.

Luke and I regarded each other shyly. "You know I still can't believe it. What a coincidence," I said. "And I loved your mother when I met her. She was so friendly. I can't believe that I've known you, sort of, for nearly ten years and never made the connection. Why didn't you say something?"

Luke laughed. "What was there to say? You hadn't met Mum then so knowing about her wouldn't have meant anything to you anyway."

That was true but it was a strange situation. I felt as if I had known him forever, when in reality this was only the third time I'd met him and while I felt close to him, and counted him as a friend, I knew almost nothing about him. Yet there was so much that I wanted to know and evidently so did Luke because he asked a question first. "What happened to your engagement?"

"Oh. That was totally unexpected," I explained. "I don't know why I said yes because I never actually loved him. We just drifted into being together, if that makes sense. He wanted to marry me and for us to have more children but I couldn't do it. I was only just getting my own life back with Jonah growing up and with my job going well... I didn't want to give any of that up so I broke it off with him."

Luke gave a short laugh. "You could have knocked me over with a feather when I saw that ring."

"He was a decent person and I felt bad about hurting him but at the same time, what I want for myself has to count, right? And anyway," I teased, "it wasn't as if you were saying anything... How old were you when your mum married Hank?" I continued, curious to know about his life.

At that, Luke filled in the gaps and although he played the story down, proceeded to describe a drunken father who made nothing of beating his cowering wife in full view of the children. Eventually, unable to stand it any longer and fearing for the wellbeing of her family, Sooky had fled to a Salvation Army shelter. After several weeks of the refugees living in the one room and sleeping in the same bed, they were offered emergency housing in a trailer park where they remained for two years until Sooky was able to secure a live in position as Hank's housekeeper.

Hank had been rattling around alone in his empty mansion for almost ten years since his own father had died prematurely of a heart attack. As could be expected for a man who didn't get out much, and for whom the chances of finding a woman independently were slim, the predictable happened and Hank fell in love with Sooky; first with her beauty, then her cooking, and finally with her calm and gentle nature. Once her divorce was final, she'd married Hank and they'd had twenty five happy years together. And if the neighbours thought anything to comment on about this unconventional pairing, nobody said a thing.

Having finished talking, Luke's face was pensive. I'd never really had the opportunity to study his features before but while I waited for him to deal with his thoughts, I did so. Not a tall man, maybe 5'8, his body was slim and lean, his arms and calf muscles well defined. His hair – dark and closely cut, eyes deep hazel and framed by neat eyebrows, smoothly curved cheeks given strength by high cheekbones. He looked slightly Arapaho in features and I wondered whether he did in fact have Indian ancestry and where. Although not a conventionally good looking man, he definitely possessed a lithe sexuality and self possession that rendered him masculine.

Noticing my scrutiny and feeling self conscious, he directed attention away from himself by inviting me to tell him about my farm.

"This is a subject I'm passionate about," I cautioned. "How long have you got? Actually," I continued before he could answer, "Why don't you come out and see for yourself?" I described where I lived and how to get there then fished out a business card from my jeans pocket and handed it to him.

"Sheriden Lewis: Realtor." He whistled. "A hotshot."

"It's only Real Estate but yeah, I qualified and I've made good money. There's a property boom on at the moment but things have cooled down a bit since the nine eleven thing."

He stood abruptly and extended his hand like a true gentleman. "Would you care to dance, Ms Lewis?" he asked with affected gentility.

I put on my best 'southern belle' voice and replied coyly, "Why, ah do care Mr Hawken. Ah'd be delighted." Then as an aside, "I really can't dance to save myself but I promise to try."

He led me to the dance floor where most of the dancing crowd had organised themselves into rows and were moving in unison to a progression of steps that anybody would have recognised as boot scootin."

"Just do what I do," instructed Luke with confidence.

As predicted, it was impossible. When the group turned left, I turned right. When Luke stepped forward, I stepped back and collided with him. In the end, I gave up and as was my way, performed my own version of the moves; accentuating the boot taps, wiggles and flourishes until we were both convulsed with laughter.

"You are very cheeky, Sheri." He said it sternly but his eyes twinkled as they smiled. After an hour of puffing and sweating we left the dance floor, thirsty for a drink. He handed me a welcome bottle of chilled bourbon and we headed out into the night air where the cool breeze on my skin made my nerves shiver. I glanced at my watch. It was ten in the evening already. I wondered vaguely where Pa and Jonah were.

"Are you cold? Would you like my jacket?"He moved to take off his coat but I lay my hand on his arm to prevent him.

"It's okay. I'm fine," I said. Then the air was thick and full of heat as such an intense desire to kiss him overwhelmed my senses that I could hardly breathe. He leaned ever so slightly towards me. *Did he feel it too?* Flustered, I spoke and broke the moment. "Shall we go and say hi to your mum? I really must head home soon. I've got work in the morning and Jonah's got school. It's getting late."

If Luke felt emotion either way he didn't show it and his 'sure' was calm and relaxed. As we approached the table where Luke had left Sooky previously, I saw that Pa was there also and the two were deep in conversation. "Mrs Stanford," I exclaimed as we drew close to them, "how great to see you again. And what a surprise; I never imagined that Luke was your son."

"Yes, we've been having a grand old catch up," she replied. "How the years do pass."

I sat down next to Pa and Luke squeezed in next to me making me acutely aware of the hairs on his arm as they lightly brushed against mine.

"I'm very sorry to hear about the loss of your husband," I said. "Luke was telling me about him."

"Thank you, dear. Hank was a very good man and we had twenty five wonderful years together. I was very lucky." She fell into silence and I could see that her mind was roving fondly over her memories.

I wished that I could find a love like that. As far as I knew, I hadn't been in love with anybody. I doubted that I really knew what love was. People said that if you had to ask the question, then you hadn't and when asked to describe being in love, could only answer with an ambiguous 'you will know when it happens.' To this I could only surmise that I hadn't because certainly I didn't 'know.' Recalling the story that Becky had told me, I wondered whether Luke had ever been in love. But there was no opportunity, and this was not the time, to ask such a question.

At that moment, Jonah ran up flushed with exertion from careening about the place in the dark.

"Where have you been?" I wanted to know.

"Playing out there, hiding with torches." He indicated in the general direction of outside.

Being reunited, the three of us rose to our feet announcing it was time to be heading home for the night. Mrs Stanford and Pa hugged amidst invitations to visit in the future. Luke shook hands with Pa and I hugged Sooky and whispered "Don't be a stranger" into her ear. Only Luke and I avoided contact, both suddenly shy; each of us knowing how we felt but uncertain of how the other felt. He walked with us to the entrance of the pavilion where, understanding his reluctance to leave his mother unaccompanied, I let Pa and Jonah walk on a few steps before turning towards him and lightly touching his hand. "Will I see you again?"I asked softly.

To which he replied, "Yes, soon, I promise." It was enough for me for now.

Pa stayed overnight and in the morning, I once again rose early to prepare breakfast and to help load the bulls back onto the Transporter. The light was breaking the darkness as we shut the ramp. Pa rolled a smoke and leaned against the door to the cab. "You was pretty friendly with Luke, girlie," he said as he put his smoke to his lips and lit the end with a match. The flare illuminated the wool collar of his suede coat.

I'd never held back from talking to Pa, from sharing how I felt. Even if he didn't agree, he never condemned and I knew I could talk to him about anything. "I know. Isn't it weird? That's only the third time I've met him but it feels like I've known him all my life. I don't know if it means anything but he has managed to tick a few boxes so far. Anyway, you can't talk. You looked pretty cosy with Mrs Stanford yourself."

Pa took a thoughtful drag on his smoke before responding. "She's a damn fine woman. Even at school she was classy. Cryin' shame she married that deadbeat loser – what's his name? That's what happens when a white woman takes up with a scum Brownie."

"Pa!" I interrupted, shocked at his attitude. "Don't be racist. They're not all like that. I thought Luke looked a bit Arapaho though. Is it his father where the Indian ancestry comes from? It suits him."

"Mm, the trouble with Luke's Pa was the drink. Beware of an Indian that drinks. They're bad news."

Beware of anyone who drinks, I would have thought. But Pa was old school. Even so, it was disturbing how deeply negative stereotypes were ingrained in my own family's beliefs, and more so, how little I knew and understood those attitudes.

"Hey. We'll come home for Thanksgiving if the snow holds off," I said. "I've got to meet up with Nessa and Becky anyway about wedding plans. To Ma's great excitement, Jet and Becky had finally set a date. Golly gosh, Pa, two grandies and Jet soon married and probably Byron too before long. I'll be an old maid!"

"Don't you worry about that, kiddo. Love will come along when you least expect it." He tossed the butt of his cigarette to the ground and extinguished it with the heel of his boot. "Well, I'd best get going." He enveloped me in a bear hug.

"Love you, Pa. Give my love to Ma and I'll see you soon."

He climbed into the truck. With a roar, the engine kicked into life and with a final wave, he rumbled away.

A few short weeks later and Jonah, Ruff and I were squeezed into the front bench seat of the Chevy and headed to Ma's. The snow had held off but the skies were dark and tinged with apricot. *Snow clouds.* Scraps of weak sunshine tore rents in the clouds and painted brilliant lime green shapes on the fields.

I thought about Luke as the Chevy ate up the miles. He'd phoned following the Harvest Dance to say he had to return to Hawaii but that he'd be back in the New Year. I envied his being able to escape the winter and wondered whether he had a girl there. Men were not noted for their penchant for celibacy so it would only be natural if he was sleeping with someone. A vague prickle of possessiveness touched me but I squashed it down and sternly reminded myself that we were not a couple.

I was glad to arrive at Ma's as the wind was bitterly cold and despite the heater being on full blast, could still feel its icy tendrils slipping between the rubbers of the doors. I suspected that it would finally snow overnight and hoped we wouldn't be stuck there.

But as predicted, it did snow and we awoke to the archetypical winter wonderland. Jonah, barely willing to wait long enough to pull on his coat and gloves, dashed outdoors to play and then, after breakfast, disappeared with Pa and Byron for the day. With the house empty, Ma and I dressed and then I drove carefully into Flagstaff for some window shopping and lunch in a warm cafe. Once we were seated and our orders placed, I proceeded to tell her about the Harvest Festival Dance and the series of coincidences surrounding Tiddly's purchase. As I spoke, I noticed her lips pursing into a thin line which suggested that she disapproved of something, but when I asked what was wrong she merely shook her head saying, "It doesn't matter. It's all history now."

"That looks good," she deflected as the waitress placed before us an aromatic toasted chicken bruschetta and Ma's order of deep fried calamari and salad. Silence fell while we took our first bites and made appreciative noises while we chewed.

"Why does food always taste better when somebody else makes it?" I commented, while understanding that I was not the best cook. Making the evening meal was usually crammed in between arriving home from work and watching the news at 5.30. It was just as well I had to cook for Jonah though or else I would have probably starved. I'd read of it happening; of elderly single women living alone who starved to death because they simply couldn't be bothered to think about eating.

"Anyway," I continued, resuming the conversation, "we're only friends. Nothing has happened between us at all. But it turns out he is not just a ranch hand. His father owned the place he was managing in Hawaii as well as Stanford Ranch so their family is old money and Luke is heir to it all because he's only got one sister and she's married and living in LA." To this declaration, Ma only commented that 'I was a grown woman who knew my own mind in such matters' before changing the subject to Jet and Becky's wedding, the date of which had been set for the end of March. After a lengthy discussion, we decided to go and have a preliminary look in the boutiques for an outfit befitting of the mother of the groom.

Traditions and celebrations mark time. Christmas closes the old year and New Years Eve heralds the new while birthdays remind us of the years that have passed and of the inexorable counting down of the remaining ones we have left. I blinked and it was 2002. Jonah was ten and I was only three years off thirty which sounded a whole lot worse than twenty seven.

My son could do the math and we were eating breakfast when he asked me how old I was when he was born. I answered truthfully and said "seventeen," but so as to make that sound as normal as possible, continued to explain that while some people had children young and others when they were older, "there was no rule to it." The answer seemed to satisfy him because he said no more about it but the conversation worried me. I wouldn't be able to conceal the circumstances surrounding his birth forever.

We plodded through the winter and I swear that if I hadn't had Jonah I would have run off to Hawaii and begged Luke to take me as the weather dragged on cold, wet and miserable. Normally, snow conditions ensured that the days remained clear and dry but this winter, the entire region was subjected to sleet and slush that melted and froze into black ice almost immediately. Work slowed to a standstill so I spent my days at home redecorating the remaining rooms in the house and waiting for spring.

By mid February, when Luke phoned to say he was back, all that remained of winter were pockets of icy drifts that clung tenaciously to the banks on the sides of the roads and patches of white that accentuated the highest mounds of the hills. The ground was still frozen with a hoar frost that refused to budge but at least the roads were drivable without chains. He told me that he was going to be in Melvin that day, 'looking at tractors' and invited me to meet him for coffee so despite it being midweek, I quickly reorganised my schedule in order to accommodate him.

We agreed to meet at the cafe but minutes before I was due to depart the office, he sauntered in and asked for me by name. Savannah, with an unerring instinct that informed her that Luke was not merely a client, bustled into my office to inform me personally that Mr Luke Hawken was here to see me, then watched with intense interest as we headed out into the street. "That was very naughty of you," I scolded teasingly as I tucked my hand into the crook of his arm. "Now I'll get the third degree when I get back."

Luke chuckled at my exaggerated angst and squeezed my hand gently against his side in a gesture that was quietly comforting. Although sunny, our breath puffed clouds into the cold air which stung and reddened our cheeks. It was pleasant to walk down the street with him, making small talk as we walked. He told me that he had employed a manager for the Hawaii farm and that knowledge pleased me. I realised how anxious I had been that he might decide to stay and run the farm himself. He was looking good; tanned, which on top of his already olive complexion made him look quite dark, whereas I on the other hand could have frightened snakes, so pale was I after over two months without sunshine.

Arriving at the cafe, we placed our orders. Luke insisted on paying so I found a booth, all the while musing that many of our encounters had taken place over coffee. It was a shared small pleasure of life. The place was warm, sundrenched and inviting. In one corner stood an old fashioned pot belly stove. Every now and then, someone sitting nearby threw in a few chunks of coal from a steel bucket causing the acrid smell of the coal smoke to mingle with the aroma of coffee. Suddenly, I was back in my childhood and the store. Luke, noticing my wistful expression as he slid into the booth opposite me said, "Penny for them," as an invitation to talk.

I shook my head. "Nothing really. Just the coal range reminded me of being a kid and the store. I was thinking how sad it is that time goes by so quickly. Aunty Harriet is over sixty now. Heck, even I'm twenty seven."

"You've got nothing to worry about," he responded. "I'm 36."

"I've always wondered why some woman hasn't snatched you up. I'd have thought a good man like you would be married with a batch of children by now," I said half joking.

He leaned back and breathed the words, "Ah well," but was saved from explaining further by the arrival of the waitress with our cappuccinos laced with chocolate syrup and a BLT bagel each. My mouth watered at the sight of the sesame speckled bagel and I realised I was starving, not having eaten anything since dinner the evening before. I took a bite and the flavours of bacon, avocado and mayonnaise exploded on my taste buds. "Mmm, mmm. Thank you. This is delicious," I mumbled with my mouth full...

"Come on. You know about me," I prodded once we had eaten. "Are you sure you don't have any Luke mini mes running around out there?"

Luke grimaced and I wondered whether I had stuck my foot in it. Maybe the story Becky had told me had some truth to it and there were painful memories he didn't want to dredge up. I hurried to correct my question adding, "If you want to share, that is. You don't have to if you don't want to."

But he leaned his forearms on the table and said quietly, "No its okay. The fact is that I did have a child once but he died. The coroner ruled it as a cot death but I suspect he was smothered or over heated because Amber, Cory's mother, used to have him sleep in bed with her."

My heart sank in sympathy. "Oh Luke, I'm so sorry," I said. "And Amber, your wife? She must have been devastated."

He nodded. "We both were. She went to England not long after that. She had family there. I haven't heard from her since. We weren't married though. She never gave me the chance."

His story explained everything; his reserve, why he kept me at arm's length and his goodwill towards Jonah. "Have you ever wanted more children?" I continued.

He shook his head. "Not really. If it happened I would be alright about it, and maybe even happy, but I'm not in a hurry to 'feel the fear' again as it were."

I could understand perfectly. To love, to have a new child, was risky. Having once opened his heart only to be cut so deeply by his son's death, not to mention the accompanying guilt and blame that must inevitably accompany such a tragedy... It didn't bear thinking about.

I said to him, "You know how I feel about children. I certainly don't want another right now. I'm only just getting a handle on how to be a parent to Jonah but that's not to say I would never have another though I'd need to be in a proper relationship first. If circumstances were right, I'd consider it. I love my little niece, Lorelei. You should see her - she's so cute. You know, it was hard when she was born. I felt more love and joy over my brother's child than I could ever remember feeling over Jonah."

"You mustn't beat yourself up, Sheri," he soothed. "You did your best and still are."

I felt completely open and warm towards Luke but then he had always been someone I could really talk to, someone I could share my true thoughts and feelings with, without feeling a need to sanitise what I said in order to make it acceptable.

"Isn't it random how life goes?" I said in a lighter tone. "What are you going to do now?"

"I don't know. Go back to Mum's I guess. Get some wood in, feed the horses," he said, missing my meaning.

"Don't forget to come out to my place one day," I reminded him. "We can go for a ride up the back of the farm. Apparently, there's an abandoned gold mine up there. The old lady who owned the place before me told me her brother once found a nugget the size of a nickel. I've been up and had a bit of a poke around but it's rocky and dangerous. I need another adult to come with me so I can explore further."

Luke expressed interest at this suggestion. "There could be gold up there, probably not in great quantities, but there are pockets of gold all over this region."

He agreed to come out the following weekend and I assured him that I would look forward to it.

The working days passed busily enough nevertheless I couldn't deny my impatience for Saturday to arrive. But then, work had that effect on me. No matter how busy I was, or how much money I was making, there was always the sense that work was something I had to do in order to be able to live my 'real' life. I couldn't wait until I was making enough off my land to leave my job.

My plans were coming along, albeit slowly. I had located a set of jumps being practically given away and all I'd had to do was pick them up; an operation that took all day so many trips did I have to make in order to ferry home the thirty drums and fifty odd poles. Then another month had been spent cleaning and repainting the pieces, an exercise that Jonah had willingly participated in. Keen to avoid disturbing the fragile new found harmony between us, I buttoned my lips when his ten year old efforts made the paintbrush veer off course and leave patches unpainted. Instead, I turned the truck radio on and we painted away companionably to the latest hits, and went back to tidy the messed up places later, without his knowledge.

With the freshly decorated jumps assembled in an unused section of the large paddock behind the barn, I placed an ad' in the local paper offering full agistment for two horses who would be given access to grazing during much of the year but would be housed in the barn during the winter and hard fed when necessary. I'd received several replies, predominantly from horse mad teenage girls living in town, and had accepted two horses for agistment as well as agreed to the incidental use of my facilities on an hourly rate to two other girls. At the moment I was making $120 per week which covered my hard feed bill.

On the Saturday that Luke was due to visit, I brushed down the horses and ensured that the tack was clean and ready. Because Jonah was home, he was compelled to come with us, a scenario that did not please him one little bit and he sulked about, making a performance of throwing himself on the hay disconsolately as I picked out the horse's hooves.

"Why can't I stay here and play on the Playstation," he whined for the sixth time.

"Because you're too young of course," I replied as patiently as I could, although my voice was developing a tetchy edge to it.

Jonah, naturally, didn't buy this line of reasoning. Like most children, he perceived himself as being older and more responsible than he actually was.

"I'm not too young," he argued. "I'm ten! I'll be okay."

"I know you are but it's the law. I'm not allowed to leave you at home alone until you are fourteen. I'll get a fine."

"I won't tell anyone."

"Jonah!" I finally snapped, exasperated. "I'm not leaving you at home and that is final."

There is only one thing stronger than a mother's will power and that is the will power of their child. Once a child has determined to break their parent's resolve on an issue, they possess the capacity to go on and on for so long that the poor parent is ready to concede anything rather than endure being tormented any longer. It was with a huge sense of relief that I heard a vehicle pull up.

"You've arrived just in time. I was ready to throttle Jonah," I commented wryly to Luke as he entered the barn.

"Why what's up?" he laughed.

"He doesn't want to come with us but he has to. Even worse, he has to ride Jasper but I'll put him on a lead rope."

"Not to worry buddy," said Luke to Jonah. "It'll be fun."

"Fun for you," he grumbled.

I'd arranged to borrow one of my agister's horses for the day. His name was Roscoe and he was a bay gelding about 16hh - bigger than Tiddly and more of a hunter type, big boned and strong. I settled Tammy's stock saddle onto his back and adjusted the cinch while Luke slipped the bridles onto the horses' heads and then their halters over the top before fastening the lead ropes around their necks. I gave Jonah a leg up onto Jasper while Ruff danced wildly about wondering why he wasn't being lifted up there with him. "You can run," I told Ruff as I handed Jonah his helmet and adjusted the stirrups to the right length. "You can ride Tiddly, Luke. It will be like old times."

He swung himself up into the saddle with ease and nudged his mount out into the open. With Ruff bounding along ahead, I led Roscoe and Jasper over to the gate so I could unlatch it and then pulled myself up on Roscoe. We were off.

Conversation was limited but it was a pleasant exercise to rock to the easy rhythm of the horse's movement and to feel the breeze on my face and in my hair and the gentle spring warmth of the sun on my back. Luke was so obviously an excellent horseman that it was a pleasure to watch him. His body moved easily with the horse and he held the reins in one hand, western style, lightly touching Tiddly's neck with the rein to indicate direction.

The horses quickly covered the distance to the back of the farm. It had been a while since I'd been up there and I was surprised to observe that the pasture was already almost thick and long enough to take a cut of hay off. After dismounting and tying up the horses, which immediately set to work munching, I pointed out the boundaries. Imperceptibly, we had been climbing steadily and the farm lay spread out before us. "There's also ten acres up there," I said, indicating the wash behind us.

Our little group climbed over the fence and scrambled our way up the dried stream bed which looked exactly the same as it had previously. Luke inspected the stones, picking up some and kicking others over with his boot. "Nothing spectacular," he commented.

I agreed, "Mostly sandy clay and granite." I showed him the decaying pile of timbers rotting away under the thorn bushes. "I thought that they could have been used for building a mine shaft."

Luke grunted. "Coulda' been, though they look a bit lightweight to me."

Towards the back of the wash, where the stream narrowed and disappeared into the bushes, he peered into the undergrowth then pulled out a machete from his boot and hacked away at some of the overhanging twigs and branches.

"I came up here in the summer time and almost died of heat exhaustion," I commented to nobody in particular.

Jonah and Ruff were busy looking under rocks and I smiled as I remembered how much fun I'd had as a child doing the same thing. The central part of the stream bed looked as if it might have recently run with water but damp soil was the only evidence of moisture. *It would take a lot of rain to get this stream to flow.* "What are you finding, Jonah?" He looked up at my approach. "Centipedes – and what's this?" He indicated a red and black beetle that I had never seen before.

"It's a beetle," I said. "Just don't touch any of them in case you get bitten. The red could mean that it's poisonous."

The sun was high overhead and I guessed it must be about noon. As before, it was very quiet in the wash with only the rustle of spiky leaves in the breeze and the irregular chopping of Luke's machete to break the silence.

Luke had disappeared from view so I followed the debris strewn pathway he had created until I came up behind him. "Found anything promising?" I asked. He wiped the sweat from his face with a bandana. I handed him my drink bottle and he took a long draught.

"No," he replied. "It all looks pretty undisturbed."

"There might not be an actual mine," I said. "I just assumed there could be because of those planks of wood but they could be there for any number of reasons."

"It probably needs a good flood to wash out some of the accumulated stones and soil. I think this stream's been dry for ages – years even."

I agreed. "Thanks for trying anyway," I said, trying not to sound too disappointed.

"Did you enjoy riding Tiddly?" I asked as we walked back to where we had left Jonah.

"Yeah it was good. I wouldn't mind going for a blat though."

"Maybe on the ride back?" I suggested.

Therefore, while we were trotting home, Luke, who was in front, called out "READY?" over his shoulder.

"Ready to canter?" I in turn called back to Jonah. "Hang onto your saddle!"

I kicked Roscoe and he leapt into a willing lope. Then we were all galloping for home, the horse's hooves pounding at the ground as we egged our mounts on, faster, onward, until with sweat flecking on their necks, we careened through the gate and skidded to a halt in front of the barn door. The horses' nostrils, flaring and snorting steam, and their heads, held high with ears pricked, communicated their excitement. And the three of us; laughing deep belly laughs as we slid weakly off our mounts, faces flushed.

Even Jonah was animated. "That was COOL" he cried. "Can we do it again?"

"If I wasn't hanging onto Jasper, I would have beaten you," I laughed at Luke.

"That'll be the day," he chuckled in response, clearly amused by my challenge and supremely confident in his ability.

"Ha! You wait," I advised sagely. "You ain't seen nothing yet. I've been riding since I was four years old. I bet I can beat you hands down."

"You're on! Name your date and time and I'll be there."

"Mum, can I go home now?" That was Jonah.

"Sure," I agreed. "We'll be there soon."

Together, Luke and I rubbed the horses down and walked them around the yard until they had cooled down. I directed him to release Tiddly and Jasper into the front paddock while I returned Roscoe to the one he shared with Smoky Joe further up the farm.

"That was fun," I commented as we walked back to the house. "Even Jonah liked it. That's the first time I've seen him excited about anything."

"Boys like adventurous activities," he said.

When we arrived at the house, Jonah was already slouched on the couch playing with his Playstation.

Luke drifted in casually and sat next to Jonah who offered him a control. "I doubt I'll be as good as you," explained Luke, "but I'll give it a go."

"Mum doesn't play at all."

"Well mums you know are busy. They've got a lot to do."

I smiled at Luke's gentle sticking up for me. *It was a shame his son never made it. He would have made a wonderful father.* I prepared the tea, keeping one ear on the conversation. Every time Luke spoke, I seemed to gain a different perspective.

Luke was asking Jonah, "Do you like these shooting games? You're pretty good at them."

Yeah, but I'd like to shoot a real gun," he answered without taking his eyes from the screen, nor his flying fingers from the buttons on the hand control.

"That's something I could teach you."

At that, Jonah all but flung his hand set across the room and jumped up with excitement at the prospect of learning to shoot a real gun. "Please! Please!" he cried, while for emphasis, he jumped up and down on the spot with his hands clenched under his chin.

"I'll have to talk to your mum first but if she says okay, then I will."

"Why does mum have to say yes?' Jonah groaned, flopping back down onto the couch. "She'll probably say no."

"Because she's your parent and is responsible for you so we have to do what she says," Luke explained firmly.

I brought a cup of tea and a glass of juice each into the lounge whereupon Luke rose from the couch and joined me at the table where he related the conversation he'd just had with Jonah.

If Luke was willing to teach Jonah how to shoot properly, I didn't exactly mind. He wouldn't be using a high calibre rifle of course and would start off shooting at targets with an air rifle. Besides, Jonah had already begun to develop a deep interest in guns, bringing home books from the school library and trolling on line for hours, absorbing screeds of facts about the different weapons and their capabilities. He'd even printed off pictures of AK47's and other military issues and posted them on his bedroom wall. Maybe learning how to use guns safely and responsibly would ease the more obsessive aspects of his interest.

And it wasn't as if Jonah was unusual. Almost every male in the Midwest either had a gun secreted in their pocket or carried one in the glove compartment of their car. Pa had half a dozen rifles locked in his gun cabinet at home and both of my brothers had been taught how to shoot at a young age, their enhanced feelings of masculinity evident in their thirteen year old swaggers and the extra heavy clump of their boots on the deck.

Even I'd had one turn with the air rifle but because I had no interest and was a little afraid of guns, that had been the first and last time. I reasoned that since I saw no point in hitting a target at fifty yards, and because I didn't believe myself capable of pulling the trigger at a person, there was nothing to be gained by learning. But I understood males were different. They loved the excitement of the sounds, the power the weapon afforded them and experienced pride in a skill well mastered - so I said yes. Luke could teach my son to shoot with an air rifle.

To be honest, I liked that Luke was willing to spend time with Jonah doing things that males like to do. I had often thought that life would have been far easier for the both of us if Jonah had been born a female. A girl, I could understand and could easily imagine shopping trips to the mall, cafes, make-up, fashion and discussions about boys. A large part of the distance between my son and I was a direct result of a lack of common ground so it was a relief to me that Luke, as a substitute extension of myself, was willing to fill that gap.

I asked him if he minded; if he was okay with spending hours of his time out in the paddock with my son shooting holes in tin cans and exulting when the pellet hit the little black bull's eye dead centre. But he just smiled and said he loved it. Perhaps, at some level, the relationship between them satisfied something missing in Luke too.

Over the following weeks, Luke's repeated visits effected an unexpected change in that they softened me. They softened my heart and my demeanour. I discovered that I had about myself a reserve – a distance from people that protected me from feeling hurt or angry. My deeper feelings had become encased in a tough, impenetrable film that I would never have known about if it were not for Luke.

The small, daily interactions we had, where he made no moves on me as we talked about our lives, our families, our hopes and dreams for the future, chipped away at my defences. Because I trusted him not to hurt me, I stopped worrying about what he wanted from me and the attendant fear that if I slept with him he would leave, abated.

These were moments when I felt safe enough to let my guard down completely and be fully myself. And it was a relief not to have to pretend that I had it all together, to relax in the knowledge that I didn't have all the answers and to know that I wasn't a bad mother just because I didn't always get it right. I was only one person doing my best in complex circumstances and Luke saw that and understood it.

CHAPTER FOURTEEN

In late March, two weeks before the wedding, Becky held her hen's party. Jonah organised to stay over at Tommy's and I set off for Becky's house. I was looking forward to the evening and to seeing Lorelei who had grown into the most adorable cherub of a toddler. At eighteen months of age, she was a blonde haired cutie with luminous eyes and it was a bit sad to think of her unspoiled, charming innocence morphing into a pierced and tattooed teenager with dyed, black hair and a bad attitude which was the way most teenagers seemed to go these days.

When I arrived at the store, it was 2 o'clock in the afternoon. Becky greeted me at the door with her hair in rollers and Lorelei in her arms so I took the baby from her and headed into the kitchen where Jet was putting on the kettle for tea. I bounced Lorelei on my knee and teased my brother about getting hitched. He told me to "eff off" so I asked after Aunt Harriet instead. But Aunty Harriet was shrinking into old age like a potato left too long in the bag and there was little of interest going on there either. Lorelei's damp little fingers were poking at my eyes and pulling strands of my hair into her wet mouth so I carried her into the family room and placed her on the mat amongst her toys.

After an hour or so, Becky appeared looking glamorous. Her blonde hair had been curled into loose ringlets that draped softly over her shoulders and I saw that she had put on false eyelashes that accentuated the sweep of her eyes and drew attention to the bronze and gold tones of her eye shadow.

Jet whistled in appreciation at his wife to be.

She was dressed in a figure hugging, hot pink sheath, gathered slightly at the hip with a plunging neckline that showed off her rounded figure to full advantage. Pink lipstick, French tipped nails, bangles, drop earrings and stiletto heels; I felt positively drab in comparison even though I had dressed for the occasion in a stylish two toned dress. The top, which comprised of a cream scoop neck bodice with short sleeves, was attached to a high-waisted black skirt that fell in a sculpted drape to calf length. I had thought it extremely elegant when I'd seen it in the shop.

After a round of kisses and admonitions to have a good time, we left. The plan was to meet at Vanessa's house in Dodge City. Never having been there, I was eager to see it and expected the place to be palatial. I was not disappointed. The stone mansion sat solidly on the apex of a hill and was surrounded by established gardens and exotic trees that were carefully situated so as not to spoil the view.

Inside, an expansive entryway tiled in cool, green marble paved the way to an ultra modern kitchen the basic colour scheme of which was silver and chrome. A brightly painted, red feature wall and lime green appliances provided splashy accents of colour. I had never seen a lime green kettle before and wondered where she had bought it.

Vanessa looked as beautiful as ever and was dressed to rival Becky in a stunning peacock blue dress with a ruffled, knee length skirt. Sapphire and white gold, tear drop earrings and a matching pendant necklace that drew attention to her enticing cleavage, complemented the ensemble.

She greeted us with animation, blowing air kisses as she drew us inside. "Where have you been?" I exclaimed as she led us to our room. "I haven't been able to get hold of you for ages."

"Oh, I had to go to Argentina," she said in an offhand manner.

"Argentina!" cried Becky. "What on earth for?"

"I had to help Santos with some business," she replied as she pushed open the door to a bedroom. I placed my bag on the floor and followed her back to the kitchen where three other women, clutching cut crystal flutes of champagne, were already seated on cream, plush leather couches in the informal seating space to the front of the kitchen bench. "He's still there," she continued. "He'll be back next week."

A large, glass topped coffee table laden with a range of canapés sat within easy reach but so far it didn't look as if much of the food had been touched. Becky introduced the seated women as her older sister Juliana and two friends, Brittany and Kendra. I was interested to meet Juliana as Becky rarely mentioned her family and I knew little about her background. Juliana and Vanessa were Becky's bridesmaids and this party was a rage for her friends. A more sedate social gathering was planned for family members the day before the ceremony.

Once the remainder of the guests had arrived, we donned our costumes and accessories. Some had brought butterfly wings, others tiaras, tutus and even wigs. I affixed a headband with fluffy pink and white bunny ears to my head and put on a pair of oversized plastic sunglasses with white frames while Becky pulled a layered net pink tutu over her skirt, positioned a plastic tiara into her hair and waved about a toy fairy wand which, she announced, was to ensure that everyone did her bidding. Vanessa carefully settled an intricately decorated eye mask onto her face, a lurid purple feather boa around her shoulders and pulled white elbow length gloves over her hands. Eventually there were a dozen of us absurdly ornamented and chattering women gathered about the table delicately devouring shrimp vol-au-vents and smoked salmon sushi in such a manner as to avoid smudging our lipstick.

The champagne flowed freely until 7.30pm precisely after which we piled into cars for our dinner reservation in the city. The restaurant Becky had chosen was an Italian restaurant called (by the not so innovative name) Casa Romano, only a short fifteen minute drive from Vanessa's home. I climbed into Juliana's Ford along with Brittany and a sharp looking woman called Felicity.

The restaurant was intimate and dimly lit. A long table had been reserved for our group and we jostled politely for position. I found myself seated next to Felicity on my right and Brittany on my left. The smells of baked dough, herbs and charred tomatoes emanating from the kitchen, enveloped the room as smartly dressed waiters flicked stiff, white linen napkins open onto our laps and poured clear white wine into our glasses. "Dinner's on me," announced Becky, "so eat up." The menu was varied but I chose pasta; a chicken fettuccini that arrived in a bowl, steaming and creamy and garnished with basil and fresh flakes of tangy parmesan cheese.

In between mouthfuls, Felicity informed me that she was an actress although she had been struggling to find work. "I've done a few television commercials," she told me in a New York accent that could only be described as affected, "but I really want to get into movies." She pronounced it 'mowvees.'

"That's where the big money is," I concurred while inwardly smiling. I could almost hear Pa's voice as he grumbled his derision at a society where 'golfers could earn millions of dollars for one game while the working man receives a pittance;' an ethic that, in principle, included actors and actresses.

The chit chat flowed around us. Outside on the pavement, a huddle of a half a dozen women had formed, each flicking a cigarette with manicured fingernails as they talked.

"Have you been to many auditions?" I asked politely.

Felicity gazed down at her plate, her expression sorrowful. "I have an agent but I don't think she is very good. I've been wondering whether to change. Actually, I must phone her on Monday."

"So you work?" I prodded. "How do you live?"

"I live with my boyfriend but I work – as a waitress in Hooters."

I wondered how she had got that job as she was not overly well endowed.

"It pays well," she continued. "I've had surgery," she added, "on my face. I've had a face lift... and a tummy tuck... guess how old I am."

I hazarded a guess, "32?"

She smiled in triumph, "47." She pointed to a petite woman sitting on the opposite side of the table wearing a bright green T shirt that was stretched thin over her swelling breasts. "That's Cordelia," she whispered. "She's had her boobs done."

Who were these women? I was suddenly curious to know how Becky knew these people.

"We used to work together at a bar called the Torpedo Bar in Reno," Felicity informed me when I asked her the question.

"Really!" I exclaimed, "When?" I couldn't even begin to imagine when she could have done so without any of us knowing about it. Did Jet know? It was a side of her that I never knew existed.

"Oh, yeah," Felicity affirmed. "Cordelia was there too. It was a good job. It paid well," she continued, leaving me to wonder whether money was her only criteria for finding work.

Having eaten our fill, the group of us, led by Becky, headed out into the night. There were a number of bars and clubs along the road so we teetered down the street in our heels, laughing and chattering loudly, to the first bar where the raucous melody of an Aerosmith song indicated that a live band was performing inside. Along with the others, I paid the ten dollar cover charge and squeezed inside a room that was already full. En masse, we struggled over to the bar and pressed up against it, in between men of various ages who were settled for the night on the available stools effectively blocking the way. Booths lined the walls but all were occupied so a couple of the girls stood guard and waited for one of the groups of patrons to leave while the rest of us bought drinks.

I ordered a premix bourbon and cola and sought out Becky who had found a stool at a table made out of a large beer keg and was busy chatting to three metro-sexual types with fashionable 5 o'clock shadows on their chins.

"Cheers," I said loudly so as to be heard over the music.

"Are you having a good time?" she shouted back into my ear. Her faced was flushed and happy, her hair unrestrained and wild. She looked like a modern day Monroe, all breathy and girly.

I assured her I was. "Very interesting; I was talking to Felicity and she told me that you worked with her at a club in Reno. Is that true?"

"Yeah," she laughed, "me, Felicity and Cordelia. Hell, we had a blast; good times." She took a swig of her drink and shook her head, remembering.

"But when?"

"Cripes, years ago. You and Nessa were flatting and Jet was at Uni."

"I thought you worked at that clothing place."

"Only in the holidays. It was so boring. Let's go dance," she shouted. She grabbed my hand and led me out onto the crowded dance floor where Vanessa and a group of others were already jiving away in time to the beat of a Guns N' Roses number that that was being performed with more gusto than talent. Throughout the course of the evening, it became evident that the reason why the band was so popular was because they played a broad range of well known pop music that got the patrons up off their seats and dancing. It was well after midnight when Becky announced that she, Vanessa and Cordelia were heading home and I agreed to go with them. It had been a long day and I was tired. One group of women had already left earlier in the evening, citing familial responsibilities. Only Brittany and Felicity elected to stay on and party.

My ears rang in the silence of the drive back to Vanessa's and my feet hurt. I was longing for a coffee and a shower. The house was ablaze with light when we pulled up but proved to be empty. Relishing the cool feel of the tiles on the soles of my aching feet, I tossed my sandals on to the floor of the entry portico and followed Vanessa into the kitchen where she put the kettle on and filled the percolator filter ready for the coffee. Becky and Cordelia collapsed on the couch.

"Do you want any help in there?" I offered, hoping Vanessa would say no.

"You can take the cream and sugar out if you would please," came the reply.

Groaning inwardly, I opened the stainless steel refrigerator and peered inside. "Is there anything to eat?"

"There's left over canapés," she said, "and some nuts and chips in the pantry."

I located the snacks and rearranged them onto new plates so that they looked presentable and carried the lot out to the table where Cordelia and Becky were discussing the floral centrepieces for the reception.

Not long after, Vanessa appeared with the coffee pot and mugs. She poured and we helped ourselves to cream and sugar.

Cordelia raised her mug and said with a smile, "Here's to Becky and your last few nights as a single woman."

"Hear, hear," Vanessa and I said in unison.

"Seems ironic to be saying that with a kid already," laughed Becky.

Cordelia turned to me. "And how do you know these two beautiful women?" she enquired.

I told her I went to school with them.

"Yep," interrupted Vanessa. "We met on our first day and have stuck together ever since."

"Through thick and thin," chipped in Becky.

"She's also marrying my brother so we will be sisters in law," I added. "How do you know Becky?" I continued, curious as to how she would respond.

"We worked together in a bar many years ago," she replied in her gravelly voice, unfazed.

"We go back a long way, don't we Cordelia?" said Becky.

"So we're practically all family – right?" giggled Vanessa who, so saying, withdrew a little plastic packet from her pocket. "Okay, ladies, who's up for a bit of fun?"

She rose and took down from the wall above the fireplace a stunning ornamental mirror that I had noticed and admired earlier. Like everything in the house, it was large and showy. The edge was decorated with highly polished, overlapping, chrome rectangles. She made to place it mirror side up on the coffee table and Cordelia hurried to clear a space.

Vanessa then opened the packet and tipped the contents onto the mirror where the white powder formed a small mound. Cordelia and Becky watched inertly while Vanessa, in a series of movements that seemed almost ritualistic, extracted her credit card from her wallet and proceeded to cut the powder into four, thin lines. I could hardly believe what my eyes were telling me. Cocaine! And she'd carried it in her pocket all night!

The blood rushed from my head, leaving me faint as I rose unsteadily to my feet. "I have to go to the loo," I mumbled.

Vanessa had taken out a $20 note and was rolling it into a tube. I hurried to the bathroom, shut the door and sat on the lid of the toilet, shaking. I'd never been faced with hard drugs before and maybe I was naive – but Becky! A mother with a baby. What was she thinking? I dithered in the bathroom unable to decide what to do.

Hearing a tap on the door, I opened it. It was Becky, concerned. "Are you alright?"

"Yes," I whispered. "I'll be out in a minute. But Becky – cocaine! Are you out of your mind?"

Becky merely laughed. "Chill, it's just a bit of fun. I'm relaxing and letting my hair down. There's nothing wrong with it."

"It's illegal," I reminded her. "And you're a mother."

"So what," she snorted. Lorelei's at home being taken well care of by her father. Honestly, Sheri, everyone does it. It's no big deal."

She stalked off, clearly annoyed.

I followed her out but instead of returning to the kitchen, I turned right and went up the passage to the bedroom and collected my bag. I guessed there must be other exits to the house and after trying a few handles, found a room that had French doors opening out on to a courtyard, beyond which I could see my truck.

I picked my way through the shrubbery, ruing the fact that my shoes were still in the foyer of the house but there was no way I intended returning for them. My fingers, made clumsy by anxiety, fumbled in my bag for the keys and it was with a sense of relief that I found them and inserted the key into the ignition. Thanking the universe that I had not been parked in, I reversed into an empty space and was well on my way down the hill before I switched on the headlights.

Through my mind ran the limited knowledge I had of the roading system in this part of the city although I had a vague idea that the back road from Dodge City to Melvin was much quicker than the way we had come and would get me home in under an hour. I pulled into an all night gas station to ask the attendant for directions. Then properly armed with the correct information, I punched in 'Old Melvin Road' on the GPS and set off into the darkness.

By the time I had been on the road for half an hour, it was 2 o'clock in the morning and I was dead tired so in some corner of my befuddled brain it came as no surprise when I overshot an unexpected sharp turn that loomed up before me in the headlights. Instinctive reactions kicked in and I yanked the steering wheel to the left only to feel the Chevy lose traction and begin to slide on loose gravel as the back wheels left the tar. Too late, I remembered Pa's instructions to turn the wheel into the direction of the slide. *Which way was that?* I turned the wheel to the right but the tail of the truck had already begun its jarring descent into the ditch on the side of the road. The engine stalled and the truck shuddered to a halt.

Once my heart ceased its panicked pounding, I turned the key in the ignition. The engine turned over without fuss so I put the gearstick into four wheel drive and pressed the gas pedal hoping the wheels would grip and clear the vehicle but all I heard was the spin of the wheels and the splatter of muddy soil against the undercarriage.

I fished the emergency torch from under the passenger seat and climbed out for a closer inspection of my situation but saw immediately that I would need to be towed as the Chevy's back wheels were buried to the axle in muddy grass and the undercarriage was resting on the ground. Only the front of the truck pointed hopefully upwards with one of the front wheels floating lightly on a thin cushion of air.

The surrounding pitch black countryside closed in with not even a sliver of a moon to cast a shimmer. The thought of a deranged, sexual deviant coming across me made the hairs on my neck prickle with fright so I re-entered the Chevy and sat there with the doors locked to consider my limited options. Pa was too far away and it was pointless asking my addled friends to come as they would be of little use anyway. Luke was about an hour away but I felt reluctant to call him, imagining that he would be asleep with his phone turned off. I was in a vulnerable situation. *If I'd joined roadside assist like I'd meant to...*

There was nothing for it. I selected Luke's number from my contacts and pressed 'call.' I heard the click as the network connected. It rang for ages; then a groggy, "Hello?"

"LUKE! Oh, thank goodness, Luke!" Overwhelming relief at having made contact with him brought a spring of unbidden tears to my eyes.

"Sheri? What's up?"

"I was driving home and I ran off the road into a ditch. I need to be pulled out." A poorly suppressed sob shook my voice.

"Are you okay?" he questioned, his voice urgent. "Where are you?"

"I'm on the Old Melvin Road, about half an hour out of Dodge City. I'm sorry, Luke. I didn't know who else to call."

"That's okay. I'll come right now. Stay in the cab, lock your doors and don't even open a window to anybody," he instructed. "I'll be there as soon as I can."

I pressed 'end call' and let the tears come; of tension, tiredness and sheer gratitude that a capable man was coming to my rescue.

After that, there was nothing to do except wait so I turned the radio on for company and lay on the bench seat shivering from a mixture of cold and fright. After an hour, I began listening out for Luke's truck but it was another thirty minutes before a vehicle slowed and pulled to a halt on the opposite side of the road. Boots crunched heavily on the gravel but all I could make out in the bright glow of the headlights was the dark shape of a figure.

A light tap on the passenger side window then, "Sheri? Is that you?" confirmed it was Luke.

Cold legs propelled me out of the cab and into the warmth of his body where I shoved my bare arms under his coat. "Luke! Thank you. Good grief, I'm frozen."

"Wait, I'll get you a blanket," he said.

He came back with a dusty rug, which I gratefully wrapped around my shoulders as he knelt and inspected the truck from all sides before confirming my suspicions. "The undercarriage is on the ground so we'll probably pull the exhaust system off when we pull her out," he said as he stood upright and dusted his hands on his jeans. He returned to his truck and reversed up, manoeuvring the bumper of his vehicle so that it was positioned in such a way that the Chevy could be pulled out straight and connected a chain between his tow bar and the Chev's chassis.

"You get in," he commanded. "Does the engine start?"

I nodded.

"Yeah, you get in and drive it in low gear as I pull. Okay?"

I nodded again and climbed into the vehicle. The engine roared into life at the turn of the key. A jerk on the connection between us informed me that the slack had been taken up by the vehicle on the road so I touched the gas pedal but on hearing the wheels spin, eased off. Presently, the creaking and groaning body of the Chev' began to inch forward so I pressed the gas again and, this time, heard the ping of hard stones being flung out from under the wheels.

Once free of their restraints, the wheels immediately grabbed traction and the truck was propelled onto the road to the sound of screeching metal.

The two of us pulled over to the side of the road where Luke disconnected the tow before kneeling and peering under the Chassis. "The exhaust pipe has come apart at the join, half way down the length of it," he reported.

"Can we unbolt it at the muffler?" I asked, thinking that although it would be noisy, I'd still be able to drive home.

Luke lay on his back on the stones and looked closely with the torch. "It's welded at the muffler," came his muffled reply. "The whole thing's stuffed. I think it's best that you leave it here and get a tow truck to pick it up in the morning."

I nodded. That was the logical thing to do. It would mean a fair amount of organisation but there wasn't much choice. I ensured the truck was parked safely then grabbed my bag and the blanket and picked my way across the tar seal to where Luke was waiting.

"Where are your shoes? And what's that thing on your head?" he asked.

I felt with my hand and realised I was still wearing the pink and white bunny ears. I laughed and took them off.

"It's a long story," I said wryly. "I'll tell you on the way home."

When we pulled into the drive it was almost dawn. I enticed Luke inside with the promise of hot coffee and toasted waffles with maple syrup. He sat at the table and watched me as I prepared the food and boiled the kettle then we ate silently, relishing the strength and heat of the coffee.

"Thank you so much for coming out and saving me," I said.

"Of course, anytime," he replied. "I'd never let you be stranded, especially in a dodgy situation like that."

His eyes met mine and the heat once again rushed between us, thick with tension. He leaned in towards me and this time I did not draw away. More than anything else in this world I wanted to kiss him, to feel his mouth on mine. I knew biology; knew it was the blood rushing from my stomach that was creating the maddening butterflies, swelling my lips and other urgently receptive organs; but biology could never have explained the crack in my yearning heart that gaped and yawned so widely that the man in front of me fell right in.

As one, we stumbled to our feet with an intense need to feel close contact, to press our bodies together and to give in to passion. We pulled apart. My lips felt chafed, bruised. I raised my hand and touched them with my fingers. Tears welled, blurring my vision.

"Now, I'm scared," I whispered.

He pulled back slightly and regarded me, his expression quizzical. "Why's that?"

"Because I don't want to lose you."

He wrapped his arms around me and pressed his lips to my hair. "Don't you worry about that, Sheriden Lewis," he murmured, "because I ain't goin' anywhere."

We didn't make love that night. I had no form of contraception and was unwilling to take the risk but we slept together, fitfully, for a few short hours, with Luke groaning in frustration whenever his hands roaming over my body tortured him beyond reason.

Later on in the morning, haggard and with a tension headache knocking on my brain, I made the relevant phone calls and organised Owen's tow truck to bring the Chevy to

Beryl's garage as well as a work car to drive while I waited for the repairs to be completed.

"You look like shit," I teased Luke as he shovelled in breakfast of bacon and fresh eggs from my newly laying hens. Then, having eaten our fill, we showered together; an x rated adventure that left both of us glowing and weak, and once he was ready to go, we lingered against his truck, kissing and holding each other like teenagers until, unable to put our parting off any longer, he drove me into town to pick up a car from the office before heading home.

CHAPTER FIFTEEN

It took most of the week but by the weekend, with a new exhaust system fitted, my Chevy was restored to me with only minor scrapes and denting along the edge of the chassis to show where it had been dragged along the ground.

My relationship with Luke resumed in much the same vein as previously but with the tacit understanding between us that we were together and that as soon as the opportunity presented itself there would be no holding back. In the meantime we touched and kissed freely.

Observing this, Jonah asked, "Is Luke your boyfriend now, Mum?"

To which I simply replied, "Yes."

On Saturday afternoon there was a knock at the door. It was Vanessa and she was dangling my shoes by the finger of one hand. "Come in," I invited. "I'll make you some lunch."

She followed me to the kitchen table where Jonah and Luke waited, curious to see who the unexpected visitor was. I made the introductions.

"Jonah," she murmured. "You were only a toddler when I saw you last. Now look at you – all grown up. And Luke! Pleased to meet you. I've heard a lot about you over the years." She pressed his proffered hand in hers.

"Vanessa and I have known each other since the first day of school," I explained.

"Yep, we flatted together in Dodge City after Jonah was born," Vanessa continued as she took a seat.

She crossed her legs and fidgeted nervously. I wondered what had brought her here. The shoes were clearly an excuse. "Did you have a good night after I left?" I asked, purposely avoiding making specific reference to what had happened.

She picked up on it immediately and carried on in the same manner. "It was okay but we all felt like crap in the morning. It must have been too much booze. I'm getting old and can't handle it any more. You left your shoes..."

"I know. It didn't matter. They're not an especially good pair."

Luke, knowing the story and comprehending that Vanessa and I had things to talk about, discreetly withdrew from the table saying, "Come on, Jonah. Let's go and see if we can get the old Jimny going. If she does, I'll teach you how to drive it. Have you got the keys, Sheri?"

I retrieved them from the hanger where they resided for old time's sake and handed them to him. "The battery will most likely be dead but there's a set of jump leads in the box on my truck."

Jonah, needing no further incentive, sprung up from the table and the two left.

"Ooh, are you and the cowboy together now?" Vanessa teased. "Tell me about it. He's cute."

I described running off the road on the way home and how the subsequent events had cemented our relationship.

"Look," she cut in when I was all but done. "I'm sorry about the other night. I didn't mean to put you in such a bad position."

"Okay," I said slowly. "The problem is, Vanessa, that this kind of thing is normal for you. You've been with Santos and all that entails for years. But lordy! Imagine if you'd been stopped by highway patrol and they found that shit in your pocket. It doesn't bear thinking about. How could you take such a risk?"

Her brilliant blue eyes looked downcast. "You're right," she said. "I'm sorry." She stood to leave. "You won't say anything, will you; to the sheriff, or anyone really? Santos would kill me if he found out what happened."

So that was it. That was why she had come; to make sure I stayed silent. And her last words, were they a threat? That Santos was capable of killing, I had no doubt. His association with the criminal world ran deep. The memory of those blank eyes from the past washed over me and my back shivered.

I encompassed the hands of my best friend in my own. "Vanessa, I've known you for over twenty years and you know that I love you to bits. I promise I won't say anything. My lips are sealed. But I have to say that as long as you stay with Santos, I cannot be a proper friend. It is too dangerous. I'm so sorry but it has to be like that for Jonah's sake."

To these words, Vanessa merely smiled brightly and breathed a sigh of what could only be called relief. "Yes. I understand. Thank you so much." *Had she even heard what I'd said?*

I walked her to the door. "Bye Sheri," she waved gaily but her eyes met mine over the window as she climbed into her car in a glance that left me feeling uneasy.

The days of the week passed quickly and then it was Friday again and I was heading once more to Ma's and fighting uncalled for guilt at missing another weekend with Luke; and Ruff too, disconsolate at being left behind in his kennel, but it had to be done.

The homestead was busy. All the relatives were present including Aunt Julie looking as happy and vibrant as ever with her aging tycoon husband, Frank. Effusive exclamations were issued over the children and how much they had grown by the women who clustered together in the kitchen while, typically, the men disappeared onto the deck to drink and smoke.

Lured by the table laden with offerings of savoury pies, sandwiches and deep fried bread, Jonah hovered nearby, reluctant to remain in the familiar company of the women but too intimidated by the men to join them. Eventually, Pa wandered into the kitchen for more booze and upon seeing his grandson standing there alone, asked what he'd been up to, whereupon Jonah, pleased at having received the invitation, announced that he had been learning to shoot and in that way was drawn into the conversation and presence of the males.

Observing Aunty Harriet sitting in the lounge, I brought a cup of tea to her. "A hive of activity isn't it?" I said, by way of initiating conversation before going on to recount some of life's recent developments. I finished with a wry laugh. "I think Luke could well be the one for me after all."

She patted my arm. "That's wonderful dear. Remember how scared you were? See it all worked out."

Amazing really," I responded. "One thing led to another. He's really good with Jonah too and does all sorts of boy stuff with him. I haven't told the rest of the family yet. I don't know what they will say about it. He's part Arapaho."

"Everything will be alright. As long as you love each other and are happy there's nothing anyone else *can* say."

A rise in the general amount of bustle announced the arrival of Becky and Jet with Lorelei and Juliana. I met Becky's eyes through the open doorway but if she had any comment to make regarding the events of a week ago she made no indication, only coming in to greet me with a hug and a smile as usual.

"Is Vanessa here yet?" she asked casually.

"No, she isn't," I replied. "At least I haven't seen her but we've only been here about half an hour.

"She's supposed to be coming," replied Becky. "I haven't heard from her."

Neither had I but that was hardly surprising considering the last conversation we'd had. I followed Juliana back out to the car and helped to carry the plastic wrapped gowns into the bedroom and hung them by their hangers on to the wardrobe door. Then we ferried in the boxes of shoes and accessories and stacked them on the floor. As we completed the task, Becky's mother and father arrived as did the florist with the bouquets so I took the flowers and stored them in the emptied beer fridge as instructed, leaving Juliana and Becky free to make the introductions.

It had been a very long time since I'd seen Becky's parents but it was evident which side she got her looks and personality from. Mrs Baldwin, fulsome, with wavy blonde hair and creamy, smooth skin was as attractive as she must have been at thirty and her voice, breathless and husky gave her the same Monroe quality that I had observed in Becky. Conversely, her tall and somewhat paunchy father stayed close by his wife's side and managed to exude an air of disapproval despite saying very little.

By the evening, there was still no sign of Vanessa nor was there any word of explanation. All calls to her phone went directly to voicemail and texts remained unanswered. Becky was agitated by Vanessa's unexplained absence and although she concealed it well, remained inconsolable by our repeated assurances that she had probably been held up and would be there by the morning at the very latest.

On the day of the wedding, I was up at dawn, excitement, competing with concern over Vanessa, making it impossible to remain sleep. I could hear Ma moving around in the kitchen so I rose to join her and the boys for the ritual morning cuppa.

Pa, Byron and Jet were already spooning sugar into their mugs. I hugged Jet. "It's your big day, bro!" He grinned widely. "Are you nervous?"

"Not yet," he replied.

Ma poured me a coffee and I stood beside her with both hands cupping the sides of the mug for warmth.

"Your turn next, Byron," Jet quipped.

"Not on your Nelly," retorted Byron. "Sheri's next."

"I doubt it," Jet inserted. "Sheri flies solo."

"Actually, not any longer," my lips announced. "Luke and I have been seeing a lot of each other since the Melvin show. I think he could be the one."

"So our baby sister is finally in luurve," teased Jet. "I was seriously beginning to think it would never happen – like Harriet – you know what I mean?"

"Jet," cautioned Ma, her voice short.

Never! Does Harriet bat for the other team? The idea was incredulous, although it would explain a lot.

"Good on you sis," inserted Byron. "I hope you will be very happy."

Pa rose thereby indicating that having finished their tea, it was time to go and accomplish the morning's essential work. I hugged my brothers' goodbye, knowing that afterwards Jet would retire to Byron's house to prepare so as to satisfy the custom that the bride and groom not see each other before the ceremony.

Once the men had clomped their way out, Ma said, "Are you sure, Sheri? He's so unsuitable."

I almost laughed out loud in the knowledge that I could have revealed certain home truths about suitability had I chosen to, but there was nothing to be gained so I only said, "He's a good person, Ma. I know we will be very happy together so don't worry." And anyway, who *was* suitable? Everyone had their mistakes and secrets, the things that were 'wrong' about them.

Our conversation was interrupted by Jonah who, having been woken by our voices, was still yawning as he padded into the kitchen. Further in the depths of the house, Lorelei could be heard wailing. The day had begun.

By 9.30 when the hairdressers arrived, Vanessa still had not and Becky was frantic. "Sheri, phone the hospital and see if she has been admitted for some reason," she commanded. I did so and when that yielded no result, thought to phone her father who merely complained that he had no idea where she was and that he hadn't heard from her in years.

"You must get ready in her place, in case she doesn't come at all. What could have happened?" Becky wailed close to tears.

That was something we all wanted to know. It was a mystery but there was no use in becoming distraught before we had any concrete information so I tried on Vanessa's dress and was surprised to discover it fitted almost perfectly with only a slight looseness around the bodice and an over long hemline which Ma said she could alter in a jiffy as she hurried off to fetch her sewing kit.

I smoothed the pastel, mint green silk gown with my hands and the fabric rippled under my touch. "It's gorgeous," I breathed, taking in the soft drape of the wide, scooped neck and the gathering at the hip that caused the gown to cascade down in all the right places.

The hairdressers positioned Becky in front of the mirror and proceeded to curl her hair with the tongs, sweeping it into an elegant French knot while allowing tendrils of curls to frame her face and neck. It looked simple but a multitude of grips and hairspray held the style in place.

I stood on a chair while Ma knelt on the floor and pinned the hem where it was to be cut. Then I took the dress off and she spirited it away for modification. The hairstylist moved onto Juliana's hair while the second woman, a young, edgy girl with a bar bell piercing one eyebrow and a bright aubergine streak in her fringe, began smoothing foundation onto Becky's face.

The women processed the wedding party as if we were an assembly line until the three of us were transformed into goddesses. "Would you like us to do your hair?" the hairdresser asked Ma and Mrs Baldwin.

"Do it, Ma," I urged. So the women took their positions on the stools and were given a makeover also, although a softer look as was befitting the mothers of the bride and groom.

At the moment when Juliana and I carefully lifted Becky's bridal gown over her styled hair, everyone turned to watch and issued a collective gasp of approval when they saw her head and arms settle into their rightful position.

The gown was exquisite and swathed Becky's body to perfection. The strapless bodice was cut into a sweetheart neckline and intricately decorated with hand sewn Swarovski crystals that sparkled like diamonds. The skirt, full and gathered at the hip, echoing the detailing on the bridesmaid's gowns was also embellished with diamantes embroidered into elaborate swirls and spirals while the back scooped down and fastened with a dense row of covered buttons.

"You look absolutely stunning," marvelled Juliana as she affixed the veil to her sister's hair with a silver tiara.

With Becky dressed, Juliana and I slipped into our gowns and slid on our shoes. As a gift, Becky had given each of us an exquisite pair of emerald and yellow gold earrings, which cascaded in a series of three gems, plus a matching necklace. They complimented out dresses and I felt like a princess.

Juliana collected the bouquets and affixed the corsages of pink rose buds to the lapels of our respective mothers, then, lifting the hem and train of Becky's gown so as to protect it from the ground, we shuffled out to the two creamy white '67 Cadillac limousines that waited outside with their bridal streamers fluttering gently in the breeze.

In our car, Ma, looking supremely elegant in a dusky, antique rose, two piece suit, the jacket of which was elaborately embroidered with fine silver thread, sat next to Pa who clutched her hand with his own. Handsome in a florid, wealthy rancher kind of way, Pa was stuffed into a cream suit that pulled tautly at the button across his middle while Jonah sat beside me, tight with tension at this unfamiliar territory of suits, white shirts, ties and cufflinks. I pressed his hand. "You look fabulous, very smart and handsome," I whispered. He made no reply but I saw the faint smile that edged his lips upwards.

Nerves tingled in my belly as we pulled up at the Flagstaff church and disembarked. I saw Jet's car already there and a quick word to the usher confirmed that he was indeed waiting anxiously at the altar for his bride. Ma and Pa, taking Jonah with them, were escorted to their pew while I waited for Juliana and Becky to arrive.

We performed the rituals, straightening the hem of the bride's gown and adjusting the veil so that it spread evenly across her shoulders and down her back. Juliana fluttered about her sister, tucking in straying strands of hair, tweaking the tiara straight and murmuring muted words of beauty and encouragement. Then we were ready.

The organist played softly as Juliana and I walked one behind the other down the aisle, all the while flicking small smiles to those who watched, before taking our positions opposite my brothers and a friend of Jet's I'd never met before. Once we were in place, the organ struck a note. "Please be upstanding for the bride," announced the pastor. The congregation stood and turned collectively to gain their first glimpse of Becky as she made her way down the red carpet flanked by her father and her mother.

"Who gives this woman to be married?" asked the preacher as they reached the altar.

"We do," her parents replied in unison. They kissed their daughter and retreated to their seat in the front pew where Lorelei, grizzling quietly reached out to her grandmother, no doubt wondering why she was being withheld from her parents barely five paces away.

I could see Jet casting awestruck, surreptitious glances at his soon to be wife, hardly daring to look at her outright.

The preacher began his talk and I took the opportunity to study the old church where Ma and Pa had been married all those years ago and where we had attended as children, bored into somnolence by the quiet solemnity that was only emphasised by the monotonous intonation of the preacher's voice. Now, extravagant bunches of white calla lilies and ranunculus garnished with draping, white bows decorated the ends of the pews and sunshine streamed through the stained glass windows creating shards of colour on the heads of the congregation. The atmosphere was solemn, intimate and beautiful.

Both sets of parents rose and approached the altar where they jointly lit a candle to signify the uniting of the two families. Then Lorelei was handed to Becky to hold while the couple promised to love and support each other until the day they died. The timeless words echoed in the restrained silence of the church as the rings were exchanged and a delicate necklace fastened around Lorelei's neck.

"You may kiss your bride," said the pastor and the couple's lips met for the first time as husband and wife.

This is what it is all about, I thought. Life was about love and family, about sticking together no matter what and supporting each other as births, deaths, marriages and separations took their emotional toll on those who strove to create beauty out of flawed materials.

While we in the wedding party were ferried off for photographs in the municipal gardens, the rest of the congregation headed for a cocktail hour at the hotel. Later on, the reception unfolded without hiccup, filled with a steady progression of food, speeches, wedding games and dancing that carried the party into the evening. I enjoyed myself, although I couldn't help but wish that Luke were with me;

thinking that there was no lonelier place for a single person than a wedding.

Seeing Aunty Harriet sitting at one of the tables along with Julie and Frank who were engrossed in conversation with Grandma and Grandpa Granger, I wandered over to sit down beside her for a chat. "How are you going, Aunty - enjoying yourself?"

"Hello Sheri. You look lovely tonight," she replied. "Yes, it is a wonderful occasion but I'm a bit tired to tell you the truth."

The tone of her voice led me to examine her more closely and I noted dark circles beneath her eyes and a rough texture to her skin. "Are you alright?" I asked, concern giving edge to my question. "Have you been well?"

She nodded. "I've been okay, much as usual only extremely tired lately. It must be old age creeping up on me. I have been thinking of cutting down my hours at the store."

"Maybe you should go to the doctors and have a check up," I suggested. "You could be deficient in iron or something. If you're sleeping alright, there's no reason why you should be excessively tired during the day is there?"

She considered my suggestion. "Maybe you're right," she agreed. "It wouldn't hurt at any rate."

I would have offered to take her home but did not have independent transport so I fetched her a cup of tea and sat with her a while, chatting about the store, family and the daily detritus of living feeling it was the least I could do for her in return for all the support she had given me over the years.

The day after the wedding found the entire family feeling flat. The house was full of flowers and discarded dresses and the fridge full of food but nobody felt like lifting a finger so we lazed our way through the hours, picking at leftovers and watching television. Ma and I sat on the deck with cups of coffee and chatted desultorily. "I spoke to Harriet last night," I remarked, "and suggested she go to the doctors. Do you think she's well? I thought she looked grey myself."

Ma said, "So she didn't tell you."

My heart sank. "Tell me what?"

"She found a lump in her breast. She's had a biopsy and is waiting for results. It could be breast cancer."

"Breast cancer," I repeated, stunned at what I was hearing.

"Of course it could be nothing serious. We won't know until the tests are returned."

"Why didn't she tell me?" I protested, hurt that she had not confided in me.

"Maybe she didn't want to spoil the wedding for you. And there's no use getting upset at something that may not amount to anything. We can only wait and see how it pans out."

"When will we know?" I asked, my voice tremulous, subconsciously including us all in the prognosis; as we all were because we loved and feared for her.

"Next week, I should imagine," Ma replied.

I lay my hand on her arm in a gesture of sympathy. "Oh, Ma, this is dreadful news," I said, remembering that Harriet was Ma's sister and therefore so much worse for her.

Feeling shattered, I drove home the following afternoon after helping Ma to restore some order to the house. The stress of the wedding, Harriet's un-wellness, and the dearth of information regarding Vanessa's ongoing absence had worn on my nerves and I felt fragile and weepy. Jonah slept for much of the trip and I longed to do the same but when I got home there would still be the animals to check and feed. As I imagined my house waiting for me, a flood of yearning washed over me, making my heart ache for my own simple life that was essentially uncomplicated and thankfully free of heinous problems.

CHAPTER SIXTEEN

Over the following week, as life fell back into the comforting routines of work, school and home, I tried intermittently to contact Vanessa with no success. Trouble, when it came, arrived on Friday afternoon with a series of demanding raps on the door. I hurried to peek through the peep hole where I saw two 'Men in Black' types complete with dark sunglasses concealing their eyes. When I opened the door, both flicked open their badges, holding them at shoulder height in much the same way as I'd seen actors perform the same action on television. "This is Federal Agent Mossman and I am Federal Agent Blakely," said the man on the left.

For a moment my mind thought it was someone playing a prank. "What's this?" I demanded laughingly. "Am I being punked?" Although why Ashton Kutcher would have wanted to punk me, I could not have provided an explanation for.

"This is no joke, ma'am," intoned Agent Blakely. "Can we come in? We would like to ask you a few questions."

"What's this about?" I asked, uneasy now. "Let me see those badges again. Do I need a lawyer?"

"I don't know, do you?" said Agent Mossman, his voice cool.

I inspected the badges. They looked genuine. I studied the car, a sinister looking black Chevy Suburban. Standing aside, I allowed the men to enter but left the door open. I wondered whether to text Luke but decided there was nothing to be gained. Mercy was over two hours away. If these men intended harm, I'd be long gone by the time he arrived.

I led the way into the sitting room where they each chose a vacant chair. Agent Mossman flipped open a black, leather bound notebook and noted down my full name and social security number; after which Agent Blakely withdrew a photograph from his briefcase and handed it to me.

My heart thudded painfully as a violent panic hit me in the chest. "It's Vanessa," I murmured. "Is she okay? What's happened? Is she dead?"

"Why would you think that, Ms Lewis?"

"She was supposed to be a bridesmaid at my brother's wedding on Saturday but she never showed up. We've gone mad trying to get hold of her but her phone just goes to voicemail."

"That's because she has been arrested," stated Agent Blakely baldly. Blood rushed to my ears. I felt like I was going to faint.

"Arrested," I echoed. "What for?"

"She was picked up at the Ministro Astorini Airport carrying two kilograms of cocaine concealed in her suitcase." He handed me a second photograph. This one was of Santos.

"Santos Haviera," I confirmed. "He's Vanessa's boyfriend."

Oh my god. Oh my god. Vanessa you stupid, stupid idiot. How could you be so foolish? I rubbed my face with my hands. My senses were convoluted with shock.

"You look pretty distressed, Ms Lewis. Can we get you a drink of water?"

"In the kitchen," I waved, mishearing. But I took the glass when he offered it to me.

"How long have you known Santos Haviera, Ms Lewis?" asked Agent Blakely politely.

"I met Santos when Vanessa met him. Vanessa and I were flatting together. But I hardly know him. I don't have anything to do with him. The last time I saw him was about six months ago at the new club he is outfitting."

"In Dodge City?"

"No. Here in Melvin."

The two men traded looks. Had they not known about the new club?

"And how long have you known Ms Goodwell?"

"I met her on our first day of school. She's my oldest friend."

The implications of Vanessa's arrest were catching up with my tongue. It had shaken me to discover that there were things I probably knew about Vanessa that the agents did not, due to nothing more sinister than length of association.

I chose my words carefully. "Look, I don't mean any disrespect and I haven't done anything wrong. I don't do drugs of any kind. I don't even smoke cigarettes but I've known Vanessa a very long time and may inadvertently say something that could be... misinterpreted so I would like to have my lawyer present if you want to ask me anything further, if that would be alright?"

The two agents exchanged a look with each other whereupon Mossman snapped his book shut and they both stood up. "Okay. We'll go now. Don't leave the country and we will be in touch if we need to speak to you further." He handed me his card.

Immediately they had left, I phoned Luke who listened quietly while I described what had happened. "Yes, get a lawyer," he agreed.

I knew several lawyers because I dealt with them all the time but they worked largely in conveyance whereas I needed a criminal lawyer. I rifled through the phone book before locating only one, a Mr Geoffrey Gattenberg.

"Who were those men, Mum?" asked Jonah who had been loitering in the passage eavesdropping. I started, having forgotten he was in the house.

"Nothing important," I soothed. "A friend of mine has got herself into trouble."

"Are you in trouble, Mum?" His voice was anxious.

"No, of course not. The police want my help, that's all."

I went into the kitchen and removed a family sized mince pie from the freezer and shook some frozen fries onto an oiled oven tray and slid them both into the oven. I couldn't think to cook anything more complicated. I wished I could phone Becky but she wasn't due back for several weeks yet. There was no one to talk to about it.

The phone rang. It was Ma and I could tell by the sound of her voice breaking that the news was not good. "It's Harriet," she said. "The lump was malignant. She's got to go in for a mastectomy at Dodge City. The hospital here isn't big enough."

"Is she going to be alright?" It was a futile question.

"I don't know. It depends if they can get it all.

It was too much to take in.

"Is she okay?"

"Well, you know. As okay as she can be, I guess. She is going to come and stay here with us while she is undergoing treatment so that we can look after her and take her for appointments."

"Alright, give her my love," I said. It was inadequate but it was the best I could do.

I hung up and slumped at the table. I'd been so happy a couple of weeks ago, without a care in the world. Now it felt as if there was a huge, black, dirty elephant sized poop hanging over my head. I desperately needed Luke but it didn't feel right to subject Jonah to the two hour drive after the hectic weekend we'd just had. I would just have to carry my burdens on my own until I saw him again.

I organised a lawyer and despite the internal anxiety gnawing away at me, managed to uphold the pattern of daily life. Business was steady, if not exciting with several good clients on my list in various stages of negotiations as well as receiving one or two new enquiries a day.

Jonah was settled at school and the latest parent/teacher interview had yielded cautiously positive results, but my greatest source of happiness remained Luke who stayed with us most weekends. During those times, we busied ourselves with a variety of pursuits and had a lot of fun conducting wood collecting expeditions into the forest, teaching Jonah how to drive, riding the horses and making love; albeit quietly so as to avoid alerting Jonah as to his mother's nocturnal activities. Each parting left me empty and aching.

I met with Geoffrey Gattenberg one afternoon and told him everything I knew about Vanessa and Santos, including the lease of the Lumberton Road property under the name of Haviera Holdings. But I did not tell him about the events of the night of Becky's hen party. For some reason, I was reluctant to reveal that I'd possessed the concrete evidence of my eyes to prove that Vanessa was involved with hard drugs.

Mr Gattenberg asked me to send him a copy of the lease and told me that he would send a letter to the FBI citing himself as my legal representative. I left after an hour, shuddering to think how much it was all going to cost.

As expected, the story broke in the media and a glamorous photograph of Vanessa that portrayed her as a page three model was plastered on the front page of every local newspaper along with lurid tabloid headlines making sensational statements along the lines of: *"Glamour Girl Conceals Cocaine for Cash."* I learned nothing about the case that was not reported on and it was impossible to make any form of contact with her, something that Mr Gattenberg directly advised against for the present, in any event.

From the news accounts, I gathered that Vanessa would be tried in an Argentinean court but that our own country was attempting to extradite her back to the US to serve her jail time here. I imagined that the Feds were hoping to get her back in the belief that they had leverage and that she would be open to cooperating with them in their enquiries involving Santos and his wider business empire in return for a reduction of her own sentence. My concern was that we, her friends and family, should at least be able to visit her.

A distressed Becky called me on my cell phone the minute she arrived home from her honeymoon. Luckily, I was staging a home for photographing and was able to talk freely but could offer little consolation. "There's nothing either of us *can* do," I said to my audibly weeping sister in law. "My lawyer told me that because I knew nothing about Vanessa's activities and had no involvement in them, and because I had nothing much at all to do with Santos, that there is nothing that they can charge me with, and I'd say the same goes for you. But if you are worried at all by being interviewed by the Feds, who've already been to see me once, then get a lawyer."

"Federal agents have interviewed you?" she gasped, shocked.

"Yes," I replied. "And I didn't even know she had been arrested when they came to my place. I got a hell of a fright."

However, not knowing that Vanessa was so involved in Santos' affairs did little to ease the uncomfortable question of whether I had done the right thing that night. *If only I had said something.* If I had gone to the sheriff, and if she had been busted for possession, then she would not have gone on that trip.

Therein lay the root of my problem. I didn't speak up. If I'd said 'no' to Mark all those years ago when he first suggested going to the river, a known trysting place, instead of merely acquiescing; and then there was the part where I had definitely turned to him and responded...

The unpalatable truth was that I had known, or at the very least seriously suspected for more than a decade, that Vanessa was more involved in the murky depths of Santos' drug world than she'd let on and I had done nothing to try and help her break free of it. A bitter feeling gnawed at the pit of my stomach; the feeling that I had let my best friend down and that I was as much to blame for her predicament as she was.

For a change of pace, I took a day off work and travelled into Dodge City to visit Aunty Harriet who had been admitted for surgery. The weather was changeable with the heat of the sun breaking through, only to be chased away by scudding clouds that swept intermittently across the sky.

Although the mastectomy had taken place three days earlier, Aunty Harriet was still heavily bandaged and hooked up to various tubes. "It's terrible to see you like this, Aunty," I said as I kissed her pale cheek, careful not to touch or dislodge any of the medical paraphernalia. She smiled weakly, obviously still in a great deal of pain.

"How did it go?"

She croaked her reply. "The doctors said it went well. The lymph nodes were all clear which means they don't think it has spread so that is good news."

I agreed. "So what happens now?"

"I will have to have a round of radiation therapy, and then they might give me a new drug that can help stop the cancer from reoccurring."

"Are you going to have a breast reconstruction?" I asked, finding the thought of being minus a breast untenable.

Harriet merely groaned. "I don't know. Maybe I won't bother. There are good prosthetics available these days and it's not like I've got anyone to look, you know, normal for."

"Well there's time to think about all that later, isn't there," I replied. "If it bothers you later, you can get it done then."

We chatted for a while longer and I filled her in on the news that Becky had returned from her honeymoon and that Vanessa had been overseas and missed her flight home but I did not tell her about Vanessa's arrest. She had enough to worry about.

"You know this is going to be much harder in a few months time," I said to Luke the next morning as we lounged around in bed. The clock on the bedroom wall and the sunshine streaming through the windows announced that we should have been up and about hours ago.

"What is?" Luke yawned, stretching his arms above his head, luxurious as a cat.

"In the winter; it's going to be almost impossible to see each other with the snow." The main roads between the towns and cities could sometimes be closed for weeks and there was no way of knowing when they would be opened again.

Luke continued to lay there, unmoving, so I prodded his lovely, lean torso with my finger nail. He squirmed and grabbed my hand, laughing.

"Okay, what? What are you thinking? Talk to me," I demanded.

He rolled onto his side towards me and rested his head on one hand. "I'm thinking – how are we going to do this? How are we going to make it work long term? Where are we going to live? You don't want to keep on like this forever do you?"

Personally, I didn't mind but then it wasn't me making the four hour round trip every weekend. I passed the question back to Luke. "What do you want to happen?"

"I want us to live together. What do you want?"

His reply imparted a surge of happiness and allowed me to agree with confidence. "I want us to live together too but I don't know where or how. I don't want to live in the same house as your mother. And you can't really live here because what will you do for work? Then there is Sooky to think about..." My voice trailed off.

"Actually, I do have an idea," said Luke with a secretive smile as he stroked my leg with his free hand. "I was thinking that if I took over the management of the ranch, we could live in the manager's house."

That was an idea although it would be a huge upheaval for Jonah's schooling and my work. "I'd have to get a new job," I said. "Would I sell my place?"

"I think it would be the most logical thing to do but you could always lease it. The only drawback would be that tenants don't always look after the place like you might want them to."

All that Luke said made sense. "I have a thought - a plan really," I said, ready to communicate an idea that I'd had on my mind for some time. "If I sold my place, I'd have enough money to put myself through college. I've always wanted to be a geologist. I'm not too old to try. If we lived with you I could study in Dodge City and I'd have enough to contribute my share of expenses while I do so."

"We'll work something out," agreed Luke. "It's only money. Anyway, it will do you good to be a kept woman for a while. Let me carry some of the burden of daily life for a change."

I straddled his body and leaned my face over his, allowing my hair to caress his skin. Our lips sought each the others and kissed deeply. I felt him respond beneath me. "I'll pay you in the time honoured fashion," I murmured.

"That's it, woman!" he commanded as he playfully slapped my bare buttock. "Now go and make your man some breakfast. All this sex is making me thin."

With a new plan in place for the future came a sense of excitement that I'd not felt in a long time. Breaking the news to Jonah provided a tense moment but I painted a happy picture of living on a ranch as big as his Grandpa's and he was satisfied. As I explained, it made sense to shift before he went to high school so that he could settle in and make friends but at his age, he was more interested in whether he could take Ruff and still learn to shoot and drive than any of the more fundamental realities.

With the end of the academic year fast approaching, the timing was awkward as it was highly unlikely that the place would be sold and everything organised in time for the new academic year beginning in August. *If worst comes to worse we will just have to struggle it through the winter and take things as they occur,* I thought. But that was life. There was always a fly in the ointment. It was with mixed emotions that I put my farm on the market. Having poured all of my energy into creating a pleasant and happy home for Jonah and I, it was going to be tough to leave it.

The spring weather through April remained changeable and turbulent with sudden thunderstorms appearing randomly out of nowhere and romping across the foothills. The pasture grew thick and verdant and I was impatient for the weather to clear so that I could order in a contractor to cut the pasture for hay. Expectant of harvesting at least eighty acres, I figured that there would be plenty to sell to cover the cost.

Luke spent long hours working in the barn and on the land, repairing fences and painting beams so as to spruce the property up ready for sale; and I marvelled at the willingness with which we got on and did those jobs in readiness for strangers to enjoy but not for ourselves.

It was about three in the afternoon and I was preparing afternoon tea in the kitchen when the bruised, dirty yellow appearance of the sky as it cast an eerie glow over the landscape caught my attention. That and the rain which had begun to fall in lazy, fat slaps that exploded violently on the roof. I went outside and looked to the west where the sky was thunderous with storm clouds. And up high, underneath, shimmered a translucent, malevolent haze.

Frightened, I grabbed my coat and ran towards the barn barely feeling the drops as they fell, gathering pace, on my head and shoulders. I shouted out to Luke who was already running towards me with Jonah and Ruff in tow. We met half way and I pointed at the threatening clouds that were rapidly changing in shape and form. "Those clouds," I cried. "I don't like it." Lightning cracked the sky, followed closely after by the deep rumble of thunder.

"Tornado cloud, I think," he shouted back. We dashed for the shelter of the orchard trees and stood watching as a definite spout began to form, pushing downwards like a finger, then retracting, before pushing down further and harder, making contact with the ground.

"Inside," Luke commanded.

We needed no encouragement. The air temperature had chilled dramatically and the rain, soaking us to the skin in stinging drops, formed into hail that drummed on the roof and pummelled the ground, piling drifts of white into the corners of the buildings. I could hear the hailstones bouncing off the roof of the Chevy. *Good thing I'm insured*, I thought with anxiety.

Once inside, we peered through the windows searching for the twister but the sky from the horizon up was so dark it was impossible to tell visually whether the wind spout had formed or even in which direction it was moving. But the noise! A steady roaring that sounded like an airliner approaching, intensifying all the while, indicated that we needed to take urgent shelter. I gasped at Luke and my face was contorted with fear.

"What is it, Mum?" cried Jonah, alarmed.

"Twister – into the bathroom," yelled Luke, taking charge.

It was the smallest room in the house. We bundled in and I pushed Jonah into the space between the vanity and the bath and crawled in after him. I wrapped my arms around his body to provide the best protection possible, and then Luke squeezed in and did the same for me. Ruff huddled close by, whining anxiously. Somewhere in the house, a door banged repetitively while the roaring wind, indescribably loud in our ears, shook the house in great gusts. Through the shrieks, I heard the sound of glass breaking.

"There go the windows," shouted Luke.

Jonah, who was clutching at my clothes, cried. "I'm scared, Mum."

"Hush, it will be alright," I lied as I pressed his head to my chest.

I prayed that the roof would remain attached to the house but the tortured creaking and groaning of the timbers as they strained against the beams attaching them to the main frame, suggested otherwise. I felt the iron bounce and jerk as it lifted on one corner, then with an horrendous screech of twisted metal, the roof ripped right off and was flung away, twisting and turning, into the howling gale where it would be found days later over five miles away.

With the roof gone, the house didn't stand a chance. The furious storm tore apart my new kitchen. It tossed appliances and household detritus into the void and kicked apart the walls and timbers of the frame until they were nothing but splinters. The ceiling collapsed with a puff. One fortuitous panel spanned the gap between the basin and the bath, wedging us into the space. Exposed to the elements, the rain pummelled our heads and backs. All we could do was cling together, heads bowed as we wept with with fear and loss, and prayed that we would survive.

The twister moved on and the winds subsided as quickly as they had arrived. Once the fury had abated sufficiently, we pushed aside the debris and emerged to a scene of utter destruction. There was literally nothing left except for a pile of jumbled timber. Everything movable had been blown away. Ruff stood close beside us, his tail wagging anxiously.

Absurdly, the sun chose that moment to erupt out of the clouds, bathing the scene with incandescent light. Somewhere nearby, a bird began to twitter. The barn and the lone maple tree were still standing, as was the chook pen, although sagging. The hens were nowhere to be seen. We picked our way through the debris finding little that was recognisable as a former possession. Dazed, I observed the Chevy tipped on its side like a toy while Luke's truck, standing immediately beside it, appeared unharmed. I could hear a distant roar of water and I wondered if it was the wash, finally alive at last.

"The house must have taken a direct hit," I groaned.

Luke held us both tightly, fearing I might collapse. "I love you, Sheri," he breathed into my hair. "Everything will be alright. I love you."

I stared, uncomprehending, at the desolation. It seemed inconceivable that an entire house could be reduced to so little in such a short time. In the distance could be heard the sound of emergency sirens. I wondered whether the twister had hit the city. A pull on my sleeve drew my attention to Jonah who was tugging at my arm.

"Look, Mum," he said, pointing.

And looking, I saw a bathtub; an old fashioned, claw footed bathtub. It was sitting alone out in the field. And wedged in the tub, upside down with its four legs pointing upwards, was a steer looking for all the world as if it was taking a bath; clearly dead, but propped upright, looking very much alive and astonished.

Jonah began to laugh. "Look, Mum. The cow is taking a bath," he giggled.

I felt a giggle erupt in my stomach and then I too was laughing, and then Luke also; deep belly laughs that gave us a stitch as we clung to each other. If we let go, we would all fall down, so we clung to each other and laughed and laughed. And the laughter, it floated up, up, up into the purple blue of the early evening sky and drifted away.

ABOUT THE AUTHOR

I live and work in the beautiful Bay of Plenty with my partner and we have five grown up children between us.

I love the arts and have painted and written all my life as a hobby but out of the necessity of finding meaningful work to do, began seriously writing as a means to keep busy and hopefully generate some income after stopping paid work as an English teacher in 2009 due to my ongoing struggles with cancer.

The world of publishing is undergoing massive changes with the advent of the internet and the ease and availability of self publishing. It is my aim to ride the waves of change and take advantage of them.

VISIT MY WEBSITES:

http://www.trilacart.com/
A site devoted to the sharing of my artwork.

http://www.trishlaceyauthor.com/
A site where I share what I am doing with my writing.

TO REPORT ERRORS OR TO CONTACT THE AUTHOR
EMAIL ME AT
trilacart@gmail.com

Thank you for purchasing my novel.

Ten percent of profits are donated to the World Wildlife Fund
in the interests of preserving habitats for wild animals.
http://www.worldwildlife.org

Made in the USA
Charleston, SC
02 December 2013